WINNING WINNIE'S HAND

Winning Winnie's Hand

MEN OF THE ISLES BOOK ONE

DEBORAH M. HATHAWAY

DRAFT HORSE
PUBLISHING

BOOKS BY DEBORAH M. HATHAWAY

A Cornish Romance Series
On the Shores of Tregalwen, a Prequel Novella
Behind the Light of Golowduyn, Book One
For the Lady of Lowena, Book Two
Near the Ruins of Penharrow, Book Three
In the Waves of Tristwick, Book Four
From the Fields of Porthlenn, Book Five

Belles of Christmas Multi-Author Series
Nine Ladies Dancing, Book Four
On the Second Day of Christmas, Book Four

Seasons of Change Multi-Author Series
The Cottage by Coniston, Book Five

Sons of Somerset Multi-Author Series
Carving for Miss Coventry, Book One

Christmas Escape Multi-Author Series (Contemporary)
Christmas Baggage

Castles & Courtship Multi-Author Series
To Know Miss May, Book Two

Men of the Isles Series
Winning Winnie's Hand's, Book One

For Dad

Thank you for everything.
I will always love you.

CHAPTER ONE

Large raindrops splattered against the windshield of Winnie Knox's emerald green Aston Martin, distorting the glass in gray, watery pools. She had long-since cranked the wipers to "high" in a futile attempt to see the black, sodden road in front of her, but the swiping arms wouldn't move fast enough to dispel the water.

Worthless things.

The raindrops pouring swiftly down the windshield resembled those calming rain simulators that higher-up executives always placed on their pretentious desks.

Ironically enough, Winnie had one of them herself at home. Although, she was no higher-up exec. And this water was definitely *not* calming.

Driving in the rain wasn't really that big of a deal—not like driving in the snow was. She'd grown up in Utah, after all, and was used to sliding and swerving across five lanes of traffic during her early morning commute to college at the U.

But after a seven-hour flight, three hours of sleep, and four and a half hours of driving on the opposite side of the road in weather that ranged from glaring sunlight to monsoon-like rain, her nerves were officially fried.

1

Driving in an Aston Martin that wasn't hers was just green-colored icing on an already burnt bundt cake.

Dad was to blame for all of this. He'd been the one to secure the rental for her. She *had* asked the Rent-A-Car people if they'd had anything less flashy than the sports car in their ridiculously wide range of vehicles. She didn't want to give the impression of being the typical "Rich American Consultant Driving a Sports Car Coming to Destroy All of Your Hopes and Dreams." But her choice had been between that and "Rich American Consultant Driving a *Minivan* Coming to Destroy All of Your Hopes and Dreams," and, frankly, her pride had won out.

With both hands still gripping the steering wheel, she darted her eyes to her phone on the dashboard. Google Maps said she'd arrived five minutes ago, yet still, there was no sign of Foxwood Hall. Was their driveway three million miles long?

The radio played over the speakers in the car, moving in and out of her attention as she shifted forward in her seat.

"We all pleyed with gret focus and determination agains' United," the man with the thick accent said. She supposed he was speaking about soccer—or football, was it? *"Bu' in the end, it weren't enough, were it? We just 'ope to stay in the league, that's all."*

A female with a fancier accent spoke next as the interview with the player ended. *"That was Gregory Lumley from Habergham FC. You're listening to the BBC news. It is now three minutes past eight."*

Winnie glanced at the clock on the dashboard. Sure enough, *8:03* was emblazoned brightly across the screen.

Well this was just perfect. She was now officially late by four full hours. What would Mr. Wintour think? Her being late was hardly the first impression she wanted to give her dad's old friend —the man who'd hired her based on that connection alone. She'd be able to prove her worth eventually, but having a leg up from the start would have been nice.

A cheesy jingle blasted through the speakers next, singing the radio station's name and announcing the upcoming host, but Winnie reached forward to turn the music off. The noise was only adding to her stress.

She shifted forward in her seat again, straining to see anything ahead of her, but as the road twisted from bend to bend, each turn remained hidden from the next by thick trees and dimming light.

She had to be on the right road. Where else could she be? Should she call Mr. Wintour again?

No, definitely not. She'd already called him hours ago, letting him know about her delayed luggage, her flight being switched to Heathrow instead of Manchester, and the traffic she'd run into time and time again. There was no need to call him for a fourth instance just to inform him that she was entirely inept and unable to find his massive house—the very house she'd been hired to improve.

She blew out a heavy sigh. "You've got this, Winnie. Chill out."

And she did. For all of two seconds.

Her father's dark, disappointed eyes flashed across her mind, and her stress returned in full force, swinging toward her like a giant pendulum.

She glanced once more at her phone. She hadn't been able to get the car's GPS to work, so she'd been using her own device to point her in the right direction. Unfortunately, the little blue arrow hadn't updated her location since she'd driven past the dilapidated brick wall—which was what she could only assume was once the front entrance of the estate.

With a frown, she glanced to the small bars at the top of the phone, tapping the screen.

Just as she'd suspected. Zero service. What kind of backwoods country estate was she being called to help if they didn't even have cell service?

She stared at the road, leaning into another bend and pressing slightly harder on the gas pedal as she returned her attention to the phone. She tried to move the screen forward to look ahead on the map, but nothing moved.

Freaking stupid worthless...

She looked back to what had to be the longest driveway in human existence, intent on curving around another bend, but all at once, the trees ahead of her drew alarmingly close.

Shock struck through her body, electrifying her fingertips and pulling her stomach to the floor as she strayed from the road's curves. She slammed on her brakes and gasped, trying to take the turn slow enough to avoid rolling the very-expensive, very-not-hers car, but the back of the Aston Martin fishtailed, pulling her off the side of the road and spinning her around.

The moment seemed to endure for an eternity. Prayers spewed from her mouth in incomplete words, her knuckles white as she gripped the steering wheel until the car finally stopped and all was quiet.

Little by little, she became aware of her surroundings. Rain tapped against the car where she sat frozen, the Aston Martin having ended up facing the same direction she'd been traveling before, though the vehicle was entirely off the road.

She looked out the window of the passenger side, experiencing further shock to discover how close she'd been to striking the trees lining the drive.

A shaky breath escaped her lips, and she set the car in park.

That was close.

After another quick prayer heavenward—this time of gratitude—she shook the adrenaline from her hands and drew deep, soothing breaths.

The car was fine. The trees were fine. She was fine. They were all fine. But she really needed to get going.

Without waiting another minute, Winnie shifted to first gear, then slowly eased the Aston Martin forward.

Only it didn't move.

"No," she stated firmly. She would not accept that sort of behavior from the sports car.

She drew a deep breath, then tried to move forward once more. Again, it didn't move.

"Come on, you worthless, too-good-for-yourself car. Move!" She slammed her high-heeled foot onto the gas as hard as she could, but the back wheels merely whirred as they spun in circles in the thick mud beneath her.

After another futile moment of watching from the rearview mirror as mud flew out behind her, she stopped, shifted the car in park, then released another sigh as she dropped her forehead on the silver-winged decal on the steering wheel.

The windshield wipers still thwapped uselessly along the window, the rain continuously tapping on the metal roof and echoing loudly around the car.

Well, this was it. She would take one moment more to enjoy the warmth of the car before she accepted the inevitable—walking without cell service in the growing darkness, down an eternal driveway to see if there really was a house at the end of it.

If she were a crying woman, she would have tear-streaked cheeks and swollen eyes by now. But she was a Knox. And Knoxes didn't cry. No matter how badly they wanted to.

Raising her head from the steering wheel, she accepted her fortune and unbuckled, checking once more for service before reaching forward to turn off the car.

Her hand froze on the button as a flash of silver between the trees caught her eye. What was that, another car on the twisting road? Were the Wintours coming in search of her?

Taking heart for the first time that day, she narrowed her eyes, straining to see through the trees as the silver flashed again in the dim light.

She frowned. That looked like a super small car. And it was driving *through* the trees, not around them.

Her jaw grew slack. That was no car. That was a...No. Her

eyes were definitely playing tricks on her. And yet, after another moment, she could no longer deny what she saw driving, or rather, *riding* toward her.

It was a man on a horse. But not just any man. He was a knight in full-on shining armor gripping a lance in his right hand.

What century had she just driven into?

CHAPTER TWO

WINNIE WATCHED WARILY AS THE KNIGHT APPROACHED her car at a steady trot. What on earth was this guy doing? Assuming it *was* a guy, of course. Did he work at the estate as some sort of cosplaying attraction, haunting the grounds at night? Was he simply a lunatic trespasser? Or had her car spun around in circles so fast that she really had traveled back in time?

She shook her head with a frown. She may be jetlagged beyond belief, but she was lucid enough to know *that* wasn't possible. Still, he had to be a crazy-pants to be dressed like this while riding around in the rain, whatever his reasons. Either way, Winnie wasn't about to stick around to find out what exactly those reasons were.

Shifting her car into first gear once more, she attempted to gently ease the Aston Martin out of the mud, but she didn't move an inch forward as her car fishtailed again.

She growled in frustration, glancing up to see the knight almost upon her. In spite of her hesitations, she couldn't deny what an epic view she was privy to, having a full-armored individual riding toward her with all the confidence of a crusader. His lance was upright, as rigid and firm as an evergreen, and his thick armor accentuated his shoulders and masculine posture. And while his face was hidden behind his helmet and visor, that merely added to his mysterious nature—a nature that screamed, "You can't handle how legit I am riding atop my noble steed right now, can you?"

Truth be told, she couldn't. She also couldn't help but wonder if he was there to help her or to strike her with his lance. If only he'd ride right past her, that would solve all of her problems. And yet, as he continued in her direction, she knew she was stuck. There was nothing left to be done but sit and await her fate.

Fate. As if the guy was going to kill her. She really needed to chill.

Drawing deep, soothing breaths, she spoke to herself logically. She was tired, hungry, and stressed. Clearly, she wasn't firing on all cylinders. If she was being honest with herself, the guy was probably harmless—just a little weird. Besides that, she was a grown woman, and she was more than capable of taking care of herself. Damsel in distress? Not Winnie Knox.

With strengthened resolve, she raised her chin and squared her shoulders, even though she still listened to the little voice of warning that urged her to lock her door—just in case.

The knight reached her car then, stopping his horse directly beside her on the road, his top half hidden by the roof of the Aston Martin until he lowered his lance to the ground beside him, dismounted, and faced her.

She peered past the raindrops speckling her window, his helmet still covering his features as he moved his fisted hand in a circular movement, motioning for her to roll down her window.

Maybe she hadn't gone back a few hundred years. Maybe she'd just traveled back in time to the nineties. After all, that was the last time she'd been inside a car with the manual windows he was imitating.

Still, she got the picture.

With her index finger, she lowered the window a mere inch.

"Hi," she stated in an even voice. She'd always been good at hiding her true emotions.

"*Arhg yhu habn chrbl?*" the knight mumbled above her.

Was she supposed to have understood that? Feeling a bit braver, she lowered the window another inch, water droplets speckling her skirt and the interior armrest.

"Sorry," she said, speaking over the loud splattering on the roof. "I can't understand you with all"—she waved her hand in front of her face, then motioned to his helmet—"this."

Finally, the knight got the hint. With the horse's reins still in his hand, he reached up and unfastened his helmet with his free fingers, pulling it off his head. She leaned forward to finally see his face, but he turned just before she could.

He secured his helmet to the side of the saddle with a small buckle, then removed the chainmail and cover from his head, revealing thick, dark blond hair that curled in the rain.

Now more curious than ever, Winnie strained to see through the small slit she'd allotted herself in the window until finally, he turned around.

Well, hello, knight.

Aside from *A Knight's Tale*, her only knowledge of knights came from old, unattractive drawings of disproportionate men from hundreds of years ago.

Heath Ledger was a pretty spectacular knight. The best, as far as she was concerned.

But this guy standing in front of her, staring at her with rain sliding down his masculine features and curling the ends of his blond hair? Well, he could hold a candle to Sir Ulrich von Liechtenstein *and* Sir William Thatcher.

All. Night. Long.

With an angled jaw covered in a perfect, dark blond beard— thick enough to not be patchy, thin enough to not be icky—the man was a veritable angel, his brow prominent and blue eyes striking.

Winnie was pretty sure she wasn't in the medieval era. Nor

was she in the nineties. Instead, she was dead and was now being welcomed to the other side by this messenger from heaven.

"I merely asked," the man began again, this time far more clearly, "is the fair lady experiencing trouble with her emerald steed?"

Winnie blinked, not only at the sound of his deep, masculine tone—his English accent strong—but also because of his dialect. He had to be leaning really hard into this knight thing, right? Or was this really how he spoke all the time?

"Uh, no, I'm good," she responded.

He didn't say anything back as he peered down at her, a half-smile on his lips, moisture clinging to their smooth lines.

Wait. Did she just say she was good? She was far from "good." What was her problem?

Clearing her throat, she looked away with heat in her cheeks. Obviously, her problem was losing her mind over a man, something a Knox should never do.

She'd just chalk it up to jetlag again.

"Oh, wait," she began, "I guess I am having some trouble. My...*emerald steed*...got stuck in the mud."

She motioned over her shoulder with a dart of her thumb, and he looked to where she signaled, then back to her. "You're from the States?" he asked, his dialect disappearing.

"Oh, so you do speak normally?" she asked.

His lips curved into another smile. "Ah, forgive me, my lady. Your accent hath startled mine straight from my lips. I only meant to ask the fair lady if she hails from the...the former colonies."

He'd hesitated, clearly trying to come up with the right words.

Winnie couldn't help her growing amusement. He had to be an actor, and a charming one, at that.

"Do I have to respond in your way?" she asked, narrowing her eyes playfully. "Or will you understand my present-day tongue?"

He thought for a moment, then pressed his gauntleted hand on his armored chest. "I shall do my best to comprehend whatever leaveth thy lips, my lady."

Normally, Winnie didn't enjoy theatrics. She didn't really have time to participate in anything so frivolous. But for some reason, she didn't mind how this conversation was playing out.

"In that case, yes," she finally responded. "I am from the States."

She lowered the window an inch more, fully aware of how judgmental she was for trusting the guy now that she saw how attractive he was.

"Thou art far from thy home," he continued. "Might I ask what bringeth thee to ye olde England?"

Winnie hesitated. She wasn't sure if Mr. Wintour had told his staff that he'd hired her. Employers typically brought on consultants in secret, as even the mere whisper of one of "her kind"—an outsider with typically limited knowledge of the company—sent people into a frenzy.

Either way, the knight had to be an employee himself, so a vague response would be her safest bet. "I'm just trying to find Foxwood Hall. I've been following the GPS, and it said I had arrived a few minutes ago, but I haven't seen any estate yet. There wasn't a signpost or anything either, so I have no idea if I'm going in the right direction or not."

"Ah," he said, peering up the road. "What a conundrum."

He wiped the rain from his face, then slicked his hair back with his gloved fingers. His armor clanked in protest with his movements, but Winnie wasn't about to complain, his features more visible now more than ever. Straight nose. Smile lines near his eyes. Ridges in his neck. Was he really as broad-shouldered and barrel-chested as his armor suggested?

"I fear I have no notion as to what this *GPS* contraption is that thou speakest of," he continued, "but I do believe my knightly intuition can help thee yet. The grand estate of Foxwood is just yonder, past the trees and final bends of the pathway. Thou shouldst arrive in a matter of moments, what with the speed of thy emerald steed."

Another smile stretched across Winnie's lips. He was entirely too charming.

"Well, that's a relief," she responded, looking at the road ahead of her instead of the angle of his jawline. "And am I to expect more of your...*kind* at the estate? I'd really love to know if I've been transported to the eighteenth century after all."

His eyes shone in the dimming light, his chin slightly ducking as his brow raised. "Did the fair lady mean to say the *eighth* century?"

He winked, and heat crawled into Winnie's cheeks at her mistake. Frankly, she was so tired, she wasn't even sure what year it was *now*, let alone when knights existed. Could she be blamed for the fact?

"Yeah, that's what I meant," she lied, raising her chin and willing the warmth in her face to depart. "I guess I was just confused with a knight from the eighth century knowing about the *former colonies*," she challenged, referring to his words from earlier.

His amused gaze lessened her embarrassment. "Ah, right you are, my lady," he said. "It would appear that I have made a mistake myself. I must beg thy forgiveness, then, if I have offended thee with my correction."

Winnie didn't like to be corrected, but that charming smile of his swiftly swept away the last of her wounded pride. "Apology accepted," she stated.

His eyes lingered on her for a moment, studying her in silence before he spoke again. "Being the noble knight that I am, my lady, I fear I must inform thee that even if thou dost make it to the estate, Foxwood does not typically accept guests during so late an hour as this."

Winnie swiped at the water still dripping onto her armrest. That was just what she needed—damage to the *inside* of the sports car. "Thank you for the warning, but I'm actually expected tonight."

His eyes narrowed. "Art thou?"

"Yep," she stated simply, unwilling to give him more information. "I guess it doesn't really matter if I'm expected or not, though, since, you know, I'm kinda stuck here."

Most obvious hint ever.

Fortunately, the knight caught onto it as his eyes returned to the back of the car. "Ah, yes. Of course. I pray thou wilt excuse my lack of proper language now, as I've grown weary of finding the correct words in reference to thy steed." He cleared his throat, his accent shifting to a more modern-day English. "Was the road overly slippy?"

Slippy? Didn't he mean *slippery*? She would have corrected him had she thought it would do either of them any good. "Yeah, I think I hit a puddle," she lied, avoiding his gaze. She wasn't about to admit that her spinout was due to speeding. "I tried to drive out of the mud, but it just seemed to make me sink deeper. I don't think I'm going to be able to push myself out either, unfortunately."

"No, I don't suppose so," he said, still looking at the wheels. "I'll check it out for you. See how stuck it really is."

"Would you? I'd really appreciate it."

"No problem." He gave a single nod, retrieved his lance from the ground as easy as one lifted a toothpick, then made his way to the back of the car, clearly shifting from theatrical knight to modern-day man with a problem to solve.

Winnie didn't mind whatever type of guy he chose to be— just so long as he kept that swagger up. She watched in the rearview and sideview mirrors as he walked around the back of the car, his armored shoulders swaying from side to side with each step he took. He rested his lance against a tree nearby, tied his horse to a thick branch, then hunkered down behind the Aston Martin.

Winnie pursed her lips together, straining to see more of him in the mirror, but with the man out of view, she settled back down in her seat with a sigh, rolling up her window and catching sight of his large, black horse instead.

The gelding was stunning. She'd always wanted one like him growing up. Dark and glistening and powerful. But that dream had dissolved a long, long time ago.

The car rocked back and forth, and her head bobbed a bit with the motion. She shifted her attention to the knight in the mirror, whose top half had finally reappeared behind the car. Despite his efforts, the Aston Martin didn't budge.

After another moment, he returned to her side. She rolled down her window halfway as he approached.

"Yeah, it's fairly stuck," he said. "But if you drive a bit forward while I push, I think we can manage just fine."

His accent, while distinctly British, had a roguish twinge to it, a little rougher round the edges than a typical English accent, with the vowels sounding slightly more clipped in some places while elongated in others.

She preferred it to the posh-sounding knightly accent from before.

"I can do that," she responded.

He made for the back of the car again, but when she caught sight of his hands, she paused, calling after him. "Oh, wait."

He stopped, looking at her over his shoulder.

"Will you make sure to be careful?" She motioned to his gloved hands, the gauntlets covering half of them. "This is a rental, so I don't really want it to get scratched."

He peered down at his gloves, then gave her an amused look. "I would never dream of injuring thy steed, my lady," he said, then he walked away without another word, his armor clanking with every step.

Winnie's brow pulled together. Her request hadn't been *that* ridiculous. What did he want her to do, accept thousands of dollars' worth of damage to a car that wasn't hers? Worse than that would be the lecture she'd receive from Dad.

"Were you driving recklessly, Winnie? You really need to pay closer attention to things."

Bleh. Nothing was worse for a twenty-eight-year-old woman.

She glanced at him in her rearview mirror again, the taillights glinting red on his wet armor, and she once again shook her head in slight bewilderment. Was this really happening right now? Was she really being rescued by a knight in *shining* armor?

She caught sight of him waving his hand in the mirror, signaling for her to move forward, so she shifted into first gear, placed her high-heeled foot on the gas pedal, and eased slowly forward.

Unfortunately, the water from the open window had pooled near her feet, so when she pressed down on the gas, her heel slid forward, and her engine revved to life.

She gasped, the moment lasting only a second as she instantly slammed on the brakes, but she knew what the result was of her slip-up.

Sure enough, as she glanced in the mirror, she saw clear as day the mud striped across the knight's face and even more of it strewn across his metal shoulders and dripping from the tips of his hair.

Oops.

Winnie rolled down the window. "Sorry!" she called out. "My foot slipped."

"No problem," came the knight's strained voice from behind the car. "Just a little slower this time."

She nodded, trying again on his signal, this time easing gently into the pedal.

Slowly, the car shifted back and forth with the help of the knight, the vehicle inching forward until the back wheels finally caught, and the Aston Martin—her trusty emerald steed— escaped the clutches of the mud.

Winnie breathed a sigh of relief, setting the car in park with all four wheels securely on the road. Now she wouldn't have to walk in her heels and pencil skirt to the doors of Foxwood and embarrass herself further with a lovely wet-dog look.

She glanced in the rearview mirror, expecting the knight—she really needed to find out his name—to come up to her car and send her off, but he had moved to his horse instead.

She hesitated. As much as she didn't want to step foot in this rain, she also didn't want to appear ungrateful to the guy, especially if he was an employee and she would be working directly above him.

And he *had* done her a solid.

She pulled her umbrella out of her bag, opened the door, then popped the canopy up before stepping out into the rain and closing the door behind her. A few drops pelted against her as she adjusted her skirt and walked swiftly toward the knight, his back to her.

Her heels clicked against the road as she sidestepped the muddy tracks her tires had left behind, then she stopped at the edge of the mud, waiting for him to face her. When he didn't, she raised her voice above the sound of the rain.

"Thank you for your help," she called out, trying to make this quick. The waiting Mr. Wintour was more important.

Finally, the knight turned. Instead of the shining armor from before, dark mud splayed out across his front, a few dots still speckling his brow as he tried to wipe the muck from his face with his wet gloves.

She winced. "I did that, didn't I?"

"Yes," he said over his shoulder, still not looking at her. "I fear that thou *hast* been the cause of my less than desirable appearance. But worry not. 'Tis nothing a little rain cannot be rid of."

He finally sent her a smile, but it faltered as his eyes traveled the length of her, returning to her face with a lingering gaze. After another moment, he blinked, then averted his stare altogether.

Winnie was no stranger to being checked out. The men she'd worked with in New York stared at any woman with legs and a head. What she *wasn't* used to, however, was a man looking away as fast as this guy did. He looked almost embarrassed for being caught staring.

Why was that more flattering than being ogled?

CHAPTER THREE

MATTHEW WAS GRATEFUL FOR THE GROWING darkness, if only to prevent his blush from being seen by the woman he'd just been caught staring at.

He'd been unable to help himself. He'd seen her beauty before in the car—dark hair twisted up in an elegant style, red lips, smooth skin, and piercing gray eyes. But as she stood before him now, tall and regal, her black umbrella sheltering her feminine frame and long legs, he'd been stunned into silence.

He knew more than anyone that women were more than their physical appearance, so he'd looked away as soon as he'd realized he'd been staring, but her image remained emblazoned in his mind's eye, despite him focusing on his horse instead.

Who was she? Was she really expected at Foxwood? And what was she doing there so late at night, speeding down the drive in a rainstorm?

"Well, I really am sorry for splashing you," the woman said with sincerity, preventing him from asking the questions swirling in his mind. "And for what it's worth," she continued, "I'm super grateful for your help."

"'Tis no trouble, my lady," Matthew returned.

He hoped going back to speaking Ye Olde English wasn't

annoying to the woman. He had discovered years before that talking in such a way allowed him a level of confidence he otherwise struggled to possess. The accent—as well as his armor and lance—helped him to replace nerdy, history-obsessed Matthew with noble, knightly Sir Matthew, and people always responded better to the latter than the former.

His horse nickered before him, Nightshade standing still and patient, ears flicking back and forth as he listened to the sounds around him. The rain, their voices, Matthew's softly clanking armor...The woman behind him clearing her throat.

"I'm Winnie, by the way," she stated. "Winnie Knox."

Matthew hesitated, then braved another look at her, allowing himself a casual glance instead of the full-on gawping he'd done before.

She stood with one heel slightly forward than the other, a small smile on her face as she extended her right hand toward him.

"Oh, and I'd prefer your actual name," she added. "Unless you wish to keep up with this knight-business for longer."

He would prefer to keep it up for longer, but clearly, *she* was done with it.

He stared at her outstretched hand but made no move to take it. "Matthew," he finally responded, raising his muddy gloves to face her. "And I'd shake your hand, but as you can see, that would not do you any good."

"Ah, I appreciate it." She lowered her offered hand, then her eyes traveled the length of his armor. "So, do you work here at the estate, or do you just find yourself dressing up like a knight and riding on other people's properties for fun?"

Matthew hesitated. He'd given her his name, she'd claimed she was expected at the estate, and yet, she still didn't know who he was.

This could be fun.

"As much as I'd love to claim the latter, I do work at Foxwood," he responded.

"And what exactly do you do here?" she pressed. "Besides dressing up like Sir Lancelot."

Matthew raised his horse's stirrup over the saddle, more questions teetering at the edge of his tongue. She'd said she was expected, but by whom? A member of the household? The staff? As a guest or as a new employee?

He had a feeling she wasn't going to be forthright in her answers until she knew his real identity, but he didn't mind hiding that from her for at least a little while longer. Most people weren't themselves when they knew who he was. He didn't want this Winnie Knox to do the same.

"Oh, I do a bit here and there," he responded vaguely. "Stable work. A few things around the estate. Simple stuff, really."

"I see."

"I can't claim to be Sir Lancelot, though," Matthew continued. "And to be honest, I'd prefer to be William Marshal. But I'd take anyone over Sir Cadogan."

She delivered a blank stare, but Matthew wasn't surprised. Her response was what he'd come to expect from most people when he showed his true colors and dropped his knightly act.

"William Marshal was England's greatest knight," he explained.

"Ah, yes," she muttered with an averted gaze, clearly trying to make it appear like she knew of whom he spoke. "But Sir Cadogan was not nearly as admirable, I take it?"

Matthew nearly laughed before realizing she was serious. He sobered at once, rushing to explain so she wouldn't think he was making fun of her. "No, Sir Cadogan was a knight in the *Harry Potter* books."

Another blank stare.

"You...You haven't read *Harry Potter*?" he asked.

"No. But I've seen the movies, and they've got to be just as good, right?"

He scoffed. As if the two mediums could even be compared. Seriously, who *was* this woman? Either way, he was finished waiting to find out because he now knew two very distinct facts about this Winnie Knox. One, she didn't have any interest or knowledge in British history. And two, her opinion could not be trusted when in reference to books versus movies.

Really, if a person couldn't be trusted in that regard, how could she be trusted at all?

WINNIE HAD SAID something to upset Matthew. The only problem was that she didn't know how she'd done it. Either way, she'd be better off changing the subject rather than risking offending him further.

"So," she began, motioning once again to his armor, "you dress up like a knight to clean up horse poo?"

Matthew watched her for a moment, and she wondered if he'd even heard her before he turned away and responded. "Not typically. I merely ride dressed this way to keep the horses used to the sounds and weight. And the lance is to keep me primed and ready for jousting."

Winnie couldn't tell if he was joking or not. "Wait, like, jousting-jousting? Like with a lance and everything?"

Her eyes darted to the six-foot-long pole still propped up against the tree. "That is how one generally jousts," he returned.

He shifted to face his horse more directly, grunting slightly as he secured the cinch around the gelding.

"Do they hold a renaissance faire here or something?" she asked, trying to make sense of it all.

"We do, but we call it a medieval festival, not a renaissance faire," he responded.

"Gotcha. So it's kinda like a real-life *A Knight's Tale*?"

His brow lowered a fraction as he paused in prepping his

horse. "No, not like *A Knight's Tale* at all. That movie is completely historically inaccurate."

She should have known he wouldn't have appreciated the comparison. "What are you talking about? Queen was totally around during the eighth century." There, she'd redeemed herself. *Eighth* Century. "And in my opinion, "We Will Rock You" is the best part of the movie."

He stared at her with a look of confusion before he seemed to realize she was teasing him. One corner of his mouth raised in a smile, and his shoulders seemed to lower in time with his defenses.

That had been fun, teasing him. Maybe she could get away with doing it again.

"I do wonder, though," she continued, "if you fault *Harry Potter* for being historically inaccurate as much as you do *A Knight's Tale*."

He held up a finger. "Ah, excellent question. I do not. That is because the amount of history and research laced throughout each story in the *Harry Potter* series is comparable to a simplified history book. So while it may be set in a fantastical world, it should still be known to a degree for its historical accuracy."

Winnie couldn't hide her smile. Honestly, he was adorable—and his passion for history and apparently *Harry Potter* were admirable. She'd had a passion for things once, too. Horses. Riding. Jumping.

But that was a long time ago.

"So," she continued, if only to distract herself from the miserable thoughts of her past, "I assume your festival takes the cake from *Harry Potter* and *A Knight's Tale* when it comes to historical accuracy?"

Matthew shifted back to his horse and continued. "Absolutely. We all pride ourselves on the quality of the entertainment we provide. Our festival is far more historically accurate than any movie you'll ever see—or any event you'll ever attend."

"That's quite the statement," she said.

"Such is the level of my confidence, my lady," he said with another wink.

He certainly was a flirtatious knight.

"I assure you," he continued in his normal accent, "if you wish to know about the medieval era, come to the festival we're holding tomorrow. You'll be an expert in no time."

Was he really inviting her to join him? Or was this more of a generic comment? Either way, Winnie was still trying to wrap her mind around the fact that someone jousted for an actual living.

She didn't know much about renaissance faires or medieval festivals, and she'd only ever watched fake jousting done by Heath Ledger. Although, in high school, she'd seen people gathering in groups, dressing up, and playing make-believe together with swords and armor.

To be honest, it wasn't really her thing. Armor, and history, and damsels in distress. But to each their own, she supposed.

"You said you're expected here, then?" Matthew asked.

"Yeah." She was more at ease, knowing the man worked there. She could be deliberate in what she shared or didn't share more easily now. "Mr. Wintour has asked me to do some work for him."

She omitted her actual job title. She didn't know of very many people who actually liked consultants. Okay, she didn't know of *anyone* who did. Honestly, she didn't even like *herself* sometimes in this line of work. But Dad was proud of her for once in her life, so what was a girl to do?

Although, now that she thought about it, maybe "proud" was too strong a word. "Tolerated" fit better.

"*Some work,*" Matthew said, repeating her words. He lowered the stirrup and unbuckled his knight's helmet from the side of the saddle, his features still hidden from her. "So you've been hired as a consultant."

Her lips parted in surprise. "I, well, I..." she stammered.

Finally, he faced her with a knowing look. "Thy hesitation revealeth much, my lady."

She fought off a smile. Fine. She would relent. "How did you know?" she asked.

"The Wintours have hired many consultants over the years. I merely put two-and-two together."

She looked away. Had they really hired that many consultants? Neither her dad nor Mr. Wintour had mentioned that. Well, it didn't matter. She was good at her job—the only one she'd ever been good at—so she knew she would succeed where every other consultant hadn't. Such was the luxury of attempting to start up one's own business a number of times and failing a number of times. With all that experience, how could she *not* know exactly how to help businesses thrive?

"Well, I wish you luck," Matthew continued. "The Wintours can be a crotchety bunch at times."

She hesitated. He was either complaining about his employers to be truthful or to try to get *her* to be more truthful. Better to be safe than sorry, though.

"Well, thank you for the luck," she returned. "But I won't need it."

He looked at her with one eyebrow raised in a challenge. "Really?"

She nodded. "I've heard of nothing but good things about Mr. Wintour, so I'm not worried."

"And who have you heard these words from?"

The light outside was growing dimmer, the rain still tapping against the top of her umbrella. Matthew—had he given her his last name? She was too tired to recall—still stood in the midst of it all, droplets dripping from the ends of his dark blond curls, though he'd pushed most of his hair away from his brow.

He looked...Well, he looked good, dang it. Moisture glinting across his features, enhancing the lines of his cheekbones and edges of his lips. Small drops of rain clung to his scruff and accentuated all the right angles of his jaw.

Why was it that men became more attractive in the rain when women just looked so soggy?

23

He watched her expectantly, and she realized all too soon that she hadn't responded to him yet, too taken with all his bearded goodness.

"My dad is good friends with Mr. Wintour," she finally said.

Matthew's eyes were impassive. What was he thinking in those blue depths?

"Well, I suppose you'd know best, then." He gave her a short smile, then turned toward his horse once more.

He might have been finished with their conversation, but Winnie had a bit more information to glean first. "I take it you've worked with Mr. Wintour directly," she said in a casual tone.

He placed a white cap over his wet hair, then pulled his hooded chainmail on next. "I have. A time or two."

"And both times were...unpleasant?" she prodded.

"Not at all," he returned. "I only said the Wintours can be crotchety. They know what they like and can be difficult to make bend. One in particular."

He was obviously talking about Mr. Wintour. But why? What had happened for Matthew to say that?

He raised his helmet over his head next, then faced her as he lifted the visor, his features framed in the small window he was allotted.

Even with her limited view of his face, his attractive traits still shone through. "I just wanted to warn you," he said. "That's all."

Warn her or scare her off? The two were synonymous in her experience.

"Well, thank you," she said. "But like I said, I'm not too concerned. I've had my fair share of working with difficult people."

"I'm sure you have."

Silence hung between them, and his pointed look made her pause. Wait, was he saying that *she* was difficult?

Before she could ask, he walked to the other side of his horse, untied the reins from the tree, and pushed himself into the saddle, his armor clanging with each movement. How had he managed that, mounting by himself?

Clearly, he was ready to get back to his knightly ride, but she still wasn't finished.

She shifted her umbrella back a degree to see him atop his horse. "Before you go," she started, inching closer to the edge of the road where the mud began, "I have to ask, since you already know why I'm here, is there anything you'd like to share with me that would make your life as an employee of the Wintours better? Anything that should be brought to my attention? Anything that could be improved?"

His horse started walking ahead, but Matthew held back on the reins, reaching for his lance. With grace that revealed he'd done the action before, he gently tossed the pole in the air little-by-little, shifting it up until he gripped the handle firmly in his hand.

"No," he finally responded, eying the top of the lance that he held straight up in the air. "The place is pretty well perfect as it is."

Obviously, the man didn't think he could trust her with the truth. But she was used to breaking down those barriers quite simply. All it took was a bit of encouragement and a whole lot of charm.

She smiled up at him, blinking slowly with a look that said, *Come on, you can trust me.*

She'd practiced this look in front of the mirror a thousand times as a high schooler. She'd learned it from one of her sisters. Samantha had achieved hundreds of dates with such a look.

Winnie had been...less successful. But it was worth a try now.

"There's not one little thing you want to share with me?" she asked sweetly.

He shook his head in silence, the lance still steady in his grip.

All right. Charm wasn't working. Maybe a little trust exercise then.

"So you don't see a problem with the GPS system not taking guests directly to the house?" she asked. "Or that the roads are unfit to travel in the rain due to puddles and pockets of mud? Or that there's not a single sign posting or welcome that lets visitors know they've arrived at the estate? None of that matters to you or the others who work here?"

The air between them grew cold. Matthew's eyes hardened, and she knew she'd offended him. But, why? Was he simply loyal to the Wintours?

"If you look for something to complain about," he began, "you'll be sure to find it. I, for one, choose to see the good in things. It makes life far more enjoyable."

Another blush threatened to rise to her cheeks, but she suppressed it. Matthew sure liked to instruct people, didn't he?

She tipped her umbrella back even farther. "I'm not complaining, merely being observant. In my experience, I've found if we don't continually look for things to improve upon, we become stagnant and filled with faults and flaws that would have been much easier to get rid of had we put in the effort in the beginning. If you look at it that way, it's really all about saving time and being more productive. And what's not enjoyable about a productive life?"

She ended with a smile, then waited in silence for him to respond.

His scrutinizing gaze would have made her squirm, were she not well-versed in remaining cool under pressure. "So Foxwood is filled with faults and flaws, is it?" he asked.

That's what he got out of her whole speech? "Not necessarily. But you'd have to be crazy to say it's perfect the way it is. I haven't even arrived fully yet, and I already know there's going to be a long list of improvements that can be made. *Should* be made."

"Is that so?" he asked.

She nodded in silence.

"Well," he began, looking away, "what a blessed relief for the lowly Wintours to have thee to rescue them." He adjusted the reins in his hands. "I bid thee adieu now, as my own steed grows weary. Good evening, *my lady.*"

26

He bowed his head in what she could only assume was a mocking nod, then clanked his visor down over his eyes and urged his horse forward—directly toward where she stood.

Swiftly, she moved out of the way to avoid being hit by the mud kicked up by the horse's hooves, but in her haste, she forgot where she stood and stepped straight off the side of the road. Her pointed heels sank into the soft mud, and she groaned as the dark grime oozed over the black toes of her footwear.

Had Matthew done that on purpose? Ridden too close to her to make her stand in the mud?

She glanced up at him, but he and his little horse just sauntered away without a backward glance, the lance high in the air like a floating, branchless tree.

He couldn't have known what he'd done, otherwise he would have offered his help to her again, right? Or had the mere mention of her being a business consultant stripped him of any desire to continue his knightly actions?

Sadly enough, in her experience, that was the truth more often than not. This was yet another reason consulting was difficult—how swiftly she made enemies.

With a sigh, she stared down at the mud once more. Whatever. She didn't need Matthew's help anymore anyway. Her shoes were far lighter than the car. She could get out of this mud herself.

One by one, she heaved her feet from the slop, her heels making a *"schlock"* sound as they were pulled from the mud's grip. Her legs were as speckled as an Appaloosa's behind, no doubt from the gelding's backsplash, but she shook off her annoyance once again.

Fort Knox. Be like Fort Knox.

She pulled a face as the phrase sailed through her mind. The words were as deeply engrained in her as was her desire to please Dad.

"Being a member of the Knox family means that nothing can penetrate your defenses," he'd always said to her and her siblings when they were children. *"It means that nothing can shake you,*

27

nothing can hurt you, nothing can rattle you. Because we Knoxes are like Fort Knox. So be like Fort Knox."

She hated those words. Sometimes, she didn't want to have a permanent defense around her. Sometimes, she wanted to let go and just be okay with not...being okay.

But ultimately, in her line of work, she needed metaphorical defenses. Heck, in *life* she needed metaphorical defenses. Because being a Knox meant that she had to deal with all the garbage handed to her—and to never get discouraged by it.

With a heavy sigh, she tramped across the road, doing her best to wipe off the mud from her heels before entering the car and using spare tissues to wipe off her legs.

As she did so, she focused on the task that lay before her with Mr. Wintour, all the while repeating to herself the words she prayed would actually help her be like the Knox she was meant to be.

"Like Fort Knox. Be like Fort Knox."

MATTHEW GRIPPED the lance tighter as he urged his horse into a trot, finding his balance instantly with Nightshade's rhythmic clip-clopping.

He probably shouldn't have done that—walked too close to Winnie to cause her to step in the mud. Such a decision had been petty and childish. And yet, still, it took everything within Matthew to keep his eyes forward so he didn't pride himself on seeing what damage he'd done to those heels of hers.

He couldn't say Winnie hadn't deserved it. She'd been far too candid criticizing Foxwood, and he wouldn't stand for it. None of the other consultants hired to improve the estate had ever been so boorish. He could only imagine what she'd say about the festival if she chose to accept his invitation to attend.

He blew out a breath, white air billowing out from his helmet and disappearing behind his armored shoulder as he and Nightshade drew closer to the stables.

The festival was one of his greatest joys. It was the only place he was free to be himself—to share his love of the medieval era with those around him, to bring history to life without being judged for being different.

And the jousting—how he loved the jousting. Dressing in the ancient, powerful armor, feeling the strength of Nightshade beneath him as they charged down the list along the tilt, using every ounce of might to grip the lance in his hands and striking the opposing knight. There was no greater feeling on this earth, no greater force Matthew had ever experienced than when he dressed as a knight and jousted.

Having that presumptuous Winnie Knox in the audience would certainly dampen that enthusiasm, though.

His stomach hardened at the thought, and Nightshade tossed his head in protest, having felt his owner's change in demeanor.

To alleviate his horse's distress, Matthew drew a calming breath, then pointed the lance straight out in front of him, cradling the handle between his arm and side for a few paces until his muscles burned. Only then did he raise the lance to stand straight up in the air once again, giving his arm the chance to rest from the strenuous position.

He always performed the exercise before a match or during a particularly stressful practice session, finding that it helped to channel his anxious energy. Fortunately, it did the same thing now with thoughts of the narrow-minded consultant.

Matthew needed all the focus he could get because he had a job to see to now, and that was alerting the household to just exactly what type of consultant had been hired to help at Foxwood—a consultant who criticized the estate and who didn't know her eighth century from her eighteenth.

There was definitely no place for her here. No place at all. And he'd be the first person to let everyone else know it.

CHAPTER FOUR

FORTUNATELY, WITH WINNIE SILENTLY AND begrudgingly chanting her family's mantra, she made it to the house without any further incidents.

Just as Matthew had promised, the estate appeared around the final bend at the end of a long, straight drive.

There it was. Foxwood Hall—a magnificent, grand house glowing warmly in the darkness. Windows illuminated the inside, while the turrets on the outside created depth and magnificence to the grand structure.

Rounded and separate hedges lined the drive leading up to the house in perfect precision, lit by uniformly staggered lights. The hedges stood straight and tall, as if they were green foot soldiers greeting guests—all the while putting off the air of, "don't mess with this fortress or else..."

Winnie got the picture. She'd gotten it when she'd Googled the place a few weeks before. This was a grand estate, and there was no mistaking the history that was involved in the making of it.

In the truest sense of the word, Foxwood Hall was spectacular. And *she* was going to be the one to help it stay afloat.

Excitement stirred within her chest, growing brighter as she drew closer to the house. She hardly ever enjoyed her job, but there were certain aspects that made it tolerable, specifically when she had the opportunity to use her creativity and intellect to help a business—or in this case, an estate—to shine brightly once again.

Of course, not everyone saw her as a helper. Still, she liked to think of herself as a rescuer from laziness instead of a dictator.

Finally reaching the house, she pulled her eyes away from the looming hall and focused her attention on where to park. A few cars were situated to the west of the house in undesignated spots. Perhaps that was just for family members, though.

However, after looking over her shoulder and finding nowhere else to go, she headed for the vehicles anyway.

This would be another thing she'd suggest to Mr. Wintour. Maybe she'd bring it up to Matthew when she saw him next. Did he not think *this* was a problem with the estate—guests not knowing where to go? Of course he didn't. He was obviously only thinking of his own well-being. Typical employee.

Focus, Winnie.

She shook the knight from her mind. She had a job to see to, and dwelling on the last few minutes of their encounter would do nothing but distract her.

Just like his curled hair and angled jaw had done.

She blinked away his image from her mind and pulled up to the other cars, taking a quick gander at the four of them. Range Rover. Rolls Royce. Audi.

The Wintour family obviously liked their cars.

Winnie wasn't super "in" to vehicles, but her dad was. Growing up, he always made it a game to find the fanciest cars on the road whenever they drove anywhere together as a family. The kid who found the most expensive car—correctly naming the make, model, and color—would win.

She never did. She had always been too focused on the horses they drove past in the fields or the sketches she drew of them on her notebook in the back seat.

"You have to put in more effort if you want to win, Winnie," Dad would always say.

She hadn't cared about winning, though. She'd cared about horses.

But that had only caused her grief.

Slowly pulling forward, Winnie focused her eyes on the final car in the row, the lights of her Aston Martin shining across the faded red paint of...What was that, a knockoff Mini Cooper?

She pulled a face. What on earth was *that* doing here with chipped red paint, what looked to be the original tires, and a side mirror that was hanging onto the rest of the car for dear life?

Maybe this area wasn't just for the Wintours, then. The staff were probably allowed to park there, as well. Actually, now that she thought about it, that was probably Matthew's car. The knight *would* drive something like that.

She chortled aloud at her joke.

Finally pulling forward, she gave herself a wide berth from the car, parking a good distance away to prevent any accidental nick from the clunker—or its driver.

Once situated, she put the car in park and turned it off, reaching for her small suitcase and bag and exiting the vehicle before trudging across the pea gravel toward the door. Rain pelted her brow in her haste, but finally, she reached the porch just in time for the door to swing open.

Light poured across the front entrance and lit the raindrops in the air, causing them to shine like falling crystals in the darkness.

A middle-aged man appeared in the doorway. "Miss Knox," he greeted, opening the door wider. His accent was fine, each word polished like silver. "My apologies for not greeting you outside earlier. I am Mr. Fernsby, the Wintours' butler." He stepped out into the rain, reaching at once for her suitcase and bag and relieving her of both. "Allow me to assist you."

Winnie nodded, her arms feeling instant relief. She wiped the rain from her brow and smoothed down her hair as she stepped over the threshold, feeling a bit like she'd fallen into a *Downton Abbey* episode.

"I'm sorry to be so late," she said, drying her feet on the rug in the entryway.

"No apology needed, ma'am."

The butler then launched into an explanation of where she would be staying—"The private section of Foxwood dedicated solely to workers of the estate"—and that the housekeeper would see to her belongings that evening.

Winnie did her best to listen, but she found herself too distracted by the gorgeous entryway to hear much of anything.

The entire space was clean, stately, and stunning, from the ornate blue and green rugs stretched across the floor to the dark wooden banisters of the staircase that curved along the wall to the upper rooms.

The walls boasted a soft, light blue shade, portraits of dogs, horses, and cats neatly hanging on each, while a gold chandelier dazzled from the center of the room.

Unlike the fake plants scattered around Winnie's small apartment in New York, the floras decorating each corner of Foxwood's entryway were large, green, and *very* real.

She should probably look into getting a butler for herself. Maybe then her plants would have a higher chance of survival.

"This way, ma'am, if you please."

Winnie followed Mr. Fernsby then, who led her up the stairs. With his back turned toward her, she took the opportunity to freshen up, smoothing down her hair and wiping away any rogue mascara that had pooled beneath her eyes, all the while observing the rooms they passed by.

Each corridor was warmly lit, each room decorated to the nines. More gilded portraits of horses, hunters, and Greek goddesses lined every passage, and time and time again, she was struck with the opulence.

Had Winnie not spoken with Mr. Wintour twice before agreeing to work for him, she would have thought he was trying to pull the wool over her eyes. Clearly, the estate was not struggling.

In her research before coming to the house, however, she'd read that many British estates were now suffering due to staff payment increases and taxes skyrocketing. She knew most upper-class families did little else but inherit their estates, but she still couldn't help but feel sad that so many grand homes were being lost to families who had owned them for literal centuries.

Mr. Wintour himself had spoken with her at length of the problems they faced—most of them similar issues. Lack of cash flow, taxes siphoning their funds, no ideas on how to generate an income to fit their family. He wished for Winnie to help prevent any chance of their estate dilapidating. Such a task was going to be monumental, but she couldn't wait to get started.

After walking through the maze-of-a-house, Winnie stood outside of a large, closed door, waiting as Mr. Fernsby knocked twice on the dark wood.

"Miss Knox, sir," the butler said at once.

"Ah, excellent! Come in, come in," replied the male voice within.

Mr. Fernsby opened the door, entered the room, then stood as a sentinel, allowing her entrance.

It was all very formal. A bit much for her taste. But as she entered the room next, she could understand why there was such pomp and circumstance.

If she thought the rest of the house was unbelievable, this room took the cake. A big ole *chocolate* cake.

The study was gorgeous. Dark bluish-gray walls. White, elaborate carvings trimming the top and bottom of the room. Warm brown shelves stuffed to the max with red, tan, and blue leather-bound books.

The rugs were a salmon and cerulean color, and a small, half-circle alcove was built into the side of the room, surrounded by more books and housing a cozy lamp, two chairs, and a table with a half-completed game of chess atop.

Drawing the most attention in the room, however, was the grand fireplace, white and crafted in the highest of qualities. A warm fire crackled inside the hearth, and dark leather chairs curved round the heat.

Most rooms of such opulence, holding so many colors and frames and trimmings, would have caused Winnie to feel claustrophobic. But this space made her feel as if she were receiving a warm embrace from an old, friendly grandfather.

As she turned around, such a feeling wasn't hard to understand as she faced the curve-legged desk with Mr. Wintour sitting behind it, a cheerful and welcoming smile on his lips.

He hadn't even said a word to her yet, and she already knew, this man was warmth in a box.

"Miss Knox, welcome," he said, standing from his desk and motioning for her to come farther into the room. "Come in."

"Winnie, please," she corrected, reaching forward with an outstretched hand. "You have an absolutely gorgeous home."

"Oh, thank you," Mr. Wintour said, taking her hand in turn. His handshake was warm and firm. "And it's Arthur."

Winnie nodded, though she had no intention of using his first name. She never did when it came to people who hired her, as per Dad's advice.

"Well, Winnie," Mr. Wintour continued, "you must be absolutely exhausted. What do you say to having a hot drink by the fire?"

Winnie's nerves had been just what they always were when starting a job—uncertain. But with the man's unassuming smile and kind gestures, it was the strangest thing. She was *instantly* put at ease.

She knew next to nothing about him, other than the fact that he and Dad had met at Oxford and had remained friends ever since. So how could Winnie feel as if she'd just stepped into an old friend's home?

"I would love that," she returned.

Mr. Wintour looked to the door where Mr. Fernsby had

remained since Winnie had been invited in. The butler nodded at once, then left the room in silence as the master of the estate faced Winnie again.

"Please," he said, his bright blue eyes crinkling at the sides, "take a seat."

He moved around his desk, and Winnie was distracted for a brief moment by the cane he leaned heavily upon. The man couldn't be over fifty-five. Did he suffer some injury to require the use of the walking stick?

She didn't allow her eyes or her curiosity to linger for long, crossing the room to the hearth before taking a seat directly in front of the fire.

Mr. Wintour took a seat kitty corner to her own, wincing slightly as he sat down, though the pained look was swiftly replaced with a smile as he lay the cane to the side of him. Salt-and-pepper colored his hair at the sides in a dignified manner, matching well with the comfortable-looking blue sweater and black slacks he wore.

"So," he began, the smile still on his lips, "you're here."

He had to be one of the happiest men she'd ever laid eyes on. Dad had said he was very respectable, but he hadn't mentioned anything about Mr. Wintour being so smiley.

"I can't believe I finally made it," she said. "I'm so sorry for the delay. I usually pride myself on my punctuality, but this trip has humbled me."

He brushed it aside with a flippant hand in the air. "Ah, it's no trouble at all. Though I was afraid I'd have to send out a search party had you taken much longer."

They shared a small laugh, and she was caught by how handsome he was. She supposed that was the British in him.

He paused for a minute, his eyes taking in the sight of her. She didn't feel scrutinized. Only...studied. "You look more like your mother than your father, you'll be glad to hear," he finally said.

She smiled. "I *am* glad to hear that. But I didn't know you'd met her."

"Only briefly. I made the trip to your father's wedding celebrations."

Her brow rose. Dad hadn't mentioned that either. "Really?"

"Yes, it was the last time we saw each other, I'm afraid," Mr. Wintour said, his smile slightly fading. "Time gets away from us, doesn't it? But I suppose with friends, it usually feels as if no time has passed at all."

Winnie could only pretend to agree. She had never been one to have many friends. The ones she had were typically work-based and disappeared whenever she moved.

"So how are your family?" Mr. Wintour asked next, his accent smooth and timeless. "Your parents and siblings?"

"They're all doing really great," she said with a nod. "We're scattered around the States and Europe, so we don't see each other in person very often, but we try to make time to get together online and in chats."

"And your parents are still working?"

"Oh, yes." She leaned back in the chair, the tightness in her shoulders easing as the warm fire and kind company soothed her soul. "I don't think they'll ever retire. My dad loves to work at their firm way too much."

"He hasn't changed, then," Mr. Wintour said with a knowing smile. His eyes took on a nostalgic look as he glanced toward the fire. "But he is happy? With his life, I mean?"

Winnie tipped her head to the side. It was a strange question. Or rather, asked in a strange way. As if her response would somehow tell him more than the simple words she would give.

Her instinct was to deliver a hearty yes. But then, *was* Dad happy with his life? He had never really expressed much joy in anything other than the Knox Family Law Firm.

Mr. Wintour's focus intensified.

She blinked, pulling out of her thoughts. "I think he is," she responded carefully.

That was as truthful as she could be, even if she wasn't comfortable with the answer.

Before Mr. Wintour could respond, Mr. Fernsby drew their attention to the doorway, entering with a tray of plates, cups, and a few cookies.

"Mr. Fernsby," Mr. Wintour said, eying the cookies as the butler placed the tray on the coffee table between them, "you do spoil me. Just promise me you'll not share with Jane that you've given me biscuits tonight."

"Of course, sir," Mr. Fernsby said with a smile. "Just as I won't tell you what treats Mrs. Wintour has been given this evening."

Mr. Wintour laughed, and Mr. Fernsby's eyes shone.

Winnie watched them curiously, surprised at their friendly relationship. They were still clearly employer and employee, but their comfort with each other merely revealed more of Mr. Wintour's goodness.

And that led to only more questions for Winnie, most specifically, how on earth had Dad ever made friends with the man? Dad only ever drew closer to people who were of benefit to him, those who could further his career or improve his societal standing—and his friends were all admittedly the same. Mr. Wintour would have certainly boosted Dad's social life back at Oxford, being the heir to Foxwood, but Mr. Wintour was so *nice*. And Dad's friends were never nice.

Had Mr. Wintour once been a shark like Dad and had since changed? Or had Dad found some benefit in befriending someone like Mr. Wintour?

After Mr. Fernsby had left the room, she and Mr. Wintour enjoyed the drinks and cookies as they conversed more about Winnie's family.

When his drink was finished, Mr. Wintour placed it on the table between them and leaned back with a satisfied sigh, though she didn't miss another flinch as he did so. "Well, I don't wish to keep you up much later," he said. "What do you say to the two of us finally getting on with a little business, eh?"

He ended his words with a harmless wink, just like Grandpa

used to. Not Dad, of course. The closest thing to a wink she'd ever seen from him was a wince when she'd done something stupid, like failing out of med school or looking into being an art museum curator during her college exploration days. Neither action was impressive enough for a member of the Knox family.

"I'd love to," she readily agreed. "You mentioned when we spoke on the phone about a comprehensive list of things you wished for me to see to?"

Mr. Wintour shifted to the side again, this time blinking hard as he clearly struck a nerve of pain. Whatever was ailing him, Winnie's heart reached out to him. She ought to speed this up, allow him to get to bed sooner.

"Yes, I do have a list." He opened his mouth, then closed it again as his eyes twinkled, despite the pain he was clearly feeling. "However, I have something else in mind for you now."

Winnie blinked. "Oh?" This had to be the first time her job description changed *after* being hired.

Mr. Wintour must have seen her hesitation, as he rushed on. "Only if you are comfortable with the changes, of course. I am still very much looking forward to your help with the estate. But before that, I was hoping you'd help me with a little side project."

"A side project," she repeated, trying to keep up with his vague description. "What sort of side project?"

Once again, his eyes shone. "Have you ever been to a medieval festival?"

CHAPTER FIVE

WINNIE'S LIPS PARTED IN SURPRISE. "WELL, NO, actually. But I have heard of them."

From your slightly nerdy, obsessed-with-history, insanely loyal employee.

But she'd keep that to herself. No need to mention her little run-in with the knight on the road, nor the fact that she had been driving too fast and far too distractedly to *not* be blamed for swerving into the mud.

"I can't say that I know too much about them, either," she clarified.

To her surprise, Mr. Wintour smiled all the more. "I was hoping you'd say that. We're holding one tomorrow, and I wanted it to be your first experience."

First experience. Medieval festival. A knight rescuing her. The thoughts flitted about her mind continuously, including Matthew's own invitation-slash-suggestion to attend the festival.

"You see," Mr. Wintour continued, the light of the fire dancing across half his features, "for over a decade, we have put on these festivals. Jousting tournaments, falconry, sword fighting, you name it. We knew a great deal of success to begin with, but over the years, the number of attendees have dwindled."

"Okay," Winnie said, trying to take his words in stride. For some reason, her stomach had started twisting like a wrung rag.

"I believe a great deal of money and enjoyment can still be had with this experience," Mr. Wintour continued. "I've set aside a fair-sized budget to revitalize the event. Now all we need is the right set of hands to secure its future." His eyes focused on her more intently. "So, I was hoping, what with your experience turning around a variety of businesses, if you wouldn't mind taking a *stab* at it. Pun intended."

He ended with a little amused smile, then waited for her to respond.

Unfortunately, Winnie didn't know *how* to respond. She'd been too distracted at Foxwood. Lulled into a false sense of security by all the hot chocolate, warm smiles, and cozy rooms. This was why she'd never be as good of a Knox as the rest of her family. *They* wouldn't have let their guards down in this situation.

"So you don't need my help with the rest of the estate, then?" she asked, trying to manage her expectations.

"Oh, no," he said, moving to lean forward, then seeming to think better of it after a soft grunt. "No, that is not what I am saying at all. I absolutely want—no, I *need* your help and your advice. I was merely hoping to push the work of the estate back a few weeks to prioritize the festival. After all, the event is on its last leg. It's draining far more money than it's bringing in, and if something doesn't change soon, we will have to end it within the month. All you would need to do is use your business expertise to help us make the event profitable."

Knowing he still had plans to have her work for the estate brought her only partial relief, as she still couldn't wrap her mind around his request. Was he really considering making her head of a medieval festival—the festival Matthew had boasted of being more historically accurate than anything she'd ever attend?

She had no expertise whatsoever in the field, not to mention the fact that Dad would die of utter humiliation if she accepted the job.

A Knox daughter, being in charge of an event that not only accepted but *encouraged* people to dress up and reenact scenes from an archaic world? How embarrassing for him.

But now was not the time to focus on Dad and his judgments. She still had a job to see to, whether she chose to accept it or not.

"If the event is siphoning money so much," she began, "the most logical solution would be to cancel it straightaway, right?"

Mr. Wintour winced, though this time, it looked more out of emotional pain than physical. "Yes, well, canceling isn't really an option. There is a sort of sentimental attachment the family has to the festival—for one of us in particular. We would really hate to see the end of it."

Sentimental attachments never did anyone any good—especially in a business setting. At least, that's what Dad always said.

Obviously, the next solution, aside from canceling the event, would be to hire someone else with more experience than her. She would never tell him to do that, though. She didn't have experience running an English estate, so what if he found someone else better suited to that, as well?

"I know this is not in your job description," Mr. Wintour said, obviously sensing her hesitation. "And I completely understand if your answer is no. If it is, we may continue on with the estate as previously planned. But I do hope you will consider it. I believe that you are just the person I've been looking for to rescue the festival and turn it into something even better than it was before." He paused with a smile. "You are your father's daughter, after all. A part of the Knox family, strong and determined."

As if that would convince her to agree. She wasn't anything like the rest of her family. She was more likely to fail at this than anyone. She knew nothing about faires.

But she did know business. And she knew how to make a company money and how to get rid of waste, no matter the industry. The years she'd spent in business school had given her enough of a leg to stand on—though failing at her other businesses had given her more knowledge than anything.

So what if she didn't fail? What if, instead, she knocked it out of the park? Helping with the event couldn't be too difficult. She'd observe the faire tomorrow, jot down a few ideas, do a bit of research, hire a few carnival rides, then boom bam, she'd be on her way to the real job, the job that would finally give her the respect she desired from her family.

"You're more than welcome to take a day or two to think about it," Mr. Wintour said. "Attend the festival tomorrow, then decide later on."

But Winnie shook her head. The man must've cast some sort of medieval witchery on her because for some insane reason, she was inclined to agree with his proposal.

"We don't have to wait for tomorrow," she said with certainty. "I'd be happy to help in any way I can."

The relief and happiness on Mr. Wintour's face was worth all of Winnie's remaining doubt. It felt nice to make someone smile for a change.

"That was exactly what I was hoping to hear," he said. "Thank you so much for being willing to accommodate us."

"It's no trouble," she said with a reassuring nod, as if to comfort her own insecurities.

"Well, excellent," he said, lacing his fingers together across his lap. Then his smile faded. "Now there is just one last thing I need to discuss with you. My hiring you may not go over so well with those directly involved with the festival."

The image of Matthew flashed through her mind, but instead of trepidation, which she was sure Mr. Wintour was expecting, Winnie's spirits lifted.

Finally, something she could handle.

"Oh, that's to be expected," she said with an easy smile. "I've had my fair share of hate mail, so you don't need to worry about me. I can hold my own."

Mr. Wintour's eyes shone in a knowing light, a light that made her slightly wary. What did he know that she didn't?

To her disappointment, he didn't explain. "Well, I'm glad to hear it," he said instead. "Let's discuss more details after you've had the chance to observe the festival yourself tomorrow, yes?"

He pressed a button on the table nearby, then pulled his cane forward and made to stand, clearly struggling. Winnie looked away to allow the man some dignity.

"Will you be joining me around the grounds?" she asked, if only to draw attention away from his grimaces.

"I hope I'll be feeling up to it," Mr. Wintour said, taking a step toward the door as she followed. "But my wife will be there if I am not."

She nodded, still following behind him. "May I ask if she is the one with the sentimental attachment to the faire? Or is it you?"

"Actually, it is neither of us."

They reached the door, and he turned to face her, an amused smile lighting his eyes once again. What was she missing?

"It is my son."

Son? Had Dad told her that Mr. Wintour had children? Now that she thought of it, she vaguely remembered a son and daughter being mentioned. Why hadn't she considered them until now?

Questions swirled in her mind about them both, but her words were stifled as soft footsteps sounded behind her, and Mr. Wintour's eyes traveled beyond her shoulder, twinkling once again.

"Speak of the devil," he said. "Here he is now. Evening, Matthew."

All at once, Winnie's insides shriveled like the ends of a dying plant. She didn't have to turn around to see exactly who stood behind her.

Matthew *Wintour.*

Of course.

CHAPTER SIX

SLOWLY, WINNIE SHIFTED AROUND TO FACE THE knight who'd rescued her on the road.

Of all the people who worked at the estate, of all the people to have found her completely helpless, and of all the people she might have seen instead to ask after the faults of Foxwood, why did it have to be him?

Had he known all along that she'd been hired by his dad? Is that how he'd "guessed" that she was a consultant—because he'd been playing her?

She glued a smile to her lips, praying it was convincing enough to show that she wasn't startled by his presence. That was another Knox rule—don't let anyone take you by surprise.

Of course, when she turned to face the guy, that was easier said than done. Instead of being covered from head-to-toe in armor, face splattered with mud, water dripping from his curled hair, Winnie was met with the sight of a knight-turned-modern-day-stud-muffin.

In the brighter light of the study, his features were even more defined. His scruff was dark along his jawline, though it faded to a slightly lighter blond as it inched toward his cheekbones. The blue in his eyes shone brightly, enhanced by the thin, light azure color of the t-shirt he wore, and his shoulders—those shoulders. Obviously, the armor hadn't been what made them broad all along.

He sure did clean up nicely.

And she sure was an idiot to not have realized who he was earlier.

Seriously. Riding across his estate at dark. Joking about his family being crotchety. Omitting his last name. *Being offended by her criticism of his home.*

Obviously all the signs were there.

Rather than admitting she was a total dolt, though, she blamed it on jetlag. That had to be why she was failing so abysmally at life right now.

"Matthew," Mr. Wintour said, breaking through the silence that had filled the air. "I'd like for you to meet Winnie—"

"Knox," Matthew interrupted. His dad looked at him in surprise. "We've met."

His voice was deep and rich, far more now that she could hear him without his armor or the rain muffling his words.

He turned toward Winnie more fully. "So you're the puddle I followed all the way here," he stated, his blue eyes shining.

Her eyes dropped to the study floor. What was he talking about? There wasn't a puddle in sight. Anyway, she'd wiped her feet in the entryway. She was sure of it.

Mr. Wintour looked between the two of them in confusion. "I'm sorry, you've met before?"

"Just a few moments ago," Matthew answered for the both of them because apparently, Winnie had lost her ability to speak. "On the drive. Apparently, she wishes to leave her mark wherever she goes."

Again, Winnie said nothing.

Mr. Wintour took a step forward to face her more directly. "Is this true? Have you met Matthew already?"

Winnie blinked, then cleared her throat. "Yeah, but I had no clue he was your son," she said, forcing a light tone.

"Clearly," Matthew responded.

His eyes were on her again, this time slightly more pointed. He was referring to the conversation they'd shared after he'd helped her out of the mud. The conversation where she'd criticized the estate.

His *family's* estate.

That was obviously when things had shifted between them. He'd been playful, kind, helpful. Charming, even. Then she'd run her big mouth and offended him.

She fought the urge to look around for a hole to crawl into and die quietly within. Everything she'd said to Matthew earlier had been true. And they were all things she was fully planning on mentioning to Mr. Wintour himself. Granted, she'd be a touch more delicate...

Anyway, it was Matthew's fault for concealing who he was to her. He was basically asking for trouble.

Mr. Wintour looked between them again. "I'm still slightly confused, I have to admit," he stated.

Finally finding her voice, Winnie answered first, refusing to allow Matthew a chance at embarrassing her further. "Your son helped me out of the mud when my car got stuck on the side of the road."

There. Simple. Straightforward. To the punch. No need to bore him with all those other details.

Matthew's eyes didn't stray from hers, his brow slightly raised. Did he know something? Namely, did he know about her speeding?

"I'm so sorry to hear that," Mr. Wintour said with a frown.

"Oh, it's totally fine," she said with a wave of her hand.

"I take it the rain was the culprit?"

She clamped her mouth shut and nodded. It wasn't *not* the truth.

Still, Matthew watched her. He absolutely knew something.

"I'm sure I know of the exact place you were caught," Mr. Wintour continued. "I've been meaning to hire someone to grass over that section for so long, but it just keeps getting pushed back on my ever-growing list of things to improve."

"I'm sure Miss Knox wouldn't have any problem adding to that list," Matthew said. "Why don't you ask her to share with you some of the items she mentioned to me earlier?"

Winnie stared up at him. She hadn't realized he was so tall before. Nor had she been aware of how bright a blue his eyes were. They were like his dad's, except they held a more sinister glint to them. A glint that said, *"I'm not afraid to betray thee by thrusting thee under thy emerald steed, my lady."*

Still, she wouldn't be intimidated. Not any longer.

She gave a small laugh and faced Mr. Wintour. "Oh, I always have a list of things to improve. The to-dos for my own apartment is so eternal, I hardly have any room to store it on my phone anymore—and I live in a one-bedroom apartment."

Mr. Wintour chuckled. "I know the feeling all too well."

Matthew's smile lessened. Ha. She'd beaten him on that one.

"Well," Mr. Wintour continued, "I'm glad you were there to help her out, Matthew."

"Mmm," Matthew hummed, his eyes lingering on Winnie. "So, Dad, when were you planning on telling me that you'd hired another consultant?"

The air in the room shifted drastically, almost instantaneously. Winnie looked between the father and son, the tension so thick, she could almost reach out and touch it.

Matthew *hadn't* known about his dad hiring her, then.

"Let's discuss this in a moment, Matthew," Mr. Wintour said with a strained smile. "Our guest has had her fair share of drama during her day of travel, and I'd love for her to receive some rest."

"Oh, of course," Matthew said with a nod and a fake look of concern. "Anyone can see how exhausted she looks."

Winnie hid her frown. This apple had fallen far, far away from the tree, hadn't it? Matthew must have been born in a completely different orchard altogether.

He turned to his dad next. "So the running total is five consultants now, right?"

Mr. Wintour cast a wary glance at Winnie, but she merely brushed aside the surprise she felt in learning the number. "There's nothing shocking about hiring multiple consultants," she said truthfully. "It can be difficult to find a good match. Hopefully I can be just that, though."

Mr. Wintour's gratitude came through in his smile. "I've no doubt that you will be. Now, Matthew—"

"Yes, but this is the first from the States," Matthew interrupted. "Tell me, Dad, where is the logic in hiring someone who clearly knows nothing about running British estates?"

Be like Fort Knox.

"That's enough, Matthew," Mr. Wintour said, then he shifted an apologetic gaze to Winnie. "You'll have to excuse my son's manners. Apparently, he's misplaced them."

"Oh, it's just fine," she replied. "I've lived in New York for long enough that I'm used to anything by now."

Mr. Wintour chuckled, but Matthew hardly looked amused.

"New York is it?" he questioned. "That makes sense."

"Matthew..." Mr. Wintour warned, but his son wasn't finished.

"So tell me, Miss Knox," Matthew said, folding his arms across his broad chest, the ridges in his forearm shifting, "what makes you think you'll be a good fit for the estate?"

"It's Winnie," she stated. "And I think a quick Google search of my name and accomplishments will tell you everything you need to know about me, Matthew. Or, you know, I could always give you my resume."

Mr. Wintour looked almost proud at her response. She hadn't received such a look from someone since she'd graduated a year early from high school and Dad had actually smiled at her.

"That won't be necessary," Matthew returned, hardly amused. "I'll just wish you luck, though, as it is no small feat to care for an entire estate."

"Oh, I can only imagine," she agreed. "Fortunately, overseeing the renaissance faire will ease me right into it."

To her surprise, Matthew's seemingly unalterable expression shifted, and a deep frown carved through his brow. His arms fell to his sides, and he turned to face his dad directly. "What?"

If Winnie had thought the air in the room was uncomfortable before, it was nothing compared to the silent tension between them now, marked only by the sound of a clock ticking on the desk nearby.

Well. She could now safely assume that Matthew had been unaware of her taking over his faire.

"Matthew," Mr. Wintour began, "as I told you before, we can discuss this later when Winnie has had the chance to rest."

Winnie didn't need to rest as much as she needed an escape. She glanced to the door. Could she slip out unnoticed? Wander around the hallways until she found her room? Or did she have to wait for Mr. Fernsby—whom Mr. Wintour had obviously rung for but was sure taking his dang sweet time getting there?

"No, I want to talk about it now," Matthew stated, ignoring his father's words. "Did you place her over the festival?"

Mr. Wintour glanced at Winnie with an apologetic look, then faced his son again. "Yes. I have."

Anger flashed in Matthew's eyes as he shifted his gaze to Winnie, his jaw twitching beneath his scruff.

"How..." Matthew broke off with a sigh, facing his dad again. "I created the entire event. What makes you think you can just hire someone to take over what is rightfully mine?"

Matthew was in charge of the event—had *created* the event? Good grief. This was not what she signed up for. No wonder he'd touted its historical accuracy and invited her to see it.

Winnie released a quiet, pent-up breath. Out of all the consulting jobs she'd had, out of all the awkward moments, the fights that had broken out, and the surprises that had been launched at employees, this had to be the worst of them all.

Stuck in the middle between a father and son, revealing things she wasn't supposed to, apparently leaving a trail of water through their stately home. Could today get any worse?

She glanced at the door again. Where was a butler when a girl needed him?

"Matthew," Mr. Wintour said softly, as if Winnie couldn't hear every single word spoken between them, "I told you months ago that this was in our future. The future is now here."

"But I clearly said no," Matthew countered.

Mr. Wintour lowered his voice. "Last I checked, I am still owner and head of this estate. The event is held here, it uses the estate's money, therefore *I* have the final say."

Go, Mr. Wintour.

Matthew pierced Winnie with his gaze, and she blanched. Had he heard her thoughts somehow?

"So, in exercising your authority," Matthew said, his jaw tight as he spoke, "you chose to hire *her*?" He pointed a condemning finger in Winnie's direction. "She has clearly never stepped foot in England before, and obviously, she knows nothing about running a festival. She doesn't even know what century the medieval era is in, for heaven's sake."

Okay, that was a low blow. He was right, of course, but still. "For the record," she began, tired of watching the conversation unfold as if she wasn't even there listening to the entire thing, "I do know when the medieval era takes place. I just...mixed up the centuries."

"Who doesn't every now and then?" Mr. Wintour asked.

Matthew looked between them with his mouth open, clearly thinking they'd both gone crazy. "You can't be serious with her," he stated.

"I am," Mr. Wintour continued. "Because Winnie knows more about reviving dying businesses than both of us combined. Foxwood needs her. We need her. *You* need her."

Winnie should have been flattered by his confidence, but

truthfully, she just felt more wary. She really needed to not screw this up.

"But she's from the States," Matthew continued. "She'll change the entire point of the festival. We'll be the laughingstock of Yorkshire. It'll be loud and brash and..." He glanced at her. "*American.*"

Winnie folded her arms across her chest and finally allowed a frown to form on her own brow. "And just what is the matter with that?"

He gave her a look. "Do you really want to get into that right now?"

What a jerk. There was absolutely nothing wrong with being American. Sure, they were a little loud at times. Perhaps a little more enthusiastic than other countries. But when had that ever hurt anyone? Matthew just needed to come off his high horse.

Mr. Wintour looked to Winnie apologetically once again, but she moved forward with a reassuring nod.

"It's okay," she said. "I'm not offended by what he's saying. Furthermore, I know why he's acting this way."

Matthew sniffed derisively. "Do you?"

She raised her chin. "Yeah, I do. You're feeling overly protective and defensive because of how much work you've put into the event, and you don't want an outsider commandeering everything you've poured your heart and soul into because you're afraid of losing the integrity of something you've formed from the ground up."

Matthew didn't respond, but she could see in his eyes that she'd hit the nail on the head.

"But you don't need to worry," she continued. "I'm not that kind of consultant."

He looked even more skeptical than before.

"I'm not," she insisted. "I value souls and people, so I'm not looking to fire anyone. And I value others' ideas and input more than my own. I'm not here to change up everything. I'm here to fix it. With your help, I have no doubt that we can turn it into something even better than what you already have."

Instead of his defenses lowering as she'd hoped, his eyes maintained their steely blue, his lips in a thin line. "We'll see."

Well, that wasn't exactly the vote of confidence she'd been hoping for, but at least he wasn't criticizing her nationality any longer.

Before another word could be said by anyone, movement by the door drew their attention, and mercifully, the butler finally arrived.

"Mr. Fernsby," Mr. Wintour greeted, sounding just as relieved as Winnie was, "will you show Miss Knox to her room, please?"

"Yes, sir."

Mr. Fernsby waited by the door, and Winnie stifled a sigh of relief. Escape at last.

She shook Mr. Wintour's hand in departure first. "Thank you for your vote of confidence, Mr. Wintour. I look forward to speaking more with you tomorrow." Then she turned toward his son. "And I look forward to working with you and your faire, Matthew. Even if the feeling isn't mutual."

She held out her hand to him with an innocent smile, awaiting his reaction. If he *didn't* accept her handshake, he would look even worse to his dad. But if he *did* accept it, he would appear to be surrendering. Either way, she'd come out on top. It was the perfect tactic.

And yet, when he did raise his hand to accept hers, his long fingers wrapping around her own, her smile faltered, and her mind froze as an energy coursed between them at their touch.

She glanced to their intertwined hands, then up to his eyes. His blue gaze met hers with such striking intensity, she knew he felt the same thing she did. A connection. An attraction. All the things she shouldn't be feeling for a coworker.

Swiftly, she pulled her hand away and averted her gaze, walking to where Mr. Fernsby waited for her before the two of them departed down the hallway.

Part of her wished to be a fly on the wall in the study as the Wintours continued their battle, but Mr. Wintour was right. She needed to rest. She would no doubt be playing host to a plethora of her own battles at Foxwood soon enough. Battles with a pompous knight who had expected her to be a silent damsel in distress when she was the furthest thing from it.

CHAPTER SEVEN

MATTHEW WAITED FOR THE WOMAN'S ANNOYING CLICK of her heels to disappear down the hallway before facing his dad again.

"I told you we should have waited until she was gone," Dad said.

"And you should have told me your plan to hire her before she stood in our home," Matthew returned.

Dad sighed. "Come. Sit down. We both need to relax."

He didn't wait for a response, moving to his usual seat on the large, red single-sofa as Matthew debated remaining in the doorway or perhaps storming out altogether.

He would have chosen the latter had he not still had so much to say, so with thumping steps, he made for the fireplace and warmed his hands that were still chilled from being out in the cold rain.

When he'd first met Winnie Knox, he had been enchanted, charmed. As if hypnotized by a snake.

Incidentally, that wasn't too far from the truth. Winnie was like a snake. Callous and sneaky. Willing to do whatever she needed to get what she wanted.

Okay, he was coming on a little strong. But how else could he describe a woman who had criticized his home, then took over his festival when she knew nothing—and he meant *nothing*—about the medieval era at all?

He'd had every intention of entering the study that evening to ruin Winnie's chances of working at Foxwood. But now? Now he was scrambling to maintain control of *his* festival. What a nightmare.

"Have you nothing left to say now that Winnie is gone?" Dad asked as Matthew's mind continued to race.

"I do," Matthew responded. "I'm only gathering my thoughts."

"I'll prepare myself for the barrage, then."

That wasn't too far from what Matthew wished to do. Honestly, Dad had lost his mind.

"I just can't understand what you were thinking by hiring her," Matthew finally said. "It makes absolutely zero sense."

"That's what I was trying to explain to you, but I couldn't very well do it with the woman standing right there, now could I?" Dad looked away. "Although, *you* had no qualms with being monumentally unkind to her."

"I wasn't unkind," Matthew said. He cringed at how petulant he sounded.

Truth be told, he had been rude, but he was still too angry to feel badly about it. He also wasn't in any mood for another lecture, nor another look of disappointment in Dad's eyes. Matthew had seen enough of that look over the last few years— specifically every single weekend the festival failed.

"Fine," Matthew relented, if only to assuage his guilt. "I was a little harsh. But it wasn't unwarranted." He leaned forward. "Do you know what she said to me on the road when she didn't know who I was?"

Dad didn't respond, simply waited for Matthew to continue.

"She criticized the estate. She kept rattling off one thing after another that needed fixing, like Foxwood was just one big flaw. It was ridiculous."

Dad stared. "That's her job, Matthew. I specifically hired her to do that for us."

Matthew's defenses slipped through his fingertips like water out of the tap. "Yes, but she was just saying it to me so freely," he said, scrambling to maintain control. "If she talks to *me* like that, thinking I was just another worker, who knows what else she'd say about our home—and to whom?"

Dad leaned back in his chair, lacing his fingers together and resting them on his lap. "If anything, I'd say you're more to blame than she is. You shouldn't have misled her by not telling her who you are."

Matthew moved away from the heat of the fire, sitting down on a chair nearby. It was getting too hot to stand near the hearth. Or was it his growing discomfort that was agitating him?

Dad's condemning look told him the truth.

"You're right," Matthew relented begrudgingly, staring into the fire's flames. "I should've told her who I was. And honestly, what she said wasn't too far from the truth. There is much to improve here."

But the festival?

His anger from before had dissipated, settling into a disappointed frustration. Dad's study had always had that effect on him. "I just wish you would have told me beforehand that you hired her to be over the festival," he continued in a quieter tone. "Or at least hired someone with more experience."

Dad watched him carefully, taking a moment before responding. "I understand how you feel, Matthew. I do. And I'm sorry for not telling you before tonight what my plans were. I should have."

Matthew had always appreciated his dad's humility when he apologized. No excuses were ever made—his words merely pure and truthful.

Matthew could learn a thing or two from him.

"I will say, though," Dad continued, "that you needn't worry about her ruining what you've created. She's a professional, as was made evident tonight with her reaction to how you treated her."

Matthew looked away. He wasn't sure he liked where this conversation was headed—turning him into the villain and Winnie into the hero.

"Really," Dad said, "I have no doubt she will improve the festival and make it profitable once again."

There it was, the word Matthew despised. *Profitable.* He knew his festival had failed, costing Foxwood thousands of pounds. He also knew that Dad, while patient with Matthew's lack of business savvy, was growing frustrated with the waste. Matthew was doing his best, and yet, his best just wasn't good enough.

"I know what you're thinking, Matthew," Dad said as his silence prolonged. "You always get that look when you're down on yourself. But that's not what this is, all right?"

Matthew blew out a snort of derision. "How is it not? You've lost faith in my ability to revive the festival and have hired an outsider before you have to cancel the festival altogether."

Matthew watched his father carefully, knowing he'd hit the truth as Dad sighed.

"Matthew, we need help."

"You mean *I* need help," Matthew clarified.

"No, I said *we* and I mean *we*," Dad insisted. "I need help with the estate, and you need help with the festival. But there is absolutely nothing wrong with needing help."

Once again, he had to agree with his dad. Foxwood was in a relatively good standing compared to other estates in Yorkshire—and England as a whole—but Dad was wise for seeking help to prevent any future failure.

Matthew hadn't been so wise with his festival. He was good at many things, but business wasn't one of them. It just frustrated him to no end that his love and passion for the past wasn't enough anymore to have his festival succeed. He'd always believed that if he put on an accurate event, with proper food, jousting, costuming, and actions, he'd be able to convince others to love the medieval era like he did. Then they would keep coming back for more. Obviously, he was doing something wrong. He just couldn't figure out what.

Would Winnie?

Matthew sighed. He hated to admit it, but he was struggling. He had been for years, ever since Dad's diagnosis of multiple sclerosis when they'd all feared the worse.

In the wake of that illness, Matthew had taken on more responsibility than he'd ever had before, giving up on his own dreams and aspirations to help Mom with her mental health, his sister, Char, with her divorce, his nieces with their lack of a father, and Dad with his illness. Matthew had also taken over sole care of the estate for a few years, which he was sure had taken ten years off his own life. All of this had led him to extreme amounts of stress with no one to rely on but himself.

Now, however, Mom was in a great place, Char and the girls were well cared for by the entire family, and being in remission, Dad had once again taken over Foxwood.

And Matthew? Matthew was left with his festival. The festival he'd built from the ground up. Was it any wonder why he was having a hard time with the idea of relying on a random stranger to help? It made sense to secure the future of Foxwood, but that didn't prevent the humiliation Matthew was experiencing for having been found wanting.

"Fine," he said, attempting to be as sensible as his dad. "I agree that I am in over my head. But surely there's someone better suited to help us."

"I haven't just hired her without any thought, you know," Dad said. "I've done my research. Winnie Knox has extensive experience with helping the widest variety of businesses I've ever seen into being highly profitable. Dental, fitness, clothing, furniture, mental health—she's done it all. Not only that, but she also comes from the most lucrative family I've ever known. I have no doubt, with her abilities and determination, she will absolutely succeed."

Matthew had never seen Dad so convinced about a person's

credentials. The way he spoke about the woman almost convinced Matthew to relent.

But Dad's actions were personal, and Winnie being hired *hurt*. Matthew's intelligence, his opinion, had been replaced in a single evening with the mere promise of a bright future and a flash of a pretty New York smile.

"So what would you have me do?" he asked, staring at the wooden floor nearby, his desire to fight slowly seeping away from him. "Stand back and let her do whatever she likes?"

Nothing sounded worse. She'd change the heart of his festival. Remove all historical accuracy. Turn it into—ugh—*A Knight's Tale.*

"For the time being, yes," Dad said. "Allow her opinions and ideas to flourish. I'm certain you'll be glad that you did. But do not hesitate to give your advice and your expertise where it's needed, as I'm sure she'll be grateful for it."

Matthew snorted in disbelief. "Yes, because consultants are known for their easy-going personalities and persuadable opinions."

Dad ignored him. "Either way, you only have to last a matter of weeks. We'll postpone the festival for a few weeks until it's ready again, then she'll be helping me with the estate."

"Providing she proves herself," Matthew said.

"I have no doubt that she will."

Matthew bit his tongue to avoid delivering another derisive scoff. Of course, his reaction was only to mask the embarrassment he still felt for not being able to succeed.

"Matthew," Dad continued, "I know this is difficult for you. But I hope you know why I'm doing it. You sacrificed so much for your family—for me—giving up your dreams the moment they were being realized so you could care for your ailing father."

In truth, Matthew didn't feel like his efforts had been a sacrifice, but he still felt humbled at the gratitude shining in his dad's blue eyes.

"I want you to know how greatly I appreciate you," Dad

continued. He leaned forward, wincing as he did so. "That is the real reason I hired Winnie. I'm certain that if you listen to her ideas with an open mind, she will change our lives—and only for the better. Just give her a chance. That's all I ask."

It took everything within Matthew to finally nod.

Fine. He would give the consultant a chance. But if she came up with some horrendous idea that tanked the festival and made her look terrible to Dad, Matthew would have no choice but to let her dig her own grave.

Yes, that's exactly what he would do. Then he'd get rid of her sooner, and Little Miss Winnie Knox would take her well-formed legs and dark bun and smooth skin back to New York.

Because that's where she belonged, and he'd be sure she knew it by the end.

CHAPTER EIGHT

FOR THE FIRST TIME WINNIE COULD REMEMBER, SHE didn't wake up to her usual alarm playing "On Top of the World" by Imagine Dragons on her phone.

Instead, the silence woke her, then the gentle tapping of raindrops against her window.

She drew a deep breath, stretching slightly as her eyes fluttered open. She felt like a Disney princess, well-rested and smiling, lying down in the most comfortable bed she'd ever slept on. Her feather pillow cradled her head like a swaddled newborn babe, and her comforter rested upon her like a thick blanket of clouds.

She shouldn't have been surprised by the quality of the bedding, what with the state of the room she was put in at Foxwood. It was in no way grand like Mr. Wintour's study, but it was clean, quiet, well taken care of, and held everything she could possibly need.

Her queen-sized bed was centered atop a blue and gold-embellished rug, and the walls were a creamy green, holding just a few paintings of English landscapes with modest frames. A wardrobe was at one end of the room, and a good-sized desk was situated beneath the window.

Did she have a view from that window? She'd been too tired

to find out the night before. She'd barely managed to stumble into her pajamas before zonking out for the entire night, barely noting that her clothing had already been unpacked, aired out, and hung up by the housekeeper.

She could do with hiring one of those, too.

She smiled to herself at her fanciful ideas. Tossing her covers aside and rushing into her slippers and robe, she stepped soundlessly toward the window and pushed back the floral curtains.

Her smile grew, and a wistful sigh slipped past her lips. From her vantage point on the second floor, beyond the raindrops dotting the window, green fields stretched across the estate's grounds, stopped only by masses of trees so thick, Winnie wondered what secrets were kept hidden beyond the branches.

Was there a red dragon guarding an underground treasure? A magic well once charmed by Merlin himself? She wouldn't be too surprised if either were true, given the renaissance faire she was about to attend.

In the midst of the dense trees emerged three thin, triangular flags just visible above the oaks. Winnie narrowed her eyes to see them better, the red, green, and yellow flashing in and out of sight as the wind played with the ends of the fabric. They had to be for the faire.

Her stomach tightened at the thought, but that was nothing new. She was always on edge at the beginning of a job. There was a surefire way to cure those nerves, though.

She needed to get to work.

After a quick shower and sprucing up in her ensuite bathroom, Winnie sat down at the desk and began her research in her usual top-knot bun, pencil skirt, and silk blouse.

With the faire not beginning until ten o'clock that morning, she had a solid three hours to do the research required of her to have an idea about what exactly she was getting into. Before, she'd dedicated most of her time on researching how to run estates in England—her original job description. But she'd be able to use all that information soon enough. For now, she focused on her task at hand, exploring website after website and reading article after article about medieval faires, knights, and jousting.

Most of her work had to be done, infuriatingly enough, on her phone, as the Wi-Fi was abysmally slow in her room, the one and only complaint she had about her circumstances. But at least her cell service was good enough to search the web for information.

Soon, with enough of a handle on what to expect from the faire, Winnie gathered her raincoat, writing tablet, and pen, and ventured to the kitchens, following the directions Mr. Fernsby had given her the night before.

The staff of Foxwood and the faire were provided with breakfast early each morning, so Winnie had intentionally waited until later on to leave her room, not wishing to meet with anyone who worked at the faire until after the event. No use putting them all on edge earlier than necessary, as she'd done with Matthew.

The image of the man in his armor flashed in her mind. His visor up. Moisture slipping down the strong ridges of his nose. Blue eyes flashing as he stared down at her atop his horse.

As much as she'd like to dwell on the attractive image for longer, Winnie pushed it aside. He was a precarious bridge she'd have to cross soon enough, so she'd be taking every second before that to tighten her defenses.

She arrived in the dining area moments later, relieved to find the tables empty, though a few clanks and clangs sounded from the kitchens nearby, the chef no doubt cleaning up breakfast with his assistants.

Winnie made herself some toast and grabbed an apple, eating them swiftly before making her way to the front doors of the estate.

Shockingly enough, she only managed to make two wrong turns before finding the main entrance, standing near the front door and looking around for Mr. Wintour, who'd agreed to meet her there at ten o'clock.

She peered down at her smartwatch, the numbers shining bright against the *Movement Circles* she had yet to fill.

10:01

Thank heavens she hadn't made him wait for her again like she had last night. That being said, she had no problem waiting for him in return.

With no sign of him descending the stairs, Winnie pulled out her tablet, jotted down a few thoughts on the digital screen, organized the notes already written, then felt a buzz on her wrist.

She raised her arm, and her neck instantly tightened at the base as she read the incoming text.

DAD

> Good luck on your first day, Win-Win-Winnie!

Winnie cringed. Dad had chosen the nickname for her in hopes of inspiring her to win more often. She hated to say, but it never worked. In truth, it kind of only made matters worse.

She slipped her tablet under her arm and swiped out a response on her watch. She hated messaging on those small buttons, but she'd become quite adept at doing so efficiently and with little to no spelling errors.

That was good. Dad couldn't stand typos.

"Why do people bother to write at all when they don't spell correctly or use proper grammar?" he'd say.

WINNIE

> Thanks, Dad!

DAD

> What's on the docket first?

WINNIE

> Just checking out the estate for now. Getting my bearings and understanding more of what's wanted from me.

65

She probably should have felt more guilty for omitting the truth of what she was now doing at Foxwood, but she didn't have the mental fortitude to hear everything Dad would have to say about her being demoted to watching over a renaissance faire instead of a stately home.

"Are you really having to prove yourself?" he'd say. *"A Knox shouldn't have to stoop so low."*

Winnie rolled her eyes. Dad had convinced himself that the Knoxes were all some special breed, set apart from the rest of the world.

If that were true, Winnie was an adopted mutt.

DAD

Sounds great. Keep me posted!

WINNIE

Will do!

And she would, just like she'd be honest with him...Just as soon as she figured out a way to make the faire sound cooler than it was.

Lowering her wrist, she shook the exchange from her mind. It was time to remove her "Win-Win-Winnie" badge and put on her "Winnie Knox, Consultant" badge—a badge that she'd actually earned by herself.

Except, of course, when Dad had connected her with Mr. Wintour as soon he discovered that her latest consultant job had fallen through. And then there were the other two jobs he'd helped her find last year.

Then there was the other time before that—but all of that was neither here nor there. The point of the matter was that she had done the work for each of those jobs, and her success was proof enough of her abilities.

Footsteps approached, drawing her attention to the present, but to Winnie's surprise, Mr. Fernsby appeared instead of Mr. Wintour.

"Miss Knox," the butler greeted. "Mr. Wintour wished for me to tell you that he will be unable to join you this morning. I'm afraid he's feeling unwell."

Winnie took the news in measure. Honestly, it wasn't much of a surprise. He'd looked so uncomfortable the night before, on the chair and afterward. She only hoped she hadn't contributed to it as his son obviously had with all the complaining he'd done.

"I hope he's all right," she said.

"Thank you," Mr. Fernsby said in his smooth accent. "He is tired but in good spirits. Instead, Mrs. Wintour has agreed to join you for the festival. However, she will be some time yet, so she is more than happy for you to go on ahead. The festival takes place on the grounds just east of the house, within walking distance. Follow the dirt pathway, and you won't miss it. Mrs. Wintour will meet you there as soon as she is able to."

Winnie instantly agreed, and the butler returned to his duties at once.

While she would have appreciated a tour with her questions being answered straightaway, nothing helped her get a true read on a business—or in this case, an event—as walking around by herself and simply observing.

With more motivation in her step than before, Winnie left the house through the double doors, a blast of cold air welcoming her into the gray, dreary world. Although, strangely enough, it didn't *feel* dreary. She'd always enjoyed rainstorms in New York—lights reflected in the puddles on the streets, the sidewalks a monochrome sea of black umbrellas.

But here in England, the rain made everything more ethereal. More magical. The overgrown trees and the lush, green grass shone like sparkling emeralds adorning a noblewoman's neck, while the misty clouds that cloaked Foxwood in a comforting embrace softened the imagery around them, as if a mystic haze had been cast across the grounds.

Winnie threw up her hood, stepping out onto the porch with

a deep breath of cool air that filled her lungs with a pleasant lightness.

First, Mr. Wintour's study had lured her into a sense of security, and now, Winnie was breathing in the cold? There was definitely some type of magic going on here at Foxwood. She was even looking forward to the faire now, for crying out loud, and that was something she didn't think was possible.

Walking across the pea gravel drive to the east of the estate, she wondered what a renaissance faire at Foxwood would look like. Before, she had visualized a pitiful recreation of a barbaric, historical pastime. After her research that morning, however, seeing videos of actual jousting that knights participated in around the world, she was brought back to the first time she'd watched *A Knight's Tale*—the splintering wood of the lance, the pounding of the horse's hooves on the grounds, the attractive men.

Jousting might not be her "thing," but at least she could appreciate what she'd seen in the videos—an immersion into the past with a healthy mixture of fun and fantastical. She just couldn't wait to see it now in person.

She continued on her way, reaching the dirt path that led toward the faire grounds. She tried to peer beyond the thick woods for any sign of the event, but nothing appeared until she rounded a bend, and the colorful flags from that morning caught her eye.

Excitement flapped in her chest, her footsteps picking up pace. Jousting, knights walking around, horses decked out in fun colors. Booths selling knick-knacks and delicious food, fire-breathers and other entertainment. She couldn't wait to see all that they had to offer.

But as she drew closer and closer to the grounds, that excitement swiftly turned to confusion—then confusion shifted immediately to disappointment.

Was this it?

After waiting in line behind a total of two people, Winnie—wanting to remain fully incognito—paid an extortionate fifteen pounds to a woman seated on a lawn chair. Not a single greeting or, "Welcome to the faire" was said by the woman as Winnie passed her by. And yet, Winnie hardly noticed, too taken with the underwhelming view before her as she finally set foot on the grounds.

Instead of manicured pathways, torn-up grass and muddy puddles lined the way forward. There were no knights in sight, or horses for that matter, and the handful of people who were in attendance wandered around with bored expressions and crying children, all the while clearly looking for something to do.

Something to do. Was there *anything* to do? Winnie slowly stepped forward, careful to avoid puddles and mud pits as she swept her eyes around her.

A total of two tents were set up—both dark green with weathered canvas that looked as if it had barely managed to live through the worst of World War II. Beyond the tents, a solitary booth stood with a sign too small to read, though Winnie was fairly certain they were advertising food—food that smelled as appetizing as the portable toilets, which, incidentally, were too close to the tents for comfort.

The biggest disappointment of all for her was the list field, which she'd learned that morning was the name of the jousting arena. In reality, it was little more than a small stretch of land cordoned off by rope and a mere rickety fence—the tilt—lined down the center of it to separate the charging horses.

Winnie shook her head in dismay. This was abysmal. No wonder they weren't profitable. What was Matthew thinking? And why had it taken so long for the Wintours to hire someone to help?

With her mind still reeling, she stood off to the side beneath a large oak tree and pulled out her tablet, shaking her head again as she peered at the nothingness that was before her.

Nothingness...

Nothingness that would be pretty easy to turn into a whole lot of *something*. With the event in such a terrible state, *any* improvement was sure to appear monumental. So monumental that Mr. Wintour would be impressed enough with her actions that he would know for certain that Winnie was just the woman to improve Foxwood, too.

A slow smile spread across her lips. With a bit of effort, attention to detail, and the appropriate usage of Mr. Wintour's budget, this was going to be the easiest, the fastest, and the most lucrative consulting job she'd ever have.

This was simply fantastic.

CHAPTER NINE

WINNIE PULLED OUT HER TABLET BENEATH THE shelter of the tree and scribbled down everything she noted about the event.

- *No shelters*
- *No vendor booths*
- *Disappointing field list*
- *Garbage everywhere*
- *Bathrooms too close*

Her list continued to grow as she listened to the people who passed her by.

"There ain't much to see, is there?" a husband asked with a young girl atop his shoulders, her little raincoat and hat covering everything but her eyes. "The flyer made the event seem a lot bigger than it is."

"It was advertised as authentic," his wife responded, a baby strapped to her chest. "Maybe authentic means small?"

- *No website*
- *No events*

- *Too authentic*

Winnie's fingers began to ache as the conversations and notes continued.

"I'm not eatin' that food. If I don't, 'ow can we expect the children to?"

"Where're the birds o' prey? They had 'em last time."

"These pathways are 'orrible. They shoulda told us it weren't suitable for prams."

After a solid twenty minutes, she lifted her hand from the tablet and shook her fingers out, intent on carrying on with her notes.

In the next moment, however, she caught sight of a short, jolly-looking woman approaching her with a large, purple umbrella and dark plum-colored boots.

Winnie paused in her writing, then smiled as the woman continued directly toward her. This was Mrs. Wintour. Who else could match Mr. Wintour's bright smile and radiating warmth?

"Good morning," Winnie said, turning off her tablet and walking forward to greet the woman. "You must be Mrs. Wintour."

"Oh, please, call me Jane," the woman confirmed. "It's a pleasure to finally meet you. My husband wished to apologize for not being able to make it out here. He's had a bit of a rough morning."

"I heard he wasn't feeling well," Winnie said. "I hope I didn't make things worse by having him stay up late last night."

"Oh, not at all. He's been in remission with his MS, but late nights do sometimes affect him. Even still, he stays awake most evenings, always drinking his cocoa and reading late until I force him to bed."

She ended with a smile—a smile Winnie couldn't really return. MS. Of course. Now all the wincing and groaning and shifting in discomfort made sense. Her heart twisted. She'd had a high school friend whose mother had MS. It had been terrible to watch her suffer through it.

"Now," Mrs. Wintour said, not appearing affected in the slightest, "I've been told I have the pleasant task of showing you around the festival. Are you ready?"

"Absolutely."

Together, the two of them wandered around the grounds, Winnie being polite and keeping her opinion of the small nature of the event to herself. Aside from what she had already found— the jousting grounds, food, and toilets—she was also shown the medieval paraphernalia displayed within one of the old tents, the stables just barely visible through the woods, and the area where the falconry took place.

"We've had to scale back on that, as well," Mrs. Wintour explained as Winnie took more notes.

- *Signs needed everywhere*
- *Return falcons*
- *Where are the knights?*

Two dozen people now walked around, far better than the handful from before, but those numbers would hardly benefit the event as a whole.

Winnie thought back to the words she'd heard, the event being called "authentic." She knew Matthew was the one behind that thought process. After all, he *had* been the one to gloat about how theirs was the most historically accurate event of all time.

She sniffed with contempt. This *authenticity* would be one of the many things they would no doubt disagree on. After all, the festival wasn't entirely historically accurate because, according to her research that morning, medieval era jousting very often led to death. Matthew obviously fudged the lines enough to ensure the safety of the knights, so he was willing to bend at least to a degree, right?

As they continued around the small grounds, Mrs. Wintour

introduced her to Mrs. Birdwhistle, a member of the festival staff with dark red lipstick and a vibrant, oversized beanie to match.

"The Birdwhistles have been here for nearly two decades," Mrs. Wintour explained. "They take care of the stables. Mr. Birdwhistle is also one of the knights here."

"Oh, perfect," Winnie said, facing the woman with an excited expression. "So he'll be jousting today?"

Mrs. Birdwhistle nodded. She seemed friendly enough as she responded in her thick, Yorkshire accent. "Yes, they should be arrivin' soon enough. They stay in't stables until just before the joustin' begins at eleven."

Winnie pulled up her watch.

10:30

"Do you know if there's a schedule of events or something, so I know what's going to happen and when?" she asked next.

Mrs. Wintour shook her head. "There isn't much need for a schedule when there's only one event. Matt—*We* thought it best to focus purely on the jousting."

Clearly, Mrs. Wintour had been about to say "Matthew." Yet another thing her son was responsible for—getting rid of anything that might take away from him being front and center of the faire.

"And the jousting is only once a day?" she asked next.

Mrs. Birdwhistle nodded. "Once a day, every Friday and Saturday from May to August."

- *More events*
- *More jousting*
- *Bring out the knights earlier*

"And you never cancel due to the rain?" Winnie continued.

Mrs. Wintour smiled. "We wouldn't be English if we did."

Mrs. Birdwhistle excused herself shortly after, and Winnie

and Mrs. Wintour continued on, passing by the food next. Winnie purchased one of each item from the menu, despite the woman behind the makeshift counter looking more than perturbed at having to do any work at all, despite Mrs. Wintour standing right there.

- *More polite vendors*
- *More food options*
- *More drink options*
- *More payment options*

As they walked away with Winnie's container of food that reeked worse than some of the subways in New York, she continued with her questions.

"Why no other food vendors?"

"We thought it better to simplify," Mrs. Wintour said after another moment of hesitation.

We? Fat chance. "Matthew is the deciding factor when it comes to the event, right?" Winnie asked flat out.

No point in beating around the bush any longer.

Mrs. Wintour opened her mouth, then closed it again. Clearly, she didn't wish to criticize her son, which Winnie couldn't help but admire. But if she was going to improve the faire, she was going to need some answers.

"I'm not asking to get anyone in trouble," Winnie said with a reassuring smile. "There's usually someone in charge of these things. If I know who it is, then I know who to work with more."

Relief shone clearly in Mrs. Wintour's eyes, despite the reticence that remained. She glanced over her shoulders to where the stables were hidden in the thick trees. "Matthew has worked so hard on this. He has such a passion for it. To have it fail..." She broke off, shaking her head with a sigh. "I just feel for him and his struggles, especially when it used to be such a grand affair."

"Did it?" Winnie asked, holding up her tablet, fingers and pen at the ready.

They stopped beneath another tree, though the rain had mostly disappeared altogether.

"Oh, yes," Mrs. Wintour said with wide eyes. "Hundreds of people would attend each weekend. We'd often sell out. The jousting was always a crowd favorite. But little by little, people just stopped coming."

Winnie jotted down a few notes. "Has anything been done to bring more people in?"

"We've advertised," Mrs. Wintour responded. "Put up flyers, had a spot or two on the local stations, but nothing has really been working. Matthew thinks people are simply out of touch with history and have lost interest altogether."

Huh. That was interesting. And also entirely wrong. "Is that what *you* think the problem is?"

Mrs. Wintour shook her head. "No. I believe that is a mere fraction of the problem. The reality is, the magic is gone, and Matthew—we—don't know how to get it back. We just want to help him. This event has been his passion for so long. To have to say goodbye would be devastating for him."

Mrs. Wintour's sincerity, her goodness, touched Winnie's heart, and her empathy soared.

"Empathy has no place in a business-centric world, Winnie."

Her dad's voice echoed in her mind, but she readily set it aside. That was one thing on which she and Dad fundamentally disagreed.

"I understand," she said softly. "I've worked with many individuals whose businesses are their passions. You have my word that I'll do whatever I can to help this event flourish again."

Mrs. Wintour's smile was worth Winnie's empathy. "My husband was right. You are perfect for the job."

At the end of the small tour, Winnie and Mrs. Wintour ended in front of the jousting grounds.

"Hopefully that was beneficial for you," Mrs. Wintour said. "I know there isn't much to see, but if there's anything else I can help you with, please, let me know."

Winnie nodded. "I think the only thing I might need is a list of the staff specifically working for the event. Other than that, I'll be great for now."

"Oh, absolutely," Mrs. Wintour said. "I can get a list sent to you within the hour." Winnie nodded her appreciation as Mrs. Wintour sighed. "Well, I'd love to watch the jousting with you, but I'm afraid I've got to see how Arthur is fairing."

Winnie thanked her for her time and help, asked Mrs. Wintour to say hello to Mr. Wintour, then faced the jousting area as the woman walked away.

That had been far more helpful than Winnie could have hoped for. She wrote down a few more things on her tablet, then checked the time.

11:06

The jousting was six minutes behind schedule. She looked around her, more people gathering toward the makeshift fence. How long would they all be waiting?

Five minutes later, a crackling sounded nearby, and Winnie looked around before finding an older man setting up an overhead canopy on the far side of the area. Soon, he stood behind a microphone, and the crackling sounded again just as his voice blared through a speaker next to him.

"Mornin', ladies and gentlemen," came his Yorkshire accent through the speakers. His thick, gray beard bounced as he spoke in the most monotonous tone Winnie had ever heard. "I've been told to inform you that the joustin' will be a bit delayed as the horses and knights prepare for this dangerous sport. We 'ppreciate your patience at this time and will keep you updated. While you're waitin', feel free to browse the tents, get yourself a bite, and stay tuned. You'll not want to miss this."

The speaker crackled again, then the mic was turned off, and the man headed into the woods.

Winnie pulled in her lips. With his lack of excitement, she

wasn't sure he was the best choice to get the crowd riled up. Sure enough, a few people grumbled around her as they wandered off. How many more guests would they lose due to their tardiness?

- *Don't keep people waiting*

To bide her time, she opened her food box and eyed the green, orange, and brown slop that had been described above the booth as

*Authentic Cabbage Chowder & Spit-Roasted Lamb
Authentic Cream Custard Tart & Rose Pudding*

Authentic. There it was again. This had Matthew written all over it.

- *What the devil is cabbage chowder?*

She had zero desire to put any of the food in her mouth, but she had to experience it all to be considered well-informed. So, with shudders and near-gags, she ate a bit of each serving, taking notes about how it was the worst meal she'd ever eaten before the knights came out forty-five minutes late.

The crackling of the microphone sounded again as they finally appeared. "As you can see, our knights are arrivin'," the announcer drawled. "You're in for a treat, ladies and gentlemen."

Winnie was inclined to believe him, if only in this regard. The rain had picked up again as the men emerged from the trees astride their horses, armor glistening with moisture and clanking in the distance.

Which one was Matthew? She couldn't tell with their faces covered by the visors.

As despondent as she had been with the state of the faire altogether, the image of the knights filing one-by-one into the list was enough to rid her mind of all else but the power and grandeur of these four armored individuals. They may as well have been walking in slow motion, so rousing was their approach.

Each man was covered from head-to-toe in armor, helmets ranging from square around the jaw to pointed around the nose. Atop each helmet plumed giant feathers in a variety of colors, matching the vibrant robes draped over their respective horses.

And heavens, those *horses*. Black, white, chestnut, brown. They were stunning, captivating. And the power they exuded from merely walking was enough to throw Winnie back into her past filled with riding, jumping, flying.

But she suppressed those memories at once, just like she always did.

A few claps sounded as the knights approached, bringing her back to the present, and she viewed the mere handful of people who remained around the roped-off area. It was a shame, really. More people ought to be witnessing such an arresting spectacle.

"Welcome, Knights of Foxwood," the announcer said in that same monotonous voice, "and welcome to our guests. The name's Albert Fogg. I'll be your announcer this afternoon."

The knights began to circle the area, riding their horses in a trot for all to admire.

Despite her entire, horrible experience with the event up to that point, Winnie felt a smile tugging at her lips. This was actually kind of enjoyable. Exciting, even. The colors, the performance, the immersion into the past. If they amped this up, there would be no reason for the event *not* to be packed every weekend.

"We have four knights ridin' today," Mr. Fogg continued, reading from a notebook with less enthusiasm than a golf announcer. "As you can see, each knight bears the color of his family, and each horse's caparison matches his knight."

Winnie observed the knights as they rode past her, her eyes settling on the black horse. He wore a deep blue cover spattered with golden lions, the animals roaring on their hindlegs.

This had to be Matthew's horse. Which meant this knight was Matthew himself.

Her gaze shifted to his helmet, the rich blue feather fluttering from the top as he rode past her. Though his visor covered his features, she could almost *feel* him looking at her.

He would no doubt be wearing a scowl, just like the night before. Would he have smiled at her, spoken with her again in that silly dialect of his had her consulting position been kept a secret from him?

The horse trotted past her, and Matthew made no sign that he had seen her at all as he headed for the top of the tilt.

"Here we have our first knight," Mr. Fogg said, the mic popping. "Dressed in red and black, Sir Hu—...cl—..."

Winnie looked to the announcer. That wasn't a good sign.

"Next, in b—...er...Si—"

Winnie shook her head. That speaker was certainly going to put a damper on things. Mr. Fogg wasn't insanely entertaining or anything, but having him explain what was going on had to be essential to watching a jousting tournament, right?

"Cl—...er."

"What's he saying, Mummy?" a little voice spoke from nearby.

"I don't know, love."

Winnie became frustrated on their behalf. Surely the guests deserved better than what they were receiving.

- *Better sound system*
- *More excitement from announcer*

She looked up from her tablet as the knights finished their circling—Matthew in his blue and gold, and the other three in black and white, red and purple, and green and yellow.

"And finally S—" Mr. Fogg paused, tapped on the mic twice, shook his head, then lowered the microphone to the table, the speakers squeaking loudly before they turned off altogether.

Mr. Fogg merely continued speaking, though his voice could no longer be heard.

When the announcer finished, Matthew and the black and white checkered knight went to one end of the tilt, while the remaining two went to the other side.

Winnie watched with anticipation, wishing she could hear what was going on. But as five minutes passed by with nothing happening, then ten minutes and soon fifteen, she pulled in her lips with frustration. Was this what all the hubbub was about, announcing the knights only to have them do absolutely nothing?

During the wait, two more families left the event, and soon, Winnie was one of the only ones remaining, still scribbling down the conversations she overheard from the others until movement caught her attention from the list.

A woman dressed in a long gown with dark blue sleeves and braided hair down to her waist ran out into the arena. She screamed dramatically and swooned to the ground before the knight in green and yellow stole her away. The other knights chased after her next in what Winnie could only assume was a horrible attempt at creating drama.

Clearly, they were implying the woman was a damsel in distress, and the knights were now commissioned to rescue her via the jousting competition.

Winnie shook her head. This was the twenty-first century. It was time they stepped into it.

- *Absolutely no damsel in distress*

Once the woman was carried from the arena, the knights returned to their places on the field. Matthew sat astride his horse at one end, while the red and purple knight faced him at the far side of the list. Their lances were handed up to them as Mr. Fogg spoke silently across the grounds.

Winnie watched the knights expectantly. Was she finally going to witness the jousting?

Sure enough, a moment later, the knights raised their lances as a salute to those few still watching, then urged their horses forward.

Winnie's heart skipped a beat, excitement widening her eyes as Matthew barreled down the tilt. The horse's hooves rumbled against the ground, ears pinned back and air blasting from his nose in puffs of white steam. Matthew appeared to float atop the black gelding, effortlessly riding even with his clanking armor as he secured his lance between his arm and side, focusing straight ahead.

She could only imagine his blue eyes unwavering from their target, his grip on the lance secure as he drew closer and closer to the other knight until...

CRACK!

Matthew's lance made contact with the opposing knight's armor, splintering into more than a dozen pieces that flew out on both sides of the tilt, splaying into the air like wooden fireworks.

Now *this* was exciting.

Breathless, Winnie looked around her at the joyful smiles on the faces of those still in attendance. Clearly, they all wanted to see more, Winnie more than anyone as she maintained her focus on Matthew.

She was apt to forget all about his mean comments the night before in his dad's study, replacing the image of his sullen frown with how unbelievably attractive he was jousting on his horse—and she hadn't even seen his face, for crying out loud.

The imagery, the pageantry, the theatricality of it all made her feel as if she was living hundreds of years ago, surrounded by gallant knights, regal women, and acts of bravery.

The sport that had veritably thrust her into the past and awakened a side of her she didn't even know existed. Sure, the faire needed a boatload of work, but the jousting? The jousting was a triumph that she could watch again and again.

Unfortunately, the time between strikes took far too long, and after a ten-minute wait, the other two knights finally took their turn riding down the tilt. While still thrilling, these men rode slower and less powerfully than Matthew had, and Winnie found her eyes trailing once more to him at the top of the list.

Matthew had dismounted his horse and removed his helmet to stand with a family on the far side, speaking to a little boy who stood anxious with his pointer finger in his mouth. Matthew smiled at him, then motioned to the horse. The little boy nodded, and, after being lifted up by his dad, reached forward to stroke the black hair of the gelding.

Little-by-little, the boy's anxiousness clearly decreased as he removed his finger from his mouth and pet the horse more willingly. Matthew nodded encouragingly as he did so, speaking with the family until he moved to the next group of individuals.

Winnie watched the display with a growing warmth in her heart. All the other knights stayed in the arena, away from the spectators. But Matthew spoke with each family on the side, spending time with the kids more than anyone else—a real knight of the people—before his name was called to joust once again.

Winnie couldn't deny the care he showed by his actions, nor what it revealed about his character. It was obvious he loved the festival. So why was he not doing more to save it?

After he jousted again, driving home the fact that Winnie was really falling for this knightly sport, only two more clashes occurred before the knights stood at the top of the arena and waved goodbye with a raise of their lances and a hand to their armor-covered chests.

Winnie stared after them, her lips parting in surprise. Was that it? Were they really done after only six runs?

Sure enough, the knights dismounted and took off their helmets one-by-one.

Winnie scoffed in disbelief. What a crock.

Once more, her tablet came up.

- *How does the scoring work?*
- *Who won the tournament?*
- *What happened to the damsel—not that I really care...*

- *Why only six jousting occurrences?*
- *Too long between jousts*

Her hand cramped with how much she wrote, but she didn't stop, the ideas she had for the faire coming fast. Carnival games, rides, treats, edible food, vendors selling goods. And much more jousting.

She had her work cut out for her, and she couldn't wait.

That is, until she felt a pair of eyes watching her. Sure enough, as she lifted her gaze, she found Matthew staring at her with a pointed scowl. He must have seen her scribbling away on her tablet and was now judging her because of it. Or maybe he was still just upset that she'd been placed in charge of his event. Either way, she wasn't going to let his sour attitude stop her from doing her job.

She delivered an intentionally over-the-top sweet smile, then raised her tablet to add one more thing to her list of things to change.

And it would be her biggest challenge of all.

- *MATTHEW*

CHAPTER TEN

MATTHEW ROLLED HIS NECK BACK AS HE WALKED across the grounds of Foxwood, heading from the stables to the house. A few joints cracked as he did so, relief only lasting a moment before the tightness returned to his shoulders. His whole body was tense, as if he'd just been standing in the stocks for the better part of a week.

If only that had been his punishment. He'd prefer it to what he'd been sentenced to—watching that consultant judge his festival.

He'd seen the disapproving shakes of her head, the perpetual turning down of her lips, the incessant scribbling away at the tablet in her hands. And what he *hadn't* seen, he'd heard from others about what *they'd* seen—bombarding guests with questions, scoffing at the size of the list, throwing away an entire box of nearly uneaten food.

Okay, that one he couldn't fault her for. Even the mere thought of Dorothy Porter's food was enough to make him gag. But still, Winnie didn't have to be so obvious about it. She clearly had no clue as to what he was trying to accomplish with his festival.

And do you know what you're trying to accomplish with your festival, Matt?

He scowled at his own thoughts betraying him.

Of course he knew. He was trying to bring the magic of the medieval era into the twenty-first century. To share his love of cracking lances glancing off metal armor, of being immersed in a past that was filled with chivalry and tales. He'd accomplished it once before. Surely he could do so again without a pompous American barging in on his territory.

His thoughts continued to barrage his mind until he drew a deep breath of the cool, Yorkshire air. He was in a right sour mood that afternoon. He needed a distraction, something to make him feel joy again.

Pulling out his phone, he checked his messages as he trekked across the wet grass. To his relief, the lads had messaged.

He scrolled down the feed, smiling as he did so, allowing the conversation between his three college friends to fill his mind and ease his stresses.

CEDRIC

Hope the festival goes well for you today, Matt. Keep us posted.

GRAHAM

Good luck, mate!

FINN

How could it not go well for our boy? He's the greatest jouster in England. Of course, he's the only jouster in England...

CEDRIC

Who's he supposed to use that jousting thing against then?

GRAHAM

It's called a lance.

FINN

Hellloooo.

FINN

GIF of Alan Tudyk with bright red hair pulling a face

Matthew shook his head with mild amusement at their quoting of *A Knight's Tale*. They often did so to wind Matthew up, and he typically could take the teasing. But the mention of the movie today brought Winnie back to his mind, so he chose to ignore mention of it altogether.

He read the rest of the messages, Finn updating them on his grandparents' health, Graham speaking about his latest white water rafting trip, and Cedric informing them of how his injury sustained on the football pitch was nearly fully healed.

Matthew read each update with real interest. The four of them had made the most unlikely of friendships from the early age of thirteen—Matthew, an English chap, rich and bookish. Finn, an Irish boy thrust into Eton's arms and kicked out within a year. Graham, a Scottish lad with a determination to live life to its fullest. And Cedric, a Welshman and poor sheep farmer's son who just so happened to land a scholarship at one of the most prestigious boarding colleges in England.

Over the years, despite the physical distance between them, their friendships had only grown, being kept alive by frequent messages and multi-yearly get-togethers where they participated in charity runs in their respective countries.

This time, they would be gathering in England, and Matthew couldn't wait to host them all at his home again.

He responded to each of their messages before finally addressing the ones referring to himself.

MATTHEW

Thanks for all the support, lads.

MATTHEW

Ced, I hope you were kidding about it being called a "jousting thing." Have I taught you nothing? Guess it's time for another history lesson. I'll be sure to have updated courses for each of you while you're here.

MATTHEW

As for the festival, it went fine. Did I mention my dad hired a new consultant? This one's from New York. She's taking over the festival.

MATTHEW

Also...pretty sure she doesn't like Harry Potter.

She probably hadn't even read the books, which was a travesty in its own right. He wasn't exactly a massive Potterhead himself, but even *he* could see the value the stories had brought to the world.

He clicked his phone off and faced forward. His friends would respond soon enough. Until then, he'd focus on finding some semblance of peace.

Of course, peace was not in his future, as the moment his house came into view, he caught sight of the woman from his thoughts—no, from his very nightmares—standing in front of the doors of Foxwood.

He groaned, slowing his pace so she might enter the house before he'd have to do the same. He really wished Dad would have put her up somewhere else—preferably in a hotel five hundred miles away. But then, every other consultant had been housed there, so why would Winnie be any different?

He watched in silence for a moment. The slower he walked, the longer she seemed to remain. What on earth was she doing? With her back to him, she peered down in front of her, struggling with something. Her purse? No. Her shirt? He didn't think so.

She dropped her hands to her sides, then propped them on

her hips as she looked up and down the length of the doors, clearly frustrated.

Slowly, understanding settled over Matthew, and a smile spread across his lips.

Now *this* was satisfying. Miss Posh Knox couldn't open a door. To be fair, those doors weren't exactly easy to open. They were old and finicky, always managing to get stuck. Still, the sight was a welcome one.

He moved forward with as little noise as possible, determined to take advantage of the situation he'd found her in. Maybe he'd tell Dad his latest consultant was defunct. Although knowing Matthew's luck, Dad would simply brush it off as normal human behavior—like speeding on their property.

"No matter your aversion to her, Matthew," Dad had said at the end of their conversation last night, *"I believe Winnie will be just the one to save the festival...If not more."*

How a woman who couldn't open a door was supposed to save Matthew's festival and "more" was beyond him. Then again, how *he* was supposed to save the festival was beyond him, as well. Would it fall to ruin like some of the great castles of old? Should he just quit now, count his losses and do something that would actually add some value to his family?

Or...or was Dad right in believing Winnie was the key to securing the future of Foxwood?

Her grunt at the door brought him back to the present as she again tried—and failed—to open the doors. He took in the sight of her as she jiggled the handle aggressively. She had a nice figure. Long legs, curvy features. She must be a runner with those formed calves. Either that, or she'd made all that muscle from wearing those ridiculous high heels all the time.

Still, her face wasn't half-bad looking. You know, if one liked that perfect flawless-skin, high-cheekbone, thick-hair kind of look.

Noting her fists once more propped on her hips, Matthew hesitated. Shouldn't he just be nice and help her inside *without* making her feel the fool?

In an instant, however, he brushed the pesky thought aside. Winnie deserved a little humbling after the criticism she'd no doubt assailed at his festival today.

With a raised chin and more confidence than he really had, Matthew stepped across the gravel drive, knowing his crunching footsteps would finally give him away.

Sure enough, Winnie turned at once to look at him, surprise registering across her lovely features.

No. Just plain, old, simple *features*.

"Hey," she greeted, looking back to the door.

He drew closer. "Having some trouble there?"

"What?" She faced him again. "Oh, yeah. I can't seem to get the door open. I think it might be locked or something, but I wasn't given a key."

He'd expected her to deny that she was struggling, perhaps even blush, but the woman held a remarkable lack of self-shame.

Good thing he had more than enough to share.

CHAPTER ELEVEN

WINNIE TOOK A STEP BACK AS MATTHEW APPROACHED in silence.

Instead of his armor or his t-shirt and jeans, he wore what she could only assume was authentic period clothing—layered pants that looked like chaps and a flowing shirt that amplified his level of attractiveness to a point where she was no longer looking at him, but *staring* at him.

She had to admit it. In this one regard, authenticity was *really* working for Matthew. The man embodied the rugged-medieval-knightly look to a T.

Obviously unaware of her stares, he walked past her, reached forward, and opened the door without a hitch.

Winnie gaped. How the heck had he done that? No matter how hard she'd tried before, the door would *not* budge for her. She didn't care to admit how long she'd been struggling with the blasted thing.

Fine, five minutes. Five flipping minutes. And now this guy just waltzed in and opened it in a split-second?

Resting a hand on her hip, she quirked her head to the side, refusing to feel any sort of embarrassment, as there was obviously some special way to open the dang thing.

"Okay, what's the trick?" she asked.

"No trick," Matthew replied, staring at her with those gorgeous, cobalt eyes of his. "You just simply have to know how to open a door."

She pulled in her lips at his snippy response, though ultimately, she chose to ignore it. She'd be better off giving him the benefit of the doubt. He'd just lost his festival to her, after all. She owed him a little grace.

"I don't know," she responded. "I'm not convinced you didn't use some sort of wizardry or something to open it. You know, like Merlin or the man Harry Potter himself."

He eyed her, no doubt to see if she was teasing, which she totally was. She couldn't help herself. His knowledge of Harry Potter had been kind of adorable. It made him more human.

He made no move to respond to her joking, which produced another question in her mind. "Can I ask you something, Matthew?"

"I don't know, *can* you?"

Winnie had often been forced to work with condescending people. So if she had to do the same with Matthew, she at least was grateful he was as nice to look at as Chris Hemsworth in that Disney+ show.

And no, contrary to what everyone thought, she hadn't just watched the series because he took his shirt off in every episode.

That was merely a bonus.

Choosing to ignore Matthew's words once again, she continued, clearing her throat. "I think we got off on the wrong foot. Well, we got off on the right foot, then swapped to the wrong foot after that."

"That's not a question."

Very observant of you, Matthew. "No, it's not," she said. "My question is, can we start over?"

Matthew shifted, folding his arms. As he did so, the scent of his cologne wafted toward her. He didn't smell like the men in New York with rich and overly powerful scents. Instead, his cologne was more earthy. More natural. And there was the distinct smell of leather about him. Was that authentic? Either way, she wasn't about to complain.

He waited a moment, clearly thinking over her proposition before shrugging. "I suppose."

Clearly, that was all he was willing to give. "Great. Then I'll—"

"I take it that's as close to an apology as I'm going to get from you," he interrupted.

"Sorry, what?" she questioned.

"Ah, so you *can* say the word."

She was about to blow out a breath, but if there was one thing she'd learned from dealing with difficult people, it was that she should never let them know they were getting under her skin.

That gave them all the power.

"Oh, I can say the word," she said with a calm smile. "When it's warranted."

He watched her carefully. "So you don't believe an apology is warranted after you criticized my home yesterday?"

Ah, so that's what he was talking about. "For the record, no," she began, "I don't believe I need to apologize for speaking the truth about Foxwood. I wasn't criticizing it. I was pointing out areas that could do with some improvement. And," she paused, debating on whether or not to continue before throwing caution to the wind. "I hate to break it to you, but I'll be saying much worse than that in the coming days about the festival. I hope you're ready for it."

He remained still, his eyes narrowing only slightly.

Wasn't she supposed to have been starting over with him? Trying to butter him up? She swallowed her pride and tipped her head to the side. "Of course, I *am* sorry if I was a little too blunt for your liking. I'll be more kind when it comes to the festival, I promise."

Matthew said nothing. After a moment, she leaned forward. "Am I to take your silence as accepting my apology or denying it?"

He drew a deep breath, his eyebrows together. "How could I do anything but accept such a generous offer?" Sarcasm hung from his every word. "Unfortunately, that doesn't fix everything else."

"Oh, there's more?" she questioned.

He nodded.

"Care to tell me so we might avoid a guessing game?" she asked.

"Absolutely. Let's see, how about you speeding on my family's property, destroying the grounds due to distracted driving, spraying mud across my armor so I was required to polish it all over again, dirtying the front hall with muddy footprints, and finally, agreeing to run a festival you know next to nothing about all while hoping you don't run it into the ground?"

He finished, his frown having grown deeper and deeper as he'd continued, all while Winnie listened with measured breaths. She was used to barrages of criticism. Heck, if Matthew thought he could get to her with his words after she'd lived in her father's home for nearly two decades, he had another thing coming. Compared to the metaphorical tomatoes Dad constantly threw at her, Matthew's words were like flowers on a stage.

"Wow," she said with a feigned heavy nod. "That's quite the rap sheet, isn't it? So one overarching apology *won't* make up for them all?"

He didn't respond, clearly unamused.

"No?" she pressed. Again, no response. "Okay, well, for the record, I did apologize for spraying mud all over you. As for everything else, what if I tell you everything that you've done to *me* so our actions cancel each other out?"

He scoffed. "And just what have I done to you, exactly?"

Now it was her turn to fold her arms. "How about tricking me into sharing more about your estate by making me believe you were a mere member of the staff instead of the owner's actual son?"

His dubious look remained, despite the slightest hint of culpability now shining in his eyes.

"Or," she continued, "how about when you made fun of me in front of your dad for accidentally tracking puddles through the house—which, by the way, I still don't think I did? Or when you teased me for getting the century wrong for the medieval era? Or when you walked so close to me on your horse that I was sprayed with mud by his hooves? Oh, and then there was my favorite— your absolute guarantee that I would fail at my job here. How about any of those? Do they warrant an apology?"

They stared at each other, neither of them wavering, eyes unflinching until, to her surprise, his lip twitched, as if he were about to smile.

"I guess we've both said things to each other we probably shouldn't have," he finally muttered.

Woah, what? Were they actually progressing toward something of an amicable business relationship? She could hardly believe it had happened so quickly.

She had some charm after all.

"I guess, then, moving forward," she began, "we can just promise to try our best not to tick each other off. It'll make working together much easier that way."

Just like that, the air between them shifted back to what it had been before, and Matthew's stoic expression returned. He licked the corner of his mouth as his jaw shifted, then his eyes sharpened. "How did you find the festival?"

So that was his next angle—to find more ways to be offended by her. She had to play this right, or all hope would be lost with working amicably with the guy.

"I found it absolutely enlightening," she stated.

"Enlightening," he repeated.

"Yep."

"That's all you can say about it?"

She pressed her lips together. Speaking openly now, before

they had even a chance to rebuild their tenuous relationship, wouldn't help anything. But then, what would lying do?

"You want me to be honest?" she asked.

He nodded. "Of course."

"Okay," she said. "Then I will be. I thought the jousting was absolutely incredible."

He looked at her with a wary gaze, as if he knew she was buttering him up.

She might as well get this over with, then. "Be that as it may," she continued, "there were significant flaws with the process and with the faire as a whole that took away from how much *more* incredible the event could be."

Matthew pulled on a look of arrogance she knew was specifically to veil the offense he'd taken. "Flaws?"

"Yes, quite a lot of them."

"For example?"

She shouldn't be flirting with fire, but then, the man was sparking already. "Well, first thing I can think of off the top of my head, the main flaw is the obsession with historical accuracy."

His jaw twitched.

"It has made the food unbearable and the activities lacking," she continued. "The faire doesn't have to be factual to be fun, you know? Have you ever even tried to put something in that wasn't one hundred percent accurate?"

"Someone tried once," he said. "Didn't work out."

"Hmm. That sounds like someone suggested something you didn't approve of, and you didn't even give it a fighting chance."

He glanced away for the briefest of seconds, revealing her accuracy. "It doesn't matter either way," he said. "You'll be proven wrong eventually."

"Proven wrong about what exactly?"

"About the historical accuracy of the event," he clarified. "And your belief that there are flaws here."

She dropped her chin with a look of disbelief. "So you think there is absolutely nothing wrong with Foxwood *or* the faire...*at all*?"

His jaw twitched beneath his beard again. She quite liked the look of it. She'd like it a lot more if, you know, he wasn't absolutely furious with her.

"That's correct," he said stubbornly. "Absolutely nothing wrong at all. But there's no point in discussing it further, as we'll just continue to argue about it. Excuse me."

He moved to the door, but Winnie took a step forward, stopping him. "Look, you told me to be honest. Would you rather I'd lied to you, told you it was absolutely perfect?"

He shot a frown at her. "I don't need to be coddled with lies. But I also don't need to hear your opinion on what you believe to be the truth. Now, if you'll excuse me."

Repeating his words more forcefully, he tried to step around her again, ready to enter his house, but indignation bubbled within Winnie.

What was she supposed to do? She had been hired to do a job, and Matthew was holding it against her. She really should let it go, and yet...

Her hand shot forward as if on its own accord, blocking him from going inside. She wrapped her fingers around the handle of the door, then pulled it closed, directly in his face.

He stepped back, a startled look in his eyes as he peered down at her. "What are you doing?"

"I'm not done with our conversation yet," she stated simply. "I wanted to talk with you so we could clear the air between us, but obviously, that's not going to work as you seem to have a little bee under your bonnet that started buzzing the second you found out I was a consultant."

Once again his jaw twitched. She wasn't going to allow it to distract her this time.

"I'll have you know," she continued, "I don't think it's really fair of you to have made a snap judgment about me just because of my job title."

"And you think it's fair for you to have made a snap judgment about my festival?"

She pulled back. "Of course not. And I didn't. I made an informed decision after a great deal of research and observation."

"As if a day could tell you all you needed to know." He looked back at the door. "You may not be done, but I am."

He opened the door again—Honestly, what witchery was he using to push it open so succinctly?—but once more, Winnie's pride swelled. Before he could take a step inside, she moved forward and closed the door on him again.

His frown grew, his gaze penetrating hers with a scowl so intense, her heart stuttered. She could only imagine what she'd do if he eyed her that intensely with a look of something else...like admiration.

She blinked mutely at her rogue thoughts. They were to be coworkers. Anything else would be highly inappropriate.

"Why are you done?" she asked, focusing more intently on the conversation at hand. "Can't you just talk to me about your concerns? What you're worried about? What you're angry about?"

He didn't respond.

"Is it because you're afraid?" she asked, knowing that would rile him up enough to give some sort of a response.

To her surprise, the anger dissipated in his expression, and he raised his chin with a calm sigh. "I won't play your games, Miss Knox."

"Winnie," she corrected.

"Consultants are all the same," he continued, as if not hearing her. "You all *work* the same."

"And how do we work?" she asked.

"Without heart."

Be like Fort Knox.

"Really?" she questioned.

"Yes. You come in, you decide what's best for everyone, you make changes based on your opinion alone, then you say goodbye to anyone who can't deal with it. It's always the same." He drew a step closer to her. "Just know, I'll not allow you to sack a single soul."

Winnie drew quiet breaths, strapping on more defenses one by one. For some reason, she had to do that more often with Matthew than with any other person she'd ever worked with before.

"I'm sorry you see me in such a way," she said. "Because as I told you yesterday, that's not how I work."

"Whatever you say."

"You don't sound convinced."

"I'm not," he stated. "But it doesn't matter. All I have to do is bide my time. You'll be gone soon enough."

Pride cinched around her heart, strapping it into place. "I can assure you, I'm here for the long haul."

"We'll see."

He opened the door again. But Winnie, in all her impulsivity and ridiculousness, reached forward and pulled it shut once more.

He stared at her with a heavy sigh. "Is this what I'm to expect from now on? You controlling every little thing you don't like that is happening?"

She smiled, attempting to lighten the mood, if only to make herself feel better from the lack of faith he had in her. "It all depends on if I get the help I need."

He blew out a soft snort of derision. "Good luck with that."

Now it was her time to blow out a breath. Honestly, this guy was going to be a lot of work. "Look, Matthew, what I saw at the faire back there—"

"Festival," he corrected.

"—was disappointing," she continued. "There were so many flaws I noticed in the first few minutes, I almost gave myself carpal tunnel by writing them all down." He didn't like that. His frown made that clear enough. "But I also saw a lot of promising things, too. Honestly, there is no reason you guys shouldn't be swimming in cash."

"And you think you're the one to make that happen for us?"

"Yes," she responded with confidence. "I am."

"And what makes you any different than every other consultant my dad has hired before?"

"One thing," she said, leaning forward. "I'm Winnie-Freakin'-Knox."

She stared into his eyes, unfaltering, willing him to see how serious she was. He didn't respond, though a strange twinkling shone in his eye. Was he amused? Impressed? She couldn't tell. Either way, it was time to make *her* exit through the door.

And yet, just as soon as her hand touched the doorknob, she remembered...she didn't know how to open the flipping thing.

She wiggled the handle down, then up, trying to mimic what Matthew had done, but the door remained closed. She could not have been more humiliated.

In a desperate attempt to escape, she jiggled the handle with more ferocity, but Matthew's hand grasped lightly around her bare wrist, stopping her abruptly. She stared at his long, masculine fingers, their warmth radiating through her skin and up her arm as her heart thrummed uncomfortably against her chest.

She shouldn't be feeling this way. She should be feeling nothing at all. And yet, heat swirled through her body like a whirlwind of fire, uncontrollable. All-consuming.

Did Matthew feel the same way?

Slowly, her gaze trailed up his flowing shirt before settling on his features. His eyes were already on her, deep and focused and unreadable.

The two of them stood close together, closer than she'd realized, and as they stared at each other, an undeniable energy passed between them.

Yes, he was feeling something, too. But neither of them should be. They were work associates, perhaps even enemies, the majority of their interactions filled with scathing words and scowls. And yet, all of those moments seemed to disappear as they stood before each other in silence.

Winnie swallowed, her throat growing dry. There was nothing more she wanted to do in that moment than to lick her lips to provide them some moisture.

No, that was a lie. There *was* something she wanted to do more.

With no further control over her sight, she felt her eyes drop to his lips, those perfect, masculine, appealing lips, and she stared at them until they moved.

"Up, then down," he said, his voice gruff.

She blinked. Up, down, what? What was he talking about?

Finally, he released his grasp around her wrist and wrapped his fingers around the door handle instead. His hand moved up, then down, and the door opened.

He stood back, creating more distance between them. "Your door, Miss Winnie-Freakin'-Knox."

A blush burned within her cheeks so deeply, she could have heated all of Foxwood with the fire radiating from them.

Without another look at him—or his lips—she entered the house, wiped her feet on the rug, and moved swiftly across the front hall, desperate to leave behind the fool she'd made of herself and the man who'd caused her to do so in the first place.

CHAPTER TWELVE

"AND HOW IS OUR LITTLE CONSULTANT DOING?"

Winnie grimaced. She'd been dreading this moment for days now, talking to her family about being schlepped with a mediocre faire instead of a grand estate. They'd be embarrassed. Dad would be ashamed. It'd be a whole big thing.

She may as well get this over with.

"Oh, I'm doing great, Dad. Thanks." Huh. She hadn't shared as much as she was planning on. Oh, well.

Taking advantage of her day off, Winnie had gone to church that morning, then wandered around Grassington—the gorgeous village near Foxwood—where she'd ultimately found a nearby park to enjoy. There, she sat outside on a bench in the middle of the large, grassy fields, enjoying the first sunshine she'd felt since arriving in Yorkshire.

She didn't mind rain or clouds, or the hush they brought over the land. But she couldn't deny how incredible a good, English sunshine felt on her cooled skin.

The fields around her were filled with soccer players kicking balls in the air, dogs chasing after sticks, and families seated on picnic blankets with their lunches spread about them. Did these people know how lucky they were to live in such a location? It was so different from New York. So quaint. So peaceful. So *perfect*.

"Are you taking charge and making changes?" Dad pressed, his voice glitching on the video call.

"Yep," Winnie responded simply again, adjusting the earbuds in her ears.

Maybe if she only gave short answers, he'd take the hint and focus on someone else.

Fat chance.

Every Sunday, the Knoxes gathered via the web to chat together as a family from all over the world. North America, Europe, Asia. Then, they would each take turns giving a list of updates on their accomplishments from oldest to youngest.

Mom and Dad had already shared the progress they'd made in their latest trials. Scott had given his spiel as an anesthesiologist at the most prominent hospital in Oregon. Samantha had told them all about her latest build as an architect in Germany. Spencer, the pilot, had no shame in showing off photos of him, his wife, and their new two-month-old baby girl riding elephants and exploring the floating markets during their trip to Thailand. And Sarah had spoken about the progress she'd made at her start-up company as a software engineer in California.

And then...there was Winnie. Win-Win-Winnie who had yet to be impressive to anyone.

"So what changes have you made so far?" Dad asked, clearly not letting her go until he received more info. He had to be desperate to discover something worth praising in her. "And how are the Wintours feeling about it all?"

"Oh, they're just fine. Pretty open to things." Minus one of them. "I'm still working through some of the changes, though."

"What's the estate like?" Mom asked, her eyes aglow, no doubt desiring to see it for herself.

Mom was just as driven as Dad was, though she was less involved in her kids' lives. Too busy planning parties and creating charities. Even still, Winnie preferred Mom's hands-off parenting approach to Dad's meddling fingers.

Taking the opportunity to distract him from her job, Winnie explained what Foxwood was like, the décor, the size, the drive.

"It's really opulent," she said. "Super impressive."

"Sounds like my kind of house," Samantha, the architect, joked.

"Wait," Dad said, and Winnie's stomach tightened. "So why do they need your help at Foxwood, then, if they're still so well-off?"

Winnie had walked right into that one. She raced to find a response that Dad would actually believe, glancing around to ensure no one was close to her. She wouldn't want anyone who might know the Wintours to overhear her words. "So the estate is in really good shape, but Mr. Wintour wants me to help prevent anything that might injure it in the future."

Dad still appeared hesitant, though he nodded all the same.

Say it now, Winnie. Before your chance is lost.

"And, uh..." She swallowed. "My first job is to improve the faire they have going on here. After that, I'll be onto something else."

There. She'd said it. No big deal. Everyone was fine. No one had died. They were all still breathing.

Although, the silence *was* deafening.

"A fair?" her oldest brother Scott asked. "As in, like, the county fairs they hold with rodeos and fried Twinkies and funnel cakes?"

There was some curiosity in his tone, but a marked judgment sounded louder. "No, it's not like a county fair," she rushed to explain. "It's a renaissance faire more than anything."

A greater silence than even before met her. She could hear their thoughts as if they all spoke them aloud.

"Wow, Winnie. What a prestigious gig."

"You didn't tell anyone you're a Knox, right?"

"Are you sure you can manage such a strenuous job?"

What was worse than all of that was the look on Dad's face—that same old expression he seemed to always wear when speaking with Winnie.

Disappointment.

She wished she was imagining it, but she knew him too well to ever be so hopeful.

"What did you do, Winnie?" he asked.

Winnie frowned. "I didn't do anything, Dad. It was Mr. Wintour's suggestion."

"But that wasn't what you and he originally agreed on," he stated, obviously annoyed.

"I know," Winnie said. "But it'll be super easy and super quick. Plus, it has the potential to be a big moneymaker, and I have a fairly large budget to manage, so I didn't see the harm in changing the plan for a few weeks."

Money always made Dad more accepting of something.

Sure enough, his frown lessened. "Still," he continued, "that was hardly fair of Arthur. Maybe I should talk to him."

"No, Dad," Winnie protested at once, leaning forward on the bench and peering intently into her phone screen. "Really, it's fine. I can handle it. Plus, it's giving me extra time and insight into what the estate needs, so it's killing two birds with one stone."

To her relief, Dad seemed to relent, though she knew this would not be the last she heard about it.

"So what exactly is at a faire, then?" Mom asked, her eyes straying down to her lap, no doubt where her phone lay. She'd never had a very good attention span.

Winnie shrugged. "It's just an event that has medieval activities and food and stuff like that. There's not much to write home about now, but I have big plans for it. Apparently, it's super important to the Wintours' son."

Mom nodded absentmindedly.

"So does it have rides and stuff?" Sarah, Winnie's closest sibling in age, asked.

"No, but I'm planning on bringing them in," Winnie said.

"That's the only way to entertain kids," Scott piped in. His wife next to him nodded vigorously. "That and food."

Winnie logged the information away.

"So if they don't have rides, what do they have?" Dad asked, still skeptical.

"Um..." she winced inwardly, knowing what would happen the moment she continued. "Jousting is their main event."

Sure enough, a few of her siblings laughed.

"Wait," Spencer said, holding his newborn over his shoulder, gently patting his back as he bounced up and down. "Like, what they did in high school, LARPing and stuff?"

"Yep. In full armor and everything."

Spencer laughed. "Those kids were so weird."

"Seriously though," Samantha agreed.

Winnie looked away, frowning at her family's lack of decorum. She'd seen those kids in high school cosplaying and LARPing to their hearts' content. They weren't weird. Just different.

And what was so bad about being different? She couldn't help but envy those kids who'd been able to throw social norms to the wind and do what they'd wanted. They had been some of the happiest, most genuine, most kind people at the school.

Of course, she couldn't say the same thing about Matthew, as he was bordering on being the rudest person she'd ever met. But she would never stoop to calling him weird for following a passion that brought him joy.

And yet, hadn't she called him that very thing when he'd ridden toward her in the rain in full armor the night they'd met? Her exact words used to describe him had been "crazy-pants," had they not?

She groaned inwardly at her cruelty. It was time to make up for it, even if no one knew what she'd done but herself.

"Actually," she began, interrupting her family's laughter, "it's pretty cool what these knights do. They ride toward each other with these huge lances and try to knock each other off their horses. It's pretty crazy."

"Crazy is right," Spencer said, shaking his head again.

Winnie frowned. She'd meant crazy-cool, not crazy-weird.

"Yeah, good luck dealing with that, Winnie," Scott said next.

"And good luck trying to make the event actually worth seeing," Spencer joked.

Winnie clamped her mouth shut. This was only making things worse, as was evident by Dad's face. With each new joke from his sons' mouths, he'd frowned deeper and deeper.

"But, hey," Spencer continued, "maybe if you finally come out on top with this one, you'll have enough experience so Dad doesn't have to get you your jobs anymore."

That was a low blow. But then, it was true, which was why no one came to her defense.

Winnie had tried to be herself around her family, but she had always been the odd one out. The one who'd failed out of medical school due to the smell of cadavers. The one who'd failed to become a chef due to not knowing the difference between baking powder and baking soda. The one who couldn't be a dental hygienist, a teacher, a computer programmer, or a thousand other things under the sun, all for one weird reason after another.

And the one thing she'd actually been good at—the one thing she'd actually wanted to pursue? That hadn't been good enough for a Knox.

But hey, she was a successful consultant. Of course, she was still bearing the brunt of her family's jokes. Never mind that her feelings were hurt continuously. At least the rest of them fit in, right?

To her relief, the conversation soon shifted away from her, and she lost interest as Dad spoke again, recounting their latest court win. Her eyes wandered away from the screen as she mentally listed pleasant things around her to bring back the peace she'd felt before.

The sunshine on her cheeks. Brown and blue birds flying

overhead, chasing each other across clear skies. A couple smiling at each other as they walked their creamy-colored dog that sniffed along the dirt path. A family playing in the grass beyond her with a soccer ball, two girls giggling as they ran across the grass.

"No hands!" shouted the father in the fields, his back to Winnie as he propped his hands on his hips.

His daughters, who had to be younger than six, ran toward the ball he'd just kicked, then picked it up again with their hands.

"I said, no hands, munchkins!" the father shouted again.

His voice was loud, but the exaggeration to his gruff tone and the laughter from the girls revealed this was part of the game as much as kicking the ball was.

The dad chased after them, and Winnie smiled as the girls ran away with delighted squeals.

A buzz in her hand drew her attention back to her phone and the conversation occurring in her earbuds—Mom speaking of the upcoming family reunion that year skiing in Park City.

Winnie hardly heard, her eye catching on the text message that popped down from the top of her screen instead.

Still on the call, she read the message from her older sister.

SARAH

You okay?

Good, ole Sarah. Winnie should've known she'd reach out.

Winnie loved all of her siblings, but she'd always liked Sarah the best. She had been the most inclusive of Winnie's different sensibilities. She didn't judge her for not being married, not having children, not knowing what she wanted to do in life.

Mostly, in part, because Sarah was the same way. Childless. Husbandless. She'd only fallen into becoming a software engineer in the last few years, but it had bumped her up in Dad's estimations instantly. Winnie had always believed the real reason Sarah remained single was because it was easier to have Dad's approval for her success as an engineer than it was to find his approval for marrying someone.

Winnie tapped out a quick response.

WINNIE

Yeah, I'm fine.

SARAH

I just wanted to check after Spencer's jerk comments. So typical of him to be so stuck-up.

Winnie looked back to the video call. Mom still rattled on about all the skiing trips she'd taken over the years and which one was her favorite and how this year would trump them all.

WINNIE

Sadly enough, I'm used to his being a butthead. Thanks for checking, though.

Sarah laughed at Winnie's text, no doubt with her use of the insult "butthead," which had fallen out of existence in the last twenty or so years.

She moved back to the video chat, noting Sarah's eyes averted as she texted instead of listened, too.

Dad was now correcting Mom, saying trips to the Caribbean in the winter were better than skiing.

Being trapped on a ship with her family wasn't Winnie's ideal vacation either. In truth, she preferred to stay at home. And by home, she meant anywhere she *felt* at home with anyone who *felt* like family—particularly ones who didn't insult her.

But when was the last time she'd felt that way?

"Now, listen here. No hands this time."

Winnie glanced back up to the dad's voice across the field. His back still faced her, the little girls still giggling behind their hands as he pointed at them.

Winnie paused, narrowing her eyes. There was something familiar about the voice. She strained to see across the field of grass, taking in the man's tall stance and broad shoulders.

Broad shoulders? Her heart thumped.

She focused harder on him, only now seeing the dark, blond curls pulled up in a man bun at the crown of his head.

That hair. She hadn't known it was long enough to be pulled back, but she could recognize it anywhere.

Matthew.

Sure enough, in the next moment, he kicked the ball to the side and watched as the girls ran after it, his profile finally being revealed to Winnie. He smiled after the girls, and Winnie's heart skipped a beat.

She thought she'd been admiring a dad playing with his kids in a way she'd never experienced herself before, in a way she'd always wanted as a child. Now, to discover that Matthew—uptight, obsessed with historical accuracy Matthew—was the guy who was lax on the rules? She was reminded again of the first moments after they'd met, how he'd smiled and winked and teased her, and her heart pinched.

She hated this part of being a consultant. Seeing people as their true, happy selves away from her, only to be treated with disdain and anger by them merely because she was doing her job. Honestly, she and Matthew would probably get along were it not for her work. But then, how true had that been for every relationship—professional or friendly—that she'd attempted to make in the last few years?

More laughter sounded as Matthew chased after the two girls running away from him, and her thoughts shifted.

Whose were they, the little girls? His friend's children? Godchildren? His...his own children?

An unsettled feeling hunkered down in her belly. He wasn't married. He didn't wear a ring. Unless, of course, he was just one of those guys who didn't like wearing them.

Images of her time with him flashed through her vision, the connection they'd shared the day before, the arguments, the battles, then that final moment when his hand had lingered on her wrist.

She frowned. He couldn't be married. She was...thirty percent sure. Divorced, maybe? Or were these his girlfriend's kids?

She glanced around, a few seconds later finding a woman who looked a couple years younger than Winnie sitting on a blanket. The woman watched the girls and Matthew with a smile on her face and large sunglasses blocking her eyes. Her hair was dark and long, pulled in a low ponytail.

The wife. The sister. The girlfriend. The friend. Who was she? Another buzz stole Winnie's attention.

SARAH

> So I doubt you were able to answer honestly with everyone on the chat. Especially Dad. But how is it there, really? And how do you feel about the faire?

Winnie's mind swirled, attempting to balance her conversation between Sarah and her family—and now the possible discovery about Matthew. She hadn't done anything inappropriate with him, but she nearly groaned at the mere notion of having been so attracted to an unavailable man.

WINNIE

> I'm actually kinda excited about it. If it weren't for Dad's judgments, I think I'd have fun. There's a boatload to improve with the faire, but I'm up to the challenge.

The video chat continued, the argument carrying on about where they really should spend their family reunion. But Winnie was hardly following right now.

Matthew had just turned around, heading toward the girl on the blanket. A broad smile was on his face—something she'd never seen before.

It was striking. Distracting. Just like that hair on him. He looked like Thor with a man bun.

Her heart fluttered, but she chastised herself immediately. She wouldn't admire him again until she was sure what his relationship status was.

Moving benches would probably make things easier for herself. But then, surely it was safer to know where he was, so she knew where to avoid looking.

SARAH

> That's awesome! I'm so glad you're excited about it. You're going to rock it, as usual. And don't let Dad or the others get you down. If this is what you want to do, I say go for it.

Sarah always knew how to make Winnie feel better.

WINNIE

> Thank you! You're the best. The jousting isn't as weird as Spencer was saying, either. It's actually really fun. The knights are awesome to see, too.

The *knights*. Plural. Not just one in particular.

SARAH

> So there really are full blown knights there?

WINNIE

> Yeah. It's pretty cool.

SARAH

> And are they as knightly as the movies make them out to be?

Winnie smiled, then hesitated. She chewed on her lower lip before sending the next text. She could tell what happened to her, all the while omitting that she found the man attractive. That was definitely okay.

> WINNIE
>
> Kinda. One actually rescued me the other day.

Three dots instantly pulled up.

> SARAH
>
> Wait, what?

> WINNIE
>
> My car got stuck in the mud at the estate, and a knight appeared and pushed the car out of the mud for me.

> SARAH
>
> OH MY GOSH. That is the most legit thing I've ever heard in my life. You were literally saved by a knight in shining armor. Please tell me he's hot.

Winnie smiled, then glanced up at Matthew, who now sat next to the woman. They weren't close to each other. They weren't even touching. And both their eyes were focused on the girls. That seemed more like a sibling relationship than anything. And Dad had mentioned the Wintours having a son *and* a daughter.

Or was she just being hopeful? Either way, she couldn't be sure. And she wouldn't risk being disrespectful to him or the woman he sat beside. Just in case.

"Winnie?"

Winnie almost jumped, looking back down to her phone where her mom had spoken to her on the call.

"Sorry, the connection is super glitchy," Winnie lied.

"I was just asking where you'd choose to have Christmas this year," Mom repeated. "Everyone's opinion needs to be taken into account."

Winnie had heard that before, but being in the minority, her opinion never mattered. "I'm good wherever," she stated, just like always.

Then she glanced back to where Matthew sat. Her heart lurched as their eyes caught.

Matthew swiftly darted his gaze away, but not before Winnie recognized the truth. He had been staring at her.

And her heart jumped again.

CHAPTER THIRTEEN

MATTHEW CURSED HIS LUCK. OF COURSE HE'D BE caught staring the one time he looked over at Winnie sitting on the bench.

Okay, he'd looked at her a bit more than once.

Fine, he'd seen her the second she'd sat down and hadn't been able to stop staring at her since. She just looked so pretty that morning, sitting in the warm sunshine, an occasional smile on her lips as she spoke on the phone.

Just like now.

He sighed in frustration, once more pulling his gaze away from her. Was it any wonder she'd caught him staring? At this rate, she'd think he was obsessed with her or something.

What was she doing over there anyway? No doubt working still. Finding more ways to destroy his festival.

"Do you know her or something?"

Matthew looked to his sister seated beside him on the blanket. "What?"

"That girl," Char said. "You keep looking over at her and leering."

Matthew pulled a face. "I'm not leering."

Especially at Winnie, a woman full of herself yet incapable of opening doors. His lip twitched at the memory of the day before.

"You're doing it again," Char said.

He cursed, pulling his gaze away from Winnie once more. Why did he keep doing that?

"So...why don't you go talk to her?" Char pressed.

He pulled back, giving his sister a look. "Why would I do that?"

"You obviously think she's cute, otherwise you wouldn't be staring at her so much."

Matthew cringed. It was true. He did find Winnie attractive. But the last thing he wanted to do was *talk* to her.

"Yeah, I think I'm fine."

"Why? Why don't you go over there? Chicken."

He sniffed in ridicule at her goading. That wasn't going to work on him today. "Trust me, my speaking with her would do none of us any good."

Char stared at him, but he focused harder on his nieces as they attempted to kick the football, first placing it with their hands on the ground.

"No hands!" he called out again.

They giggled, and he couldn't help but smile. Dad had taught him to play football the same way, refusing to allow him the use of his hands. Matthew never had, but how could he fault his adorable nieces for not being as strait-laced with the rules as he was?

Despite his adherence to the rules, he'd never made it far in football. His friend, Cedric, on the other hand, was an entirely different matter. As a professional footballer from Wales, if the man touched a ball with his hands while in play, he'd be bullied from one end of the country to the next. He'd already been torn apart by the media for pulling a muscle and having to sit out for a season for Habergham FC.

Matthew had always admired his mate's stamina and grace,

even under intense media scrutiny. Matthew wasn't sure he'd be able to do the same.

He couldn't even handle Char's scrutiny right now.

"Am I missing something here?" she asked, still watching Matthew with narrowed eyes.

Matthew looked at her with feigned naivety. "What are you talking about?"

She looked at Winnie, then back to him. "Do you know her or what?" she asked again, clearly growing impatient.

He didn't want to get into this. But then, he couldn't lie to his sister.

With a side-eye toward her, he shrugged. "Maybe."

"I knew it. Who is she?"

He contemplated remaining silent, but then, what was the point? Char would find out who she was eventually. "That's the new consultant Dad hired."

Char's eyes rounded, her mouth dropping open. "Her? She's the American?" She leaned back to see Winnie beyond him. "She's definitely not who I pictured."

Earlier that morning, Matthew had told Char all about Winnie and her desire to change everything, hoping to get his sister on his side early on. Who knew if Winnie would win Char over like she had Dad and Mum.

"You made her out to be a lot older than she is," Char continued, staring. "And a lot uglier."

Maybe he had, maybe he hadn't. "I think I painted quite an accurate picture."

"'Bitter, fake, and *old*?'" Char said, quoting back the exact words he'd said to her. She folded her arms, shaking her head. "Boy, do you have a chip on your shoulder."

"I was describing her personality more than her looks," he defended weakly.

"And what's so wrong with her personality?"

"She wants to change everything," he said, acutely aware of how childish he sounded right now. "I already told you that."

Char exaggerated a gasp. "No, a consultant wanting to change things? Call the constable!"

Matthew stared at her with a blank expression. He was not amused.

Char, however, laughed. "Look, you know I'm on your side with this whole thing. Dad should've told you, just like he'd said. But it is what it is. You can't change it now."

Matthew knew that. But it didn't make it any easier to accept. He'd already forgiven Dad for doing what he thought was best for the estate, but that didn't mean Matthew had let go of Winnie being there—or would ever let it go. She should have said no to taking over the festival.

"She'll probably have some good ideas," Char continued. "Ideas that might actually save the festival."

That little New York snake had already gotten to his sister. How was that possible?

He glanced back to Winnie, who removed an earpiece from her ear but still stared down at her phone. It was a good job she was so attached to her device, otherwise he might've been caught staring again.

"The only thing she's going to do is run it faster into the ground," he said.

And he felt that now more than ever. Last night at approximately 11:58 PM, Winnie had sent a lengthy email to everyone on the festival staff, explaining who she was and that she wanted to meet together first thing Monday morning.

"I'm thrilled with the prospect of working with you all!" was how she'd ended her email.

Matthew shook his head. It was a joke. All of it. She would have nothing of value to add to the festival. She was a New Yorker, running on New York hours, living on New York fumes, and bringing her New York vibes where they didn't belong.

Well, she was in for a rude awakening.

"I'm going to introduce myself to her."

Char's words broke through Matthew's thoughts, and his stomach dropped. "What?"

"Yeah, I'm going to see if she's really as bad as you made her out to be."

That was exactly what Matthew was afraid of. Winnie would be on her best behavior, and he'd look like a child again. "No, don't."

"Why not?" she asked with an accusatory brow. "*You've* met her."

"Yeah, and I regret it very much."

"Well, I highly doubt I will. She's not challenging *my* existence at Foxwood." She gave a haughty little smile, clearly proud of her teasing, then stood.

Matthew groaned, standing too. Winnie was still sitting on the bench, typing out something on her phone.

Was she pretending to be busy? She hadn't looked back at him since their eyes had met a few minutes before.

Not that she ought to have. But still, after their touch yesterday, he could've sworn he'd seen something in her gray eyes—a level of attraction, perhaps? Whatever it was, it hardly mattered to him. He doubted it had even been real. Women like her never went for guys like him, and he was glad of it.

Wait, where had Char gone? He glanced around him, finally spotting his sister walking across the grass to her girls.

"I'll be just over there," she told them, pointing to Winnie on the bench.

The girls nodded, still kicking the football as Char made directly for Winnie.

"Char, wait," Matthew said softly, trying to catch up to her.

She looked at him over her shoulder. "What?"

He tried to think of what to say. "Just...You don't want to speak with her."

She stopped, propping her hands on her hips. "Why not?"

"Because...she'll be mean to you." That had to be his weakest argument ever.

"Why, because she was mean to you?"

"Well, yeah."

She narrowed her eyes. "And were *you* mean to *her*?"

He opened his mouth, but no words left it. Worthless brain.

"Just as I suspected," she said, then she turned around again and headed toward Winnie. "You can join me if you want," she called over her shoulder. "Or you can cower over here with the other little girls."

Matthew stopped, glancing between his nieces and Char, who was fast approaching Winnie.

He gritted his teeth. He'd much rather be spending time with Char's girls, but then, what would be said about him between his sister and the consultant who clearly didn't like him?

Well, that decided it.

With a heavy sigh, he picked up his pace, reaching Char's side the moment they stood before Winnie.

The consultant looked up with a pleasant expression, clearly distracted by whatever she'd been doing on her phone, then surprise lit across her features as her eyes shifted from Char to Matthew.

"Hi," Char said with a cheery smile. She was far too bright to be meeting this woman today.

"Hey," Winnie responded with uncertainty, turning off her phone and standing to face them.

She glanced to Matthew—for an explanation or for reassurance, he wasn't sure. Well, she wouldn't be getting either from him. He remained silent behind Char, a watchful eye on Winnie.

"Sorry if this is weird," his sister said. "I'm Char Wintour. Matthew's my brother."

For a split second, Winnie stared, her lips parting and eyes lingering on Char. Then a genuine smile stretched across her lips, no doubt to make a good impression. She'd done that with Matthew, too, before she'd opened her mouth and revealed what kind of viper she was, criticizing his home and festival.

"It's so nice to meet you," Winnie said. "I'm Winnie Knox, though I'm guessing your brother has already told you all about me."

Matthew cringed. Time to put on his armor.

CHAPTER FOURTEEN

"He has, actually," Char said, not bothering to look behind her at Matthew. "Which is exactly why I needed to come here to see for myself what you're really like."

Matthew gave a subtle shake of his head. He never should have spoken with Char. She trusted people far too easily.

"I can only imagine what he's said," Winnie returned.

She looked different today. Carefree, maybe? No, that wasn't the right word. "Slightly relaxed" was closer to it. Maybe the jetlag had finally left, taking with it the sleepy circles beneath her eyes.

"Oh, don't take it personally," Char said. "He's always been judgmental."

"I gathered."

Matthew frowned. "You two are aware that I'm standing right here, aren't you?"

Char waved a dismissive hand over her shoulder. At least Winnie had the decency to look at him, though neither of them still said a word to him.

He folded his arms. He'd come here to steer the conversation in the right direction, not to be subjected to his sister's teasing in front of Winnie, making him look even worse in front of her. Although, how that was possible, he wasn't sure. She probably blamed him for the whole state of the festival. Not that it *wasn't* his fault...

"Mummy! Lilly won't share the ball with me!"

Thankfully, the attention shifted to Matthew's nieces, who ran toward them to stand beside their mum.

"Lilly, Ava wants a turn, love," Char said as the three-year-old gripped tightly to the ball.

"No, my turn!" Lilly shouted with a scowl.

"And who are these beautiful girls?" Winnie asked, smiling down at his nieces.

Instantly, Lilly and Ava stared up at Winnie with curious eyes, the argument over the ball apparently forgotten.

"Oh, aren't you kind?" Char said, falling at once for Winnie's compliments. Was Matthew the only one who wasn't a sucker for the consultant?

"These are my little girls, Ava and Lilly," Char continued. She leaned down to her daughters. "This is Winnie. She'll be staying at the house and working as Matthew's boss for a bit."

Matthew pulled a face. *His boss.* He knew Char was trying to annoy him on purpose, but blimey, he didn't think it'd be working so well.

At least Winnie didn't react. Instead, she bent her knees and lowered herself to be at the girls' levels.

How did she manage that, then? Those heels would have toppled anyone.

"Hi, girls," she said with a warm smile. "Do you live at Foxwood, too?"

Ava, who had just turned five, nodded with a shy smile. Lilly, the three-year-old, had hidden herself entirely behind her mummy, clinging her little arm around Char's leg.

"Wow, so you get to live with your grandparents?" Winnie continued with a bright smile.

Char was smiling now, too, peering down at her girls, who had also started to grin.

But Matthew's frown had only grown. Sneaky woman, trying to get in with the kids. She was good. He'd give her that.

"Yeh," Ava said with a nod.

"That is so fun," Winnie said. "I bet you love that."

"Yeh," Ava repeated. She drew a deep breath, clearly trying to gather her courage. "And we get to live with my uncle, too."

Winnie glanced up to Matthew, then back down to the girls. "Well, that makes you even luckier! Do you joust on those big horses like he does, too?"

Ava gave another smile and shook her head, clearly losing her shyness by the second. "No, I don't joust. But I do ride!"

"You do?" Winnie looked more than amazed. How did she do that? Act so genuine when she was so...fake? "I bet you are the best rider."

"I am," Ava said with no shame.

"Yeh, me too!" Lilly piped in finally, drawing on her sister's strength.

"You, too?" Winnie said with excitement, shifting her attention to the little girl. "That's amazing!"

"And I have my own horse!" Ava said with bright eyes.

"Yeh, me too!" Lilly repeated.

Winnie pulled on a look of surprise. "You both have your own horses?"

Ava continued. "No, *I* do, but Lilly has to share with Mummy 'til she's old enough like me."

"Yeh, me too!" Lilly said with all the excitement a three-year-old could muster.

Winnie laughed. Matthew had never seen such a genuine look on her face, and curse his inability to deny it, but the woman was gorgeous. Her gray eyes squinted playfully at the edges as she grinned, and her nose did this cute little scrunching up thing as she laughed.

It was infuriating.

As was how genuine she seemed with his nieces. How was she so good with children?

"Well," Winnie continued, "you girls are so lucky to have so many family members to live with and so many horses to ride."

Ava pumped her head up and down. "Do you have your own horse?"

Winnie's smile faltered. It was only for a brief moment, but Matthew was sure of what he saw. What he couldn't figure out was why she'd had that reaction to such a simple question.

"No," Winnie said, her smile returning. "I once..." She seemed to think better of what she'd been about to say, shaking her head and beginning again. "Anyway, I'll have to see you two ride sometime before I leave Foxwood, just so I can see how good you are."

The girls nodded, the excitement in their eyes pushing Matthew to the edge. Why did they care about Winnie watching them? She was no one to them. Just a woman who'd managed to trick them, too.

His frustration mounted like a child throwing a tantrum until he spoke without thinking. "Yeah, we'll see if you don't leave too early for that."

Char turned to look at him with a frown. Winnie merely rose from the girls with ease and faced him with an unreadable expression.

All right, maybe that had been a little too harsh. He just couldn't help it. This woman had taken over every aspect of his life, and now, even his nieces liked her.

Granted, she *was* charming. She'd been charming sitting in her ridiculous Aston Martin stuck in the mud asking him to avoid scratching the green paint with his gauntlets.

"I hope you don't mind my brother," Char said, breaking through the silence his unkind comment had caused. "He's not always a grump. Hopefully you get the chance to see a nicer side of him. He comes out every few weeks. You have to coax him from his cave, though. Like a yeti."

Winnie laughed. "Thanks for the advice."

Matthew's irritation only grew.

Lilly tugged on Ava's arm. "Ava, come pyay?"

Ava nodded. "May we play again, Mummy?"

"Yes, love," Char said, and the three of them watched the girls run toward the football on the grass nearby.

"They are beautiful girls, Char," Winnie said with a sincere smile. "You must consider yourself very lucky to have them."

"Oh, I do, even if they're a handful." Char stared off at them for a moment. "If only their dad knew how great they were." She glanced back to Winnie. "He gave up all his rights to move in with a...less-than-desirable in London a few years back."

Matthew nearly pressed a hand to his brow. Char had always been an over-sharer, which was definitely not a typical British trait, but she hardly cared.

Would Winnie? He scrutinized the consultant, wondering how she'd react, but she nodded in measure, not hesitating a moment before responding.

"His loss, though, isn't it?" she said with more understanding than Matthew could comprehend. "Missing out on the girls and you."

Char smiled, clearly touched by this near-stranger's words. "I knew I'd like you, Winnie."

They shared a smile, and Matthew stared between them again, wondering at the swiftness with which their relationship had formed.

"So how are you finding Foxwood?" Char asked next.

"I'm loving it," Winnie said with a nod. "It's a gorgeous house in the most stunning location."

"That's not what you said when you first arrived," Matthew murmured.

Char looked back at him with a look that said, *"You're embarrassing yourself, Matthew."*

But he merely looked at Winnie, challenging her to disagree with the truth.

Winnie merely smiled. "I never made a complaint about Foxwood. I only mentioned the spotty cell service and the mud on the side of the road."

"Oh my gosh, yes," Char said with a shake of her head. "I can't tell you how much I've complained to our dad about the cell service. And the mud? It's entirely out of hand. I'm glad you're here to fix it." Then she looked back to Matthew. "*And* the festival. It's seen better days."

Matthew pulled back. Char was being brutal today.

It was a good job he was a kind brother, or he'd be at her, too.

"Well, I hope I can help," Winnie said.

She was showing far more humility than she had the day before.

Winnie-Freakin'-Knox. He was never going to be able to forget that. The level of confidence she'd shown, the spark of pride in her eye that had somehow made her look all the more attractive. Honestly, if it wasn't for their current circumstances, he could almost admit to admiring her for her courage.

Almost.

He still couldn't believe how spot on she'd been in her assumptions about him. The Birdwhistles and a few others had once suggested adding more fantastical elements to his historically accurate event, while someone else had pushed to bring in more well-known foods, but he'd set the proposals aside without giving them a chance, just as Winnie had guessed. He couldn't risk losing the authenticity he'd pushed for. That was the only thing they had going for them now—the only thing that was still *him* about the festival.

"I'm sure you'll be able to help, Winnie," Char continued. "Just don't let this chap get you down." She threw a thumb over her shoulder at Matthew.

"Oh, I'm not worried about him," Winnie said, as the two continued once more like he wasn't there. "I've been placed in charge of far more difficult individuals."

"I'm not being difficult," he muttered.

Winnie shrugged. "I've got different words if you prefer. Challenging. Impossible. Mulish."

"Oh, this is going to be fun," Char said, her eyes dancing as she glanced between Matthew and Winnie.

"What is?" Matthew asked gruffly.

"Just you two working together," she replied cheerfully.

"Yeah, so much fun," he returned.

Char glanced to Winnie, somehow sharing a knowing look with her. He knew women understood each other in ways men could never possibly comprehend, but the girls had only just met. What were they sharing? And what *more* would be shared?

Nothing he was willing to find out.

"Well," he said, clapping his hands together once, "we'd love to stay and chat, but Char has her daughters to look after."

"Yes, yes," Char said with a wave of her hand. "Typical Matthew, always slaughtering the fun."

"That is him, isn't it?" Winnie gave him a look.

He took a step away, hoping to force his sister to leave, but she paused again. "Do you want to come sit with us?" she asked Winnie.

Good grief, she was trying to kill him, wasn't she?

"Oh, thank you so much for the offer," Winnie responded, "but I've got some things I need to do back at the estate. Plus, I think if I stayed with you a minute longer, Matthew might blow a gasket."

The girls laughed, but Matthew was over it. He wrapped his hands gently but firmly around his sister's upper arms and coaxed her back. "All right, come along, Char."

His sister waved goodbye, taking a few steps back.

"It was so nice to meet you, Char," Winnie said with a wave of her own. Then she looked to Matthew, her eyes taking on a different light. "And nice to see you again, Matthew."

He grumbled a response, then turned his back on the woman, not bothering to read her expression.

"It's official," Char said as they walked away. "She's my favorite."

Matthew shook his head. "Fantastic. She pulled the wool over your eyes, too."

"Yep. I'm fully convinced. You need to marry her."

Matthew nearly choked on his own spit. "You're insane, Char. I would never marry someone like her."

"Exactly. Which is why you should. She'd keep you in your place."

He shook his head, though he chose not to respond. He'd come out there that afternoon to play with his nieces, and that was exactly what he was going to do.

All he needed was for that American to leave so he could stop being distracted by her runner legs, smooth hair, bright eyes, and charming smile.

A smile that he knew existed only to sugarcoat what she was going to tell him tomorrow during their meeting. Because he had a feeling that meeting was going to be the worst he'd ever have in his life.

And that was all due to Winnie Knox being his...*Ugh*...Boss.

WINNIE WALKED AWAY from the park and the Wintours, smiling as she pulled up her phone to respond to her sister.

She stole a quick glance over her shoulder, watching Matthew kick the ball to his nieces. He stole a glance at Winnie over his shoulder, then hurriedly darted his eyes away.

Winnie hid her widening smile and faced forward.

Nothing would ever happen between her and Matthew. Not only would that be entirely unprofessional, but they were far too different to make anything work between them.

But now that she knew who Char was, Winnie could stop suppressing her thoughts.

Matthew Wintour, great with kids, a good sport with his sister, and able to pull off medieval hair and a modern man bun.

She pulled up her text thread with Sarah, smiling as she responded.

WINNIE

Yep. He is absolutely hot.

Then she let out an airy sigh and walked through the rest of the park, feeling lighter than she had in days.

CHAPTER FIFTEEN

THE FOLLOWING MORNING, WINNIE STOOD AT THE front of the meeting hall, greeting the faire staff with a smile as they entered the large room and made their way to the seats she'd set up an hour before.

The meeting hall—which had been refurbished a few years before from Foxwood's old carriage house—was warm, inviting, and large enough to be an event venue in its own right. At two stories tall, the hall boasted shining wooden floors and black, brown, and white stone walls. Wooden eaves framed the roof in perfect uniformity while three large candelabras cast light across every inch of the setting.

Why they didn't hold weddings, receptions, work parties, or other events there was beyond Winnie. That would be one of her first suggestions to Mr. Wintour as soon as she finished with this little project on the side.

That's what she'd decided to call her work with the faire—a side project. Not only did it help her manage her expectations, but she was also fairly certain it would drive Matthew a little crazy, and that was always fun.

She recognized a few of the faces as the staff began to file in, though she consulted the list Mrs. Wintour had given her the day before to name the rest.

Mrs. Birdwhistle sat on the front row with her husband, Hubert. Mr. Fogg, the monotonous announcer, and his wife, the also-emotionless woman who'd sold tickets at the front entrance, sat beside them. Two teenage stable hand boys came in next, then Dorothy Porter soon after, looking every bit as annoyed at having to be there as she had selling food to Winnie a couple days before. The woman rolled her eyes, then took a seat in the back row, pulling out her phone instantly.

More continued to fill the room, and Winnie fought the urge to make herself look busy. Instead, she stood calmly beside a table, papers situated neatly across it with a projection ready on a blank screen behind her. Avoiding eye contact and fiddling with papers would ease her discomfort, but it would also make her look unprofessional, so she maintained focus on those walking in, smiling to help put the staff at ease.

This was always the most nerve-wracking part of the job— meeting the group of individuals whose lives she was going to change.

"Good morning," she greeted with a smile as more entered. A few of them responded with hesitant nods. "Come in. Have a seat. Is it warm enough in here for you all?"

Mrs. Birdwhistle spoke as the rest of them merely nodded. "Quite toasty, yes."

Winnie had come in earlier to ensure the place would be as warm as the stables next door. The Wintours certainly cared for their horses. After speaking with little Ava and Lilly the day before, Winnie now knew the love of the animals stretched from old to young at Foxwood, which was always lovely to hear.

She'd been like that once, entirely in love with horses. Before Dad had hit her with a reality two-by-four. Now she avoided them at all costs, aside from the occasional stolen glance here and there.

Setting her thoughts aside, she greeted a few others—Jess, the woman who'd played the damsel, and her husband, David Newell, who played another knight, both of them appearing around Winnie's age.

"Come on in," she encouraged as the final knight—James Pryor—hesitated in the doorway.

He moved forward and took a seat on the back row, glancing to the others with uncertainty.

Winnie knew she had Matthew to thank for much of the staff's reluctance. She could only imagine what he'd said to them about her.

At this point, though, it hardly mattered. Her plans had already been greenlit by Mr. Wintour earlier that morning, so they were good to go.

"I'm going to let you run with this," he'd said. *"I trust you to make the best decisions for the festival. But I will say, you'll be met with resistance."*

She fully expected as much—from one individual in particular who had yet to show his face.

Big shocker there.

Mr. Wintour had encouraged her again that morning to stay strong. *"If my son gives you any grief, simply send him my way."*

Matthew would just love to be sent to his daddy for misbehaving, wouldn't he? As appealing as it sounded, Winnie wasn't sure she'd ever do such a thing. They had made some major progress yesterday in the sunshine at the park. She'd received some good insight from Char, found out Matthew *wasn't* married after all, and realized if she teased him, she could maintain control of their professional relationship.

Of course, that was easier said than done with a man who looked better in a bun than she did.

Eight o'clock rolled around, and each member of staff had arrived apart from Matthew, but she wasn't going to wait for him.

She faced forward with a smile. "Good morning, everyone. I..."

Her words faded as, true to form, Matthew appeared in the doorway with an innocent expression, wearing jeans, a dark green jacket, and a thin white t-shirt. He looked at the group, paused, then sauntered in as if he owned the place.

All right, technically, he would one day, but that was beside the point.

She waited as he scooted past the others on the back row and finally took a seat with a loud sigh. His frown from yesterday was gone, replaced with an easy half-smile that revealed he knew *exactly* what he was doing by coming in late.

Well, so did she.

"Glad you could join us today, Matthew," she said.

"Me, too," he responded.

Be like Fort Knox.

She drew a settling breath. "All right, allow me to start again." She smiled at the twelve individuals before her. "Welcome, everyone. I just want to begin by thanking all of you for coming in this morning and getting here on time. I know it's not easy some days."

No one responded. That was fine by her. She could get through her plan quicker if they listened more than talked.

"So," she continued, "as my email said, I'm Winnie Knox. I've been hired by Mr. Wintour to help with Foxwood, specifically the faire, over the next few weeks."

The woman in charge of the faire's entertainment—Sue Jones—pulled open her phone, her purple fingernails swiping up and down on her screen.

A promising start.

"First, I'll share a little about myself," Winnie continued, telling them all about where she grew up and where she now lived before moving on. "I'm a hard worker, quick on my feet, easy to adapt, and I love team playing. My philosophy in life is, if everyone works hard together, nothing is unachievable."

Mrs. Birdwhistle smiled up at her, but no one else reacted.

"In my experience," she pushed on, "as a consultant, my presence is usually met with a lot of reticence and fear. Hopefully I can ease both to a degree by letting you all know right now that

I'm not here to fire anyone or to make your lives more difficult. I am purely here for the benefit of the faire."

A sniff that sounded suspiciously close to a scoff echoed from the back row. She couldn't be sure who'd done it, but Matthew looked far too innocent sitting there in the back row.

"That being the case," she continued, ignoring his behavior, "I *do* expect you to work hard, to be open to the changes that are going to be made, and, most importantly, to be honest with me. If something's not working for you, let me know, and we can adapt. This first event is going to be a lot of work, but I'm sure you're all capable of rising to the occasion. I can promise you if we put our heads down and work together, we'll be fighting fit, and you'll be thrilled with the response we get." She gave an encouraging smile and a nod to the group. "So...are you ready to get to work?"

A few heads bobbed here and there. Mrs. Jones, who had since put her phone down, folded her arms stubbornly with no reaction, and Mrs. Porter stared out of the window with a look of boredom that rivaled a child in church.

Everyone else appeared hesitant. Everyone but Matthew, that is. He whispered something to the knight beside him, and both of them smiled with ducked heads.

That was fine. She'd give Matthew his freedom for now, allowing his confidence to grow. But if he didn't stop soon, she knew what to do.

"I'd love to ask you all a question as we start," she said. "What is your favorite part of the event?" She waited in silence. "Anyone?"

Finally, Ben Watson, one of the teenagers, raised his hand. "Picking up the horse manure."

His joke landed him a few snickers from the group, especially from his friend beside him.

Winnie smiled. "I'll be sure to keep that in mind. Anyone else?"

Mr. Birdwhistle spoke next, his thick, gray mustache covering his entire upper lip. "It may seem biased," he said in a deep, thick accent, "but I enjoy the joustin'."

"Not biased at all," Winnie said with a shake of her head. "I expected this would be a favorite. How many of you would say the same?"

Everyone aside from Matthew and Mrs. Jones raised their hands, her purple nails now being chewed on absentmindedly.

"Wow, so almost all of you." Winnie looked to Mrs. Jones. "And yours?"

She shrugged. "All of it."

"I won't fault you for that," Winnie said with a friendly smile, even though she received nothing in return. "And what about our fearless leader, the man behind the plan. What do you think, Matthew?"

She was fully expecting a half-baked response like Mrs. Jones, but instead, he said, "The history."

"Ah, yes. Hence where the *authenticity* comes into play."

He gave a single nod.

"What is it about the history that's appealing to you?" she asked.

"The magic of it all. It's what makes the festival worth it."

Winnie couldn't help but notice the irony in his statement. He loved the *authenticity* of the faire because of the *magic* of the past? How was magic in any way factual?

Still, the entire group nodded in agreement with their leader, the tension in the room finally lessening.

"It may come as a surprise to you all, but I agree with Matthew," Winnie said.

A few people smiled at her joke. Matthew's eyes merely narrowed with suspicion.

"I loved the jousting," she continued, "but it was the *magic* of the jousting, of the past, that really got me excited. That magic is what makes people want to come back."

She faced the projector, holding up her clicker to shift to her first slide. Dozens of photos from other renaissance faires she'd found on the internet appeared on the screen, everyone smiling, participating, and cheering.

She paused, avoiding Matthew's gaze and drawing a deep breath as she sent a prayer heavenward. This was where things usually got dicey.

"Unfortunately, that magic is what is missing from *our* event. So that is our goal—to bring the magic back. Because—"

"And you know this how?" Matthew's words cut through her own, daggers from his blue-eyed gaze threatening to crumble her defenses.

She'd expected his response, so she fortunately had one of her own.

"Evidence," she stated. "As pure and simple as that."

She clicked to her next slide, her "evidence" stacked up in conversation bubbles that appeared one at a time.

"Each and every one of these are direct quotes from guests who attended the faire on Saturday." She turned and read them aloud to the others. "Not worth the money. There was nothing to do. Even my kids were bored. Absolute pants." She paused. "That one, I assume, means terrible?"

A few nods moved about the room, then she continued.

The quotes went on and on, the staff reading along as Winnie continued. Mrs. Birdwhistle was nodding. A few of them were scowling. Mrs. Jones wasn't even bothering to read the board at all.

And Matthew? His jaw was twitching beneath his whiskers more ferociously than she'd ever seen before. More than anything, she'd put these quotes up for him. He needed to see that his obsession with historical accuracy and authenticity was killing his faire.

Luckily, she knew how to resuscitate it.

"As I'm sure you can all agree," she continued, "we want this at our faire." She shifted back to the photos of joy and laughter. "But in order to get this, a lot of change is going to be required of each of us."

One by one, she picked up the packets she'd compiled for each staff member, delivering them as she explained further. "We'll go over each person's individual tasks more in depth later, but right now, we'll just have a brief overview so it's not super overwhelming, all right?"

A few heads bobbed up and down.

Matthew whispered something again to the knight beside him, whose shoulders shook with silent laughter. Matthew met Winnie's gaze, then, a clear challenge in his eye, which she met without hesitation, handing him his own packet. He took it with a smirk at the knight, then flipped through it with a disinterested gaze.

But Winnie wasn't worried. She'd receive the last word. Matthew just needed to wait and see.

CHAPTER SIXTEEN

OVER THE NEXT THIRTY MINUTES, WINNIE MOVED swiftly over the changes of responsibilities for each staff member. The teen boys would be esquires, Mrs. Birdwhistle would help ready the horses and knights to get them out earlier, and Mrs. Fogg needed to find better non-WWII tents.

"We want a lot of them," Winnie explained, "in bright, happy colors, like a circus."

A few looks were exchanged, but Winnie pushed forward.

Albert Fogg was next. "We're going to be giving you a mic that actually works," she said, and his face brightened. "But of course, that means your level of enthusiasm has to increase, too."

He gave a short nod, then peered down at his paper.

Winnie blew out a quiet breath. Those had been the easiest changes. Now for Mrs. Porter and the food.

"I know we've been pushing the authenticity factor, but after trying the food myself, and hearing a lot of feedback from guests, we're going to be changing up the menu...entirely."

Matthew crossed his arms over his chest and leaned back in his chair. Mrs. Porter's lips thinned so much, they were no longer visible.

"Are you sayin' me food ain't quality enough?" she asked.

Winnie squared her shoulders. "Unfortunately, it's true, as was evident by the uneaten portions of cabbage chowder—mine included—filling the garbage cans."

Looks were exchanged, but Winnie continued. "I need to warn you, Mrs. Porter, that at the next faire, there will be more food options from other vendors apart from yours. I'm planning on bringing in your usual event foods, hot dogs, hamburgers, cotton candy. You'll have to up your game if you want to stay relevant, which, by the way, I have full faith in your ability to do so."

With Mrs. Porter still pouting, Winnie shifted to Mrs. Jones, ready to rip off another Band-Aid.

"We'll need more entertainment," Winnie said. "A lot more."

"We need nothing more than the jousting," Mrs. Jones said stubbornly.

Winnie made to explain how her reasoning was flawed, but she caught Matthew staring down at his packet, shaking his head in silence.

"Any thoughts you'd like to share, Matthew?" she asked.

He shook his head.

"All right, well you let me know when you do."

"Oh, I will."

Winnie returned to Mrs. Jones, reminding her of the boredom experienced by the guests. "With more to do, they'll actually want to stay for longer," Winnie explained. "We'll have falconry, archery, carnival games, fire breathers, jesters, merry-go-rounds, maybe even bumper cars. There needs to be enough for adults and children to be entertained at all times."

"Carnival games and rides?" came a whisper from the back. "She'll turn it into ruddy Blackpool."

Winnie had no idea what Blackpool was, but she didn't think it was meant as a compliment.

"Rides are cheap and effective," she said, defending her choice. She'd had to do the same with Mr. Wintour that morning, but she was sure they'd be a big hit. "More than anything, kids love them. If children are happy, their parents will be happy, and if parents are happy, they'll be more likely to come back, stick around, and spend more money."

The group fell silent again, so she moved on to her final and most challenging of topics—the jousting.

"Now I know we all love the jousting, but even that spectacular event can be improved upon. We're going to up the tournament to twice a day with *much* more than the six clashes I saw on Saturday. There will be a script to follow with the winner pre-determined. And finally...we're removing the damsel in distress."

It was as if a thick, dark cloud of smoke slipped into the room and hovered above each person, so quickly the tension returned.

Seven hands shot up, Jess's being the first. "Um...no damsel?" she asked.

"Don't worry," Winnie reassured her. "You're not being let go. I've got so much more for you to do that I know you'll love. We're going to turn our damsel into a knight in disguise who will win some of the matches and reveal exactly who she is at the end of the tournament. It's so much more modern and inspiring to allow our damsel to receive equal treatment."

"But..." Jess began, "I've never jousted before. And I don't have any of the armor or expertise or anything."

"Oh, that's fine," Winnie said with a wave of her hand. "When you're up against the men, we'll be fudging the rules anyway, so you'll be able to win and won't be hit."

Jess sent a furtive glance to her husband, who rested a reassuring hand on her knee. Winnie knew this one would be a hard pill to swallow, but she had complete confidence that it would be a crowd favorite.

One-by-one, she responded to the other concerns shared.

"The original damsel has always been a favorite."

"You can't tell me the majority of people wouldn't rather see more jousting than a waif."

"How are we supposed to score correctly if the winner is already chosen?"

"No one knows how to score jousting in this day and age anyway."

"*The knights can't handle that much jousting. Twice a day, every weekend, for five months?*"

"We'll build up your stamina. And we will no longer be holding the events weekly. It drains too much money and resources. Instead, we'll be holding the faire twice a month, only on Saturdays, throughout the summer. The knights can handle that. I have faith in you."

"*What about the historical accuracy?*"

"What about it? We'll still have it to a degree, of course. Otherwise, we'll be adding in fantastical elements based on your own recommendations, and cosplayers will be encouraged to attend, as well."

The tightness in her neck crept higher as the questions continued, and all the while, she struggled to keep Matthew's continuous scoffs and shakes of his head out of the corner of her eye.

After today, things would be better. She just had to keep reminding herself of that. Things would get better. They had to.

"We have three weeks to make all of these changes and pull off a spectacular faire," Winnie ended. "We'll be postponing the event until then, allowing us more time to finish everything before the busy season picks up. It will be a lot of work in the beginning, but I promise, with all of us working together, you won't regret the effort you put into this." She smiled encouragingly, though most eyes remained on the packets in their hands. "Before I meet with each of you individually to go over more details, are there any other questions, comments, concerns?"

No one said a word aloud. Matthew whispered something to the knight beside him again, but his friend barely managed a smile this time.

Winnie sighed. It was now or never. "I've seen you whispering a lot back there, Matthew. I'd love to hear what you have to say, if you can be brave enough to share it."

Matthew peered up at her, confidence emblazoned across his features. "I was just saying that none of this is going to work."

Winnie drew steadying breaths, though what she really wanted to do was chuck her clicker at Matthew. Still, words would pack far more of a punch and reveal that she was still in control—of her mood, of her emotions, *and* of the faire.

"All right. Tell me, then, Matthew. Why won't any of this work?"

He remained leaning back in his chair, a bored look on his features. "The festival isn't about bumper cars and carousels and twenty-first century damsels. It's about immersing people in history."

Nearly every single person in the group nodded, but Winnie didn't let it faze her. "I can see that," she said, "but don't you think a faire could—"

"Festival."

She paused at his interruption. "Excuse me?"

"It's not a faire." For the first time since arriving in the room, he leaned forward in his seat, speaking very carefully. "It's not a faire, a carnival, a Wild West event, or even a renaissance gathering. It's a *medieval festival*."

Winnie stared. The entire staff exchanged wide-eyed glances, a few individuals shifting uncomfortably as the tension grew palpable between her and Matthew.

"So this minor detail is so important to you that it trumps all the other things you could have brought up?" she challenged.

He raised his brow. "Perhaps if you were more focused on the *minor* details of what the event actually is, you wouldn't be attempting to change what is at its heart."

She could almost hear the other staff members calling out, "Oooh burn," like her older brothers would have.

Unfortunately, the thought only made her defenses rise.

She pulled on her metaphorical boxing gloves and peered down at him. "What is at the heart of this *festival*, Matthew, is a dying, failing event."

His eyes turned an icy blue.

"I know it's difficult to hear," she continued unapologetically, "but the magic is gone. It is not there. Not a single person looked like this"—she waved a hand up to the screen where the happy faces from the first slide bore down on the group—"at your *festival* two days ago. And I can almost guarantee that you haven't seen so many looks in the last year. Tell me I'm wrong. Any one of you."

She looked around her, but no one said a word—including Matthew.

"You see?" she said, knowing she was pouring lemon juice in an open wound now. "You must want the magic to return. You said yourself that it was your favorite thing about the event. Not the accuracy of the past, but the *magic* of the past. I think you know deep down that the only way to do this is to lose this authenticity obsession you have and add just a small amount of *modern* magic."

Mrs. Birdwhistle delivered a barely discernible nod in response to Winnie's words, and it was just enough to settle her nerves as Matthew continued to stare her down.

After a moment, he shrugged, leaned back in his chair, and pulled on his carefree look once again. "I'm glad you're so confident, Miss Knox. You should know, though, before you make any of these changes, my father will hear, about this."

Don't, Winnie. Don't you do it.

And yet, she couldn't help herself.

"Careful, Matthew," she began. "Your Malfoy is showing."

She didn't know about Sir Cadogan in *Harry Potter*. But she certainly remembered the antagonist.

To her sheer delight, she managed to coax a few snickers from the group. Matthew, however, turned a deep, delicious red. Like an apple ripe for the picking.

"Now," she said, "if no one else has any questions, I'll excuse you all to go about your work, take some more time to read through your packets, and prepare a bit for when we meet individually. Sound good?"

Half of them nodded, and the other half stared at their papers still with bewildered stares. Matthew merely kept his gaze on her.

"Thank you all again for coming," she said. "I'll be in touch."

She gave a nod, then the group stood as one and filed toward the door.

Winnie rolled out the tension from her neck the moment their eyes left her, and she stacked her belongings together before noting the others speaking with Matthew as they left the room.

He nodded at them reassuringly, worried brows across the mark, and Winnie shook her head, her teeth clenched. There they all were, seeking reassurance from their boss after the big, bad Winnie shook up their lives.

This faire, the festival—whatever the heck they all wanted to call it—was never going to work if he continued to undermine her. They needed to know she was in charge now, and Matthew needed to be the one to tell them. Otherwise, who knew what revolution would be on her hands?

Honestly, as the American, wasn't *she* the one who was supposed to revolt?

She cleared her throat. "Matthew?"

All eyes fell on her, a few people darting out the door to no doubt avoid being caught in the crossfire.

"Yes, Miss Knox?" he asked.

How she hated that. It was as if he was trying to elevate her above the others. "Can I speak with you for a minute? Alone?"

Matthew audibly sighed, and the others left him with hesitant glances as he rejoined her at the front of the room.

"You beckoned," he said, hands behind his back.

His hair wasn't pulled into a bun today. Instead, it looked even more like the knights in the movies. Long enough to reach his ears, curly, unkempt—yet perfectly appealing.

Winnie knew she ought to keep their conversation civil—to speak with him in a light, teasing manner as she had the day before or to be as calm and polite as she'd been throughout the meeting.

However, her irritation over his lack of respect had mounted all morning, and frankly, she was over it.

"You can drop the act, okay?" she said, her lips void of any smile as she folded her arms across her chest. "I know you're upset with me for being here and for the changes I've made. But this is our reality now, so we may as well stop fighting each other on everything, or it's going to be a very long, very miserable few weeks for us both."

"Perhaps," he said. "Or I just need to outwait you."

Good grief. The man was utterly impossible.

Instead of rising to his bait again, however, Winnie raised her chin. She was the consultant. It was her responsibility to put out the fires that she'd started—whether she'd done so inadvertently or not. And she knew exactly how to do just that.

"I'm sorry," she stated.

Matthew narrowed his eyes, obviously trying to decipher if she was lying or not.

She didn't blame him for being suspicious. Not when they'd argued only days before about her refusing to say sorry for words she believed were justified. While she still felt the same way, she also knew that nothing softened a person more than a heartfelt, truth-based, excuseless apology.

And Matthew needed a little softening.

"Really," she said. "I'm sorry about all of this. I'm sorry that your dad gave me this job. I'm sorry that I accepted it. And I'm sorry that you now have to work with me, a tasteless American who likes *A Knight's Tale*, has never read *Harry Potter*, and could not care less about getting her centuries correct."

His shoulders lowered a degree, his eyes less cold than before as he searched her expression, clearly attempting to see if she was in earnest or not before he finally nodded.

"Thank you," he mumbled. "I appreciate that."

A weight began to shift off Winnie's shoulders. "You see? I *can* apologize."

He gave her a knowing look. "But only when you believe it's warranted."

"Exactly."

They swapped small smiles, and the weight lifted even more.

"I suppose I ought to say my own apologies, then," he said, averting his gaze. "And be more sincere than last time." He cracked his knuckles in front of him. "I am sorry for being rather...inattentive during your meeting. And for being less than supportive. I will behave better next time."

"I appreciate that," she said, her heart softening.

Sure, he was mostly a pill, but really, he was just a guy who'd lost his figurative baby. She should be a little more considerate of that.

"For the record," she began, "I don't blame you for being so upset about this whole thing. I would absolutely have the same reaction as you, were our roles reversed. But I just know that if we could find a way to work together, we could make the festival even better than it was before. We just need to focus on what we can agree on first."

His shoulders lowered. "I suppose you're right. The difficulty will simply be in finding things to agree *on*."

"On the contrary," she said. "I already know something we feel the same about."

"And what is that?"

"Two words: cabbage chowder."

A smile broke out on his lips. "You're right about that."

"Cat's meat and hot wine would be better." They shared a laugh before she continued. "But there's more than that. I'm sure we both feel the same about getting Mr. Fogg a new microphone. And his need to be more enthusiastic. Not Geoffrey-Chaucer-level, but just a little more passion."

Again, Matthew relented with a nod. "Yeah, I can agree with you on that, as well."

"You see?" she said, feeling lighter than a lance looked in Matthew's hands. "This is only the beginning. I just need to be more tactful, you need to believe in me, and together, we can create something amazing."

For the first time since the start of their conversation, Matthew's eyes met hers and remained. A storm seemed to be raging within him as he watched her before he finally spoke aloud.

"I do believe in your abilities," he said, much to her surprise. "My dad wouldn't have hired you otherwise. The problem is believing in my own."

She waited, tipping her head to the side as she listened intently to what she could only assume was a very difficult confession to make.

"The truth is," he continued, "I'm at a loss. I don't know how to make the festival profitable again. Everything I try to do just brings more failure, and I don't know what to do anymore. No one has more to lose than myself, which is why..." He paused, his blue eyes focusing even more intently on her. "Which is why I need you to understand something."

Winnie sobered further, nodding as she waited in silence for him to continue.

He drew a deep breath. "While you may know business, and while some of the changes you've suggested *will* do the festival good, some of them will take away the heart of what we're trying to do here—which is to share our love of the medieval world with those around us. Without that beating heart in the center, there is no amount of quid, success, or prestige that will comfort us if this fails. I know I speak for the entire staff when I say, if our passion is no longer there, if our heart isn't in this project any longer, we will lose the desire to make it succeed. I'm sure you and I can both agree on this as well—that if there is no heart or passion involved in what we do, then why would we do it at all?"

His words were like an ax to a tree, cutting down Winnie's defenses and chopping her to the ground. He'd taken her whole existence, summed it up in one sentence, lit it on fire, and now watched the branches burn to ash, just to prove that she'd been wasting away the last decade of her life.

Of course he had no idea what he'd done. How could he have any clue as to how miserably she'd lived her life, coasting from job to job, trying to find passion and heart but always out of luck? And what sort of hypocrite would she be if she agreed with his words—that there was no purpose to the last ten years of her life because there had been no *passion* in the last ten years of her life?

"So what do you think?" Matthew asked, completely unaware of the turmoil raging within her.

Winnie scrambled for a response. His words were sound. But they weren't hers. Nor were they a part of her plan or her research. How was she supposed to keep the passion and the heart at the center of the festival when she couldn't even do that in her own life? If she agreed with him, she would render herself completely useless for the job, and she'd fail. Again.

Be like Fort Knox.

Dad's words snuck through her mind, reminding her once more to be blunt. To stick to her guns. She couldn't flop this time. She couldn't waste the money Mr. Wintour had entrusted her with. She couldn't disappoint their family and allow the faire to fail.

More than anything, she couldn't risk Dad's reputation being negatively affected by her messing things up. He'd vouched for her abilities. If she didn't succeed, who knew if he'd ever help her find a consulting gig again? Then she'd be right back to where she was years before, jobless, passionless, heartless. A major disappointment to the Knox family as a whole.

Swiftly, she picked up the branches of her defenses, then stuck them around her chest in a makeshift protection.

"I see where you're coming from," she stated diplomatically, her voice as wooden and hollow as her fortifications. "I agree that heart is very important, but...you need an event that earns money. Not an event that offers a history lesson."

The second the words left her mouth, Winnie's heart shriveled in her chest. She sounded just like Dad.

"You don't need to ride horses, Winnie," he'd said. *"You need a reality check."*

How painfully she'd received those words as a teenager. How excruciating they'd been. And now, she was reciting the same thing back to Matthew, who'd finally had the courage to humble himself and ask to keep the heart of the festival the same. Was she really so stupid to have responded so defensively?

Matthew didn't react for a minute, his expression remaining unchanged until he looked away with a single nod, the ridges in his jaw returning.

"Well, thank you for that," he said, backing away with his eyes on the door behind him. "Now I know what to expect from you in the future."

Then he turned around and left her in the assembly hall alone, the echoing of his shoes reverberating in her ears and in her soul.

Long after cleaning up the meeting, long after speaking with each staff member alone, Matthew's words remained swirling around in Winnie's mind because she just couldn't find an answer to his question. If there was no heart or passion involved in what she did—then why was she doing it at all?

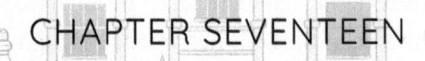

CHAPTER SEVENTEEN

PROGRESS WITH THE FESTIVAL WAS STEADY, EVEN though Winnie felt like a chicken running around with its head cut off, trying to accomplish all of her tasks and everyone else's beside, all while dealing with money constraints as she fought to strategically save every pound of Mr. Wintour's she could.

Fortunately, Jess was a massive help, renting rides, finding other food options, and being a positive influence on others. That is, when she wasn't being forced to joust. Getting her on board with being an undercover female knight was taking a great deal of convincing, but Winnie continually put her faith in the woman.

Mrs. Birdwhistle and the teenage boys, too, were pulling their weight with the horses and tournament planning. But Mrs. Porter wouldn't let go of her cabbage chowder, Mrs. Jones refused to hire more entertainment, and Mrs. Fogg couldn't find tents to rent because she didn't even know how to search for them on the internet. Furthermore, Mr. Fogg couldn't animate his voice to save his life, and the knights didn't hesitate to express their disapproval of a scripted event, jousting with Jess, and predetermined scoring.

Along with each individual and their very strong opinions, Winnie was also having to deal with last-minute cancellations of carnival games and hiring overly priced sideshows, all the while dealing with money constraints.

The only person she didn't have to fight with, surprisingly enough, was the one person she'd expected to fight with the most —Matthew. He went along with each of her suggestions, never saying a word unless it was to encourage others to follow her ways.

The only reasonable explanation to his change in passion was that his spirit had been broken, her words having finally done the trick. Turns out, she was more like Dad than she thought.

She'd tried to apologize to Matthew for being brash, for not listening to him and agreeing to follow along with his plan at least to some degree, but due to her tight schedule and the time constraints laid on her—and her complete and utter humiliation at having to say sorry again—she had zero opportunity to do so.

Nearly a week after their meeting in the assembly hall, on a drizzly Sunday, Winnie spent the morning at church, then headed straight back to her room at Foxwood. She was glad for the weather and the nice excuse it was to remain indoors. She didn't want to chance seeing Matthew at the park again, or his delightful family. They reminded her too much that she had to chat with her own family today.

Despite her best attempts to slow down time, the call eventually came. At first, she tried to remain in her room, but the rain must have lessened her cell service *and* the internet, as she was continuously kicked out of the chat due to poor connection. After the fifth time of attempting and failing to connect, Winnie debated on whether or not to bother trying again.

The option of a peaceful sabbath with no questions about her job and no comparisons between her life and her siblings' was astonishingly tempting. But Dad would just end up calling Winnie for an update—or worse, he'd call Mr. Wintour to demand proper internet and better cell service for his daughter.

Winnie grimaced. It was better to try again, but this time, she'd go somewhere she knew she'd find success.

Grabbing her earbuds and laptop, she headed downstairs,

having learned over the last week that the only reliable place for a stable internet connection was in the small dining area situated right off the kitchens.

Being two in the afternoon, she was fairly certain she'd receive enough privacy there. If not, she'd have the excuse not to speak. Either way, she'd get credit for trying.

Win-Win-Winnie.

Within a few minutes of arriving, she had established a secure connection to the video chat and sat on one of the benches behind a wooden table set aside for Foxwood's staff.

"There she is," Mom said with a smile.

Her siblings and parents shifted in fluid movements, as opposed to the jittery messes they were before.

"You got it working," Spencer said.

"Yeah, finally," Winnie said. "I just had to walk to the other side of the estate."

Even though she was alone in the dining area and no sound came from the kitchens nearby, she attempted to put in her earbuds for an added measure of privacy. However, she realized all too late that she hadn't charged them the night before.

Ah, well. It was worth it to listen to her latest audiobook, *England's Gardens: How to Transform Your Space to Work for You —and Earn for You.*

Just another resource on how to help her figure out what more to do with Foxwood when the festival was over. If she proved her worth, that is.

"All right, Winnie," Dad said, as if on cue. "You're up."

Winnie grimaced. What would she share this week? How she'd presented her plan to a group of individuals who had zero faith in any of her ideas? Or how she'd beaten up the heart of a man until he was devoid of passion for a project he'd created from the start?

"Have you made any progress with Foxwood yet?" Dad asked.

She stifled a sigh. She'd already told him she wasn't over the dang estate. Why was that so difficult for him to accept?

"No," she said, "but the festival has been coming along nicely."

He didn't respond. Winnie glanced to the window, rain dribbling down the glass, blurring most of her view. Too bad she couldn't escape outside with the excuse of watching the knights practice their jousting astride their horses. That had been her favorite part of the job so far, observing both man and animal working hard, living their best lives as horse and rider.

That had once been Winnie, feeling that same satisfaction back when she used to ride. All before it had been snatched from her fingertips after a simple mistake.

"So what changes *have* you made?" Mom asked, interrupting her thoughts.

Winnie cleared her mind of her past, then mentioned a few of the alterations she'd made, but she didn't go into more detail than that. Why bore everyone—and why disappoint Dad—any longer?

"Well, that sounds amazing," Mom responded. "You seem to be doing a fabulous job."

"Which is a good thing," Spencer quipped. "If you want to keep any job, you *have* to prove that you're good."

"Which, of course, she will," Sarah added.

Winnie sent a smile of gratitude to her sister which she knew Sarah would know was for her. Then Spencer's words hit Winnie in a way she knew he hadn't been intending.

Did she want to keep this job? Not specifically the job at Foxwood, but her job as a consultant altogether. She'd only ever kept it because Dad wanted her to, not because she enjoyed it.

The thought gnawed on her mind, just as Matthew's words had about passion and heart, incessant and unyielding, like a rat chewing through a wall.

She'd lived in an apartment once that had housed a rat. She'd moved out of the complex the very next day—and she'd quit the teaching program soon after that.

She could still hear Dad's words when he found out what

she'd done. *"You have a name to uphold, Winnie. Stop being a disappointment and start sticking to your commitments."*

That was the exact reason she couldn't fail at Foxwood—nor quit the festival. And it was the exact reason she had to remain a consultant.

"How are the Wintours?" Dad asked. "Is working with them difficult?"

Winnie hesitated. "No, for the most part they're great. I'm only struggling a bit with Matthew. He's the—"

The door opened, cutting off Winnie's words. She looked up in surprise, expecting to be caught by one of the Wintours' household, but when Matthew himself walked in, all broad-shouldered, bearded, and curly-haired, shock struck through her limbs and pulled her heart straight down to the floor.

Oh, boy, was she in trouble if he'd heard her.

MATTHEW REMAINED STANDING STILL in the doorway, staring at Winnie in surprise. Obviously, he hadn't expected to see her there, otherwise he would have never come in.

After his conversation with her in the assembly hall and her slamming down his request to keep history at the center of the event, he'd realized then and there that she didn't really care about the festival. What she cared about was the money. And while that initial knowledge hurt, he had since learned to accept it. He couldn't deny the woman's tenacity and competence in being able to accomplish the tasks she'd set about. Her sheer determination was admirable, if not annoying. But ultimately, when her ideas would undoubtedly fail in the coming weeks, she'd have only herself to blame.

He took a step back from the room, ready to withdraw instead of being forced to carry on an obligatory cordial conversation with her, but when he took note of Winnie's deer-in-the-headlights look, he paused.

She looked absolutely stunned. Embarrassed, even. As if...as if she'd been caught doing something she shouldn't have been doing.

Suddenly, he had the strong desire to stay and see just exactly what she was up to.

"Hey," he said with a toss of his head, taking a step farther into the room.

Winnie didn't respond, her eyes falling to her laptop, then back to him. He was interrupting whatever she was doing, but did she actually expect him to leave her alone when it was *his* home?

"Winnie?" A voice spoke from the laptop, and both of their eyes dropped to it.

"Is she there?" another voice asked.

"I think she's frozen."

"No, there was another voice. Didn't you hear it?"

Realization struck Matthew. She was on a call. But with whom?

"Winnie are you there?" came yet another voice.

Finally, Winnie looked down at her laptop. "Yeah, I'm still here. Just a sec."

"Winn—"

The voice was cut off mid-word as Winnie muted the conversation. She looked back up at Matthew expectantly, as if to ask what he was doing there.

He had a mind to ask her the very same question, but then, after the last week of maintaining his stellar silence on how she was ruining his festival, he wasn't in the mood to get into an argument with her.

"I was just grabbing a bite to eat," he said, pointing to the fridge. "Am I interrupting something?"

"No, of course not," she said, glancing back down to her screen.

"I can come back when you're finished if you'd like me to," he offered, wondering if she'd accept his ridiculous suggestion.

Fortunately, she shook her head. "No, you're totally fine. I was just talking to my family."

Ah, her family. "Well, I'll just be a minute." He motioned to her laptop. "Please, don't let me interrupt."

She hesitated. "Okay."

He made his way across the room, feeling her eyes on him as he approached the fridge before Winnie unmuted her family.

"—I just don't know how skiing is *not* the best option," a female voice said loudly before coming down a few notches. "Ah, Winnie's back!"

"Yeah, sorry," Winnie said softly.

"We were just talking about our skiing trip again," the woman continued. Her voice dropped in the middle of her sentence as Winnie lowered the volume of her laptop again.

She obviously wished for more privacy, but the kitchens were bare and quite echoey. Matthew could still hear their words as clear as day, but did Winnie know this?

A buzz in his pocket drew his attention to his phone, and he pulled it out, standing in front of the open fridge.

He wasn't surprised to see more texts from his mates. They'd been messaging non-stop today, prepping for the coming weekend when they'd finally be together for the charity run—the charity run Matthew had yet to start really preparing for. He'd been too busy doing Winnie's bidding for *her* version of *his* festival.

FINN

> I hope you've got better accommodation for us this year, Matt. I don't want to be sleeping in the servants' quarters again.

Matthew smiled. The Irishman always teased him about his family's wealth.

> Nope. I've got somewhere even better this year. It's the dungeons for you.

> Typical Englishman.

Matthew nearly laughed aloud. It was a good feeling, after the week he'd had. He only hoped that having his friends there for the weekend would be just the thing to boost his spirits for longer.

> All you commoners asked for it.

He sent the text, then smiled to himself. He couldn't wait to see them. And truth be told, he was more than a little relieved that Winnie had canceled the festival while they were there. That would save Matthew more than a little embarrassment of having his friends witness how his event had fallen from grace over the last few years.

"So what were you saying before, Winnie?"

The voices from the computer reached Matthew's ears again, and all other thoughts disappeared as he tucked his phone away and focused on finding the food he'd come in search of.

"Oh, I can't really remember," Winnie said.

Matthew moved aside the Branston Original Pickle jar, the plate of cherry tarts, and the Hartleys' strawberry jam, looking for the block of extra sharp, cave-aged cheese from Cheddar.

"I remember what it was," a younger female voice said. Her sister, perhaps? "You were saying the only difficult person was Ma—"

"Oh, no," Winnie said loudly, cutting her off. "No, I was done. Hey, Sarah, what happened to that guy you were dating? Troy or something?"

Matthew had to hide his smile at Winnie's panicked diversion. Ducking farther into the fridge, he reached for the cream cheese with slow movements.

"Oh, I dumped him months ago," this Sarah said. "He was so boring. Not an interesting bone in his body."

"Not even his clavicle?" asked a male voice.

A bit of laughter sounded, and Matthew's lips twitched. That had to have been a brother. How many siblings did she have?

Finally finding the cheese, he pulled out the block and set it on the counter, rooting around next for the Jacob's Cream Crackers in the cupboards.

"No, for real," Sarah continued. "You guys would have hated him. Anyway, that's enough about me. Winnie, we haven't heard nearly enough from you. Are you enjoying all the rain?"

"Yeah, I am," Winnie said.

Was she always this tight-lipped around her family, or was it just because Matthew was there?

"And..." Sarah pressed, "how are the knights? Particularly the one who saved you?"

The silence in the room was deafening. Winnie's eyes shot up to Matthew's, but he continued moving between cupboards, feigning complete ignorance.

"Wait, who saved you?" an older woman said. That had to be Winnie's mother. "And what did they save you from? Are you in danger, Winnie?"

The sound on the laptop lowered again. Once more, Matthew had to hide his smile.

"No, I'm not in danger, Mom," Winnie said. "It was nothing."

"Nothing, my foot," Sarah continued.

How Matthew could still hear their words was beyond him, but he wasn't about to complain. He reached for the crackers in the top cupboard as Sarah continued.

"She was rescued by a knight when she slid off the road. Winnie said he's totally hot, too."

The moment the words reached Matthew's ears, he unwittingly released the package. It slipped from his fingertips, landing with a loud thud as the crackers no doubt crumbled to pieces inside. That was hardly any of his concern now, though, as pride welled within him.

So. Winnie thought he was *hot*, did she?

He retrieved a plate nearby, his back still turned to her as he placed the crackers and cheese onto the dish in a uniform fashion, all the while fighting off another broad smile. Was that all she'd said about him, or was there more?

Winnie didn't respond to her sister's words, and their voices lowered from the laptop until he was sure even Winnie couldn't hear them.

"Rescued...road..."

Matthew didn't care. He'd heard what he'd wanted to—something to boost his wounded ego. Something to finally give him the upper hand against Winnie Knox.

He couldn't wait to use it to his advantage.

Piling the items he'd gathered onto his plate, Matthew turned to face Winnie with an innocent smile, her ruby-colored cheeks and dazed expression satisfying him to no end.

"Thanks for letting me interrupt," he said louder than he probably should have.

Winnie gave a solitary, silent nod as he moved to the door with his food.

A quiet voice came from the laptop. "Wait, who..."

"No one," Winnie said, speaking to her family with clipped words.

Matthew reached the door, balancing his food in one hand as he made to open it, hearing someone else speak.

"No...someone..."

"Hey! Who's there?" shouted another so loudly, he could finally hear it.

He paused and turned toward Winnie.

"You can go," she said with a shake of her head, her voice tight, like a rubber band stretched too thin.

He should give the woman a break, but her desperation to have him leave made him linger.

Besides, after the week he'd had of holding his tongue, letting go of his will, and practicing as much patience as he possibly could, Matthew deserved a win.

"Show us who it is, Winnie!" shouted the female voice again.

"No, he's busy," Winnie said, her expression mixed between an apology and a pleading for him to *leave now.*

Matthew should have, but his desire to one-up the woman won against his conscience.

"I'm not busy at all," he said with another innocent look. "I can meet them."

Then with an audacity he didn't recognize, Matthew placed his plate on the counter and strode directly toward Winnie.

Her gray eyes widened in a panic. "You don't have to."

"Oh, I wouldn't wish to be rude," he said. He stopped directly in front of her with a focused gaze. "Besides, I'm sure they'd love to see who the most difficult person is for you to deal with here."

Her blushing response was well worth whatever guilt Matthew might feel after this moment. Well worth it by a longshot.

CHAPTER EIGHTEEN

WINNIE HAD NEVER BEEN SO HUMILIATED IN HER LIFE. Not only had Matthew caught her saying he was difficult to work with, but there was also no way he hadn't heard Sarah proclaiming that Winnie said he was attractive. *Hot*, to be exact.

How was she ever going to live this down?

Before she could even muster up an apology, an excuse—heck, even a *word* would've been better than her silence—Matthew moved to stand behind her, his torso shifting into view on her personal screen before he bent down so their faces appeared side-by-side.

Each of her family members waved in silence on the screen.

"Ah, there he is," Mom said, her voice barely audible. "The man behind the voice."

"You can turn up the volume now," Matthew said quietly in Winnie's ear.

Her skin prickled, and she jumped forward to the volume control, if only to try to dissuade her ever-present blush and the effect his proximity had on her.

"Winnie," Dad said first, "aren't you going to introduce us?"

She blinked. "Oh, yeah. This is Matthew Wintour, Mr. Wintour's son. Matthew, this is my family."

Matthew leaned closer, resting his left hand on the table next to the laptop as his face drew level with hers. She'd been close to guys before this. She'd *kissed* guys closer than this. So why did it feel as if she was a new teenager, being attracted to a boy for the first time?

"Hello, everyone," Matthew greeted, his voice close to her ear. "Lovely to meet you all."

Nothing good was going to come from this. She just knew it. Matthew was far too comfortable appearing in front of a bunch of strangers. It was almost as if he was *trying* to make her uncomfortable.

She should have turned the dang computer off the second he'd appeared. She'd just been so flustered, her brain entirely addled.

"Nice to meet you," came the response from each of her family members.

"I love your accent!" Sarah said with an easy smile.

"Oh, thank you," Matthew responded. "But I can't take credit for it. My parents gave it to me."

Winnie's family laughed again, and Matthew responded with a grin. She hadn't seen him smile in more than a week. She'd truly sucked the life out of him, so what was bringing him back now?

"So you're Arthur's son," Dad said, his eyes calculating. "I don't know if he's told you, but he and I have been good friends for a long time."

"Yes, sir," Matthew responded. "He's told me how much your friendship has meant to him over the years."

His cologne drifted under Winnie's nose. She parted her lips to breathe through her mouth instead, then shifted a degree to the right to create more distance between them.

"So you're the one who rescued my Winnie?" Mom asked next.

Matthew shrugged with a modest chuckle. As he did so, his shoulder brushed against Winnie's, sending shoots of warmth across her skin.

"I suppose I am," he replied, apparently unaffected by their touch.

Winnie shifted in her seat again. "It wasn't really a rescue," she said, hoping to maintain some shred of dignity with her family. "I could've gotten out of the mud eventually."

"Not in those heels," Matthew retorted.

Her family laughed, and Winnie peered at him in the screen. She could've sworn he was looking directly at her, the small smile on his lips driving her crazy.

She hadn't seen the two of them like that before, side-by-side, a smile on Matthew's face and a forced smile on hers. It was like staring at one of those moving Harry Potter portraits, but way more engaging. Way more...appealing.

Harry Potter portraits. Matthew would certainly appreciate that reference, wouldn't he?

"So are you one of the jousters there, then?' Spencer asked, interrupting Winnie's thoughts.

"Yes, I am," Matthew responded.

In her ear, so close to her senses, his deep voice was far richer, his accent far more delicious, than she'd ever realized.

"Must be quite the easy gig, playing dress-up for a living," Spencer continued.

Winnie caught sight of her brother's smirk, followed by Scott's stifled laugh, and she frowned. She may have squashed all of Matthew's hopes and dreams a few days ago, but she wouldn't allow her own family to make fun of him for those dreams.

To her surprise, however, Matthew didn't need defending. In fact, he hardly even looked offended.

"I don't know," he began, pulling in his lips with a shake of his head. "Putting on that armor, riding horses, receiving so much attention from all the ladies. It's more difficult than you can imagine."

Sarah laughed aloud, and even Spencer cracked an impressed smile, as if to say, "Touché."

Before another word could be spoken, Dad chimed in next,

ending all laughter. "So, Matthew, Winnie was just going to tell us all about the changes she's been making. How are the others taking it?"

Ugh. Winnie would rather go back to Spencer's taunting.

"They're taking it very well," Matthew responded.

That was an outright lie. Had he said so for her sake?

Matthew leaned forward again, this time, his shoulder fully resting on hers. "Although," he continued, "between you and me, Mr. Knox, no one would dare cross her if they *didn't* agree with her changes."

Her family laughed, but Winnie hardly heard, too focused on the tingles rushing across her skin and the warmth spreading from his body to hers.

She'd known about the connection and energy between them from the beginning, but this lingering heat and that smile on his features had stirred something in her heart she wasn't ready to accept. The two had fought nearly non-stop since day one, and now, with his smiles, teasing, and touch, it felt like there was something more.

But there *was* nothing more. *They* were nothing more. Nothing but coworkers.

"Well, look," Matthew said, their shoulders still pressed together, "I'd love to stay and chat, but I'm sure Winnie would like to get back to speaking with her family alone. It was such a pleasure to meet you all."

Her family said goodbye in scattered harmony, and he waved his hand in departure as he sidled behind Winnie. Cold air pressed against her shoulder at his absence.

Her parents and siblings picked up their conversation again, but Winnie wasn't listening, focusing instead on Matthew as he reached the door and faced her.

"See you later, Miss Knox," he said with a knowing look, then he was gone, leaving Winnie behind to acknowledge the fact that he'd just gained the upper hand in their professional relationship.

And she dreaded to see what would become of it.

CHAPTER NINETEEN

OVER THE NEXT FEW DAYS, WINNIE KEPT A LOW PROFILE as much as she could, maintaining her distance from the rest of the staff and not speaking with Matthew at all. The last thing she needed was for him to talk to her about the call with her family, reviving her embarrassment all over again, so she dove headfirst into preparations for the faire, doing her best not to dwell on him.

She did her best not to think about him as she reviewed the knights' scripts. She did her best not to admire his finesse on his horse as he charged down the list over and over again during practice. And she did her best not to notice how appealing he looked as he broke for lunch each day. Helmet off, curled hair dripping with masculine sweat, sunglasses hanging from the front of his breastplate.

Obviously, her best wasn't good enough—nor could she avoid him forever, as discussions with him had to occur and meetings with him needed to be held.

On the following Thursday, a little more than one week before the festival, she called a meeting in the assembly hall, sharing with the staff what else needed to be done before the big event.

Everyone seemed in good enough spirits, if not a little tired, as they listened to her seemingly endless list of items until she excused them for the day. She'd kept her gaze mostly off of Matthew throughout the meeting, and he'd shockingly maintained his silence, leaving quietly with the rest of the group when the time came.

While Winnie appreciated his lack of snarky comments, she hadn't been able to understand it. She'd thought for sure he would have used his newfound power over her to put her on the spot and embarrass her in front of the others even more. Was he waiting for a better chance, or was he taking the high road after all?

Her rumination continued as she stood alone in the assembly hall, gathering her tablet and a few papers across the table before the door opened with a loud creak.

She glanced up, half-expecting to see Matthew and only half-disappointed when his dad appeared instead.

"Mr. Wintour," she said with a smile. "I didn't expect to see you today."

The two of them had met nearly every other day to discuss the progress being made toward the event—if they were within their budget, how the staff was handling their workloads, and about a thousand other things—though their meetings were usually held in his cozy study instead. To see him anywhere other than that room was an anomaly for Winnie.

"I needed to get out and stretch my legs a bit," he said. "And I wanted to see if there's anything I could do for you."

Winnie smiled, thanked him for his generosity, and gave him an update on the meeting and all that needed to be accomplished.

"Everyone seems really eager to help, though, so I have no worries that we'll get it all done," she said with a confident smile, hoping it looked more convincing than it felt.

The pressure had increased tenfold over the last couple of weeks, and her nerves had been marinated, grilled, and burned because of it.

"Excellent," Mr. Wintour said, leaning on his cane, though

not as heavily as he'd done the day she'd arrived. "And...*everyone* is helping?"

Winnie knew at once who he was referring to, so she was quick to answer. "Surprisingly enough, yes. Everyone is helping. Matthew, too."

She could have sworn she'd seen disbelief in Mr. Wintour's eyes for a moment, but he blinked it away in an instant.

"I'm glad to hear it," he said. "I know I speak for my entire family when I say we have high expectations for the festival. We can't wait to see what you've pulled off."

Winnie knew his words had been meant as an encouragement, but she could have done with maybe a little less faith. She wasn't used to such lofty hopes—not with her family, at least. Was she going to be a monumental letdown to each of them, the Wintours included, when all was said and done?

After Mr. Wintour took his leave, Winnie was left alone again to a buzzing phone and a mile-long list of to-dos which she checked off little-by-little until her stomach rumbled—her only indication that she was in need of a break.

Still staring at her phone, signing off on the carousel delivery and another food booth, Winnie headed out of the assembly hall. As she did so, just like every day she worked in there, the smell of horses, leather, and feed from the stables drifted past her nose.

Most days, she walked straight past the smells, ignoring the wave of nostalgia that always rushed over her, but this time, whether it was due to hunger or simple exhaustion, her strength wasn't what it usually was.

She stopped, staring wistfully—and perhaps a bit fearfully—at the stable entrance. She hadn't willingly been within any stables since she was eighteen years old and her heart had been crushed. It was too hard, the happy memories that returned, the peace and joy she hadn't felt since those days of blissful horseback riding. Somedays, those memories were so powerful, so potent, it was hard to breathe.

And yet, today, her eyes remained on the stable doors, the

nickers and whinnies from inside tying a rope around her heart and tugging her toward them. The pull had always been there, but it had grown stronger each day at Foxwood as she'd been surrounded by the animals that had once filled every part of her life.

Still she hesitated outside. No good could come from flirting with temptation by going inside to take a look around.

She turned away with her chin held high, settling on her decision to leave. That is, until another nicker from within the stables cinched its hold tighter around her, and she paused.

Then again, what harm would occur if she *did* go inside? After all, she'd been around horses for the last two weeks now and had been perfectly fine. She hadn't been thrown back into her past too uncontrollably or anything. She was sure she could handle it.

Besides, once the festival was over and she was tasked with improving Foxwood, the stables would inevitably fall under that umbrella. It was only logical for her to get a sense of how many horses they had and what the stables were like. One quick look around would be fine, she was sure of it.

With hesitant steps, she moved forward, reminding herself she was a decade older and wiser now as she finally entered the stables, and instantly, all other thoughts fled her mind.

When she was younger, the stables she'd trained at had been impressive with clean cement flooring, white posts separating the horses' stalls, and large windows in the ceiling.

But Foxwood's stables? They were unmatched. The same gray, black, and brown stone that covered the interior of the assembly hall now filled the aisles of the two-storied structure. Each horse's stall had been constructed of gorgeous, dark wood, while the individual gates were made of black wrought iron, the doors curved low and centered to allow the horses to pop their heads over into the aisle whenever they wished.

Ornate lanterns hung from the walls near the stalls, casting warm, glowing circles across the stone flooring, and every inch of the place shone with cleanliness and care.

What really caught her attention, however, was when she let out a sigh of appreciation, and one by one, horses poked their heads out of their stalls to see who had come to visit them.

One, two, three, four. She counted faster. *Seven, eight, nine.* And that was only the first aisle. How many horses did they have? How many did they *need*?

She was one to talk. She'd had lofty goals of housing hundreds of horses when she was younger.

Her heart twisted. She moved to turn away, but when she caught the eye of the third horse down, jet black face and mane, she paused. That was Matthew's horse.

She knew she ought to turn away right then, having learned long ago that ignoring horses—no eye contact and no touching—was far better than to pine after them, as she'd done when she was younger.

But Matthew's horse continued to stare her down, as if to say, *"Hey, you disturbed us and got our hopes up. The least you can do is give us a pat."*

Could she? *Should* she?

She drew a deep breath, a hint of manure on the air. She'd never been offended by the smell. It had an earthy scent to it that brought to mind summer trail rides and shared sugar cubes.

A few of the horses in the stables pulled back into their stalls, but Matthew's remained, still watching her. She'd purposefully not learned his name. Names only brought attachment—as did touch.

Did proximity?

Biting her lower lip, she stepped forward, the black horse still watching her as she approached. He had as penetrating a gaze as his master.

"Hey, there," she whispered, drawing closer and closer to him. "I've seen you around here. I'm sure you've seen me lurking, too."

He made no movement, his ears pointed toward her.

She shifted her belongings to her left arm, slowly raising her right hand toward him before hesitating once again. She hadn't touched a horse since...since quitting. But surely one stroke of his hair wouldn't tear down all the walls she'd placed around her heart.

Using more courage than she cared to admit, Winnie shifted her hand to below the horse's nose, allowing him to sniff her. But the second he blew a soft breath back onto her fingertips, a rush of emotions overcame her. A lump formed in her throat, tears flooded her eyes, and she was taken straight back.

Straight back to when she'd been encouraged to ride as a child, wearing her black velvet hat and tall black boots. Straight back to when she'd performed for thousands at countless shows. Straight back to when she'd had a purpose, a passion for life.

The black gelding shifted to the side, as if encouraging her to pet him, and her mind struggled to remain in the present. This reaction was what she'd feared all along—dwelling on the past, being filled with so much regret and sorrow, she could hardly stand it.

And yet, the gates had been opened. There was no stopping the pain, the intense ache in her heart at how badly she missed riding. With shaking fingers, she reached her hand toward the patient horse's neck, flashing from the past to the present with each stroke of his hair. Her fingers glided across his silken coat, the rhythmic movement of her hand mimicking his breathing until the tightness in her chest eased, and the sorrow in her heart soothed.

How had she forgotten that horses had that effect on her, the ability to calm whatever was ailing her? The pain remained, but with her proximity to the gelding, she could regulate her feelings better. She could sit in them for a moment without longing to flee from the discomfort.

Soon, her tears dried away, and though her sorrow remained, a different emotion arose, one she'd shelved long ago on the dusty recesses of her childhood memories—an emotion of deep love and respect she'd always had for the animal.

How she missed them.

"I'm Winnie," she said softly to the horse. "I'd ask for your name, too, but I don't think you'd be able to tell me."

He blew out a breath, and she smiled, moving her hand to the bridge of his nose, then to his forelock.

He accepted her affection, leaning toward her with a nudge of his broad nose to receive more. "You're an all-in kind of guy, then, huh?" she asked with a smile.

She lowered her belongings to a bench she found nearby, then returned to the horse at once, using both hands to stroke him.

For longer than intended, she remained there, petting him, breathing in his scent, allowing his sensitivity to adjust her emotions.

Everything was working fine until reality slowly settled in, and the reminder of what had occurred in her past crept up behind her like a stalking cougar.

Dad's words. His heart-wrenching actions. Her pleading that had never been enough.

She winced at the pain tightening around her chest. She never should have come in here. She never should have touched him. It was too great a reminder of all she'd lost—all she hadn't been allowed to do.

The black horse nudged her again, as if to break her from her thoughts, but she didn't stroke him again. Her heart was weary, though her tears had dried. It was time to go.

As she took a step back, the gelding raised his head, his ears pointing down the aisle, as if he knew she was about to leave...Or as if he knew someone else was coming.

She turned in the direction he looked. Not a soul was down the aisle, but still she watched, trusting the horse's ears and instinct until she heard the footsteps herself.

Was it a groom? Mrs. Birdwhistle? Perhaps one of the boys still hard at work?

All of her guesses were wrong as Matthew appeared around the corner instead.

CHAPTER TWENTY

WINNIE'S STOMACH LURCHED IN SURPRISE AT THE sight of Matthew. When was she going to stop being surprised by his sudden and frequent appearances? He *did* live at Foxwood. She knew that, right?

With two buckets in hand he moved toward her, his gaze downcast and muscles bulging from the sleeves of his t-shirt.

He didn't notice her for a moment, so she took the opportunity to step away from his horse until he finally looked up at her.

Surprise registered across his features, and his footsteps slowed. "Hey," he said hesitantly, looking between her and his horse.

She definitely should have left before now. What was she going to do one-on-one with the man? Would he mention the video call with her family? Or mention again how her ideas were all going to fail?

"Are you still working?" he asked, eying her laptop, papers, and tablet on the bench nearby.

"I was. But I just came in here to..." To what? Why *had* she come in there? To torture herself? To see if she really was Knox strong?

174

He waited for her response, but her mind continued to draw a blank.

"To...look at the horses?" he guessed, closing the distance between them and setting the buckets on the floor next to the stall.

"Yeah," she said. She'd go with that. "Are you still working?"

He looked to the buckets he'd set down, one filled with water, the other with grooming supplies. "I guess you could call it that. But I don't really consider grooming horses work. It's more..."

"Therapy," she finished aloud without thinking.

Their eyes met, and a strange light appeared in his. "Exactly."

She knew the feeling well—brushing down horses as she thought through problems or simply practiced mindfulness. The shine on the black horse's coat told her Matthew must come out for therapy often.

A horse nickered nearby, his chestnut head sticking out over the stall door down the aisle as he eyed Winnie and Matthew.

"Do you groom all of them?" she asked. "'Cause that one looks a little jealous."

Matthew smiled, entering the stall of his own horse. "That's Char's horse, Prince. He's jealous of everyone. But sadly, no, I don't have the time. Their owners or the Birdwhistles take good care of them, though."

Winnie paused. "Their owners?"

He secured the horse with a lead on either side of his halter, then reached for the buckets, hanging them on latches inside the roomy stall. "Most of the horses here are being boarded by members of the staff, residents of Grassington, and friends of my dad. We only own about a third of them."

"I was wondering about that," she said. "I just thought you guys really loved your horses."

"We do. Just not that much."

That same twinkling in his blue eyes from Sunday appeared now. Was that his way of showing that he was playing? Or was it a warning that he was going to embarrass her again?

"Well, you guys are lucky," she said, trying to keep the good mood going. She didn't want to jinx it, but they'd actually been carrying on a civil conversation for the last few minutes. "I mean, that your family can share that love of horses."

He studied her, his gaze remaining past the point of what she was comfortable with, purely because she knew another question was perched at the edge of his lips.

Whatever that question was, she was pretty sure she didn't want to answer it. "And this one is obviously your horse," she said, distracting them both.

Fortunately, he took her bait. "Yep, this is Nightshade."

"I thought you would have gone for something more historical or knightly. Or something from Harry Potter."

"I did toy with naming him Sirius—you know, Sirius *Black*—but Nightshade fit him better," Matthew replied.

Sirius Black. She thought she recognized the name from the films, but she couldn't be sure.

"Do you ride?" he asked.

"I did. When I was younger."

"Ever had a horse of your own?" he asked, rummaging through the bucket beside him before pulling out a hoof pick.

Discomfort pressed at the bottom of her heart. "One. Once upon a time. She was a palomino. Goldilocks."

She had been the most gorgeous horse Winnie had ever seen —even more so than the black ones she used to pine after. Creamy golden coat. Silvery mane and tail. White socks above her hooves and a white stripe down her nose. She had been tall, regal, majestic. Perfect.

"A clever name," Matthew said.

"For a seven-year-old," she returned.

"Do you still have her now?"

A twisting ache pierced her heart. "No, I lost her when I was seventeen."

Matthew didn't respond for a moment. "There's nothing worse than saying goodbye to a horse that passes away."

Winnie nodded, though she couldn't agree. There was something worse than that. What Dad did was much, much worse.

Winnie blinked, distracting herself from the past as she watched Matthew stroke Nightshade, rubbing his forelock and standing close to him. The bond between them was obvious. Matthew was gentle and affectionate, and his horse respected and trusted him in return.

She still found it hard to believe that this was Matthew she was standing by—the same Matthew she'd argued with a number of times, the same Matthew who'd teased her, the same Matthew she'd crushed with her unkindness.

Because right now, it was as if none of that had happened and they were speaking cordially, even friendly, like they had when they'd first met.

She could chalk it up to both of them being too exhausted to maintain their animosity that night. But it was more likely that the horses had something to do with it. They had a magic of their own.

"So, you know horses, then," Matthew stated.

"Um, I *did* know horses," she corrected.

Before she knew it, he reached into the bucket and tossed her a rubber curry comb, which she caught just in time against her chest.

"Once a horse girl, always a horse girl," he said, then he tipped his head toward Nightshade. "Come on. You can help me out."

Winnie stared down at the brush in her hands. She wasn't sure about this. If feeling a horse's breath on her fingers had launched her into the past, what would *grooming* one do to her?

"What?" Matthew asked, seeing her hesitate. "You'd rather pick the hooves?" He offered the pick to her, then eyed her up and down, his eyes lingering a moment on her legs. "Don't get me wrong, I'd love to see that as much as the next person, but I do think a curry comb is better suited for you tonight."

Her heart stuttered at his words.

He didn't wait for a response, merely turned his back to

Winnie and faced Nightshade's back right hoof. He slid his hand down the back of the leg, and the horse lifted it instantly in response. Matthew braced himself, leaned forward, then began to pick out the hoof.

Winnie, however, focused on what faced her the most, namely, Matthew's backside.

She blinked, realizing all too soon that she was kind of, sort of, most definitely admiring what she was staring at before she looked again at the comb in her hands.

At this point, with Matthew bending over like that and talking to her the way he was, she didn't think she'd be focusing too much on the horse if she brushed Nightshade after all.

Silently, she stepped into the stall with Matthew, moving in front of the horse to cross to his other side.

Matthew didn't respond. He simply reached down to Nightshade's front hoof next. Winnie stole another glance at him before pressing the curry comb against the horse's already pristine coat.

Flashes of brushing down Goldilocks flickered in her mind's eye, but she set them aside as Matthew spoke again.

"I appreciate your help," he said, grunting as he worked to clear out the hooves—though what little dirt was still there was beyond Winnie. "I've somewhere to be tonight, so I'm glad to have it."

Winnie tipped her head to the side. "Oh? Got yourself a date or something?"

She frowned. What the devil had made her ask that? Now she sounded like she was more interested in him than she was.

Matthew straightened, looking at her over his horse's neck, his features slightly red from exertion, though his eyes bright. "Maybe."

Something akin to jealousy stewed in Winnie's belly, though she told herself it was just hunger. "Well, good for you. It's not easy finding time to date *and* work."

Matthew smiled with a watchful gaze, but she didn't acknowledge it. After a minute, he moved to the other side of Nightshade

—the side she was on—and picked up the horse's back leg. Matthew's rearend once more faced her, though this time much closer than before.

She averted her body away from him, avoiding temptation altogether. He *had* to be doing this on purpose.

"I take it *you* find the balance difficult," Matthew said, still cleaning out the hoof.

She fought the urge to look back at him. "I do okay," she lied. She'd much rather talk about his dating life than her nonexistent one. "So is this a first date, then?" she asked, trying not to picture what type of girl Matthew was into. Probably a blonde.

"No, I've been out with her before."

She paused, finally facing him as he put Nightshade's hoof on the ground and straightened. "Oh. So, second date, then? Or hundredth?"

"She's definitely not old enough to have gone on a hundred dates with me."

Winnie pulled a face. He was that kind of guy, then, was he?

"I can see your confusion," he said, his eyes shining. "Allow me to explain."

"Oh, don't feel like you need to defend yourself."

"I don't, but I'm going to explain anyway. My niece passed off learning her letters today, so my family and I are going out with her to celebrate."

Instantly, the tightness in Winnie's chest dispelled, and warmth spread throughout her like water pouring over a smooth surface. That was...that was really sweet, actually. But then, would he be bringing—

"And no," he said, interrupting her thoughts as he leaned against the side of his horse, his arm across the back of him, "I won't be bringing an actual date."

She glanced at him, feigning neutrality. "Why would I care about that?"

"Because you think I'm...What was it your sister said again? Oh, that's right. Hot."

Winnie nearly groaned. She had begun to think she'd gotten out of that conversation. "I think you need to get your ears checked, Matthew," she said, attempting to cool down her blush. "My sister was the one who called you that."

He raised a brow. "Oh, just your sister, was it?"

"Yes," she stated stubbornly.

"Are you sure?" he pressed. "Because I recall her stating specifically that you described me in such a way."

He took a step toward her, and she froze in place. Why was he looking at her that way? With that knowing smile and with those warm blue eyes?

"Nope," she said. "I just think...that you smell like horse."

That was the weakest defense she had ever had. Ever.

Apparently, Matthew thought so, too, his smile growing to twice its size. "I have it on good authority that women like men to smell of such manly things as horses."

"Who did you hear that from?" she asked, taking a step back. "Other men?"

He gave a soft laugh, taking a step closer to her. As he did so, his smile faded, though a softness lingered in his eyes as he continued to stare at her.

Her mind threatened to lose its grasp on reality with such a look, so she took another step back.

"What are you doing?" she asked, hoping her direct question would bring them both back down to reality.

He didn't respond, his eyes searching hers, focused and determined until, for a split second, they dropped to her lips, and her mouth dried.

"I just want..." he began in a soft voice that filled her senses to breaking point.

She swallowed hard. What did he want? The same thing she did? What they both *needed* was to create distance between them, but with the stall door closed, Winnie had nowhere else to go.

What was even worse was that she didn't *want* to have anywhere else to go. As coworkers, they should definitely not be entertaining such a proximity—or such thoughts. But she couldn't help herself. If Matthew was willing...perhaps she was, too.

"What?" she asked when he didn't continue, her voice huskier than she would have liked. "What do you want?"

"I want..." he began again, drawing a step closer to her so she had to crane her neck to maintain her gaze on him, "to get to that final hoof."

Winnie blinked. The final hoof? What was he...

Realization rushed over her, and energy spilled from her limbs, causing her legs to tremble inside like gelatin.

"Why?" he asked, his eyes bright with feigned innocence. "What did you *think* I wanted?"

As if he didn't know.

She raised her chin, hoping to maintain some shred of dignity as she pretended she wasn't affected by his closeness, even though his teasing thrilled her. "Maybe you wanted me to know that you have no knowledge of personal space."

He chuckled. Why did it feel so good to make him laugh?

Before he might have reached for the hoof with her right there, Winnie swiftly ducked beneath the horse's head and continued her brushing on the other side.

Matthew picked up Nightshade's hoof, carrying on with his work as if he hadn't just almost caused her to melt into a puddle at his feet.

He must not have been affected in the same way she had—which was more than disappointing, even though it shouldn't have been.

"So I take it you ride western, being from the States," he asked, straightening as he finished Nightshade's hoof.

He dropped the pick in the bucket and pulled out a hard brush, swiping down the side Winnie had prepped.

"No, actually," she said, trying to keep up with the swift change in his demeanor. One minute, she was thinking he was going to kiss her, and the next, they're speaking of her past with horses again. "I learned both, but I prefer riding English. *Preferred* English," she corrected. "Like I said, I don't ride anymore."

His eyes stayed on his horse. "Why not?"

"I don't have much time now."

That was a lie. She could find the time. She just couldn't find the courage to face Dad.

"Did you take lessons?" he asked next.

"Yeah."

"How many years?"

"Thirteen or so."

His brow shot up. "Wow. I take it you competed in shows, then?"

"A few." Understatement of the century.

"Were you any good?" He rested his arms on the horse's back, his attention finally focused on her.

"I was okay," she responded, eying the ridges in his arms.

"Win any trophies or tournaments?"

"Almost each one I participated in."

"Which was how many?" he pressed.

"Oh, I wouldn't begin to know."

"Come on," he urged. "Just a range."

"Um. Over a hundred?"

He gave her an impressed look.

She should have just shut her mouth after that. He didn't need to know any more. But truth be told, she wanted more of his admiration.

"I also placed high enough to go to the qualifying rounds for Equestrian Eventing at the Olympics," she said matter-of-factly.

His eyebrows shot up, his lips parting. "Seriously?"

She nodded.

"That's incredible."

"Thanks," she murmured.

"No, really. You must have been amazing." He blew out a breath, then his brow pulled together. "So, what happened?"

She knew this would come next. "Goldie spooked. I fell hard on the ground and lost my chance." She shrugged. "That's all."

He shook his head. "But you didn't try again?"

"Nah, I didn't bother. My dad..." She froze, forgetting to censor her words. "*We* thought it wouldn't be worthwhile to train again for so long. I just had too much else going on with school, and work, and family stuff, so I quit."

"You quit the competitions?" he asked in clarification. He was no longer brushing the horse, fully enveloped in her story.

"Yeah. And riding."

His brow furrowed. "Altogether?"

"I just didn't have the time anymore," she lied again.

In truth, it was Dad. It had all been Dad.

The memory of his cruel words rushed over her in unrelenting waves.

"It's time to get your head out of the clouds and stop embarrassing the Knox family name, Winifred. You can't make a career out of riding horses."

Winnie winced at the memory. She'd begged him to reconsider. She'd joined honors societies and special clubs, participated in countless extracurricular activities, created service projects, earned her Associate's before graduating early from high school—all of it to impress Dad to allow her to continue riding on the side.

But none of it had been enough. *She* hadn't been enough. The minute Dad had seen her fall off the horse during qualifiers, he'd stopped her riding altogether.

"I'll quit training, then," she'd said. *"Just let me keep riding for fun. I'll pay for Goldie's boarding, food, everything."*

"And who is going to pay for the embarrassment you're going to keep causing us?" Dad had retorted. *"Honestly, Winnie, falling off a horse in front of so many people?"*

Winnie had been riding since she was a child. She knew being thrown and horses being spooked was bound to happen, but Dad didn't care. He sold her palomino that same week and forbade Winnie from ever riding again.

The pain from the memory fully returned as Winnie took in the sight of Nightshade, his kind eyes and relaxed ears, gorgeous coat and smooth hair. And suddenly, she was overcome with a regret so poignant, she could hardly breathe.

She never should have stepped foot in the stables. Not only had she erased more than a decade of building up tolerance for not being around horses, but she'd also just revealed way too much to Matthew—a guy she wasn't sure she could even trust with such knowledge.

She pulled the comb away from the horse at once, taking a step back as tears pooled in her eyes. She couldn't do this any longer.

"Are you all right?" Matthew asked, concern in his tone.

Winnie strapped on a smile and tossed the comb into the bucket nearby, averting her gaze at once. "Yeah, of course. I just... I-I remembered I've got a few emails to respond to before the end of the day."

Matthew nodded in silence. He didn't believe her, but Winnie didn't care. She needed to get out of there.

"Thanks for your help," he said softly.

Winnie nodded. "Tell Ava congratulations on learning her letters," she said, gathering her belongings on the bench outside of the stall.

She waved over her shoulder and fled from the stables, not daring another glance back at Matthew or his horse. She wouldn't allow herself to fall into this miserable trap from her past.

Not again. Never again.

MATTHEW STARED at the empty space Winnie had left behind, shock still fresh in his system.

She'd cried. Winnie Knox had actually cried. But, why? What

on earth had been going through her mind those last few minutes to have made her so overcome with emotion—emotion he didn't know she was capable of experiencing?

The memory of losing out on going to the Olympics would make anyone upset, as would speaking of a beloved horse dying or choosing to quit riding altogether. But in Matthew's heart, he knew there was something more to her tears and her quitting. Something deeper and far more traumatic.

He picked up the comb she'd used on Nightshade, the rubber still warm from her grip as he finished brushing down the horse.

They'd been having such a civil and friendly conversation. No talk of business, no arguments, no criticisms. He'd even further tested the tenuous waters between them by pretending to draw close enough to kiss her. He'd done so purely for his own vanity's sake, to see if she really did consider him attractive—enough to even kiss him.

But that had been a major mistake, as his feigned desire turned into a very real yearning to have her red lips press against his. The biggest problem had come when she hadn't retreated like he'd stupidly assumed she would have. When had he ever known Winnie Knox to retreat from anything?

Although, tonight she'd been so different. So kind. She'd even taken the time to congratulate his niece on her letters—remembering Ava's name, on top of it all. That spoke measures about a person. But that was the problem. Winnie was becoming more of a human being than the devil he'd made her out to be, created to make his life miserable.

He wasn't supposed to think of her as a woman with desires and talents and heartaches of her own. He was supposed to want her gone, out of Foxwood in less than two weeks. That's why he wasn't helping her as he ought to be, letting her know that most of her ideas would cause the festival to fail even harder than before.

Because without telling her, she would be gone all the sooner.

Then he'd be free from all this headache—free to get back to the heart of his festival.

He tossed the curry comb into the bucket with a shake of his head. It was time to shape up. No more teasing Winnie with flirtatious looks just because he wanted to see her blush. No more thoughts about how he admired her ability to work under pressure. No more conversations about horses and Olympic qualifying events.

And, more than anything, there would be absolutely no more thinking of Winnie Knox as a woman he would like to keep around. Even if that was beginning to change.

CHAPTER TWENTY-ONE

MATTHEW STOOD ON THE GRAVEL DRIVE NEAR THE front doors of Foxwood, smiling as the car appeared around the corner. They were finally here.

He'd offered to pick up his friends from the airport that Friday evening, but Cedric had insisted on driving up from Wales himself and collecting the others from Manchester Airport before heading to Yorkshire.

Seeing Cedric's beloved Tesla, Matthew finally understood. The man was obsessed with the car. He would take any chance he could to drive it.

Matthew raised his hand in greeting as the white vehicle approached much faster than he would have expected, but when he saw who has actually driving, a grin spread across his lips.

He should've known. Cedric wasn't driving. Finn was. How in the world had he convinced Cedric to agree to that?

As Finn reached the end of the drive, he turned sharply, skidding to a halt in front of Matthew as the disrupted pea gravel flicked toward the front porch, clacking in protest.

Matthew walked forward with an amused shake of his head as Finn opened the driver's side door first, his face alight with exhilaration. "Woo, what a rush!"

Matthew laughed. "I was wondering how you all made it here so quickly. Quite the entrance, O'Meara."

Finn raised his eyebrows in a flex. "You like that? I thought I'd try to give wee Cedric here a heart attack, but it didn't work."

Cedric leapt out of the passenger side with a frown. "That's the last time I give you the keys, Finn." He faced Matthew with a shake of his head. "Nearly wrecked it fifteen times. He does me head in."

Graham exited the car last. "Both of you just need to relax," he said, his Scottish accent thick. "Clearly, Finn had it under control."

"What, nearly dyin'?" Cedric questioned, gently closing the passenger door. "You blew past so many speed cameras, I'll be fined hundreds of quid."

"I'm sure you can afford it," Finn returned. "Just sell one of your autographs and you'll be right."

Matthew grinned, greeting each of his friends with a short embrace and a clap on their backs. To have the four of them back together was exactly what he needed right now.

"Have you driven one o' these, Matt?" Finn asked, his Northern Irish accent all the more prominent with his excitement.

He jutted a thumb over his shoulder toward the car, still not over their conversation. "It handles better than a tour bus, I tell you that."

"Of course it does, you plonker," Cedric said, opening the back of the Tesla as they gathered their belongings.

"It might even rival Matt's beater over there," Graham teased, motioning to the rusted, red Mini Cooper. "I can't believe you still have that."

"Of course I do," Matthew defended. "She's worth more than your pipes."

The Scotsman snorted in disbelief. "You mad bampot."

A long, low whistle sounded from Finn behind them. "Who's drivin' *that*?" he asked.

All eyes shifted to the Aston Martin in the drive. Matthew hesitated. "That would be the...consultant's."

Looks of understanding passed between the lads and Matthew. "Ah, 'course," Finn said. "And do we get to meet this infamous consultant today?"

Matthew scoffed. "Absolutely not. Nor will you be meeting her ever."

After he had spoken with Winnie's family on the video chat, she'd avoided him. After Matthew had spoken with her in the stables, she'd full-on ignored him. It was just as well. He was ignoring her, too. It seemed that they both wanted to pretend that their conversation hadn't occurred—the conversation where they'd behaved more as friends than standoffish colleagues. Who knew what sort of trouble his real friends would concoct if they *did* meet her.

"Oh, come on," Graham protested. "You're really going to deprive us of the pleasure of seeing her for ourselves after all we've heard about her?"

That was even more of a reason to keep his friends and Winnie separated. Matthew may or may not have exaggerated certain aspects about the woman to his mates.

For example, she wasn't the worst human being he'd ever had the displeasure of knowing. At least, not anymore.

"That's exactly what I'm going to do," Matthew said. "I've mapped out our whole weekend, so I'm afraid we haven't the time."

"So now we don't get to see her *or* her festival?" Finn asked.

"Precisely," Matthew returned.

Before, he'd been relieved that his friends weren't going to be seeing his failure-of-a-festival. Now, he was just glad they wouldn't be there either for Winnie's *faire*. He'd never be able to live it down if her event actually turned out better than his— which was a fear he was praying wouldn't be realized.

"What if I promise you can drive the Tesla before we leave?"

Cedric asked, attempting to sweeten the deal. "*Then* can we meet her?"

"Not a chance," Matthew said.

He led the way forward to where the ever-vigilant Mr. Fernsby waited for them by the front door of Foxwood.

Despite their pressing to meet Winnie, Matthew had a good feeling about this weekend. Time with his friends he hadn't seen in months, a charity run to participate in, a break from the festival —and most importantly, time away from Winnie.

It was going to be great.

So long as he kept his mates away from the consultant, that is.

Matthew leaned back against the cushion in the booth of the White Hart, listening to the chatter of the pub around him and his mates. The charity run had come and gone that morning, the weekend having flown by, and now the four of them were enjoying their final night together, banter and laughter abounding.

"I didn't lose," Matthew defended. "There were three others behind me."

"Mate, they were in their eighties," Finn said, shaking his head. "That means you lose by default."

Matthew shook his head, even though he agreed with him. He'd raced abysmally that morning. But what else was to be expected when he hadn't trained a lick in the last couple of weeks?

Fortunately, he didn't care about winning or losing in that moment. What he did care about was eating. White Hart over-flowed that night with customers—as was the norm for the pub on a Saturday evening, being one of the best in Grassington—and the waiter had yet to come to their table. While Matthew tried to remain patient, his growling stomach had other plans.

With his friends still in conversation about the charity run, Matthew glanced around for any sign of a worker, hoping to ask for a time estimate so he could prepare himself for the wait.

He looked past the pub's old stone walls, wooden support beams, and amateur paintings of Yorkshire landscapes before spotting a waiter at the bar, chatting with a few other customers. Matthew was about to raise his hand to get his attention, but he paused when he caught sight of the woman the waiter stood beside.

Her back was toward Matthew, her dark hair in a top bun, and a silk shirt was draped gracefully across her slender shoulders.

His heart stuttered. Winnie. He hadn't seen her in three days —thanks to his very calculated actions—though in some ways, it felt like weeks had passed by.

She sat alone, her phone resting on the bar as she tapped out something on the screen. He tried to decipher if she was working still, but his view of her was soon blocked by the waiter finally reaching their table.

"Evenin', lads," he greeted.

He took their orders for drinks, dropped off the menus, then wandered away to his next table.

Matthew peered down at the menu, pretending to be paying attention to the food listed on the page, but he was much more invested now in seeing what Winnie was doing.

She took a sip out of her bottle of J2O—orange and passion-fruit, his favorite—then focused again on her phone.

Had she eaten already? Or was she waiting for her order to be taken, too?

"Who's the bird you're starin' at, Matt?" Cedric asked, his voice cutting into Matthew's focus on Winnie.

Matthew's eyes darted toward his friend. "What? Oh, no one."

He stared harder at his menu. That was his first mistake. His second was to think that his friends would let his obvious denial slide.

"Is that the consultant?" Finn asked next. "She looks like a New Yorker."

"It has to be," Graham agreed. "Why else would Matthew be cowerin' behind his menu like that?"

Matthew frowned. "Maybe it's because I want to order my steak."

"Would you like it in the shape of the consultant, perhaps?" Finn asked.

The men laughed, and Matthew fought the urge to quiet them. He didn't want to draw her attention toward their table. Then he'd *have* to invite her over. That would be the nice thing to do, especially because she was eating alone. But he'd hate to imagine the sort of mischief his friends would create. He'd managed to keep them separated the entire day. He wasn't about to stop now.

"You didn't tell us she was a looker," Finn said next as Winnie looked to the side, her profile becoming visible.

Graham and Cedric hummed in agreement. Matthew would have, too, but then, admitting that Winnie was attractive aloud to his mates would be the final nail in his coffin.

"She's eatin' alone, so she is," Finn said next. Then he faced Matthew and tossed his head toward her. "Why don't you invite her to sit with us?"

Matthew scoffed. "As if I'd ever agree to that. You guys'd take the mickey right out of me."

All three of them feigned looks of innocence. "As if we'd do that to you," Cedric said. "She does look lonely."

"Aye, go on, then," Finn pressed.

"She's working," Matthew said, shaking his head. "I know better than to interrupt her."

"Oh, aye?" Finn said. "Are you afraid of the wee bird?"

Again, the men laughed.

Matthew ignored them. "So what're you all ordering? I highly recommend the gammon."

"No matter," Finn said. "I'll go get her if you won't."

"Finn," Matthew began in warning.

But Finn ignored him. He headed straight for Winnie as Matthew watched in frustration, glued to his chair like the worthless coward that he was.

CHAPTER TWENTY-TWO

MATTHEW WATCHED FROM THE SAFETY OF THE BOOTH as Finn stopped next to Winnie. She looked up at him in surprise, a hesitant smile on her lips before he pointed to the lads. Her eyes fell on Matthew, and she visibly relaxed.

She raised her hand in a wave, and Matthew awkwardly responded with a wave of his own.

Finn said something to her, no doubt inviting her to join them, but she shook her head, obviously declining. Another moment passed by, however, and Finn apparently convinced her as Winnie gathered her bag, phone, and drink and followed Finn toward the booth.

"If you guys utter so much as a word about my supposed attraction to her..." Matthew began through gritted teeth to Graham and Cedric, but he couldn't finish his threat as Finn and Winnie arrived that very moment.

"Hey," he greeted, shooting a look at Finn that said, *I'll get you for this later.*

Finn didn't see, too busy retrieving an unused chair from a nearby table.

"Hi," Winnie said in return, looking at the others with uncertainty. "Sorry to interrupt, but your friend here was adamant."

194

Finn returned with the chair, sliding it in for her as she took her seat at the head of the table, diagonal from Matthew. Her knee bumped against his leg, and he shifted away at once, shaking out the warmth shooting up his limb.

"You're not interruptin'," Finn said. "Is she, Matt?"

Matthew shook his head at once. "Not at all. I was going to invite you before Finn rushed ahead."

That seemed to ease her discomfort. Unfortunately, *his* only grew as his friends exchanged knowing looks at his lie.

"So," she said, looking around the table, "I take it these are your friends."

Matthew gave his head a little shake to pull out of his stupor. Where were his manners? "Yes, you've met Finn already. But this is Graham and Cedric. Boys, Winnie Knox."

Nods and "Hiyas" were shared as Winnie smiled in response. "So you're the ones who pulled Matthew away from practicing his jousting the last few days," she said with no hint of malice.

"Sorry about that," Graham said to her. "We told Matt to practice still so we could watch him joust from the sidelines, but he wouldn't allow it."

"I didn't want to deal with your heckling," Matthew retorted.

"What?" Graham asked with innocence. "Heckle? Us?"

The waiter returned then, interrupting their conversation to ask for their orders.

As the others shared what food they wished, Winnie leaned toward Matthew. "I really don't have to stay. He just insisted..."

But Matthew shook his head. "You don't need to worry. We're glad to have the company."

Cedric, who sat beside Matthew, nodded in agreement. "So long as you don't order a salad for supper. That doesn't belong at our table."

Matthew was about to explain that Cedric was joking, but Winnie smiled straightaway. "You don't have to worry about that. I already ordered a steak."

"Ah, that's what Matt was orderin'," Cedric said. "Two peas in a pod, you are."

Fortunately, the waiter asked Matthew what he wanted right then, so no awkwardness was allowed to linger. Though, he would be adding Cedric to the conversation he was planning on holding with Finn immediately following dinner.

After the orders were placed, the five of them sat in silence for only a few seconds. Fortunately, despite Matthew being annoyed with his friends, he knew he could count on them to keep the conversation going when his brain refused to work.

He wasn't used to being like this near Winnie, lacking in all confidence. He far preferred it the other way around, but having his friends there just unnerved him.

"So we saw the car you drive," Finn said to her, leaning back against the booth. He sat across from Matthew, diagonal from Winnie's other side. "Aston Martins are gorgeous cars."

She nodded. "They really are. Unfortunately, it's just a rental, though."

"Still," Graham added, "it must be fun to drive."

"Especially compared to the ridiculous beater Matthew forced us into today," Cedric said.

"Ah, the old Mini Cooper?" Winnie asked.

How had she known that was his?

"Yes," Cedric continued. "I still can't understand why we had to drive that lemon here when I've got a Tesla to enjoy."

"Because you need to keep yourself humble with the rest of us in the real world, Ced, that's why," Matthew retorted.

"Says the man who lives in a castle," Winnie said.

The boys raised their glasses in cheers and laughter, but Winnie's bright eyes focused solely on Matthew. He had no retort, too distracted by the way she glowed in the temperate light of the dark-walled pub. Her lips were a warm shade of red, and her gray eyes glimmered.

She was in a happy mood tonight. No doubt trying to win

over his friends, just as she had his sister and parents. Just as she had *him* when he'd helped her from the mud.

What would have happened between them had Dad placed her over Foxwood instead of the festival? Would they have been friends? Or would they have found something else between them?

"So," Winnie began, pulling his attention away from his dangerously straying thoughts, "I hear you boys ran a charity run today."

"Yep," Graham said. "Cedric here won, despite pulling his hamstring a few months ago."

Winnie's brow rose. "Well, that sounds painful." She gave a little laugh as Cedric shrugged. "But congratulations all the same."

"And Matthew here nearly lost to a few elderly folk," Finn added.

Thanks, Finn.

"Well done to you, as well," she said with a teasing smile at Matthew. "Was this your guys' first, or..."

"No, we run every year as an excuse to get together and participate for charity," Cedric said. "The hosting individual is in charge of finding the charity run."

"Oh, I love that idea," she said.

"Do you run, Winnie?" Graham asked.

Matthew sat back in silence. He wasn't doing much speaking. He was far too on edge, wondering what teasing comment would come next from his friends to make Winnie even more confident than him that evening.

"Oh, just for exercise," she responded. "I've never really had time to train for a marathon or anything like that."

Too busy with work. Was that why she didn't have time to ride any longer, too?

She glanced at Matthew as if she'd heard his thoughts, then looked to Cedric. "So how did you all come up with the charity run idea?"

"It was Cedric," Finn explained. "None of the rest of us can

keep up with him, but he insists on keepin' it going twice a year."
He leaned closer to Winnie, and Matthew's eye shifted to watch
his friend more carefully. "He plays for the Premier League, so he
does. Finest striker there is."

"Premier League...I assume you're talking about soccer?" she
asked. "Or football, I guess?"

The men nodded.

"The *real* football," Cedric added.

Winnie grinned. "Don't let my brothers hear you say that. They
both played in high school and have the concussions to prove it."

More laughter sounded. Even Matthew cracked a smile this
time.

"So what's the equivalent of the Premier League in the
States?" she asked next.

"Probably the NFL," Cedric responded.

Her brow rose. "Oh, wow. So you're, like, famous here?"

Cedric shrugged humbly again. "Moreso in Wales. That's
where I'm from, see. But in most circles I don't get recognized."

Graham scoffed. "Everywhere we go, he gets stopped. He was
busy signing Habergham shirts at the charity run."

"Blessin' seniors," Finn teased, "kissin' babies. It's a hard life,
so it is."

Winnie laughed. Had Matthew imagined her eyes lingering
on Finn?

"So *you* play football," she said, pointing to Cedric. "And
Matthew jousts. What do the rest of you do?"

"I lead bus tours 'round *Norn Iron*," Finn said.

Winnie narrowed her eyes. "Around where, sorry?"

"Northern Ireland," Matthew translated.

"Ah, of course." She looked back to Finn. "That's where
you're from, then?"

"Right you are," Finn replied.

"I love your accent, but I'll be honest..." She paused with a
wince. "I'm only catching about a tenth of what you're saying."

The group laughed.

"Join the club," Graham quipped.

"Sorry," Winnie said with a sheepish grin.

"Ah, no bother," Finn said with a wave of his hand. "Half o' what I say isn't important anyway."

Then he winked at her again.

Matthew shook his head. What was with these guys? Were they each going to take their turns flirting with the woman? He obviously didn't have any claim over her, but still. They could have a little decorum.

"And you enjoy leading tours?" she asked, her eyes taking on that same light of interest she had while staring at Cedric.

Looking. Looking at Cedric. Just as she was *looking* at Finn.

"Aye, it's a craic every time, so it is," Finn said. "I get to sing, share me knowledge of *Norn Iron*, tell tales, and—"

"Be the center of attention," Matthew finished, "which is your favorite thing to do."

That wasn't super nice of him to say, but the lads laughed anyway. Finn flashed him a grin. "Matthew's only jealous I can capture people's attention so well. Most people fall asleep the second he starts to drone on about history. I'm sure you've been a victim o' that, Winnie."

Winnie made the motion of zipping her lips, and his friends laughed again.

"And you, Graham?" she asked next. "What do you do?"

"A bit of everythin', really," Graham responded. "Skydivin' instructor, bagpiper. Overseein' the Highland Games in my hometown. I just go for whatever strikes my fancy at the time."

"I love that," she responded, her smile warm. "Being able to do everything that you want to. It sounds like a dream."

"It certainly keeps me occupied," Graham returned.

"That's enough about us, though," Finn said as a lull in the conversation returned. "Matthew says you're a consultant?"

Winnie waved a passive hand in front of her. "Oh, we don't

need to talk about that. Besides, I'm sure you've already heard an earful about how I'm ruining his festival."

Matthew shifted in his seat uncomfortably as his friends exchanged looks and mumbled weak words in the contrary.

Winnie smiled. "It's okay. You don't have to lie for him. I'm used to his fussy ways by now."

Matthew frowned. Fussy? He wasn't fussy.

"I don't know how you could be used to it already," Finn said. "He was impossible at college. How do you manage workin' with him?"

She smiled at Finn again. What would it take for Matthew to receive those lingering, impressed, interested eyes like she had with the others?

"Oh, we manage just fine," she answered. "I think our working relationship has gotten much better ever since we've acknowledged the fact that he doesn't like me. Wouldn't you say, Matthew?"

Her eyes finally met his. And yet, the minute they did, he wanted them off of him. They were reading him too directly.

He opened his mouth to reply, but nothing came out, words failing him yet again, so he took a sip of his drink instead.

"Come on, Matt," Graham said. "Where are those knightly manners you're always boasting of?"

"Wasted on you lot," Matthew returned.

He was sounding like a right pompous lout tonight. But he couldn't help it. He was just in a mood, and that mood was annoyed.

Annoyed that he wasn't as confident around Winnie as he had been before. Annoyed that his friends had invited her over. Annoyed that he wasn't getting the attention he wanted from a woman he shouldn't want attention from at all.

"See?" Winnie said. "He doesn't like me."

Her eyes remained on him for a minute before shifting to his friends, whom she asked more questions to as Matthew stared at his drink, basically pouting at the bubbles sliding up the glass.

Yes, he was annoyed at a lot of things. But more than anything, he was annoyed that he couldn't contradict Winnie's words. Because truth be told, despite everything they'd been through, he did like her.

He liked her too much.

But admitting that aloud, what can of worms would that open?

He knew it was far better to stay silent.

So why didn't he *feel* better?

WINNIE HAD NEVER EXPERIENCED A MORE delightful meal in her life. All of her business dinners in New York City had centered around, well, business. All small talk, all boring plans, rigid and dull. Her family dinners were even worse with words of accomplishments as her siblings one-upped each other.

But here, the conversation was entertaining, the food delicious, and the company an utter delight. Not only had she found her confidence around Matthew again, but she was genuinely enjoying her time with his friends.

As for Matthew, she had finally managed to coax him slightly from his shell. She still wasn't exactly sure why he'd retreated so much in the first place, falling silent and appearing so discomfited, but she didn't mind. After all, she enjoyed the payback she was now receiving after how uncomfortable he'd made her while speaking with her family.

With their meals delivered and drinks refilled, their conversations moved from subject to subject, starting with the charity run, circling around their jobs again, then shifting to their time at Eton, the boarding school they'd met at when they were all fifteen.

"What are the chances that the four of you would meet from

all different countries, then end up as friends?" she asked, looking between them all.

"It's not that surprisin'," Finn said with that same teasing smile on his lips. "We were very exclusive. Stopped others from joinin', so we did. Once we had one from each country, we put a cap on our group."

"Yeah, we asked everyone where they were from," Graham jumped in, playing along.

"'You're from England?'" Cedric roleplayed.

"'Nope, you're out,'" Finn continued. "'We've already got one o' them.'"

The men laughed, and Winnie joined in. "Sorry, but there's no way I'd believe that any of you are the type to exclude others." She paused. "Matthew, though..."

They laughed as Matthew frowned at her, though not as deeply as he had before.

Winnie couldn't deny that she'd been slightly offended when he hadn't refuted her comment about him disliking her. The news came as no surprise, though, so she was doing her best to pretend like she hadn't been hurt by it.

"I'm the most inclusive of them all," Matthew said, drawing her focus back to him. "Look at all the rubbish I have to deal with here."

"Yeah, but you wouldn't be without us," Finn said.

Matthew snorted in protest. "I almost didn't graduate because of you lot." He shifted his attention to Winnie. "I was the only one who did any schooling whilst at Eton, and I basically tutored each of them in every single subject."

"Yes, like a good little mummy," Finn teased. "Makin' sure we did our schoolwork, makin' sure we got in before curfew, makin' sure our lights were out at nine o'clock."

"How else could I get the sleep I needed?" Matthew questioned. "Studies show if you receive a solid—"

"Yes, we've heard it before, Matthew," Graham said with a roll of his eyes. "All through college."

Winnie laughed. "So how long were you at Eton?"

To her delight, Matthew was the one to respond—although he'd only done so since his friends were all taking bites of their food. "I was there until I graduated at eighteen. Graham, as well. Cedric left after two years, and Finn, one."

"You were only there together for one year?" she asked.

The four of them nodded.

"It would've been longer had Finn not gotten kicked out," Graham explained.

Winnie laughed in surprise. "What on earth got you kicked out?"

Finn flashed a grin—that same, harmless, flirtatious one he'd been sharing with her all night. "Fraternizin' with the ladies."

Matthew rolled his eyes.

"How did you manage that?" she asked. "Isn't Eton an all-boys college?"

"It is until you help sneak a few girls in," Cedric said. "Right, Finn?"

The men laughed, and Matthew cracked another smile.

The conversation continued, as did Winnie's laughter as they recounted their school days and beyond. All too swiftly, though, the evening wound down, and her time with the friends came to an end.

She leaned back in her chair with a sigh. "Well, boys, I'd love to stay and chat more, but unfortunately, I have work to do."

"On a Saturday night?" Finn questioned, turning to Matthew. "What kind of ship are you runnin' here, mate?"

Matthew held up his hands. "She makes her own schedule. And ours beside."

Winnie delivered a pointed smile. "Yes, and I work late into the night so you guys don't have to."

Another lingering look passed between them before she scooted back in her chair. "Thanks again for letting me join you all tonight. I haven't had this much fun in a really long time."

His friends expressed the same sentiment as she stood and

gathered her things. "Good luck on prepping for your next charity run," she said with a smile.

"If you find yourself in *Norn Iron*, feel free to join us," Finn said with another wink.

"I will," she said with a laugh. "Goodnight, guys." Then she turned to Matthew. "See you Monday."

He nodded. "Yeah, I'll see you."

Or at least, that's what she thought he'd said. She wasn't exactly sure, as it all tumbled out of his mouth at once.

After another wave goodbye, she sidestepped her way through the crowds of the pub, leaving the warm atmosphere for the cool air outside. She rooted around in her purse for the rental car's keys, still smiling to herself at the memory of the evening.

"Winnie?"

She paused, whirling around in surprise. "Matthew?"

He walked toward her, his hands in his pockets as he approached, a curl blowing across his brow in the soft breeze. "I just wanted to make sure you got to your car safely." He motioned over his shoulder. "The lads wouldn't lay off until I did."

She smiled. "That's nice of you guys. But I'm all right." She tossed her head toward her car she stood in front of. "I made it."

He nodded, looking away. "Right. Well, have a good night."

He began to walk away, then paused. She watched him with amusement. "You all right?"

Matthew looked up at her in surprise, as if he didn't know she still stood there. "What? Oh, yeah." He turned to face her more fully. "I just...I wanted to say, I like you."

Winnie paused. What? He liked her? Like, *liked*, liked her?

"You mentioned to my friends that I didn't," he said. "So I just wanted to clear the air. I like you, you know, as a person. You're all right."

Disappointment settled on her chest, heavy and thick, like hot tar pressed onto a fractured road. So. She was *all right*. That made her feel...feel what, exactly? Why had he even felt the need to tell her as much? Because he felt bad about saying nothing before or because his friends had told him to be nicer?

Either way, she hardly felt better.

"I was only kidding," she said, trying to blow off her own embarrassment. "I didn't expect you to answer me or anything."

"I know," he said, his eyes lingering.

Those blue crystals captured in the light of the streetlamp above connected with her in a way that made her hope that maybe...maybe he did feel something more. That maybe he was out there because he wanted to be truthful about his feelings.

"Okay," she said simply, hoping he'd say more.

Instead, he turned away. "Anyway, I just wanted to clear the air while I could. You know, in case you leave Foxwood early."

Winnie's heart dropped, and she chastised herself for allowing it to lift in the first place. He still expected her to leave early, then, to fail the festival altogether.

"Well, thanks, I guess," she said, unable to come up with anything else.

He nodded, then left in silence toward the pub.

Winnie stared after him for a moment, then unlocked the rental, all the while telling herself she should be glad that he liked her as a business associate and only that.

But for some reason, she couldn't convince herself that it was a good thing at all.

CHAPTER TWENTY-THREE

THROUGHOUT THE FOLLOWING WEEK, WINNIE HAD never been busier, and she was glad of it, wanting to swallow any memory she had of Matthew and their interaction that night at the pub. Their conversations were kept to a bare minimum and *always* centered around work. They weren't friends, after all, and he expected her to fail and leave early, so why try to create any sort of relationship from such a basis?

Besides, her success with the festival would tell Matthew everything he needed to know—she wouldn't be failing, and she wouldn't be leaving early. In fact, she would succeed so greatly that Matthew would finally be handed back the reins, and Winnie would be well on her way to working directly with Mr. Wintour and Foxwood. She couldn't wait.

Of course, her confidence was now proving to be a slippery devil as each day, another problem arose. Food booths falling through, grounds being unprepared, fire-breathers bailing, rides being late for delivery.

Even with the many setbacks, however, she continued to lob the problems back into the atmosphere, refusing to give up as Saturday came and the festival finally arrived.

Six o'clock arrived swiftly, and Winnie was up straightaway, heading out to the faire grounds in the hope of finishing the seemingly endless list of items she needed to accomplish before nine o'clock that morning.

On her way out, as she strode across the pathway through the trees, her dad called, wishing her good luck, which she thought had been rather kind of him. That is, until he added the unnecessary, "You're going to need it," at the end of his well wishes.

"Thanks," she muttered.

"How's progress with the estate?" he asked next.

Winnie shook her head, grateful he couldn't see her rolling her eyes, as well. "I'll be in charge of it after the festival, remember?"

The other end of the line went silent. "Well, maybe something will come up earlier than that," Dad said.

Winnie barely registered his words as she received a text from Jess, telling her there was a problem with where the vendors were being set up.

"Listen, Dad. I'm sorry, but I gotta go. I'll call you after, okay?"

"Yeah, do that. Talk to you soon, Win-Win-Winnie."

She hung up the phone and walked to the festival as swiftly as her heels allowed, leaving any thought of Dad on the pathway behind her.

Unfortunately, not even *that* helped to improve the event from the beginning.

With her advertising work beforehand—updating Foxwood's social media profiles, throwing up ads in newspapers, websites, and on the radio, and more—they'd sold three times as many tickets as the last festival, if not four times. But even as the gates opened and the guests filtered in, Winnie's hopes for a smooth event lowered little by little as more problems arose.

First, the carousel broke down after only three cycles, then the line for the pony rides and the bounce house—which had to be swiftly called in to replace the bumper cars that couldn't make it in time—grew to an unmanageable size.

The food was better, though not by much, as Mrs. Porter had still insisted on providing her cabbage chowder, and the typical carnival food was being described as "the same as everywhere else." The falconry had gathered a large crowd at first but was cut short due to the wind.

To add to the drama, the rest of the entertainment had been postponed due to Mrs. Jones missing an important phone call from the lost carnival games.

Fortunately, the cosplayers had shown up in droves, providing some much-needed immersion as crowds wandered around the craft booths and local art sales.

By the time the jousting rolled around, however, Winnie was being held together by a mere thread. The crowds surrounded the entire arena with looks of excitement, but the knights were late coming out of the stables again, driving away a number of people before Mr. Fogg's monotonous voice finally announced their arrival.

She had been hoping for the tournament to wow people, but the feedback she overheard from passersby caused her insides to twist with worry.

"The scorin' don't make any sense."

"The winner's chosen before anyway. None of it's real."

"Mummy, I'm bored. Can I go back to the bounce house?"

"Look, they're not even tryin' to strike the small knight. No, the one who can't even hold the lance up."

Winnie chewed the inside of her cheek, if only to keep from relieving the contents of her stomach across the tournament grounds. This wasn't what she'd planned at all. She'd poured all of her efforts into this, so why was it failing? Where was her success? Where was her praise?

Halfway through the jousting, the carousel started working again, much to the delight of every child in attendance. But when music, loud and plunky, blared out across the grounds, drowning out Mr. Fogg's words—despite his new microphone—Winnie grimaced. With no volume control on the ride, one-by-one, families left the joust for the carousel, children tugging their parents away to something they found far more appealing.

Winnie could only imagine the staff's words occurring behind her back.

"So much for Winnie's promises of success."

"You see? Now no one cares about the jousting when it's scripted."

"Just like Blackpool."

Matthew would be thinking the same thing. After all, he'd called her out on her failure from the start.

But, no. She wouldn't fail again. She was a good consultant. She knew too much, had learned too much, had *given* too much, to not succeed. The festival would be a triumph if she just worked harder and stuck to her plan.

And yet, despite her scrambling to improve matters throughout the latter half of the day—closing down the carousel for an hour, encouraging Mr. Fogg to explain the jousting points, and trying to boost interest in the big reveal at the end of who the small, secret knight was—the majority of the guests quit the festival as a whole, hours before the festival was scheduled to end.

When Jess *was* finally revealed as the winner, though she hadn't managed to strike a single knight in the process, the response was so underwhelming, Winnie couldn't take it any longer.

With worry clouding her common sense, she ducked behind one of the tents and pulled out her phone, anxious to read the feedback the guests had been given via the QR code on the back of the schedule of events. She'd promised herself not to read any of them until the end of the day, knowing they wouldn't do her any good, but she could no longer keep herself from knowing the truth.

With each new sentence she read, stress clawed at her chest like a wild animal, dragging her spirits lower and lower until they were devoured altogether.

"Carousel was too loud. That's all the kiddies wanted to do."

"Wanted my children to experience a little culture from the past, didn't get it."

"The jousting was great. Too bad we couldn't hear it."

"Would've liked to see them making contact more."

"Wish the jousting scores had been real."

"The whole thing was just too much."

"The small knight wasn't believable enough."

On and on and on the list went until Winnie finally stopped, her cheeks burning with humiliation.

Had Mr. Wintour read these comments already? She'd given him the link to the feedback that morning, having full confidence that he'd be reading over her praises. What about now? How would he feel, knowing his faith in her had been entirely wasted— that she couldn't even revive a measly, dinky little faire? There was no way he would entrust her with Foxwood. Not when she didn't even trust herself.

All of her ideas, all of the changes she'd made, all of the things she'd sworn would succeed had failed. The staff had tried to warn her—Matthew, even—but had she listened? No. She'd bulldozed her way forward in true Knox fashion and willfully ignored every word of concern, all the while naively believing that she knew what she was doing.

How could she *not* know? She was supposed to be good at consulting, good at figuring out problems and solving them. She'd helped every other business until now. How had she failed at *this*?

She squeezed her eyes closed, pressing a hand to her brow that pulsed with a fresh headache.

Matthew had been right all along, and it killed her to admit it. Just as it killed her to imagine his all-knowing eyes silently, accurately judging her. He would have his way now. She would be headed back to the States soon enough, just as he'd predicted, just like he'd always wanted.

Back to the States. Back to *Dad*.

Her stomach churned as she groaned audibly. He'd vouched

for her to Mr. Wintour. What would Dad say when he found out she'd embarrassed him again?

"When are you going to change, Winnie? When are you ever going to learn?"

Her shoulders sunk low, her soul even lower. She didn't have what it took to be a part of the Knox family—and she'd just proven it again.

At the end of the day, when the festival had been cleaned up and everyone had gone home, Winnie quietly slipped into the house.

After her moment of panic behind the tents, she'd pulled on her big girl pants and faced the rest of the event with quiet dignity, just as she faced her future now.

What that future held, she didn't know. What she did know was that she was finished at Foxwood.

She opened the door to the estate—up, then down—and stepped foot in the entryway, not surprised to see Mr. Wintour standing at the top of the stairs, cane in hand.

Her heart thudded hollowly in her ears. "Mr. Wintour," she greeted, closing the door behind her.

He gave her a warm smile. "Do you have a minute? Just a quick chat in my study."

A quick chat. Firings never took long. "Of course."

He nodded, leading the way as Winnie joined him, feeling as if she were being led to the gallows. It wasn't too far from the truth. Her life at Foxwood was ending. If that wasn't enough of a punishment, Dad would be sure to add more.

Maybe she just wouldn't return to the States. Maybe she'd change her phone number, her name, her identity. She'd become

Winnie...Winnie Smith. That had a nice ring to it. Perfectly normal, perfectly average, Winnie Smith.

But of course, Dad had his fingers gripped too tightly around her to ever run away from the Knox name.

They reached Mr. Wintour's study in a matter of minutes, that same warm room she'd been in over and over again for the last three weeks now holding a different feel to it—one of sorrow and of goodbyes.

They moved to their usual seats by the fire, and she sat before him, blinking repeatedly as she averted her gaze.

"So..." Mr. Wintour began.

Winnie tried to keep her mouth closed, tried to listen to his words, but she couldn't handle it.

"I know," she said, beating him to the punch. "You don't have to say anything. I'll pack my bags and be out of here before the end of the night."

Mr. Wintour didn't respond for a moment, a soft expression touching his features. He was probably grateful that she'd fired herself so he could avoid getting his fingers dirty.

"While I appreciate your determination," he began, "I do need to say, that's not why I brought you in here."

She paused. "It isn't?"

"No. I merely wished to see how you were doing. You may be used to criticism in your line of work, but that feedback was a lot to take in, even for myself."

Winnie didn't know what to say. Why was he being so *nice*? She'd wasted his money, his time, his resources. She didn't deserve his understanding. She deserved to get the boot.

"I'm just sorry I couldn't live up to your expectations," she said, unable to say anything else.

Mr. Wintour frowned. She didn't see that expression often from him. Matthew, on the other hand...

His blue eyes flashed in her mind. What did he think of her failure? Was he hosting a victory dance party in the assembly hall for finally getting rid of the wicked witch of the wild, wild west?

"Now why would you think that you didn't live up to my expectations?" Mr. Wintour asked, still frowning. "You've *exceeded* my expectations."

Winnie gave a mirthless laugh. "Thank you for being so nice, but I know that isn't possible."

"It is possible," he defended. "You made more money, grew more interest, brought in more people than I ever could have hoped. Just because there were a few hiccups along the way—many of them beyond your control, by the way—doesn't mean you were a disappointment in the slightest. I'm sure the next festival will be even more of a success."

Winnie wasn't sure she was hearing him correctly. The next festival?

He leaned forward, his wince barely noticeable. "I know the plan was to have you switch to overseeing the estate. But seeing how disappointed you are has me wanting to give you a second chance with the event."

She stared. Was he serious? Was he actually giving her another opportunity to prove herself?

"I can see your hesitation," he continued. "And really, if you'd like to leave behind the festival altogether so we can focus on the estate instead, I'll gladly accept that. After all, Foxwood was the original agreement we had. But if you have any desire whatsoever to see the festival through to its success—to work with it over the next few weeks and try again—I would love to see you do so."

Winnie couldn't say a word. She could hardly formulate a thought. He wanted her to try again. He still had faith that she could do it. But, how?

"Winnie?" he asked as she remained silent.

"I'm sorry, I just don't understand," she said, still reeling. "I've used so much of your money. Who's to say I won't fail again and waste more?"

And who was to say that Matthew wouldn't have a stomach ulcer if she chose to stay? She didn't know if she had the mental fortitude to battle with him any longer.

"You know," Mr. Wintour began, tipping his head to the side, "I didn't have to spend much time with your dad to find out how driven he is. He expects nothing short of perfection from himself and everyone around him. He doesn't need second chances because he succeeds the first time—always."

Winnie listened to his words, a growing pressure on her chest. Was this supposed to make her feel better? She knew how Dad was. She also knew how she could never live up to his standards.

"I can see that same drive in you, Winnie," Mr. Wintour said, "and also that same pressure to perform perfectly the first time. But you'll find that in the Wintour household, we don't believe in succeeding the first time. We allow failure and mistakes. We give second chances, third chances. Even hundredth chances, so long as the person is willing and able to keep trying."

She looked up at him, humility blanketing her soul.

"So my question for you, Winnie, is this. Would you like to have another go at it?"

Winnie didn't know what to say. She'd never been treated more like a human being than with the man seated before her. But his confidence in her was too great—especially when she'd done nothing to earn it.

"We can still hold the event in two weeks which should be enough time to prepare," he suggested when she remained silent. "And I can be more or less involved. Whatever will help you out the most."

Winnie shook her head, guilt rendering her nearly speechless. She didn't deserve to work for someone so generous.

"I really am so grateful for your offer, Mr. Wintour. But I don't know if I'm up to doing it again."

"I understand. But may I ask you to take the rest of the weekend to decide? Come Monday, you can either leave Foxwood, help with the estate, or have another go at the festival. Whatever you choose, I will be happy to accept your decision."

Winnie had been lulled into a false sense of security again with his kindness and talks of second chances. But she couldn't handle the fact that she'd done something she'd never done while being a consultant. She'd failed. She was used to not succeeding in every other aspect of her life. Why did she have to suffer in this job now, too?

"So, what do you say?" he asked, his tone hopeful.

But Winnie had already closed off her feelings.

Be like Fort Knox.

"I'll take until Monday, if that's okay?" she responded, then she stood, signaling her desire to end the conversation.

She couldn't remain there any longer. She had too much to hide and too much to feel.

As they made their way to the door, Mr. Wintour continued, his eyes still soft.

"Keep your chin up," he said with another encouraging smile. "Perfection is nice to strive for in theory, but all it really does is cause us disappointment. Humans weren't born to thrive on such feelings, no matter what the world tells us." They stopped at the door, and he leaned forward, his voice barely above a whisper. "Or no matter what our fathers tell us."

The understanding in his tone, the words he spoke, struck a chord within Winnie's heart, strumming it with such care and compassion, tears sprang to her eyes.

She looked away, embarrassed by her emotion. "Thanks, Mr. Wintour. I'll keep that in mind."

He pulled in his lips and gave a single nod just as she started down the hallway.

Now Winnie could only pray that, come morning, Mr. Wintour would show her the same forgiveness he'd shown her today because she wasn't going to wait until Monday to make her choice. She'd already decided that Winnie-Freakin'-Knox would be leaving England tomorrow. For good.

CHAPTER TWENTY-FOUR

MATTHEW WATCHED FROM AROUND THE CORNER AS Winnie slumped down the corridor, stopping a distance away from Dad's study and slipping off her heels one-by-one. He had never seen her without them before, nor had he seen her shoulders so low.

It was his fault. All of it.

When it was clear to everyone that the festival had not been as monumental a success as Winnie had hoped, she'd still held that typical Winnie Knox confidence in front of them. Now it was clear how she really felt.

Instead of the satisfaction he'd hoped to enjoy at her dejection, guilt swirled in Matthew's chest. She shouldn't feel disappointment at all, really. Even with the small hiccups that had occurred, she'd quadrupled attendance and brought in more joy and laughter than he'd seen on the guests' faces in years. All of this was due to her courage to try new ideas, advertise in new places, and make big changes—all of which he'd been unable to do himself.

He could only imagine what she might've been able to accomplish with Matthew actually *trying* to help. But it was too late for that. And now? Now it was time to eat crow, his least favorite

216

meal ever. He only prayed he'd be able to stomach Dad's look of disappointment, too.

With a sigh, he moved to the study and gave a gentle knock. "It's me."

"Come in, son."

Matthew did as he was told, entering the study to find Dad sitting on his chair, staring into the fire with a book on his lap—open, though unread.

Matthew sat across from him. "I need to speak with you about something."

"What is it?"

Matthew drew a breath. "Did you..."

"No. I didn't let her go. And I hope you're not here to tell me that she deserves to be."

Matthew winced. Of course Dad would assume that's why Matthew was there. He scooted forward on his seat. "Actually, I'm here for the opposite reason. To convince you to give her another chance at the festival."

Finally, Dad's eyes shifted toward him, his brow raised in surprise. "Is that so?"

Matthew nodded.

"And why is that?"

"Because she's not to blame for the feedback the event received. I am."

Dad stared, clearly waiting for him to continue.

"I didn't help her when I should have," Matthew said. "I did once, but after that, I made the conscious decision to allow her to do what she wished because I knew her changes wouldn't be responded to well. I wanted her to fail so she would leave earlier, then I could have control over my event again." He lowered his eyes with a self-disgracing shake of his head. "I know I shouldn't have, and I regret it now, especially seeing what she was able to accomplish even with my scheming. But you have to give her a second chance. Let her prove to you what she's capable of doing, and I'm sure this time, she'll fully succeed."

He'd hoped to experience relief at the end of his speech, but he only felt worse. How could he have acted like such a child? No, he hadn't done anything truly dastardly, but his was a sin of omission—doing nothing when he should have done *something*.

"Well," Dad breathed out. "I have to say, I wasn't expecting you to admit what you did. Though, I had suspected you of the behavior from the start." He raised a brow. "You went along far too willingly with her plans. Even she noticed."

Matthew looked away. And here he was, thinking he'd been so clever. At least Dad didn't look utterly gutted.

"So," Dad continued, "you'll be glad to know that I have already offered her another chance with the festival."

Matthew's eyes darted up. "You have?"

He nodded.

"Well, that's great, then," Matthew said. So he *hadn't* needed to go into full-blown confession mode after all.

Dad stared back at the fire. "I gave her the weekend to think on it. Though, I will say, I'm fairly certain she'll choose not to. Unless…"

Matthew waited. "Unless, what?"

Dad's eyes fell on him, and suddenly, Matthew understood.

"Unless *I* help her," he finished.

"More than that," Dad said. "I want you to convince her to stay, then I want the both of you to work together. Not one over the other, and not in competition. Side-by-side. As a team."

Matthew stared. "Honestly, Dad, I don't know if that's possible."

"On your part or hers?"

"Both? Neither of us responds well to criticism, and neither of us knows how to tactfully share our opinions. Put those together in a high-pressure situation, and we've no hope of success."

"Rubbish," Dad huffed. "All I'm hearing from your lips is the fear of what might happen."

"Fear based off of reality," Matthew defended.

Dad sighed, closing his still-unread book and placing it on the small table beside him. "Well, the way I see it is this, you either work harder together or fail greater apart. One will result in a festival that lasts many years to come, and the other, well, I'm sure you can guess the outcome."

Matthew didn't have to guess. He knew. But still, working with Winnie? How was such a thing even possible? They'd tried and failed a number of times. The same would happen again, wouldn't it?

Unless, of course, he lowered his pride and accepted the fact that she knew business better than he did. Of course, she'd have to lower her pride and admit that he knew the *festival* better than she did.

Blowing out a slow breath, he nodded. "Fine. I'll try—*actually* this time."

Dad smiled, clearly pleased with his decision. "Then I suggest you begin this evening. I don't expect her to last through the night."

Matthew's brow rose. "I thought you gave her the weekend to make her decision."

"I did. I also gave her the option of continuing with the festival or moving on to helping Foxwood. But you need to understand something, Matthew." Dad stopped, hesitating. He looked to the closed door, then lowered his voice. "I only tell you this in the strictest of confidences."

Matthew leaned forward. What was going on? Dad never spoke like this.

"It's about Winnie's family," he began. "Or rather, her father. I've always respected his intelligence and success, but over the years, our relationship has weakened due to distance, yes, but also difference of opinion. Namely, how we view the outside world— and how we treat others."

He paused, staring at the floor with a distant look before continuing. "He also puts too much pressure on his children. When I spoke with him on the phone a few months ago, he had no difficulty touting their many accomplishments, but when he got to Winnie, it was made clear that she hasn't impressed her dad like her siblings have. Surely you've seen the self-doubt she suffers with, hidden by false confidence created by a father who expects too much of his children."

Matthew grimaced, rubbing his chest as his heart pinched. His mind flew over the last few weeks with Winnie, their interactions, her behavior, the insecurity in her eyes all falling into place like pieces of a jigsaw. How could he have been so blind?

"I brought her here with the genuine hope of having her help us," Dad continued. "But now, I wonder if we cannot help her in return."

Matthew stared into the fire, hoping the lapping flames would distract him enough from the guilt pressing on his mind. If only he'd known. If only he'd been a little more patient. A little more kind. But he shook his head.

To live in a world of *if-onlys* never brought peace. But changing his present to alter his future *would*.

"I'll do my best to help her," he said humbly, "and to convince her to stay."

"Thank you, son," Dad said. "I'm sure your words hold much more weight than mine do when it comes to Winnie."

Matthew didn't bother to ask Dad why. Instead, he stood, said goodnight, then headed down the same hallway Winnie had.

He wished he could go to bed right now, but he had one more stop to make on this apology train, and it was the worst one yet. He drew a deep breath.

Let's get this over with.

MATTHEW FOUND Winnie's room with the door

unsurprisingly shut. He hesitated a moment as he raised a hand to knock, rustling coming from within her room.

Was this really what he wanted to do, try to convince Winnie to stay? There was no going back if he did. He'd have to deal with any disagreements or arguments that came up. More than that, he'd have to try to *solve* those disagreements and arguments.

But when Dad's words about Winnie's situation drifted into his mind, and the image of her slumping down the hallway, shoeless and shoulders low, filtered in next, he settled firmly on his decision.

Yes, this was exactly what he wanted to do.

He knocked. The rustling silenced inside her room, but there was no response.

Matthew wouldn't accept that. He knocked again.

A few seconds later, she answered. "Who is it?"

Her voice sounded harried, as if she'd just been interrupted doing something important. He had an inkling as to what exactly that was.

"It's Matthew," he responded.

Silence met him again. No rustling, no response.

"I just wanted to talk for a minute," he continued, hoping his soft tone would convince her to open the door. "Preferably face-to-face, if you're willing."

Another few seconds passed by in silence, then footsteps sounded, and she finally opened the door.

Matthew stood frozen to his spot as he took in the sight of her. From the moment he'd seen Winnie in that Aston Martin, she'd been so put-together. Even when she'd been wet from the rain, she'd been pristine—her clothing, her bun, her makeup.

And now? Now, her dark, silky hair fell down past her shoulders in crooked waves from the bun she perpetually wore, and her skirt and shirt had been replaced with gray sweats and an oversized sweater with a large, red "U" on it. Her eyes no longer wore makeup, and the whites held a tint of red, hinting at the tears that had been shed that evening before he'd arrived.

She looked positively in disarray.

She looked positively...irresistible.

"Yes?"

Her words brought him back to the present. Clearing his throat, he looked away. "I just...wanted to see how you're doing."

"I think you can tell how I'm doing." She waved a hand in front of herself.

That didn't do Matthew any favors, as he just took to staring again. What was the matter with him? It must be the shock of seeing her in such a different light. Physically and figuratively. She just looked so perfectly approachable. He supposed that was better than how she normally looked—so perfectly unattainable.

His eyes shifted to behind her, and he caught sight of her suitcase half-filled on her bed. "You're packing already?"

She glanced over her shoulder. "Your dad gave me the weekend to decide if I wanted to stay, either to work at Foxwood or with the festival again. But I figured I may as well get out of everyone's hair and leave without doing either."

Matthew didn't know where to begin.

"So, why are you really here?" she asked, walking back into her room, though she left the door ajar.

Was she inviting him in, or just not pushing him out? To be safe, he remained hovering in the doorway. Her room was clean and tidy, her bed made, and curtains drawn neatly. Even her gathered belongings that she was clearly in the process of packing were spread out in an orderly row.

"Are you here to gloat?" Winnie asked, her back to him as she piled a stack of pristinely folded clothing into her suitcase.

"No," he said with a frown.

"To make fun of me for failing?" she tried next.

"Of course not."

"To convince me to leave tonight instead of tomorrow morning?"

He sighed, but more due to the fact that these questions were completely and entirely warranted. He'd been an absolute rat to her.

"Actually, I'm here to convince you to do the exact opposite," he said.

He'd expected her to turn around in a sort of pleasant surprise, but she merely scoffed, still turned away from him.

"It's true," he pressed.

"I'm guessing your dad pressured you into doing this."

Matthew hesitated. He needed to say this next part delicately, but truthfully. Was he capable of doing both at the same time?

"I did talk with him just a minute ago," he began, "and he did tell me to come down tonight, but I had every intention of speaking with you before you left."

She placed another stack of clothing into the suitcase. "Well, you should probably get on with that, since I'll be leaving tomorrow morning."

Matthew thought for a moment. He knew Winnie more than he cared to admit, just as he knew simply asking her to stay wasn't going to work. He'd have to try another route.

"Wow," he said, folding his arms and leaning against the door frame.

Finally, she turned around to face him, her brow furrowed. "What?"

"I didn't peg you for a quitter."

A spark of pride flared in her eyes, reminding him of the Winnie he was so accustomed to seeing, but in a flash, she was gone. Her shoulders fell again, and she moved to the wardrobe at the edge of the room.

"I know what you're trying to do, but it won't work," she said.

"And what exactly am I trying to do?"

She gave him a sidelong glance. "You're trying to make yourself feel better by convincing me to stay so you can be guilt-free when I *do* leave."

Matthew blinked, trying to hide his surprise. She was more

astute than he'd given her credit for. "That's not entirely true," he said.

"Only mostly," she added.

"Well, I would like to be guilt-free if you choose to leave, but I don't think that's in the cards for me."

"And why is that?"

He drew a deep breath. "Because I *should* feel guilty."

She faced him, her features sharp—yet still just as appealing.

"I'll be honest," he continued, "I was more than ready to see you riding off into the sunset a few days ago."

"What made you change your mind?" she asked disbelievingly. She folded her own arms and turned to face him more directly. "Daddy scold you again?"

His defenses flared. He didn't need to deal with this. He could say goodbye to the woman forever and do the festival on his own.

"Surely you've seen the self-doubt she suffers with, hidden by false confidence created by a father who expects too much of his children."

Dad's words made him pause. Reminding himself of what he'd learned about her, Matthew looked to Winnie again. All at once, he *could* see that self-doubt in her eyes, and his heart softened.

"I scolded myself enough for the both of us," Matthew replied.

Her eyes narrowed, but she turned away to pull a few more items from the wardrobe. "And why would you need to do that?" she asked, sarcasm in her tone.

"I think you know that already," he said. "I haven't been exactly helpful."

"No, really?"

Again with the sarcasm.

"Would you like to hear what I have to say, or do you want me to leave?" he asked.

Winnie shrugged. "Do whatever you'd like. Either way, it's not going to change my mind about leaving."

Once more, Matthew's pride knocked at his door, but he refused to answer. It was time to start behaving like an adult. "All right, I'll talk, then. First off, I think you did a..." He paused. This compliment would come out if it killed him. "A fine job with the festival."

She looked over at him. "Wow, don't strain yourself with the praise."

"I'm British, what did you expect?"

For the first time that evening, a ghost of a smile haunted her lips, but it was gone in an instant.

Still, it was progress.

"Really, though," he said, "it pains me to admit it, but you brought more people in today than we've had in years. And a lot of your changes improved the festival as a whole."

She narrowed her eyes, a wary look crossing her features. "But?"

"But," he repeated, "I think you've seen now that some of the changes weren't responded well to, and I'd like to apologize for that."

Her brow twitched. "Apologize for my own poor judgment?"

"No, apologize for not explaining to you more why those changes—the rides and the scripted tournament—wouldn't work." He unfolded his arms and tucked his hands in his pockets. "I knew they wouldn't, and still, I kept my mouth shut because I'd hoped it would drive you out faster."

Her eyes reflected the hurt he'd hoped not to see. "Well, you got your wish," she said, flopping her arms out, then back to her sides in a retreating gesture.

He blew out a sniff from his nose. "If only it *had* worked. My poor attempt at sabotage only sabotaged myself. Had I been honest from the start, explained to you the reasoning behind my hesitance, the event would have been more of a success because I..." He paused, waiting until she met his gaze. "I have no doubt that with your abilities, and my support, you could pull off the best festival we've ever had."

She watched him for a moment, as if to see if he was joking or not, so he kept his gaze on her, praying she'd see the truth in his eyes. Finally, she looked away, but not before he noted her softening expression.

"*That* wasn't very British of you," she said.

He smiled. "What can I say? I'm growing as a person."

Their eyes met, and a level of understanding passed between them before she looked away, staring at her suitcase as her expression slowly fell.

"I appreciate you coming down here," she said, "but I don't know if I can do this again."

"You can," he said. "With my help, you absolutely can."

"So, what, you're suggesting that we work together?"

"That's exactly what I'm suggesting."

She scoffed. "You're crazy."

"We'd both be mental if we go along with this plan," he agreed. "The two of us working together, can you imagine?"

She eyed him curiously as he continued.

"And yet," he said, "it might be so crazy that it works."

He could see the cogs churning in her mind. "How so?"

He took a step forward before realizing it was her room, and he most definitely had not been invited in. Standing in place, he began again. "If you continued sharing your ideas for how to improve the festival, and I listened without getting defensive, and if I shared my ideas on *your* ideas without *you* getting defensive, we wouldn't have a problem at all."

"Sounds way easier said than done," she said with a shake of her head.

"Aren't most things in life that way?"

"I guess. But the two of us would have to do a whole lot of tongue biting."

He raised his brow with a knowing look, wishing to ease the tension between them further. "I don't know if that sort of thing ought to be required, but if you insist…"

Her lips parted, a stunning blush stretching across her

features. "I didn't mean..." She trailed off when she caught sight of his teasing smile. "Yeah, we have no hope of working together."

He grinned. "We do. I promise, we do. Listen, I am unbelievably stubborn. But not so much that I can't admit that I am a terrible businessman. That's why my dad hired you instead of me." He took a step forward, gaining steam from the light now shining in the stormy depths of her eyes. "But I *do* know history, and I *do* know England. And I know how to mix the both of them to bring an immersive experience. I just don't know how to execute it. If we can help each other with our weaknesses and give only our strengths, I really do believe we could excel."

He finished, searching her features for any sign of what she felt inside, but her expression was a closed book.

So all Matthew could do was pray. Pray that Winnie would forgive him. That she would take a chance on him. And that she would show compassion for his desperately failing festival.

"So," he prompted, "what do you think?"

CHAPTER TWENTY-FIVE

WINNIE DIDN'T KNOW WHAT TO SAY. THE OFFER WAS SO generous and Matthew so complimentary, how could she respond in any other way but "yes?"

Then again, they'd tried to work alongside each other for three weeks now, and it had led from one disaster to the next. Granted, he had intentionally stopped helping her so he could get rid of her, but still. Who was to say things would be any different?

Well, Matthew was saying that, wasn't he? And he *did* seem different now. Heck, he'd even managed to lift her spirits after the crushing defeat she'd suffered with the festival. She'd been humiliated—was still now. But the sting was no longer so terrible. If she worked with him again, and if they both promised to be on their best behavior, could they really succeed?

Of course, she'd have to break the news to Dad that she was still working on the festival instead of Foxwood. That had been the exact reason she'd chosen to leave early, despite her desire to help Mr. Wintour in the way he deserved. She figured if she could find another consultant gig by herself, something prestigious in New York, Dad would forgive her failure before he became too angry.

"You're being awfully quiet," Matthew said, still standing in front of her, awaiting her response.

It was strange to have him there, tall and imposing, in a room she'd claimed as her own for nearly a month. In reality, no part of the room belonged to her, nor did the festival.

All of it, everything belonged to the Wintours.

"I'm just thinking," she said.

"About what?"

He was talking so softly, so differently from the sarcasm and pride she was used to hearing from him. Maybe she could do the same, lower her defenses and speak with him openly, as he had spoken with her. After all, what pride did she have left to fortify those Knox defenses that were supposed to be impenetrable?

Taking a deep breath, she began, voicing her concerns. "You said so yourself I don't know anything about faires or festivals. I just think we'd all be better off if I just went back to the other consulting jobs in the States, where I'm encouraged to be cutthroat."

Matthew tipped his head to the side, a spare curl falling against his temple. "Is that what you enjoy?"

"Does anyone enjoy destroying people's hopes and dreams?" she asked with a raised eyebrow.

"I'm sure some people do."

She sighed, flopping down on her bed, a mere section of it uncovered by her belongings—belongings she'd been so intent on packing away. Now she didn't know what to do with them.

"Well, *I* don't," she said, "contrary to everyone's beliefs."

"I didn't think you did," he said.

She gave him a dubious look.

"Not anymore," he added with an irresistibly sheepish grin. "Anyway, it doesn't matter what people think of you. What matters is what you think of yourself. Where do your values lie? Who is the person you want to be? That sort of thing."

Winnie listened to him as if he was speaking a foreign language. He might as well have been, what with how little she understood him. What did it matter what people thought of her? Who did she want to be? He couldn't have asked her more difficult questions.

"And if I don't know the answer to either?" she asked.

He merely shrugged. "Just keep moving forward until you do."

Keep moving forward. Figure out the person she wanted to be. Don't let Dad's opinion muddy the water. What a life she would lead if she could tackle that fear.

Good grief, was she really taking life advice from *Matthew* now?

"So," he pressed, "what do you say?"

"To what?" she asked, half-teasing. "You've said a lot."

"To working together," he said patiently. "To staying and helping me with the festival."

She looked away, still grappling with her fears. As nice as it was to imagine being able to stand up to Dad and one day become the woman she wanted to be, it was just a pipe dream.

"Aren't you the least bit curious to see what could come of us working together?" Matthew asked next, giving her a look of intrigue. "We really could put on one amazing event."

Winnie must have been utterly exhausted, for her mind actually started to linger on Matthew's words. What if she put her heart and soul into this event—her true heart and soul—just as Matthew did, just as Mr. Wintour had asked her to? What would happen *then*?

"I don't know," she said, still hesitant. "I just don't think it's possible for us to work and not fight with each other."

"Oh, I'm sure we'll still fight," he said. "We have to keep our lives interesting, after all. But I think you'll find me to be quite the agreeable gentleman when I'm not trying to sabotage innocent individuals."

He gave a harmless smile, and she fought off a laugh. He was too adorable. Who would have ever thought—Matthew Wintour, adorable?

"Soooo..." he said, dragging out the word expectantly.

The hope in his eyes almost made her give in instantly. He really did want her to stay, didn't he? She could hardly believe it.

Honestly, she wanted to stay, to follow through with the festival and do what she'd promised. But Matthew was becoming an even larger driving force in her desire to remain. She wanted to see what would become of the two of them actually working side-by-side. To see if they really could succeed together.

"Okay," she said slowly, her pride dropping to her feet as quietly as the start of a gentle rainfall, drip by drip. "I have to admit, I...I do want to see this through."

His eyes brightened, but she rushed on, knowing there was still much to consider. "I just don't know where to start. I don't know festivals, I don't know the audience. Heck, I don't even know England."

He studied her for a minute, then a slow smile spread across his lips, as bright as the sun rising over the hills and spreading its light directly on her features. "I might have just the thing to help with that. Once you know England, all the pieces will fall into place."

She eyed him suspiciously. He looked far too excited for his own good. "What are we going to do, then?"

"You'll just have to wait and see," he said enigmatically. "Only be prepared for a very busy, very English holiday."

"A holiday?" she asked.

Intrigue poured over the last of the trepidation simmering in her belly.

"Yes. Just give me a day to work through a few details."

"Okay," she said in a daze.

He smiled broadly, taking a few steps out of her room before turning back toward her. He pressed his hands against both sides of the doorframe, the ridges in his forearm shifting. "And pack an overnight bag, warm clothing, and shoes to walk in. We leave Monday at seven o'clock sharp. Will that suffice, Miss Knox?"

Winnie's mind spun with the information. Overnight bag, strong shifting forearms, warm clothing. *A holiday with Matthew.*

"I guess," she said. She wasn't leaving England quite yet, then. "But I don't even know where you're taking me or who's going."

"We'll be alone," he said with a sure nod. "As for everything else, just leave it to me."

"All right," she mumbled.

"Monday. Seven o'clock sharp," he repeated. "Do you need to set an alarm?"

She rolled her eyes. "I'm a big girl. I think I can handle being on time." Then another thought occurred. "Wait, what about hotels and food and stuff?"

He tapped excitedly against the doorframe with his fingertips. "I'm a big boy. I think I can handle it." Once again, his eyes twinkled. "I'll see you Monday. Seven o'clock."

He backed away, leaving her door open as she called after him. "So eight, is it?"

His laughter echoed down the hallway.

When he was gone, Winnie closed her door, shaking her head in utter shock. She'd just agreed to spend time alone with a guy who hadn't liked her for the last three weeks.

She pressed a hand to her brow, staring at the piles of clothing and toiletries on her bed and in her suitcase.

Well, she'd better get started unpacking right now because apparently, she had something else to pack for entirely.

CHAPTER TWENTY-SIX

"Is that what you're wearing?"

Winnie paused in the doorway of Foxwood, looking down at Matthew, who leaned against his horrible beater-of-a-car that was pulled in front of the estate. It was Monday, two minutes until seven o'clock in the morning, and Winnie had just appeared before Matthew for their...their what, exactly? Matthew had called it a holiday. She thought it was better to call it a business trip.

That was the safest option.

Whatever it was, she wasn't sure she was ready for it, especially when she caught sight of Matthew in his tall boots, thick blue raincoat, and jeans. She thought he looked rather perfect.

But apparently, he took issue with how *she* looked.

"What do you mean?" she asked, peering down at her heels, skirt, and shirt.

She had to look way better than she had in her sweats Saturday evening, despite the fact that she hadn't slept last night due to nightmares. She'd dreamt that she'd shared her failures with her family during their Sunday chat, despite the fact that she hadn't attended their virtual call the day before.

She hadn't been able to stomach it.

Matthew motioned to her person, drawing her attention to the present. "I said to wear warm clothing and shoes to walk in."

She frowned, moving toward him and his car, her small carry-on bouncing against her leg. "I'm warm enough with the raincoat, and I *can* walk in these shoes. See?"

She stepped closer to him, but he shook his head, pushing away from the car and motioning to her heels again. "Those will not work for what we're doing today. First off, you absolutely need to wear trousers, and don't you have any wellies?"

"Wellies?" she asked, pulling up her lip. "I don't even know what those are."

"Wellies," he repeated, as if that would help her. "Wellingtons. Rain boots?"

Oh. She looked over her shoulder at the closed door of the estate. "I have some boots—"

"Not high-heeled," he said with a knowing lift of his brow.

She shrugged. "Well, I guess we'll just have to cancel, then, 'cause I don't have anything else."

"You don't even have any trousers?"

"Of course I do. They just..." She hesitated. "They don't speak 'professional,' do they?"

"Where we're going, you don't need to look professional." He reached up, taking her suitcase from her. "At least for today's activities."

Their fingers brushed against each other, and their eyes met, but Winnie looked swiftly away, ignoring the way her heart leapt. This was a business trip, after all. A business trip with a business associate. Nothing more.

Matthew placed her small suitcase in the trunk of his car, then closed the door with a loud creak. "We're going for function over fashion," he continued, eying her heels. "What shoe size are you?"

She eyed him. "Eight."

"US eight," he mumbled, pulling out his phone and typing onto the screen. "All right, you're a UK seven." He swiped up, then typed out more. "I might have a solution for you. Just change into something that's more practical, and I'll meet you back here in five."

He disappeared inside Foxwood without another word, and Winnie stared after him in surprise. If she'd had a leg to stand on, she would've protested. She did everything in a skirt and heels, and she'd never had any problem with it up to this point.

But Matthew was doing her a favor by taking her around. Heck, he was the only reason she was still in England at this point. So the least she could do was take his advice when it came to what she ought to wear.

In less than five minutes, Winnie had changed into her jeans —she'd forgotten how much warmer they were than skirts— pulled on a cozy sweater beneath her raincoat, smoothed back her hair in its bun, and returned outside to meet with Matthew again. She had slipped on her high-heeled boots, despite his protests, and smiled when she saw him once again waiting for her against his car.

"See?" she began. "These will do...just...fine..."

Her words faded as she noticed what was in Matthew's hands. Before her were the loudest, gaudiest, most rubber boots she'd ever seen in her life.

"What are those?" she asked.

"Wellies," he said, raising them higher, as if she couldn't see the hot pink of the boots well enough already.

Vivid orange and yellow flowers speckled in a continuous pattern across the pink footwear, and Winnie winced as if the brightness of it was blinding her.

"Your old schoolboy boots, I assume?" she asked.

He smirked at her joke. "Here." He shoved them toward her as she reached the car. "They're Char's. She told me these should fit you just fine."

Winnie still stared, unwilling—unable—to accept them.

He wiggled them at her again. "Come on, they'll keep you warm and dry all day long."

With the skies fully overcast that morning, Winnie didn't

mind the sound of keeping dry. But she'd given up so much of her pride over the last forty-eight hours, she had to keep at least a sprinkling of it.

"Um, thank her for me, will you?" Winnie asked. "But I think I'll take my chances in these."

He stared down at the high-heeled boots now covering her feet. "You'll sink into the mud and grass faster than you can say 'ridiculous,'" he stated.

"They'll be fine."

He shrugged. "Mark my words. You'll want the wellies before long."

He obviously didn't know the extent of Winnie's pride.

Opening the trunk of his Mini Cooper again, he tossed the boots inside, and only then did Winnie register what he was doing.

"Wait, why are we taking your car when we have my much nicer rental?" She motioned to the glistening green of the Aston Martin.

It's not that she really wanted to take the sports car, but it seemed much safer than his beater.

"Because I'm the one leading the tour," he responded. "If I was on your insurance for the emerald steed, perhaps I'd consider taking it, but alas."

He closed the trunk—or boot, she supposed—and went around to her side again.

"*I* could just drive, then," she said, eying the rusted red paint and the crack of his side, back window. "You can give me directions, or I could follow the GPS."

Matthew raised his brow in disbelief. "And have you swerve off the road again into a pile of mud? I don't think so." He turned back to the car he nearly towered over and patted the hood with affection. "No, we'll be taking Minnie here."

Winnie looked at the car back and forth. "Are you sure it can still drive?"

236

He hardly looked pleased with the comment, then his previous words finally sunk in.

"Wait," she began, "did you say Minnie, M-I-N-N-I-E, or mini, as in, M-I-N-I?"

He stared. "Minnie, as in, her name, Minnie. I-E."

Winnie had never heard of anything so adorable. She'd known of others naming their cars, but a man naming his *Minnie*? She could hardly stand it.

"You think that's funny?" he asked.

"Not at all. A car like this certainly deserves the name."

"She does," he defended. "She's been in the family almost as long as Char has."

"And likely your great-grandparents, too."

"All right," Matthew said, shaking his head and opening the door. "You either get in and stop making fun of her or you can take the tour of Yorkshire by yourself."

She smiled to herself. It felt good to tease someone, to feel some semblance of normalcy after the weekend she'd had.

"Come on, then," he said, waving her forward. "Let's not wait for the sun to shine."

Winnie paused. She hadn't realized he was on the passenger side until that moment. It had been a long time since someone had opened a car door for her. Her high school date to the prom, maybe? She usually walked to her dates in New York, and...

The thought made her pause. Date? This was no date.

"I can get it myself, you know," she said.

"Oh, I'm sure you can," he responded. "But Minnie's very particular about who touches her."

Winnie gave him a look. "Seriously?"

"No. But her door handle is hanging on by a thread, and it doesn't work unless it's handled with finesse, so I'm going to have to do this each time."

Winnie smiled, amused. "What is it with you guys and doors?"

With a sigh, she relented, slipping in and easing herself into the low seat with a mumbled, "Thanks."

Matthew closed the door behind her and walked around the car as she took a look around her. It was clean, she'd give him that, even if it was the smallest car she'd ever seen.

The door handle from the inside was rusted, as was the crank-down window lever. Now his gesture of rolling down the window on her first day made sense.

She adjusted her legs in the small space she was allotted just as Matthew slid into the driver's side.

"Ready?" he asked, buckling before hooking his phone onto the dashboard stand.

"If you're meaning to ask me if I'm ready to ride around this car like I'm Fred Flintstone because I'm so close to the ground, then sure. I'm absolutely ready."

He shook his head again, but the twinkle in his eyes was undeniable.

Winnie buckled up, then Matthew made to start the car, but it merely sputtered in response.

He tried again, and again, but there was no start. "Come on, Minnie," he muttered. "Not again."

Winnie watched in silence for a minute. This did not bode well for the rest of their trip. "Maybe you should call her Grannie instead," she said.

"Hush. She just takes a bit of warming up, that's all." He stroked his fingers down the steering wheel. "Come on, girl. We've got a busy two days ahead of us."

"Do you think maybe—"

"I'll have no more cheek from you, Miss Knox," Matthew said, turning to look at her with a stern look.

She clamped her mouth shut at his feigned scolding as a smile begged to be let out on her lips.

Matthew tried once again to start the car, and this time, it roared to life. Well, perhaps *roared* was the wrong word. Minnie coughed and sputtered more to life than roared.

"There, you see?" he asked with a triumphant look in Winnie's direction.

"Oh, yes. Super reliable, this one," she said.

He didn't respond, merely turned the radio on and put the car into gear before easing across the drive.

With no stalling car or broken handle to focus on, Winnie's mind finally settled on the man beside her. For the first time in their professional relationship, they were alone. Like, alone, alone. Before, there was always the chance of someone happening upon them—someone from the festival staff or household staff, or one of Matthew's family members.

But now, in the car, they were officially by themselves, and for some reason, the thought made her uncomfortable. There was no out now. No escape. No chance of running away if things got awkward or uncomfortable. This was it. An entire overnight excursion with a man whom she could barely handle—a man who could barely handle her.

A man by whom she was sitting far too closely.

She had to hold both hands on her lap, tucking in her elbows to avoid touching him, especially with him adjusting the gear shift so often. One swift turn, and she was sure she'd lean right into him and his distracting, muscular arm.

"Comfortable?" Matthew asked, shifting the gears again as they made it off the gravel and headed along the windy road out of the estate.

"I mean, I'd be more comfortable in the Aston Martin..."

He shook his head. "Trust me. One day with Minnie, and you'll rue the day you have to get back inside that sports car."

"I think the fumes from old Minnie here have gotten to your head," she returned.

To her surprise, he cracked a smile. The car clanked loudly as he shifted gears again. "She needs a new transmission. Don't judge her for it."

Winnie glanced to his hand that rested on the gear stick so near her leg. The tendons across the back of his hand shifted as he controlled the speed at which they traveled, his fingers, long and capable, curving around the top of the handle.

What was it about a man driving a manual car that was so attractive? Even in Minnie here, she had to admit Matthew looked good.

They drove in silence, "Golden Years" by David Bowie playing on the crackling stereo before a loud buzzing occurred beneath Winnie. She paused, unsure of what the vibration was until she remembered that she'd slipped her phone into her back pocket. She so rarely wore jeans, she wasn't accustomed to the sound or feel of it.

She leaned toward the door and pulled out her phone, careful to avoid any touch to Matthew as she looked at the screen.

Dad's name lit brightly across the front of it.

Instantly, her stomach churned. She'd been doing so well focusing on the present, laughing and enjoying her time with Matthew, and now, she was back to where she'd started.

Dad had called her for their Sunday chat yesterday, but Winnie just hadn't been able to get herself to answer it, just like right now. She couldn't deal with the disappointment in his voice, the scolding she would inevitably receive like she was a child.

She had to focus on the task at hand, on really improving the festival and no longer wasting Mr. Wintour's money. If she spoke with Dad, her thoughts would muddle, her insides would knot, and any instinct she might still possess would most assuredly vanish.

And more than anything? She just didn't want to talk to him. Period.

Without a word, she pressed the side button of her phone to stop the buzzing, then slipped it back into her pocket.

"Everything okay?" Matthew asked beside her.

"Huh?" She looked to him, once again taken aback at their proximity. "Oh, yeah. It was just my dad, but I can call him back."

Matthew paused. "Isn't it nearing midnight there?"

"I think so."

He didn't respond for a minute. "You can answer it now if you need to."

But Winnie shook her head. "No, it's okay. I'll talk to him later."

He nodded, though she could almost feel his desire to ask her why she'd silenced her own dad's call. No doubt Matthew had never done that to *his* dad before.

"So where are we headed first?" she asked, anxious to put his call behind her.

"Malham," Matthew replied. "We can grab a bite to eat there for breakfast, then head up the cove for a nice, leisurely walk."

Winnie nodded. She'd never heard of Malham before, but it sounded nice enough. "And how is this going to help us with the festival?" she asked.

"It's not."

She paused, unable to help herself from looking at him again. His profile was lined in the soft, gray light of the morning, enhancing the angle of his square jaw. "What? Then why are we even going there?"

He shifted again as they pulled out of the drive, officially on the road. Minnie ground her gears in protest. "Because I think it'll help you get out of your head."

She pulled a face. "I'm not in my head."

He scoffed, and their eyes met for a brief moment. "The very fact that you are already asking how to improve the festival and we haven't even been with each other for a quarter of an hour proves to me that you are most definitely in your head."

Winnie had been called out. Not in a rude way, by any means, but she folded her arms and stared straight ahead all the same. "Well, forgive me for trying to help your beloved festival."

A moment passed by in silence. "You're right," he said softly. "I'm sorry. I should have spoken with more care."

Winnie blinked, stunned. He'd apologized. Like, *really* apologized. "Oh, it's okay," she mumbled, unsure of how to respond. "I wasn't really offended."

"That's good because I..." He paused, beginning again. "I want this trip to be a sort of recharge for you. I really believe that if you immerse yourself in England, Yorkshire specifically, and the way we live here, you'll be able to remove the pressure more easily from off your shoulders."

Winnie chewed the inside of her lip. He wanted to take the pressure off? He wanted her to *relax*? Honestly, his words sounded like a dream. An unachievable, unattainable dream.

"If you're all right with it," he continued, "I'd like it if we kept the conversation about the festival to a minimum. Only chat about it when we absolutely have to."

She paused, biting her cheek in hesitation. "But how will we get anything done? That's a whole two days wasted."

"I've already spoken to my dad and told him what we're doing," he assured her. "There's nothing you need to do for the time being except enjoy the experiences you'll have."

Winnie hesitated. "I don't know if I'm capable of fully turning off my work brain."

"That's all right. Just do the best you can."

Winnie drew a deep breath. She wasn't sure about this, really. But then, who was she to protest? She'd already failed at her attempt to revive the festival. Maybe Matthew's idea would be just the thing to help them both get what they wanted.

Either way, she was willing to give it all a shot.

The car clunked as Matthew shifted gears again, and the tension eased from her shoulders.

"So how far is this Malham place?" she asked.

"About a quarter of an hour, give or take. Why?"

"I was just contemplating whether or not Minnie was going to last that long."

Matthew hid another smile with a shake of his head, and Winnie beamed as Minnie clanged again in protest.

CHAPTER TWENTY-SEVEN

THE DRIVE TO MALHAM WAS SHORT AND BEAUTIFUL, the thick trees that lined Foxwood's border eventually shifting from dense wood to incredible open fields of lilting, green grass, gray stone walls, and small homes that dotted the landscape.

They traveled down a supposedly two-car road that was barely big enough for even Matthew's small car to fit, then finally arrived at their first destination. He pulled into the little lot, then turned the Mini Cooper off.

"Are you sure you're going to be able to turn it back on?" Winnie asked.

"You keep carrying on that way, and she's going to throw a fit," Matthew warned.

Winnie only laughed. She reached forward then, trying to open the door, but nothing happened.

"Handle doesn't work, remember?" Matthew said.

He sent her a smile, then exited the car himself. Soon, he arrived at her side and opened the door for her.

Another memory flashed through her mind of high school and boys opening doors for her on dates, but she suppressed the thought. They were on a business trip, that was all. Despite the fact that he'd prohibited them from speaking about business at all...

She expressed her gratitude, then made to step out of the vehicle, only to freeze with her boot hovering in the air just above the muddiest ground she'd ever seen.

"Hence why I suggested the wellies," Matthew said, waiting for her to exit the car.

With what little pride she had left, Winnie pushed aside her reservations and placed both boots on the ground, pushing herself out of the low vehicle.

The heels stuck directly into the mud like needles into a pincushion, but she faced him with an easy smile. "Ready?"

He shook his head. "You're not going to make it far in those."

"Look, I've walked miles in these shoes in New York. I can handle however long it'll take to get to Malham Cove."

"I'm sure you could. But the terrain is a touch different than New York City's streets." He looked to the boots with a shake of his head. "You'll aerate half of Yorkshire with those on. Just put on the ruddy wellies."

Winnie wrestled with herself. She was supposed to be taking his advice. But...those wellies. They were hideous. She took a step forward, her heels making it far more difficult to move than she'd thought.

With a sigh, she closed her eyes. "Fine. I'll wear them."

"Finally," Matthew muttered.

He made for the trunk and pulled out the gaudy creatures, handing them to her with far-too-chipper a smile.

She mumbled another thanks, sat back down in the car, and one by one, exchanged her sleek, black, leather, high-heeled boots for the rubber, flower-covered monstrosities.

Matthew left to pay for parking, and by the time he returned, she was standing in the mud with Char's boots donned.

Matthew's amused smile didn't help. "Now *those* look good on you."

She grimaced. "I should not be seen in public like this."

"I don't know," Matthew said, placing the parking stub on the inside of the dashboard before locking up his car. "I think they fit your personality perfectly."

She glared at his smile. "Where do you even buy stuff that looks like this?"

"I think Char purchased them from a charity shop," Matthew responded.

"That checks out," she muttered.

"You ought to be grateful," he continued. "You'll be able to make it to the top of the cove. And, bonus—now I won't lose you in the crowds."

After all the comments about his car, Winnie absolutely deserved his teasing. But as she stared down at the boots, the pink, yellow, and orange contrasting harshly with her classy black raincoat and dark blue jeans, she shook her head.

"I'm sorry. I can't. I can't be seen like this."

She made to open the car to switch back to her own boots, but Matthew cut her off, wrapping his fingers around her hand, and pulling her across the lot.

"Come on, you muppet," he said with a laugh. "No one cares what they look like but you."

She would have protested, but his hand around hers had rendered her completely senseless.

As soon as they'd crossed the parking lot and tramped through the worst of the mud, he released her, but the warmth around her remained.

Fortunately, the rain boots she now wore distracted her enough from the fact that Matthew Wintour had just held her hand.

"How do you even walk in these?" she asked.

She stepped awkwardly in them, feeling as if she wore snowshoes.

Matthew looked down at her. "How long has it been since you've not worn heels?"

"Does being barefoot count?"

"No."

"Then I can't remember."

"You're kidding."

"No, seriously," she said. "I can't remember. Maybe when I was riding horses?"

"A decade ago?"

"Probably."

He shook his head. "Well, just go slower until you get the hang of it."

It took longer than she cared to admit, but eventually, Winnie was finally able to step more naturally.

"There you go," Matthew said beside her. "Now you've learned not to trudge, we'll reach the top of the cove before nightfall."

Winnie ignored his teasing, and the two of them continued down the quiet road as she took in the sights around her.

It was a gorgeous area, filled with massive, towering trees, full green leaves, and a small river that trickled gently beside the road. They crossed by a few people who nodded their heads in greeting, most of them walking small dogs who stopped to sniff at every branch, tree trunk, and spare rock on their path.

She and Matthew fell into a comfortable silence, and it continued as they reached a small café off the side of the road. They ate their breakfast—scones and hot chocolates—on the small, white tea tables set up with sunshades atop, as Winnie looked around her in amazement.

Everything was just so *quiet*. In New York, cars constantly honked, police sirens whirred, and crosswalk signals incessantly beeped. If people spoke, it was only on their phones, eyes focused straight ahead or on the sidewalk before them.

Here? Here, not a phone was in sight as the people sat on their small tables outside, quietly murmuring their conversations. A gentle breeze rustled the leaves in the tops of the trees, and even the water softly trickled instead of raged as it trailed down its path.

That near reverence continued as they left the café behind, following along a tan-colored pathway lined on both its sides with grass, thick, full, and rich.

Most people whom they passed by along the way tipped their heads in greeting, their dogs as quiet as the owners. Others greeted a soft, "Hiya," or "All right?" before continuing on their way in further peaceful silence.

If she tried to say hello to even one stranger in New York she'd either be ignored or stared at like she was crazy.

She wasn't sure how she felt about how friendly everyone was here, but as the cool air kissed her cheeks and the green and gray atmosphere filled her soul with a peace she hadn't known to exist since she was a child, she had to admit, she could get used to it.

"You're not thinking about work, are you?"

Matthew's words broke through the silence, though it did nothing to detract from the quiet around them.

"No, I was just thinking about how slowly everything seems to move here. More intentional, you know?"

"That's what I believe you New Yorkers like to call *mindfulness*."

He wasn't wrong.

"Although," he continued, "I will say that it's easier to be at peace here surrounded by such beauty. But that's Yorkshire for you."

Winnie peered up at him, his wistful tone intriguing. His blue eyes looked distant as he stared at the stone walls climbing up the green fields and the skies textured by both dark and light clouds. A look of tranquility stretched across his features, soothing any worried wrinkles he might have had and easing a small smile on his lips.

She'd never seen him like this before, as if he was at one with his surroundings. But then, as she observed the people around them, they *all* had that same look.

What was it about this place that cast that relaxing spell on everyone—herself included? Not even the memory of Saturday's

247

failure or of Dad's calls could diminish the feeling. It was as if her heart slowly opened to allow stillness to drift in like the trickling of the brook by the café.

"I love your boots."

Winnie was pulled from her thoughts at the compliment delivered by an older woman walking by.

"Oh, they're not mine," she instantly responded.

"Well, I think they're lovely," the woman insisted, then she walked on.

Winnie had been so caught up in the spell of Malham, Yorkshire, and seemingly England as a whole that she'd forgotten all about the blasted wellies.

Matthew nudged her with his elbow. "See? They're the height of fashion."

Winnie rolled her eyes. "Nice try."

But as they continued, more women, both young and old, complimented her boots. Winnie continued to respond on the defensive until the fifth comment, where she finally held her tongue and merely expressed her gratitude.

"There you go," Matthew said with an approving nod. "Just accept it."

Their eyes caught, and they shared a smile before a large, gray and white cliffside loomed in her peripheral vision.

Matthew followed her gaze. "There it is. Malham Cove."

Winnie wasn't sure what she'd been expecting, but the view of the beautiful cove outdid anything she could have imagined. Reaching heights that had to be more than two hundred feet, the cove boasted of a curving cliffside, white limestone that was stained gray, and a waterfall pouring down the center of it. Full, craggy trees filled the area at the base of the cove, and a river led away from the waterfall, gentle and curving, with steppingstones placed deliberately across it.

On one side of the cove, sheep speckled the land like white stars in a green sky, and on the opposite side, a long stretch of stairs led directly to the top.

"Are we going up there?" she asked, pointing to the stairs.

He smiled. "Hence why I suggested wellies."

"How many steps are there?"

"Four-hundred," he said assuredly. "Can you manage?"

She scoffed. "Please, I've climbed more flights of stairs in New York."

Only a slight exaggeration. Still, she couldn't let him know how intimidated she was by the prospect of climbing so many steps.

They neared the cove closer and closer, Winnie still marveling at the tranquility around her before they reached a stone wall that blocked their way. As she drew closer, however, she noticed that the walls overlapped with a wooden gate in the middle of them, only one person being able to fit through at a time.

"So what's the point of this?" she asked.

He looked back at her as he went through first. "You've never seen a kissing gate before?"

She gave him a dubious look. "Kissing gate? That's really what it's called?"

He nodded in earnest, sidling through part of the gate as she waited for her own turn. "Really. They're used to keep animals contained. But it's also tradition for a gentleman to hold the gate closed until he receives the proper payment—usually a kiss—from a lady. Only then does he let her through."

Winnie paused, looking at Matthew as he remained where he was, preventing her progression as he held the gate closed, just as he'd described in his story.

He had to be joking, right? There wasn't any way he was actually considering making her pay in the way he'd explained. And yet, as their eyes connected, those blue depths staring into her soul, her breath caught in her throat.

She had a feeling that was *exactly* what he was considering.

CHAPTER TWENTY-EIGHT

As alluring as those blue eyes were, as attractive as Matthew's chiseled lips and jaw appeared, there was no way Winnie was going to turn this working trip into a...a...a one-kiss stand.

She raised her chin. "This is a business trip, Matthew, and tradition or not, I don't think it would be appropriate to give in to it."

In an instant, Matthew's lips curled. "You don't think *what* would be appropriate?" he asked innocently. "All I was doing was telling you a story, Miss Knox."

He lifted his hands from the gate and took a small step back, finally allowing her passage.

The little tripe. He knew exactly what he was doing to her. This was like grooming Nightshade all over again.

"So it's going to be like that, is it?" she asked. "You teasing me only to deny it later on?" She pushed the gate open and slipped through it, bumping him softly on the side with the wood.

He skittered out of the way with a little laugh. "I have no idea what you're talking about."

"Really?" she asked pointedly. "So you weren't just asking me to kiss you, then?"

He focused straight ahead, his eyes still shining. "If I wanted to kiss you, believe me, I wouldn't have to ask you for it. You'd give it of your own freewill."

Her breath halted. What were they doing, chatting away so comfortably about *kissing*?

"You think very highly of yourself," she said, trying to prove she was more at ease than she was.

"No, I'm just a realist."

Winnie shook her head, wanting to say something more, but as the pathway narrowed and the steps began, she didn't get the chance.

It was just as well. He'd have some response waiting anyway that would blow hers out of the water. He always did.

With the idea of kissing Matthew still at the back of her mind, she focused all the harder on the scenery around her until they reached the top. Propping her hands on her hips, she stood with her feet securely on the limestone, the years having eroded the pavement into bumpy blocks and deep cracks. Breathless from exhaustion and the sight, she stared out across the valleys and marveled at the view.

"You can see for miles," she breathed out, shaking her head in amazement.

Her eyes followed the bent trails of the tanned pathway they'd walked across to the cragged river that curved through the land like a silvery snake.

She'd heard of the green that England boasted, but she'd never expected this. Utah was very often yellow and brown. New York was metal and silver. But England...England was life.

"You approve, then?" Matthew asked.

"How could anyone not?"

"You're right about that." Then he paused. "Pop trivia question. What movie was filmed on top of here?"

She instantly shook her head. "Oh, I'll definitely lose at that game."

"Not into movies?"

"No, I like movies enough." She raised her voice to be heard above the wind whistling in her ears. "I just wasn't allowed to watch many growing up, so I haven't seen as many as most people have."

"You weren't allowed?"

She should have known that's what he'd fixate on. It *was* strange.

"Yeah," she said with a shrug. "My parents wanted us to focus on more important things than media, so we could only ever watch documentaries and things like that. I made up for it in college, though. My roommates made sure of that."

Since her parents didn't believe in watching films that had no educational purpose, she and her roommates had stayed up every night, binge-watching all the shows and movies from every genre they recommended. Chick-flicks, historical romances, horrors, adventures, sci-fi, fantasy. She'd seen more in those few years than she had in her entire life. While she loved it, watching so many films also made it more difficult to continue getting straight A's, which her parents required.

Matthew didn't respond, the wheels in his head still clearly turning.

"So are you gonna tell me what movie it was?" she asked, desperate to divert the attention away from her controlled life.

"Oh, *Harry Potter*," he responded. "He and Hermione sit atop here in *Deathly Hallows, Part One*." Then he looked at her sidelong. "I take it you don't remember the scene."

"Um, no," she said. "I don't remember much of the series."

"Well, you ought to watch them again. Or rather, you ought to read the books."

She shrugged. "If I had the time I would. Probably."

"Maybe I'll make it a goal to make you a Potterhead by the end of this trip."

"And how would you manage to accomplish that?"

He shrugged. "I have my ways. Just like I'm going to convince you to bring the damsel in distress back to the jousting tournament."

She laughed. "Good luck with that. But, wait, I thought we weren't supposed to talk about work?"

"All right. Correction. *I* can. You can't." He walked across the cracked top of the cove. "What's your problem with having a damsel anyway? Too un-feminist for you?"

She followed after him, focusing her eyes on the large gaps between the limestone to avoid tripping. "Exactly. And like I said before, we're in the twenty-first century."

"What's so outdated and terrible about being a damsel in distress?" he continued, sidestepping a large crack.

"It just insinuates that women can't take care of themselves when we're perfectly capable of doing so."

"And can you always?" he asked.

She thought for a minute. "We ought to be able to."

"Then is it wrong for men to need help every once in a while?"

"No."

"So what's with the double standard, Miss Knox?"

She pulled in her lips, staring at the back of his head. Honestly, he had a point. But it was different. Wasn't it? "I dunno. I just—Oh!"

Her foot caught against one of the crags sticking up, and she launched forward toward Matthew. He turned just in time, wrapping his hands around her and steadying her.

She breathed hard, righting herself at once and smoothing down her jacket. "Blasted boots."

"Oh, come now," Matthew said. "Don't be blaming them when the limestone is at fault."

She glanced up at him, seeing him fight off a smile.

"What?" she demanded. He had to be laughing at her tripping.

"I just think it's ironic. For someone who doesn't like being

253

rescued, you do find yourself in a lot of situations requiring rescuing."

Winnie pulled on a frown. "I can take care of myself," she said weakly.

He stared at her, and his features softened. "There's nothing wrong with needing help, Winnie. Or accepting it. To need help is to be human. To accept it is to be humble. I learned that from you."

Winnie's heart raced. That was the first time she'd heard him call her by her given name in...how long? Ever? But his words were what lingered the most.

"So you're coming to understand that it's good to accept help, then?" she asked.

He walked past her with a hidden smile. "I'm beginning to see the value in it, yes. Ready to go?"

Winnie could only follow in silence.

On the way down, she received three more compliments over her—no, *Char's*—boots, which she accepted with a smile and a gracious, "Thank you," and when they reached the kissing gate again, she pushed through before Matthew had the chance.

"I'll be going first, thank you," she said with a pointed look.

"Why, so *you* can demand a kiss?" he asked with a knowing smile that made her heart curl warmly in her chest.

She hadn't been able to muster a response, so she'd merely slipped through and marched on, forcing the image of kissing Matthew Wintour from her mind once and for all.

Or, for her sake, she *hoped* it would be once and for all.

CHAPTER TWENTY-NINE

"I've never been inside a castle," Winnie said as she and Matthew walked toward their next destination, Skipton.

They'd parked their car in the lot nearby and now stood in front of the gatehouse—two large, circular towers holding up a portcullis at the back.

"Really?" Matthew asked. "Never?"

"The closest things I've seen in Utah are granaries, so I guess you could count those."

He chuckled at her joke.

They neared the large precipice of the castle, and Winnie stared up at the brown and black stones, marveling at the alternating raised spaces of the towers, the coat of arms, and eventually the writing at the top.

DES OR MAIS

"'Henceforth,'" Matthew said, motioning to the writing. "It's the Clifford family motto. Lady Anne had it created as a defiant slight against Oliver Cromwell, who wanted the castle destroyed."

Winnie smiled. "I like the sound of this Lady Anne."

"You *would*," Matthew said with a roll of his eyes, then he motioned her forward. "Come on. There's much more to see than the gatehouse."

He was right. Winnie couldn't believe the sight before her as they passed beneath the portcullis and were greeted by the sight of a full-blown, real-life castle.

Stretching across the length of a pristinely cared for lawn, the castle boasted multiple drum towers, light brown stone, and a Union Jack that waved proudly at the foremost tower. Small windows speckled a few of the towers, and a broad staircase led up to the front entrance.

The medieval fortress—according to Matthew—had been preserved for over nine hundred years and was open for guests to explore every room, aside from those off to the side, where a family privately resided.

"It's incredible," she breathed.

"It really is," he agreed. "I've been here countless times, and it still doesn't get old."

They moved forward, the noise from the town outside being cut off as the grounds of the castle echoed that same peaceful silence from Malham.

The area wasn't full in the middle of the day, but those who were there still spoke in hushed tones. Was that just the English way? She couldn't deny that it was a refreshing change to what she was used to.

"You mentioned Utah before," Matthew said in his own lowered tone as they climbed the castle steps. "That's where you're originally from?"

Winnie nodded. "Yep. Born and raised. I graduated college there, then moved all over until I found consultant work in New York."

"There weren't consulting opportunities closer to home?" he asked next.

Oh, there were opportunities. Plenty of them. Especially

being near Dad with all the many connections he had as a lawyer. But she'd chosen New York for a reason—and that was to get some space between her and her family.

Of course that had never stopped her dad from still giving her his contacts left and right.

"New York just called my name I guess," she replied.

"Does your whole family still live in Utah?"

"My parents do. But my siblings are scattered everywhere now. Oregon, Germany, Florida, California."

They reached the top of the steps and turned to face another set. Winnie had to admit, she was kind of over stairs after Malham, but if these led to another view like the cove had, then she wouldn't complain at the top.

"Do you ever get to see them?" Matthew asked.

Why the sudden interest in her family? Or was he simply making polite conversation? "We get together once in person every year, but other than that, we just see each other during video chats." She looked at him from the corner of her eye. "As you well know."

He smiled, though he had the decency to look slightly sheepish. "I've been meaning to speak to you about that. I'm sorry I made you uncomfortable."

"No, you aren't," she said with a small laugh. "You were eating the whole thing up."

He shrugged. "Well, any man would when he hears a beautiful woman finds him attractive."

Winnie looked at him, her lips parting at his words.

Beautiful. He'd called her beautiful.

Obviously, he wasn't aware of the effect he'd had on her, as he motioned straight ahead and pulled her attention elsewhere. "You'll like this."

Winnie followed his gaze, still reeling before catching sight of the enormous tree in the center of the open-roof courtyard. "It's a tree," she stated, "just...growing right there."

He laughed at her stating the obvious. "That's a yew tree, planted in the sixteen hundreds, reputedly by the very Lady Anne who erected the sign in the front."

"Yeah, I really like her," Winnie said, propping her hands on her hips and nodding her head as she admired the towering tree above them. Its trunk twisted toward the sky like a giant licorice.

The inside of the courtyard boasted of far more windows than the outside of the castle had, countless, skinny frames lining the walls to the doors that led to even more rooms.

They stepped across the stone flooring, moving to the stairs at the left as Matthew continued to share his wealth of knowledge about the enormous fireplaces tall enough for children to stand in —"It's been said that the fires were so hot, the chefs used to cook without clothes on"—to the toilets on the top floor that sent their waste down, down, down, where "individuals used moss to clean themselves up afterward."

Winnie listened to everything, even when she was squirming in the darkness of the dungeons, completely enraptured by the history Matthew shared with her.

"Now I know why we've come here," she said, moving to yet another room, this one labeled *Lord's bedchamber*.

"Why is that?" Matthew asked.

"So you can teach me all about the medieval era and make me fall in love with history, too. Then I'll want the festival to be as authentic as you do."

His gleeful smile made her laugh. "Is it working?" he asked.

"Maybe," she lied.

It was *totally* working.

They passed by a few more rooms as Matthew continued his questioning of her family. "So, I assume your siblings left Utah for work, like you did?"

Honestly, he was probably just curious, and his questions *were* harmless. But Winnie always felt crummy after touting her siblings' experiences. She always looked so dowdy afterwards.

"Yeah, Scott is an anesthesiologist, Samantha is an architect,

Spencer is a pilot, and Sarah is a software engineer. They all found more money everywhere else but Utah."

The driving factor for most people. And yet, did it ever make them happy? Had it made *her* happy?

Matthew moved to stare out one of the windows nearby, the courtyard tree's vibrant green leaves visible at eye-level from the warped glass. "They all have *S* names? Was that a coincidence?"

"Um, no." She moved to look at the tree, too, watching as a young girl pranced around the stone barrier at the base of it.

"Is Winnie a middle name, then?" he pressed.

"Nope," she said. "I was the accident of the family as the youngest. They said they chose Winifred because it means peace and joy, but I called their bluff a few years ago and found out they just couldn't think of any other *S* names they liked."

Yet another reason she was on the outside looking in with her family. Her mood shifted, as it always did when she spoke of them. "They told me with five kids, and with me as the youngest, they wanted me to stand out in all the best ways. Fat bit of good that did me."

MATTHEW COULDN'T STOP STARING at Winnie.

Dad had been right. He'd been right about everything. Mr. Knox's pressure, her siblings' successes, her own insecurities being hidden by the pride she was forced to exhibit. But now, listening to her speak of her family and their jobs, he could see clear as day the self-doubt in her gray eyes.

How it pulled at his heart.

"Ready to go to the next room?" she asked, her smile clearly forced.

She moved on before he had the chance to respond.

He felt bad for asking so many questions about her family

when her spirits were clearly lowered, but he'd wanted to hear the truth from her own lips. Now that he had, he longed for the Winnie from before. The Winnie who'd made fun of his car and the Winnie who'd marveled at the sights.

Honestly, their trip so far had exceeded any expectations he'd had, especially in regard to Winnie's response to things. She'd been impressed with his home, with Yorkshire and England, and he couldn't begin to explain how happy that had made him.

Now he needed to bring her happiness back.

They continued moving from room to room, and Matthew shared more of the history with her, relieved when she finally shifted from unhappiness to intrigue once again.

"So, did visiting here inspire your love of the medieval era?" she asked, peering through one of the many turrets they passed by.

She leaned forward, and Matthew had to pull his gaze away from her jeans once again. Even those terrible wellies she still wore didn't distract him from how good she looked today.

"Matthew?"

He blinked, staring at her as she turned around with a quizzical look. "Hmm? Oh, yes. There were other things, of course, but visiting here definitely helped nurture my love of history."

It was strange to be speaking with her like this, as if they were actually friends. Shocking what being nice to a person could do to another.

"So you're obsessed with all of history, not just the medieval era?" she asked.

He nodded. "Yeah, all of it. I know, it makes me even more boring, but that's the truth of it."

He was used to women finding him boring, his love of history apparently repulsive. He'd never had droves of girls chasing after him like Cedric for being a striker or Graham for being a piper, or even Finn for being in a small Irish band. Women just didn't take an interest in what Matthew had to say, it was as plain and simple as that.

And yet, the notion of Winnie feeling the same was disappointing.

"I don't think it makes you boring," she said as if hearing his thoughts. She looked through the next turret. "I think it's refreshing. You know what your passion is and you're not afraid to pursue it. It's admirable."

Matthew didn't know what to say. Did she really feel that way?

"So when did you first know you wanted to start jousting?" she asked next.

Was she asking her own questions to avoid answering his? Even if she was, he owed her a break.

"Well," he began, "it always fascinated me when I was younger, but that grew when my dad hired the Birdwhistles to work in the stables when I was...fifteen, I think it was? Hubert had been a knight for quite a while before that and had participated in other tournaments. Once I found out, I'd return home from Eton for summer holidays, and he'd show me how to joust, training me up little by little."

He paused, wondering if he was speaking too much, his voice echoing around the small room they stood within. But Winnie leaned back against one of the stone walls and listened to him with focused eyes.

It had been a long time since he'd had someone even pretend to show interest in his love of history and the joust. Dare he keep going?

"I proved good enough in the sport to participate in a few events alongside Hubert," he continued. "We had a great time jousting together and against each other."

His mind strayed for a moment to those early days of jousting. The feel of the solid lance in his grasp, the focus required to succeed, the satisfaction of the cracking and splintering of wood when he struck his opponent directly on target.

"It was and has always been rewarding," he said. "But my favorite part is the feeling that comes when I dress in the armor and ride down the list. I'm just entirely and completely immersed in history, as if I was actually a knight chosen to fight for king and country."

He stopped again, wondering if he should be embarrassed by the things he was sharing, but Winnie still listened, her eyes even more intent than before.

"Anyway," he continued, "I wasn't able to do as much once I started uni. I dreamt of becoming a history professor next, graduated with my degree, and shortly after, I received a job offer at a university where I got to teach for a few months, but life obviously had other plans for me."

"What plans?" she prompted.

"My dad being diagnosed with MS."

Winnie's brow furrowed at once. Matthew could understand why. Dad's diagnosis had been a traumatic thing for the Wintour family as a whole, but together, they'd managed to grow stronger because of it.

"He needed a lot of help in the beginning," Matthew continued, "so I moved back home to help with the estate and his recovery."

"That must have been so hard for you to give up your dream," she said.

But Matthew shrugged. "It wasn't difficult, just more sad than anything. I'd worked a long time to realize that dream, but in the end, I found another one. I created the medieval festival, brought Hubert on as one of the knights, and eventually built up the event from the ground up." He looked away. "Until I ran it back down into the ground."

To his surprise, she laughed. "You think that's funny, do you?" he asked, unable to hide his own smile.

"Sorry," she said, covering her mouth with her hand. "It's not funny, just the way you said it. In reality, you didn't run it into the ground, or it would be completely dead. All it needs is a little...resuscitation."

Matthew stared at her, still marveling at the change that had come over the two of them. "I think that is the nicest thing you've said to me about my festival, Miss Knox."

He hoped she didn't mind his little nickname for her. He'd used it first to annoy her, but now, he found it suited her so well, it was hard to break the habit.

"Well, it was overdue," she said. "I'm sorry I took so long to say it."

Their eyes met, another level of understanding passing between them before she looked away, her eyes traveling over the stone walls, flooring, and ceiling.

"I still can't believe I'm standing inside of a real castle," she murmured, shaking her head.

Matthew smiled at the way she took everything in, like a child in a candy shop—or like himself in a history museum.

"Do you know what Char and I used to play here as kids?" he asked.

"What?" she asked.

"Hide-and-seek."

Winnie laughed. "Hide-and-seek? Here? That can't be allowed."

"Oh, it absolutely isn't," Matthew said, his grin growing. "We played it anyway, though."

She smiled, just imagining the young Wintour kids hiding in the nooks and crannies of an actual castle. What a childhood that must have been.

"Did you ever get caught?" she asked.

"By our parents, yes, but it didn't stop us from playing again. We added more rules, so if other people were around, we had to walk when trying to tig each other."

"Tig?"

"You know, tap them so they're out."

She nodded her understanding.

"We had to be deathly quiet," Matthew continued, "no matter how few or how many people were here. It was always best when the castle was quiet, though. Like today."

263

His eyes took on a faraway look, then he cast a sidelong glance at her.

"What?" she questioned.

"I wonder what it would be like to play now..." he said, then he ended in a loaded silence.

CHAPTER THIRTY

WINNIE'S BROW FURROWED, AND SHE INSTANTLY shook her head. "No way," she stated at once.

But the light in Matthew's eyes wouldn't cease. "Oh, come on. Just one quick game?"

She looked around them, even though she already knew no one was there. "Are you kidding me? There's no way I'm gonna play a game in a castle we're not allowed to."

"The worst you'd get is a warning," he said with a flippant wave of his hand, his smile becoming more appealing by the second. "Come on. One quick game. No running. No shouting. It'll be fun."

Man, he was convincing. But there was no way she could play.

She folded her arms, unable to bend. "Sorry, but I can't."

Matthew delivered an exaggerated sigh, then he shrugged and sauntered away from her. "Fine. Suit yourself. But you're not getting out of Skipton until you find me."

Winnie dropped her arms to her sides. "What? What do you—"

Her words ended abruptly as Matthew flashed a smile. "Good luck," he said, then he was gone.

Winnie stared at the open doorway he'd disappeared through,

shaking her head in disbelief. Was he really going to make her do this?

"Matthew, I'm not going to find you," she said, her voice only slightly raised.

He made no response. Instead of the trepidation she probably should have been feeling, excitement bubbled within her, and a smile etched across her lips.

Fine. She'd play his little game, and she'd beat him at it, too.

She rushed to the open window, peering at the ground below as she anticipated where he'd go first.

Sure enough, she found him walking swiftly from the ground floor out into the courtyard, looking over his shoulder, as if expecting her to be following him.

She tapped lightly on the glass. "Found you!"

Matthew paused, looking from window to window until seeing her. "Cheat!" he said, pointing at her.

She shook her head, putting a finger to her temple. "Smart," she said.

"You still have to tig me," he returned, then he walked swiftly to another door and disappeared within.

Winnie remained where she stood, watching as he popped in and out of the rooms, his head appearing every once in a while in the windows, and she couldn't help but laugh.

After a few minutes of not seeing him, however, she knew he must've wised-up. Leaving her vantage point, she went the opposite way Matthew had, hoping to catch him that way.

Before long, she caught sight of him, pointing at him and calling out, "Found you!" in her softest whisper she could manage.

Matthew grinned, then disappeared through the door.

Winnie scurried after him, having to stop for a moment as she allowed a mother and her two young kids to pass her by before she continued in his direction.

Of course, he'd vanished by that point, so Winnie took up her search again. Unfortunately, this time, she couldn't catch a break.

She circled the castle once, then twice, all without a single glimpse of him.

She tried watching from the window, then moved to the courtyard, sitting down on the small circle barrier around the base of the tree, breathless but only from excitement. Despite not being able to find him, she still smiled. This was the most fun she'd had in years.

Going through a mental list of rooms she'd already been to, Winnie narrowed down her options as to where to look next. The banqueting hall, the kitchens, the withdrawing room, the watchtower. She'd been everywhere.

Well, everywhere but the dungeons.

Her stomach tightened. The dungeons. Of course that's where he'd be. She'd been so uncomfortable walking down there before with him that she hadn't even stepped foot on the floor, remaining on the stairs before ushering Matthew out herself. They were just so creepy. Dark and damp and filled with all sorts of harsh history. So now she had to walk all the way down there to find and tag Matthew? Nope. No way.

And yet, if there was anything she'd learned about him in the last few weeks, it was that he was as stubborn as she was—maybe even more so. If she ever wanted to leave Skipton, and if she wanted to win, she'd have to find him. It was as simple as that.

With a heavy sigh, she pushed herself off the stone and headed for the dungeons. At the top of the steps down, she paused.

"Matthew?" she called out quietly. "I know you're down there."

No response.

"I'm not coming down," she continued.

Still, nothing.

Winnie sighed. He was really going to make her do this, wasn't he?

She descended a few steps, pulling out her phone and shining her light down the stairs.

"Come on, we're gonna be late for whatever we're doing

next," she said. She listened for any sound of him, but there was nothing. "Don't you wanna come out and teach me more about history and stuff?"

Not even *that* worked.

She pulled in her lips, taking the remaining steps down to the dark, windowless room.

She shone the light across the space, lighting up as much of it as possible, though the corners remained black.

Still, there was no sign of him.

"All right, you win," she said. "Just come out already."

She took a step forward, her heart thudding uncomfortably against her chest as she stared at the dark walls, imagining the type of things that had once occurred down there. Torturing, deaths, hauntings...

A shadow moved in the corner, and her stomach dropped, her heart echoing in her ears. Matthew could stay down there for the rest of his days, for all she cared. She was done.

Spinning on her heel, she had every intention of flying up the stairs to escape whatever ghosts now surrounded her. But when she came face-to-face with Matthew instead, his features half-covered in shadow, she yelped, launching toward him on instinct. Her phone plummeted to the floor, and she reached forward, landing a sound slap on his cheek.

He grunted, backing away from her in shock as she gasped.

"Oh my gosh," she said, rushing toward him, realizing too late what she'd done. "I'm so sorry!"

To her relief, he laughed. Then she realized what *he'd* done.

Lit by her phone still on the ground, Matthew straightened, holding a hand to his cheek as he beamed with utter delight at having scared her so badly.

Indignation ran through her. "You jerk!" she said, reaching forward and pushing his broad shoulder back. "You scared me to death."

He laughed again, lowering his hand from his cheek and reaching down for her phone. "I'm sorry. I couldn't resist."

She snatched her phone from his fingers. "You do realize you just lost the game."

"It was absolutely worth it."

She fought the smile off her lips. "You're lucky I didn't punch you. You can't mess with a girl who's lived in New York, you know. I could have pepper-sprayed you, too."

"You have some on you?"

"Usually."

He smiled in response, rubbing his cheek. "Sorry. I really didn't think I'd scare you that badly."

She had a mind to reject his apology on principle, but when she shifted the light of her phone onto his face, the redness beyond his beard shone brightly.

She winced. "I suppose *I* did that."

He rolled his jaw. "Yes, you did. But I deserved it."

"Well, I know that much. But I'm sorry just the same."

He waved a passive hand, but Winnie still eyed his cheek. Now she really did feel bad.

Without another thought, she reached forward, intending on stroking the skin to see if she could dispel the redness, but as her fingertips stroked his beard instead, every inch of her froze aside from her racing heart.

What on earth was she doing? She shouldn't be staring deeply into his eyes, feeling the soft prickles of his facial hair on her fingertips. This was a business trip. A business trip that involved talks of kissing, playing hide-and-seek, and assaulting her business associate, apparently. But a business trip all the same.

She dropped her hand and took a step away from him, shifting her phone's light away to hide her embarrassment.

"Sorry," she mumbled.

"For slapping me?"

"Sure."

Matthew's smile grew tenfold at her words.

CHAPTER THIRTY-ONE

Shortly after their escapade in Skipton's dungeons, Winnie and Matthew headed straight for York. Despite feeling guilty still for the redness lingering on Matthew's cheek, Winnie had enjoyed every minute of their drive.

Matthew had taken a longer route to the city, showing her more incredible views of Yorkshire's greenery before they finally reached York. Together, they headed to the bed and breakfast just on the outskirts of the city where they parted for their separate rooms and agreed to meet downstairs for dinner shortly after.

Winnie took a quick shower, changed into fresh clothes, and replaced the wellies with a pair of red heels, having been reassured by Matthew that they were finished with stairs and muddy puddles—at least for now.

Truthfully, were it not for the small blisters now forming on her heels from the rain boots, Winnie would have probably worn them throughout the night. They were comfortable, sensible, and produced more compliments than Winnie had received in her life.

In those boots, she was no longer Winnie Knox. Instead she was Winnie: Gaudy Wellies Wearer, and she loved it.

Unfortunately, the city called for something a bit nicer, and those floral attention-getters just did not match with the sleek black dress she'd changed into that night for dinner.

As she peered into the mirror, she made to pull her hair back into her typical bun, then paused. Wasn't there something different she could do? Something a little less boss-y? Besides, if she wasn't supposed to think about work, why did she have to *look* like work?

She dug through her toiletry bag, finding a claw clip inside before twisting her hair up loosely and allowing a few tendrils to frame her face.

There. Now she didn't appear so fierce.

But as she closed and locked the door behind her, Winnie wondered if she'd put in a little too much effort that evening. Hair, lipstick, clothing. Was she trying to draw too much attention to herself? What if Matthew still wore what he had before? She'd look like a try-hard.

Fortunately, her worries were set aside when she saw him standing at the base of the stairs waiting for her, wearing slacks and a striped button-up shirt, though his curly mane was only slightly tamed.

He caught sight of her as she stood at the top of the stairs, a smile growing on his face as his eyes settled on her heels. "Got tired of those wellies, did you?"

She smiled. "I figured I'd go for something a little more subtle tonight."

He looked her up and down. "Then you probably shouldn't have worn that dress."

Her heart skipped a beat in response.

"Ready?" he asked.

She nodded, unable to speak as the two of them headed out the door.

Winnie did everything she could to distract herself from Matthew—from his compliment and from the way his slacks hugged his thighs to his ability to make her not only feel heard but also *seen*.

That was all easier said than done until they reached the inside of the city, where Winnie was shocked to discover that York was, in fact, surrounded by a large wall. Matthew explained the history as they walked down the streets, both sides of the small roads lined with countless shops, their windows boasting of Christmas décor, antique books, and hand-crafted teapots.

It reminded her of New York in a way, but this *old* York held a definite magic to it, a magic that she was sure came from how ancient the city was and the history it held. Instead of towering, metal skyscrapers, York overflowed with quaint shops, over-hanging signs, and cobbled roads, and Winnie fell in love with England just a little bit more because of that.

As for her time with Matthew, she felt as if she were living in a dream. The last thing she wished to do was return to reality tomorrow, to her job, to her stress, to her decision to stay or to go.

But then, who was she kidding? How could she ever choose to leave now, after all the work Matthew had put into helping her?

Instead of telling him her decision, however, she kept silent about it throughout their dinner at a nearby pub, centering their conversation around more trivial matters—matters that didn't cause her to fear failing again. Because, frankly, she was enjoying this frivolous time with Matthew, so much so that she didn't want the evening to end when their meal did. Fortunately for her, he appeared to want the same, suggesting a walk around the city walls instead of going to bed, which Winnie readily agreed to.

"I thought you said no more steps," she said as they climbed the twenty-or-so up to the top of the walls.

"Quit your whinging," he'd said with a smile, then he motioned for her to precede him up the stairs.

At the top of the thirteen-foot walls, Winnie marveled at the pink and purple sunset across the city, lighting up the glass windows of the minster, the brown tops of the terraced homes, and the trees that popped up across the city like green flowers blossoming from stone.

"It's beautiful, isn't it?" Matthew asked, motioning to the sights. "New York doesn't hold a candle to the *real* York."

Winnie had to agree.

They continued on, and Matthew took to sharing more facts about the city as they walked along the fortifications.

"They're the longest city walls in England," he said. "They were built in seventy-one AD, but only a small degree of stonework remains from actual Roman origin. It's pretty amazing, though, that in the medieval times, there were already the four gatehouses that allowed traffic inside and out of the city."

He continued for a few more minutes, then abruptly stopped with an averted gaze. "Sorry. I could obviously go on for hours about this stuff."

"Oh, please, don't apologize. I love listening to you talk."

Their eyes met, and only then did she realize how ridiculous her comment had sounded, like she was fawning all over him.

"The history is fascinating," she quickly corrected.

He nodded, though his eyes lingered on her. "No, it's the accent. I've heard it can make anything boring sound entertaining."

That was true enough. She could listen to him read Minnie's owner's manual, and she'd still swoon at the sound. Still, she didn't want to risk sounding like she was throwing herself at him. She'd better tease him again. That was always the safest option.

With a shrug, she responded. "I guess that could be true. For some people. I mean, I prefer Finn's. Northern Irish, right? But yours is nice, too, I guess."

"Northern Irish? Over my proper English?" Matthew scoffed. "I'm going to pretend you didn't just say that."

"Whatever suits your pride. Now tell me more about these walls."

Matthew swiftly obliged. With bright eyes, he continued his happy instruction, and Winnie listened with as much enthusiasm as ever until they paused on the path with the perfect view of the minster.

Matthew took a moment to catch his breath, and unfortunately, Winnie's mind took the silence as an opportunity to wander.

There they were, walking around an ancient city's walls with Matthew—basically breathless with how happy he was speaking of the history of the city, revealing his passion every minute—and Winnie...heartless, passionless, lifeless Winnie.

"See, *now* I've talked too much," Matthew said. "I can see the will to live fading from your eyes."

He'd said it as a joke, but it struck a little too close to home.

"No, it's not you," she said, trying to pull up her spirits like she would a pair of tights, both nearly impossible to accomplish without a strong sense of determination.

"Can I ask what it is, then?" he questioned.

Winnie hesitated. She didn't like to voice these things aloud. It made her seem vulnerable, which she wasn't supposed to be. But then, wasn't that what she wanted—to be seen as human, to be treated with kindness and patience? Who was better to speak with this about than Matthew?

Winnie moved to the edge of the wall, leaning against the elbow-length height of the stone. Drawing a deep breath, she shrugged to play off how deeply her feelings really ran. "It's nothing. I was just thinking about what you said that first time in the assembly hall. When you'd asked why do something if there wasn't heart or passion involved."

He joined her by the wall, leaning against it as well. "What about it?" he asked softly.

She chewed on her upper lip. "It just stuck with me, that's all. Because...I don't really know what it's like to do something with my whole heart. At least, not anymore."

"So, you're worried about the festival?" Matthew asked, filling in the gaps she couldn't voice aloud. "If you can put your heart into it to have greater success?"

She nodded, responding in a heavy sigh. "Pretty much."

He pulled his gaze to the view before them, a calming light coming across the city and quieting the busy streets.

"You haven't failed at much, have you?" he asked.

She huffed out a laugh of derision, a bitterness rising inside of her she couldn't silence. "On the contrary. That's *all* I do—fail at things. Law school. Culinary school. Medical school. Horseback riding. Becoming a realtor. After all that, I tried business school, which I almost graduated from before starting and failing my own businesses. And now I'm even failing at consulting, which I always thought I was good at, up until two days ago. I am a hot mess with nothing going for me."

She stopped. With Matthew's attention focused solely on her, embarrassment flushed over her. "Sorry," she mumbled.

"There's no need to apologize," he said at once. Then he paused. "Did you really try to do all of those things?"

"Over the years, yes. And more. All of it was a monumental waste of time."

"I don't know about that," he countered. "Failing is good for us. It helps us learn each time we do."

She looked away. "Not in the Knox family. It only makes you more of an outcast. More of a disappointment."

Matthew was silent for a minute, and she was about to apologize for being a massive bummer again when he spoke.

"I have a confession to make," he said softly, staring down at the wall they leaned against.

She waited, wondering what on earth he had to admit to now.

"My dad told me a bit about your family," he said. "Mostly your own father, who has very high standards as to what constitutes an accomplishment."

Winnie wasn't surprised Mr. Wintour was talking about her and her dad. In fact, she might have already expected such a thing to occur. After all, Mr. Wintour must be no stranger to Dad's ridiculous criteria.

"That's why I was asking about your family earlier," Matthew continued. "I didn't want to assume that I knew the truth without hearing it coming from your own mouth."

Despite their topic of conversation, Winnie's heart softened. How much more admirable could Matthew get?

"Anyway," he continued, "I'm sorry if my bringing up your family earlier has produced more of these feelings in you."

"Thank you," she said, "but you didn't cause this. It's been there all along."

He nodded, looking toward the minster again. "For the record, I don't think you failed at the festival or at being a consultant. Just because one event didn't go entirely as planned doesn't make it out to be a failure."

"You might be right," she said, validating his words. But something else chipped away at the peace she'd felt that day, the peace she so desperately wanted to bring back. "But that's just the thing. I have no real passion for consulting. Sure, I love helping people. I love seeing the growth that comes when good advice is taken. And I love finding creative ways to improve businesses. But all of that is surface level. Definitely not enough to move the dial of passion."

Matthew nodded, seeming to think about her comments before responding. "Can I ask how you came to be a consultant?"

"I'm sure you can guess. It was my dad's doing. After all my failed attempts pursuing other career paths, I thought I'd start a few businesses. Each one failed in the end, whether it was selling wholesale on Amazon, opening up an ice cream restaurant, or putting up custom blinds. I found out that I knew exactly what *not* to do when running a business, so I started reaching out to people, giving free advice here and there about their businesses and finding relative success.

"Anyway, Dad told me about a friend of his in New York who owed him a favor. I was hired and ended up doing a fine enough job because the pressure wasn't there to make my *own* business work. Dad saw this, then pushed me to follow the career because it was the first time I'd actually been okay at something he approved of. I didn't really want to, but it was time I stopped embarrassing my family."

"Embarrassing your family or your dad?" Matthew asked.

She thought for a minute. "I guess just my dad."

Matthew laced his fingers together as he leaned them over the side of the wall. "Have you ever tried to embrace your failures, see them for what they are?"

"I know what they are. Evidence of my flaws."

"No, they're not," he returned softly. "Failures are merely stepping-stones propelling you towards the person you're meant to be. I'm sure you know that a person learns more from failing than by succeeding."

"Yeah, but it's a heck of a lot less painful to succeed."

He cracked a smile. "I'll give you that." Then he peered down at her, his features softening. "You ought to give yourself a break, Winnie. Believe in yourself. My dad does. That's why he gave you a second chance." He leaned in closer to her, his shoulder and arm pressing against hers. "*I* believe in you, too."

Winnie could hardly breathe, the warmth from his touch seeping through their jackets and swirling around her soul. He was leaning into her on purpose. He was *lingering* on purpose. Was that to drive home his words? Or did he touch her because he wanted to be close to her—because he felt the same stirring in his heart that she did?

She swallowed, unable to keep her eyes from his any longer. Slowly, she looked up at him, meeting his gaze.

"All you need is to believe in yourself now," Matthew whispered, his eyes flicking between hers before ultimately settling on her lips.

Moments ticked by. Winnie's heart sputtered like Minnie's exhaust.

They were on a business trip.

A business trip.

They were coworkers.

Coworkers.

But the words echoed meaninglessly in her mind now, no longer holding any power over her—Unlike Matthew. The words he'd said to her, the help he'd given her that day, the way he'd made her feel alive for the first time since she was a teenager—all of it had rendered her incapable of withstanding his goodness. She'd never experienced that with anyone before. And she couldn't keep herself from him any longer. She needed to experience his kiss. She needed *him*.

In the waning light of the sun, she waited until he finally leaned toward her. Her eyes closed, and she drew in what little breath she could as he inched closer. She could almost feel the soft tickle of his beard on her lips and the gentle breath from his nose on her cheek, as if they were already kissing. So why were they not?

Slowly, she opened an eye, then two.

The hesitation on Matthew's brow was enough to yank her from the dream that might've been the best she'd ever had. She leaned back, snapping her gaze away and pulling their shoulders apart.

"I'm sorry," he said.

"It's okay," she responded. As if he was the only one to blame.

"No, I..." Matthew hesitated, pulling out his phone. "I just remembered, I think the gates close at sundown."

CHAPTER THIRTY-TWO

WINNIE BLINKED. "THE GATES? WHAT DO YOU MEAN?"

"The gates to the wall," Matthew clarified. "I'm pretty sure they close before dusk."

She pulled her eyes to the sun that had already set. "What, so we're locked up here?"

He looked at her with hesitance in his gaze, and her heart sunk.

First, they didn't kiss. Now, this?

"Do they not do, like, a sweep around the wall or something?" she asked, looking up and down the path. Come to think of it, they'd been alone for some time now.

"All two or three miles of them?" Matthew questioned with a doubtful look. "Unfortunately, I think they give people more credit to watch out for the approaching darkness themselves."

Winnie pressed a hand to her brow. "So, now what?"

Matthew appeared to think for a second. "Let's just go check the gates. No point in getting worked up for nothing."

And yet, when they reached the steps leading down to the city, it was made perfectly clear that the gates at the bottom had, indeed, been locked.

Matthew rubbed a hand at the back of his neck. "Sorry," he

mumbled, clearly embarrassed. "I should've paid attention to what time it was."

But she wasn't about to let him take the fall. "Oh, it's fine. I'm sure we'll find a way down. Maybe we could call someone?"

"I have no idea who."

"The police?" she offered.

He gave her an amused look. "Probably not for this." He paused, looking around them, then back to the top of the wall. Finally, a smile grew on his lips. "I have an idea that might actually work."

She followed him a ways along the wall, then he stopped with a beaming smile that revealed just how proud he was of his idea he had yet to share.

"What?" she asked, clearly missing something.

"This is our way out," he said.

He waved toward a large tree sticking out toward them, its long branches stretching over the wall, just above their heads.

Winnie stared, calculating the distance she'd have to jump to reach up to the tree, shimmy along the branch, then fall to the ground below.

"I don't know about this," she mumbled.

"You'll be fine," he reassured her.

"Even in these?" She motioned to her high-heeled feet. "And this?" Then she waved a hand across her dress.

Matthew frowned. "You and those ruddy heels. Well, never mind. You can take them off. The dress, of course will have to stay on." Winnie wasn't sure he knew what he was actually saying as he looked back to the tree.

"Come on," he urged, "let's get down before it gets too dark. I'll go first. Then I can spot you from the bottom."

Winnie stared at him in disbelief. He was out of his mind. But then, what other option did they have?

In a state of mild panic, she watched Matthew climb onto the ledge of the wall, facing the outskirts of the city and gripping the branch that stretched toward them.

Slowly, he steadied himself, eying the grass below.

"Is it a far drop?" she asked.

"Nah. If I fall, I'll survive. Might have a broken bone or two, though."

She winced. "Matthew, I don't know about this..."

"I'm kidding, Winnie. I promise, we'll be fine." Then he looked back to the tree.

Winnie leaned over the edge herself. That drop looked a lot farther than Matthew had let on. Honestly, the things he was making her do today—wearing wellies, playing games in castles, now climbing trees in heels. What would he concoct next, breaking into a museum that night to spend even longer learning about history?

The street beyond the walls was situated more than two dozen feet away, and a few cars drove by, the people inside entirely unaware of her and Matthew escaping the city walls. At least, she hoped they were unaware.

"What if we're caught?" she asked.

"Escaping from the place we were locked into?" Matthew asked. "I don't think we'll be faulted for that. Now hush. I have to focus."

Winnie clamped her mouth shut, watching in silence as he tested the strength of the branch by pulling it up and down. It hardly moved an inch, even with his pressure.

"All right, here we go," he mumbled, as if to hype himself up.

Finally, he jumped up, grabbed onto the branch more securely above him with both hands, then shifted his way slowly over the wall.

Winnie fought the urge to close her eyes, not wanting to see him fall, but needing to ensure his safety.

In what seemed like years, but in reality was mere moments, Matthew finally reached far enough away from the wall to drop toward the ground.

As he did so, she gasped, peering over the edge and holding her hands over her mouth in horror before seeing him land on his feet. He teetered slightly back and forth, but in the end, remained upright.

"Are you sure you'd not rather be a gymnast than a knight?" she called down to him. "You stuck that landing perfectly."

He grinned up at her. "Your turn."

All humor was lost to her at that point. "Maybe I'll just camp out up here until morning."

"Nope. Come on, you can do it. I'll catch you if you fall. Trust me."

"Trust you? I barely know you," she said pointedly—albeit untruthfully.

"That's not entirely true," Matthew said. "You know more about me than most people do. Besides, you almost just kissed me back up there, so don't give me that, 'I don't know you' business."

Her cheeks burned. What was with this guy being so blunt? Why couldn't he be more normal like the rest of the world—never mentioning awkward moments aloud and pretending they just didn't happen?

"Now," he continued, "stop stalling and throw me your beloved pumps."

"I don't wear pumps," she mumbled, relenting and removing her heels, tossing them down to him one by one. "Keep them safe."

Matthew caught each one, then set them on the grass beside him before waving her down. "Now, come on."

Her bare feet were cold against the stone, though she would have kept them there, frozen until the turn of the century, to avoid doing what was required of her. Still, she had no choice but to follow Matthew down.

Carefully, she mimicked his movements, climbing up the wall and steadying herself on the lower-hanging branches.

"Steady now," cooed Matthew from below.

She braced her bare feet apart atop the wall, grateful she'd had the foresight to wear her short leggings beneath her dress, even though the darkness around them would have prevented her showing anyone anything.

She stared down at Matthew, his arms up, already ready to catch her as soon as she dropped, but the height difference from the top of the wall was much different than what she'd been expecting.

It was a good thing she wasn't afraid of heights. Really, this wasn't too different than being bucked off a horse and shot fifteen feet into the air.

Her brain clicked. That was it. She'd just pretend she was riding a horse. A surge of confidence burst through her, and she leapt up to grasp hold of the thick tree branch above.

"There you go," Matthew said, his pride for her clear in his tone. "Now just shimmy your way toward me, and we'll be out of this pickle for good. Just remember, I'm right here to catch you if you fall."

Winnie nodded, drawing steady breaths and groaning only occasionally as her hands pinched painfully into the thick branch.

"How did you make this look so easy?" she asked with a grunt.

"Because of my manly strength," he joked.

She smiled, but as her fingers started to weaken, she knew she couldn't hold on much longer. "I think I'm gonna fall," she squeaked out, her smile vanishing.

"That's all right," Matthew reassured her. "I'm right here, remember?"

Remember? Of course she remembered. How could she forget? And yet, the image of her plummeting through the air, only to have Matthew miss her as she fell to the ground, breathless and broken, flashed through her mind.

"I'm gonna fall," she repeated.

"I'll catch you."

"No, Matthew, I'm gonna fall!"

"Winnie—"

Her fingers slipped.

Fear sailed throughout her, and she was taken straight back to the last time she'd fallen so frighteningly through the air—when Goldilocks had spooked and launched Winnie from her back.

In those moments of being thrown so many years ago, Winnie didn't have fears of if she'd be okay. Instead, she'd had one thought—*Please, don't let Dad be watching.*

Even now, she closed her eyes, clenched her hands tight, and braced for another fall that would inevitably lead to more disappointment from her dad.

Instead of landing on the hard earth below, however, strong arms wrapped around her, cushioning her fall until she stopped just as the tips of her toes poked against the grass.

She breathed heavily, still squeezing her eyes shut, holding onto...What was she holding onto? And why was there a soft, soothing breath brushing against her cheek?

"It's all right," came a soothing voice. "I have you, Winnie."

Matthew. He'd caught her. Just like he'd said he would.

Slowly, she opened her eyes, realizing only then that her arms were wrapped around his neck, and his arms around her middle.

His breath brushed against her cheek again as he calmly held her.

The feel of his arms around her, his strong chest against her, was enough to drive away any negative feelings, and little by little, fear seeped from her person, carried away by the vessel of Matthew's comfort.

"You okay?" he asked after a moment, no doubt feeling her breathing as it steadied.

Winnie wanted to pretend that she wasn't okay so she might stay in Matthew's arms forever, but she knew their separation was inevitable.

Slowly, she drew back, moving to stand on the flat of her feet as he stared down at her, his arms shifting to hold her around her waist. She told herself his lingering grasp was due to his wanting to secure her, not hold her. But she couldn't help but wish for the latter.

The grass curved around her feet, even colder than the stone from the wall now beside them, but she didn't care. All she could feel was the warmth of Matthew's fingertips searing into her sides.

His eyes delved into hers as they stood in silence, their bodies still touching.

"Thank you," she said, staring up at him. "I kinda lost it up there."

"That's understandable. It's a long drop."

"You said it wasn't that far," she returned, her heart skipping a beat as his gaze dropped to her lips, then lifted back to her eyes.

"I had to say *something* to convince you to jump down from a wall meant to keep Romans out."

"If I hadn't freaked out, I probably would have landed it like you did."

"Oh, no doubt. You aren't a damsel in distress, after all." Again, his eyes dropped to her lips.

"Not even a little bit," she breathed, though she was beginning to wonder if that was true.

His words from before echoed in her mind. *"If I wanted to kiss you, believe me, I wouldn't have to ask you for it. You'd give it of your own free will."* How could he have been so right? Because with his eyes on her mouth, and his hands on her hips, there was nothing more she wanted to do in that moment than to fall into his arms all over again and be rescued by the knight standing before her.

But once again, disappointment crushed her racing heart as a car revved its engine nearby, breaking the silence between them. Matthew looked away, losing his focus and dropping his hands to his sides.

Winnie drew a deep breath. How did they keep getting into this situation? Almost kissing and then...nothing.

It was a good thing, though. Business trip, remember?

"You ready to head back?" he asked, taking a step away from her.

"I just need my heels."

285

"Right." He bent down and delivered them to her, their fingers brushing against each other's, though Matthew no longer met her gaze.

On their short walk back to the bed and breakfast, Winnie itched to walk with her hand outside of her jacket pocket, longing to see if he'd hold her hand if given the option, but she withstood the temptation and kept her fingers tucked securely away.

After all, no good would come from holding hands with a man like Matthew Wintour unless she was allowed to *fall* for a man like Matthew Wintour. Because as much as Winnie hated to admit it, she *was* falling for him. And that was where the problem was. Knowing that Dad got her the job at Foxwood was bad enough. Having Dad believe that she'd kept her job at Foxwood because she'd kissed the boss's son would be even worse.

So she'd keep away from Matthew if it was the last thing she did. Which, honestly, it very well could be, seeing as how each moment she spent with him and didn't kiss him, was another moment she died a little bit more inside.

Not a damsel in distress, her foot.

CHAPTER THIRTY-THREE

MATTHEW DIDN'T SLEEP VERY WELL THAT NIGHT. HIS thoughts and dreams were filled with too many thoughts of Winnie. Her gray eyes, those wellies on her feet, the way her hair hung around her face loosely as they'd walked around the wall... the kisses they'd almost shared.

He'd become so restless throughout the night that when the sunshine finally peeked through his curtains the following morning, he no longer bothered trying to rest, getting ready for the day instead.

Soon, he met with the woman who'd plagued his thoughts all night, and it was little wonder why she had. Once again, she wore those jeans, a classy shirt tucked partially in the front of them, and the wellies from yesterday.

He'd hoped she would wear them again.

"This is in case we have to jump down more walls today," she said, motioning to her outfit.

Matthew could only smile. He'd been astounded at her bravery yesterday, climbing into that tree, carrying herself beyond the wall, falling into his arms. He knew her fear had been less about actually falling and more about trusting him. Which was why it had meant all the more when she did rely on him.

But dwelling on *why* he'd wanted her to rely on him in the first place wouldn't do him any good. It was why he'd pulled away from her last night when they'd nearly kissed.

Twice.

If they gave in to that clear desire the both of them shared, where would it lead, to a relationship? Or to a few non-committal kisses before she left back for New York, never to be seen again?

He wasn't sure he had the heart to find out.

After a full-English breakfast, and before they traipsed about the city, the two of them gathered their belongings and secured them in the car.

"Keep them safe, Minnie," Winnie said, patting the rusted bonnet.

Matthew grinned. "Nice to see you're embracing her."

"It took me a minute, but I'm beginning to see her appeal."

After saying goodbye to the car, the two of them made their way back into the city, along with the throngs of early morning shoppers holding their cups of Costa coffees and bags of Gregg's pastries.

Matthew had filled the day full for them, starting out at York Minster, where they both admired the beauty of the white, vaulted ceilings, the intricate details of the medieval stained-glass windows, and the stunning, Gothic exterior of the structure.

He'd wondered if her excitement that morning would continue throughout the day, so he was immensely pleased when it did as they visited Guy Fawkes's birthplace, countless shops, seventeenth century inns, and eventually the Shambles and Little Shambles, where she'd actually laughed with delight at the sight.

"I honestly had no idea a place like this even existed," she said, shaking her head in amazement as they walked down the narrow street, timber-framed structures jutting forth on each side, only a few feet apart from touching one another in the center.

Signs hung out across the street, alerting potential customers of sweet shops, fudge pantries, and tea rooms. They walked past a shop filled entirely with Harry Potter merchandise, and her brow raised.

"Your favorite shop?" she guessed.

"Oh, of course."

They moved farther along, stopping at the fudge shop for Winnie to purchase a bag before the two of them stood outside together, staring at the quaint and cozy atmosphere the Shambles exuded.

"I bet you can't guess how far back this dates," Matthew challenged, leaning closer to her to be heard above the crowds and the musician playing "Viva la Vida" on his harmonica in the street over.

"Let me guess," Winnie said, popping a small piece of fudge in her mouth. "The medieval era?"

"Wait, how did you know that?" he asked with narrowed eyes.

Her gray eyes sparkled as they met with his, a bit of fudge sticking to her lower lip, and his heart leapt. He should not be looking at her lips right now. Fortunately, he knew just the thing to distract himself.

"This street used to be called the Great Fresh Shambles," he began. "That was because butchers would hang their meat out for people to purchase. At one point, there were thirty-one butchers' shops here, and the blood from all the meat would just drain right down the road."

She fell silent, a look of disgust on her face as she chewed another piece of fudge half-heartedly, the other half of the sweet between her thumb and forefinger.

There. That had put a stop to his mind wandering. "Really makes you have an appetite, huh?" he asked.

"Not really," she mumbled.

"In that case..." He reached forward and stole the other half of her fudge, slipping it into his mouth before she could protest.

"Hey," she exclaimed in protest.

He merely walked away with a brighter grin.

After the Shambles, the two of them headed for the museums, ending with the York Castle Museum, where Matthew was more than happy to discover Winnie just as enthusiastic about what she saw within the buildings as she was with the outside of them.

She read every detail of the pamphlet she was given, looked at every sign of every exhibit, and commented on everything she found that was even remotely medieval related.

Matthew was dying. How often had he wanted to take a girl on a date to a museum but had stopped himself, knowing they'd lose their sanity from utter boredom?

But not Winnie. She was taking it all in stride and was making *him* slow down.

Not that they were on a date, of course. This was still purely business-centric. But if they *had* been on a date, this would have been the best of his life.

At one point, as the two of them walked past displays designed to throw the observer directly into the past—Victorian streets, prison cells, candlestick makers' shops—Winnie paused, looking up at him with a curious gaze.

"What?" he asked, ducking in his chin. Why was she looking at him like that? Did he have something on his face?

"I was thinking last night before I fell asleep," she began.

He narrowed his eyes, waiting. "Yes?"

"I was thinking about how you shouldn't give up on your dream of teaching."

"Oh?" Matthew asked, slightly distracted. Did she just admit to thinking of him last night...while she was in bed?

Get ahold of yourself, Matthew.

"There are different ways you could make it happen, you know?" Winnie continued. "Instead of a fancy university at first, you could settle for a while with one of the local schools near enough to commute to. Or you could teach virtually so you wouldn't have to go anywhere at all. You could even set up online courses with your own curriculum and find people interested in the same things you are."

Matthew didn't know what to say. That level of thoughtfulness he was used to from his family, but Winnie?

They stopped in front of one of the displays, a dining room decorated with dark-paneled wood on each wall, an old piano at the back, and a table filled with all manner of delicious-looking wax food.

Instead of facing the room, however, he faced Winnie, his eyes roving over her features. He still couldn't believe this was the same woman as before. The one he'd despised and expected the worst from.

He'd been so stupid, so blind as to not have seen the real Winnie until now.

"I hope you don't mind my suggestion," she said hesitantly. "I just figured, if it's something else you have a passion for still, why not pursue it?"

She winced, and Matthew pulled out from his thoughts. She must think he was upset with her for her suggestion. "No, I don't mind your thoughts at all," he quickly corrected. "I actually really appreciate them. And truth be told, I've considered doing the online thing, especially during the winters when we don't hold the festival. I usually spend those months working around Foxwood, but now that Dad is more self-sufficient and I have more time, teaching would work even better. I just..." He shrugged. "I don't know if I could actually pull it off. Or if my dad would approve of another foolhardy idea from his son that he'd later have to bail him out of."

Winnie peered up at him, her eyes taking on a serious note. "You really think he wouldn't support you?"

Matthew didn't have to think for a minute. "No. He would. He always has. I guess I just don't want to disappoint him again like I did with the festival."

"I highly doubt you could ever be a disappointment to your dad."

He gave her a knowing look. "Hiring a consultant to replace me sort of proves you wrong, Miss Knox."

She smiled. "No, but really. He loves you so much. He clearly just wants to help." She looked away, her features sobering. "Even if you were a disappointment to him, I hope you wouldn't ever let it stop you from doing what you really wanted to do. Like I did."

Matthew stared. Was she referring to the careers that hadn't worked out or something else entirely?

He wanted to ask, but she turned to face the darkened display room more directly.

"Anyway," she said. "If you ever need any help getting anything like that started up, I know of a consultant who considers herself slightly well-versed in helping businesses, whether they're brand new or highly seasoned."

He peered down at her with a smile. "It's good to hear you talking about yourself in a positive light again."

She shrugged. "I figured it was about time Winnie-Freakin'-Knox made another appearance."

A chuckle pulled from his chest.

"Seriously though," she continued. "I'd be more than happy to lend some advice. No pressure, though."

"Well, I appreciate it," Matthew said sincerely. "I'll be sure to take you up on the offer."

They walked to the next exhibit, but he still stared after her, just as he did while they made their way through the museum. Her whole demeanor, her whole person had altered so greatly, he could hardly comprehend it. Then again, had he not changed, too? He wasn't being a total cretin now, criticizing her and finding fault with her at every turn. Instead, he was doing exactly as Dad had taught his entire life—something Matthew should have done from the beginning.

Giving Winnie a chance.

He was only glad he could do so before she left England for good because now, her opinion mattered to him.

It mattered to him more than he cared to admit.

CHAPTER THIRTY-FOUR

THE REST OF THE DAY PASSED BY SWIFTLY, AND SOON, the two of them were headed outside of the museum.

As they left the warmth and comfort of the building, they were met with cooler temperatures, a storm having blown in to cover the sunshine and fill the city with rain. With the afternoon drawing to a close and the poorer weather creating puddles across pathways, the streets that had once been filled were swiftly deserted by tourists and residents alike, allowing Matthew and Winnie to reach the car much faster.

She thanked him for opening her door for her, then lowered herself into the vehicle, peeling off her raincoat and buckling up as Matthew got in on the other side.

He made to start the car, but unsurprisingly, Minnie struggled to meet expectations yet again, stalling for what seemed the hundredth time that trip.

"Come on, girl," Matthew soothed, rubbing the steering wheel again.

"Do you really think that helps?" Winnie asked.

He held up a finger to silence her.

She did as she was told, but when the car stalled again, Winnie had to hide a smile. "She's quite temperamental, isn't she?"

"Aren't all women?" Matthew asked. "Weren't you just saying that she was growing on you?"

"That was before when she was actually doing what she was told."

In the next moment, the car started. "Ah ha!" he exclaimed in triumph. "See? A little patience goes a long way."

"No one should have to be as patient with their cars as you are with this one."

"I can be patient with an ever-reliable vehicle," he returned.

Over the next hour, after a quick bite to eat, the two of them continued through unrelenting rain. Darkness fell, and still, the windshield wipers thwapped back and forth, back and forth.

They drove along a quiet street, turning slowly with the curves that followed stone walls and crooked trees that were only visible in flashes.

Winnie peered out into the darkness, and a nugget of worry hunkered down in her belly.

"Is Minnie safe in this kind of weather?" she asked.

This was too similar to how she'd spun out on the road to Foxwood.

"Far, far more than your little green sports car," Matthew assured her.

Winnie nodded, still trying to calm her rattled nerves.

"Are you worried?" Matthew asked after she fell silent.

"Slightly. Are you not?"

"Not with Minnie."

The car rattled in response. Matthew looked down in confusion. "What is it now?" he muttered to himself, his brow furrowed.

Winnie stared. Had the sound been different than any other that day? It must have been. Matthew looked genuinely troubled.

After another sputter, a loud *pang!* and *cling!* sounded near the bottom of the car. Winnie gasped. Matthew merely frowned. "Come on," he said louder.

But the car had had it. Little by little, it slowed until finally coming to a stop, and Matthew pulled off to the side of the road just in time.

Winnie was about to make some sarcastic comment about the car's reliability, but the sight of the frown marring Matthew's forehead made her hesitate.

After a minute of silence, however, she couldn't help herself any longer. "Is she officially...kaput?" she asked as gently as possible—and with only the slightest hint of irony.

His frown stayed the same. "I'm sure she's fine. She's probably just acting up. First time she's had to share attention from me before, you know."

"Oh, so it's my fault," Winnie returned.

He glanced at her sidelong. "I'm not saying it is, but I did warn you about offending her." With a sigh, he unbuckled. "I'll go see what the problem is."

"From the sound back there, I would guess Minnie coughed out her engine."

"Hush," he said with a pointed look, then he got out and closed the door behind him.

Winnie smiled happily to herself. He *was* fun to tease. Then again, maybe she shouldn't under the circumstances. If the car really was dead and they ended up being stuck wherever the heck they were, what were they going to do?

Her concern didn't last long. She knew Matthew would take care of them both.

Choosing to be a damsel in distress again, Winnie?

Fine, she'd put forth some effort, too. She pulled out her phone to search for what was nearby—a car garage, a hotel, Foxwood—but, to no surprise, she had zero service.

The first time she had experienced no cell service on the road to the estate, she'd been utterly and absolutely frazzled. Now, she didn't know if it was the slower paced two days she had or her time spent with Matthew, but she was completely at ease.

A few minutes later, Matthew lowered the hood and came back to the car, giving a shiver as he left the cold air outside for the now-lukewarm air inside. Rain beaded in his beard and dripped from his curls.

"So what's the verdict for our Minnie?" Winnie asked.

Matthew's shoulders lowered. "I think she's going to require some major work to recover from this."

"Of course she will," Winnie returned. "She's, like, two-hundred years old."

He pulled in his lips. "A little respect for the wounded, please?"

"My apologies," she said, her hands raised in a gesture of retreat. She looked at the rain now pouring down the windows in droves. "So what are we supposed to do now? Call for an Uber?"

"No, they're too hard to find all the way out here. Of course I had to take the scenic route in the dark," he mumbled. "We're only about thirty minutes from Foxwood, though. Char should be able to pick us up."

Thirty minutes alone in the dark with Matthew Wintour? Winnie didn't mind if she did.

He pulled out his phone, clicked on his sister's name, then held the device in his hand against the steering wheel. He placed the call on speaker as the other end rang throughout the quiet space of the car.

"How do you have service?" Winnie asked.

Before he could answer, his sister picked up. "Matthew?"

"Hiya, Char," he said.

"Hiya, you okay?"

"Yeah, we're all right. You're on speaker with me and Winnie."

"Oh, Winnie! Aw, I love Winnie. All right, Winnie?"

Winnie beamed. She had only spoken one other time with Matthew's sister since the park, yet she felt as if she and Char were the best of friends.

"Hi, Char," Winnie greeted back.

"Is my brother behaving himself?"

"Well..." Winnie began.

"Char, listen," Matthew interrupted. "Before you and Winnie get into another *Matthew-Teasing-Fest,* I just needed to tell you, Minnie has finally died on me."

"Wait, what?" Char asked. "You're breaking up, Matty. I just *talked* to Winnie. How did she die on you?"

A guttural laugh sounded at the back of Winnie's throat.

Matthew shot her a look, but his eyes wrinkled at the sides, a clear sign he was finding this humorous, too. "Not *Winnie. Minnie.*"

"Oooh," Char said. "That stupid lemon? Why haven't you gotten rid of it already?"

"That's what I've been saying this entire time," Winnie piped in.

"Shh." Matthew put a finger to his lips.

"Are you telling me to hush?" Char asked, her voice taking on an attitude.

"No, I'm telling Winnie to hush," he clarified.

"I thought Minnie was dead? Why would she need to hush?" Char asked.

Again, Winnie laughed.

"Oh my giddy aunt," Matthew said, pressing a hand to his brow. "Listen, Char. My car has died, and Winnie and I are stranded near Littlethorpe, I think. Is there any way you could pick us up?"

"Oh..." Char clearly hesitated, and Matthew met Winnie's gaze. "I...Um, yeah, I can do that."

Matthew frowned. "Wait, what's the matter? Are you busy?"

"No. Well, just a bit. I was about to leave on that date I told you about, but I can cancel."

Winnie instantly shook her head in protest, but Matthew was already on it. "Oh, I forgot you'd mentioned that. No, don't cancel. We'll be fine. You should go on the date. Winnie agrees, too."

"Your car has feelings about who I date?" Char asked.

"No, *Winnie,*" Matthew stated loudly.

Char's voice hinted at her own smile. "I know. I was joking that time. Really, though, I'm sure I can reschedule."

"No, please. We'll be fine. I'll just call Mum or Dad," Matthew said.

"They're in Manchester for the night, remember?"

Matthew grimaced. "That's right. Well, we, uh..." He seemed to think for a minute. "I think there's a small bed and breakfast in Littlethorpe. We can just stay for another night and have you pick us up in the morning." He glanced at Winnie, clearly seeking her approval, which she gave with a ready nod.

Anything to get Char on the date. A single mother of two children deserved that at the very least.

"Are you guys sure?" Char asked. "I don't want to put you out."

"No, we'll be right," Matthew said with a reassuring nod, though Char couldn't see.

"Right," Char said, still hesitant. "Well, give me another call when you get sorted at the B&B, just so I know you made it."

"Will do. Thanks, Char. Love you, bye."

Winnie's heart nearly exploded at his expression of love for his sister. She couldn't remember the last time her siblings had shared their love for her—or she for them, for that matter.

He hung up the phone and faced Winnie with an expectant look.

"What?" she asked.

"Are you ready to walk in this downpour for ten minutes to the B&B?"

Ten minutes? Eesh. But what choice did they have? "Yep," she stated with a smile. "Good thing I've got my wellies."

He grinned, and together, the two of them left Minnie at the side of the road with their suitcases and umbrellas in hand, both of them praying the inn held some vacancies. Otherwise, they were in for a very long, very cold night in what little-to-no shelter with which Minnie would provide them.

Come on, B&B.

CHAPTER THIRTY-FIVE

WINNIE AND MATTHEW REACHED THE BED AND breakfast after a cold, wet walk, both of them relieved to see the *"Vacancies"* sign bright at the front of the red-bricked, white-trimmed home.

Newly energized by the mere thought of a warm bed and dry clothes, they rushed forward. Matthew opened the door for Winnie as a bell jingled above, and instantly, they were greeted by the warmth of a crackling fire and by the smell of wet wood and brown sugar.

"It's freezing out there," Matthew said, closing the door behind them and giving his head a little shake as raindrops flew out to the side of him.

They looked around the small waiting area of the bed and breakfast where three claw-footed chairs were arranged before a modest fire that cast a glow across the wooden floor. A table sat in the middle of the chairs, holding a tray with clean, floral teacups and lace doilies beneath it.

At the other end of the room, a small front desk was situated with no one behind it, though a white cat sat on top, flicking its tail toward them. A vase of flowers was perched at one end, and a bell on the other, which Matthew moved forward to ring.

A few moments passed by, but no one responded.

"I guess we'll try again," he said, dinging the bell once more.

By the third time, Winnie began to worry they'd have to walk back to the car, but a moment later, a door opened in the back room, and a harried looking woman appeared around the corner. Her raincoat was sopping wet, along with her wellies and hat that barely covered a bush of gray hair.

Her brow rose in surprise when she caught sight of them. "Oh, oh my goodness. I'm so sorry. Have you been—Oh, Angel!"

Winnie nearly jumped out of her skin as the woman ran forward, pulling the cat into her arms with her eyes heavenward. "Oh, I thought I'd lost you for good, my darling boy." She cast her eyes at the cat, giving him a stern look. "Don't you ever scare me like that again."

Once more, she held him close to her chest, breathing out a heavy sigh of relief. Finally, she looked back to Winnie and Matthew, who both stood staring at the woman in stunned silence, though they still tried to smile politely.

"I'm terribly sorry," the woman said. "I've been out in the rain looking for this little rascal for the last thirty minutes. Thought he'd got lost in the storm." She pulled him away from her and scowled at him again. "Did you just slip right past me as I walked out? Cheeky mite." Once more, she held him against her chest. "I couldn't live without my little boy, despite him causing me turmoil day in and day out."

She breathed another sigh, then finally placed the cat on the floor and began to shed her wet clothing. "Now, where was I? Oh, yes. Welcome to Robin's Nest Bed and Breakfast. I'm the owner, Agnes Kitchingside." She smiled, then raised her eyes up and down the length of them. "I take it you're here looking for a room and shelter from the storm yourselves?"

Winnie paused, heat crawling up her neck, despite how chilled she still was. Did she say *a* room? As in one?

"Yes, we are," Matthew said.

Winnie's eyes rounded. Had he not caught Mrs. Kitchingside's words?

"Alright," the woman said, placing thin glasses at the end of her short nose and pulling out a binder filled with paper. Had she no computer system to book people into the rooms?

"Um..." Winnie said, moving forward with a finger in the air. "Two rooms, that is."

Matthew stared at Winnie, as if to say, *"That goes without saying."* But he nodded all the same. "Oh, yes. Of course. Two rooms."

Mrs. Kitchingside eyed them above her glasses, a wince marring one brown eye. "Oh, dear. I'm so sorry, but we've just one room available."

Winnie's ears started to ring. One room? Would they have to walk back to the car, spend the night in Minnie's cold clutches? She wasn't sure she had the tenacity to even step foot in that rain again. She was chilled to the absolute bone.

"Just one?" Matthew repeated, as if he was coming to terms with what that meant, too.

"Yes, I'm afraid so," Mrs. Kitchingside explained. "We've one under construction and the other is occupied." She stared at them, clearly wondering why the two of them were having a difficult time accepting her words. "The room I have to offer is equipped with a king-sized bed, however."

Matthew nodded absentmindedly. "Do you know of any other places to stay nearby?"

"Not for miles, deary. I'd give up my own bed, but I don't think either of you would take kindly to Angel as a sleeping companion."

Winnie nearly laughed, thinking the woman was joking, but at Mrs. Kitchingside's sincere expression, Winnie swallowed her chuckle and took to staring at the cat, instead. Angel now slept comfortably before the fire, curled into a warm, hairy ball. At this point, Winnie would take the cat's place at the front entryway before returning to the car.

"Winnie?"

Winnie pulled her attention back to Matthew, who stared down at her expectantly.

"What do you think?" he asked, motioning to Mrs. Kitchingside.

Winnie hesitated, glancing at the woman, who still watched them curiously over her glasses.

"Excuse us just one second," Winnie said politely, then before awaiting a response, she led the way back to the door.

She faced Matthew once they were far enough away from the woman's prying ears, intent on stating in no uncertain terms that she could not fathom walking back to the car, but he spoke first.

"You take the room," he whispered. "I'll sleep in the car."

Despite his gallant offer, she instantly shook her head. "And have you freeze to death at my expense? Absolutely not."

"I'd most likely be fine," he said with a flippant shrug.

But Winnie was adamant. "No. That's not an option."

He stared down at her, their voices still low. "Okay, but what other option do we have, short of sharing the room tonight?"

Honestly, the very notion was ridiculous. Absurd. Absolutely asinine.

And yet...

She sighed. "That's fine."

"What's fine?"

"We can just share the room."

He stared down at her, his brow raised in surprise. "And you'd be okay with that?"

"Of course," she said, determined not to make it a big deal.

Who cared that they were once enemies and now friends? Or that there was all this tangible, warm, sparkling chemistry between them? They were professional, working adults. They could handle one night in the same room in order to keep the both of them dry, safe, and warm. Not to mention alive.

"But," Matthew began, still clearly hesitant, "wouldn't it be a little...inappropriate?"

Bless his heart. "Only if you make it so, Matthew Wintour," she teased.

He smiled, and the awkwardness from before seemed to drip off them with the rain.

"Anyway," she continued in a whisper, glancing back at Mrs. Kitchingside. The woman's eyes darted swiftly away as she pretended not to listen. "It's not like we have to share the bed. One of us can sleep in it, and the other can sleep on the floor with pillows. Anything is better for the both of us than sleeping with that traitorous Minnie for the night."

Matthew grimaced. "She *is* traitorous. The little minx."

Winnie nearly laughed. "So it's decided, then. We share the room."

"You sure it won't make you uncomfortable?"

"Nope. I trust you."

The words startled her as much as they seemed to startle Matthew. His eyes darted toward her, lingering and softening as the seconds ticked by.

"You do?" he asked.

Winnie had no idea where the words had come from, other than the center of her soul. She didn't really have a problem trusting others. She'd trusted some boyfriends in the past. She trusted her sister Sarah. But trust the guy who'd openly admitted trying to get rid of her?

Yet, it was true.

"Yep," she said flippantly. "Any guy who names his car *Minnie* can't possibly be a threat."

He chuckled, and they returned to Mrs. Kitchingside. "We'd love your final room, thank you."

"Excellent," the woman responded, though her curious eyes remained on them.

Winnie looked away, unable to respond to anymore probing. She was questioning herself enough, wondering once again how she'd managed to go from practically hating Matthew Wintour to liking him...If not more.

After providing their information and paying for the room, Winnie assuring Matthew she'd reimburse him for half, they followed Mrs. Kitchingside to the room upstairs.

Winnie didn't think they would have had any trouble finding the way on their own, but Mrs. Kitchingside had insisted—no doubt to lob more questions at them.

"So are you in Littlethorpe for any particular reason?" she asked with a smile over her shoulder.

"We had a spot of car trouble on the way in," Matthew responded politely. "Had to leave it on the side of the road a couple miles back."

"Oh, dear. I can recommend the motor mechanic we use, but he won't be available until morning."

"I'd appreciate that," Matthew returned.

Before long, after a few more investigative questions from Mrs. Kitchingside, the three of them arrived at the room.

"Toilet's down the hall, breakfast is served downstairs in the dining room from six o'clock to nine o'clock, and I'll be up shortly with complimentary cake and a hot drink for you both."

"Oh, lovely," Matthew said with a smile, taking the ancient-looking key she extended toward him. "Thank you so much for your hospitality, Mrs. Kitchingside."

She nodded, her eyes flicking between them before she left, though it looked like it pained her to do so.

Matthew unlocked the door, then motioned for Winnie to precede him inside the room. With a grateful nod, she ducked past him and entered the cozy space, her eyes sweeping across the room in pleasant surprise at the clean, inviting atmosphere.

The walls were painted a soft olive green, dotted with a few frames holding pressed leaves from oak trees and bracken, and the king-sized bed was covered with a white duvet, a large, floral comforter was folded neatly at the foot of it.

At the far side of the room, near the single black, diamond-paned window, was a small seating area with two thin chairs and a table that didn't look like it could support the weight of a single crumpet, let alone two meals.

The size of the room wasn't very grand at all, the bed taking up most of it, but it was tidy, smelled of lemons and musty wood, and—most importantly—was warm and dry.

"Not bad, is it?" Matthew asked behind her.

Winnie nearly jumped. She'd been so taken with the quaintness of the room, she'd almost forgotten she wasn't alone.

Almost. Because who could ever really forget when they were around Matthew Wintour?

"It's really nice," she agreed, still turned slightly away from him.

"And look," he said, motioning to a twelve-inch television with a video player beneath it. "We could even fall asleep to a movie tonight. No, wait. I've forgotten my VHS collection at home."

She grinned. "Are you sure you didn't leave it behind with your other antique?"

He turned accusing eyes on her. "You'd best not be speaking of my Minnie."

She laughed, and they shared a smile, their eyes catching as neither pulled away.

Winnie's breathing shallowed. She tried to lean on that same confidence she had downstairs, but the reality of their situation continued to thwap her right in the face.

This had not been a part of the plan, to spend the night with Matthew. Not a part of *the* plan, *her* plan, or *any* plan.

But tonight, with those once-glacial blue eyes now looking at her with all the warmth of the deep, crystal pools of the Caribbean, she wasn't sure that she didn't want this—that she didn't want *him*—to have been a part of her plan all along.

"You're not going to make this awkward now, are you?" Matthew asked.

She placed a hand on her hip. "Nope, definitely not. Are you?"

"Why would it be awkward?" He walked to the other side of the room, sliding her suitcase—which he'd carried up the stairs for her—against the bed. "We're just two enemies turned business associates turned...friends? Question mark?"

She nodded, laughing at his words, as if he was voice texting.

"Yes, friends," he continued, "who just spent two days together *not* on a date, and who are now going to end it by sharing a room together." He glanced at her from over his shoulder as he moved his own suitcase toward the opposite side of the room. "There's nothing strange about that at all." He looked up, staring at nothing in particular. "And yet, if my mum knew where I was..." He blew out a slow whistle and shook his head.

"If she did, she'd be just fine with it," Winnie said, taking a few steps forward. He seemed to be owning the room as he walked about, but she was going to pay for half of it. She could own it, too. "Because that's literally all we're doing. Sharing a room. Nothing else."

"Nothing else at all." He turned to face her, tucking his hands in his front pockets as his eyes took on a glint she wasn't sure she liked.

It was a good thing she *did* trust him because otherwise, with a look like that, she would have gone running for a distraction from Mrs. Kitchingside and Angel.

With an amused shake of her head, she turned away from him, feeling slightly overheated, despite her clothing still being soaked through.

Speaking of.

"I'm gonna go get changed," she said, pulling out her pajamas and bag of toiletries from her packing cube at the top of the suitcase.

Then she paused. Should she get in her pajamas? Or should she just sleep in a change of clothes? No, that would be ridiculous. Besides, her pajamas were perfectly fine. Sweats and an oversized sweatshirt. He'd seen her in them already, hadn't he? The night she'd almost quit.

With a nod of resolve, reminding herself that this situation was only going to be awkward if she *made* it awkward, she excused herself from the room and walked down the hallway to where the shared bathroom was situated.

She didn't like the idea of sharing a toilet with all the tenants, but beggars couldn't be choosers. And tonight, she was a beggar.

Closing the door behind her, she took a quick glance in the mirror, horror rushing over her at the sight of herself. She looked *worse* than a wet dog tonight. Her hair was slicked back and half-fallen from her bun, her makeup leaked down from her eyes and slid down the sides of her cheeks, and her silk shirt stuck to her shoulders with wrinkles galore.

Swiftly, she tried to fix her appearance, pulling out her bun to reset it, but her wet hair wouldn't cooperate. With a sigh, she ran a comb through it, instead, fluffed up the strands with her fingertips, wiped off her failed mascara, and changed into her pajamas.

She and Matthew were friends, and if they were friends, it really didn't matter what she looked like. Maybe tonight, she would be fine with being average.

Actually, that could be her new mantra.

Step aside, 'Be like Fort Knox.' Make room for 'I'm fine with average.'

Her hand paused above the door handle at the thought, and she turned to look at herself in the mirror, surprised at what she saw now.

Instead of a wounded fawn trying to hide exactly who she was, impressing others with a wealth of business knowledge and pencil skirts and pulled-back hair, she saw a simple girl with imperfect locks down to her shoulders, comfortable, oversized clothing, and eyes that reflected the joy she'd felt with the most perfect man and the most perfect two days of her life.

She could get used to seeing this side of her—the real, true version of Winnie Knox.

With confident steps, feeling lighter than the air around her, she made her way back to the room, opening the door with that same smile on her lips.

And there it froze, as did her feet, body, and heart, all of them immobilized by the sight before her—Matthew half-dressed, standing in the middle of the room they would share that night.

With his dark blue sweats fortunately in place, he lowered his shirt, turning toward her as he revealed just a glimpse of his chest and abdomen.

He looked…Well, let's put it this way. He looked exactly how a person would expect a knight to look putting on his shirt. Except multiply that expectation by three thousand and maybe, *maybe*, you'd get close to how Matthew looked right now in front of her.

The moment lasted shorter than two blinks of an eye, and yet, the image of the contours of his back, the angles across his abs and chest, the shifting of his many muscles as he put on his shirt would be engrained in her mind for all eternity.

And she wasn't mad about it.

She wasn't mad about it at all.

CHAPTER THIRTY-SIX

"YOU ALL RIGHT?" MATTHEW ASKED.

Winnie blinked, shaking herself mentally from her stares. "Sorry, I figured you'd dress in the bathroom. I can come back."

"No need. I'm finished."

She nodded, walking in and closing the door behind her.

He straightened his thin, gray t-shirt over his torso, revealing just a sliver of his skin, but Winnie forced herself to look away all the same, hanging her wet clothes near the wall heater, where Matthew's shirt and pants already rested.

He motioned to the brittle table near the window, cake and teacups now balanced precariously atop the small surface. "It was a good job I was here when Mrs. Kitchingside brought the slices of cake. She might've come in and rifled through all our luggage to see what we're really doing here."

Winnie smiled, though still frazzled. She took a few steps forward, blinking away the image of him once again and staring at the cake slices, the smell of sugar and strawberries tickling her nose.

There was nothing that could distract a girl more than sugar.

And yet, when she sat gingerly down on one of the toothpick-legged chairs, not even a bite of the delicious, homemade cake could distract her as he took a seat across from her and his knee pressed up against hers.

She looked up at him furtively, wondering if he had touched her on purpose, but when he didn't move, taking a bite of the cake himself, she had to assume that he thought he was pressed up against the table's leg instead of hers.

Her flesh burned, heat coursing through her heart, reminding her again of the other night, how close they'd been to each other, how his lips had looked drawing toward her.

"You mind if we crack the window open?" she asked, stuffing another bite of cake into her mouth.

Come on, *sugar. Work.*

Matthew nodded, standing to push one side of the window open a few inches, the cool breeze brushing past Winnie's face at once.

The minute he moved, Winnie shifted her legs to no longer sit beneath the table, allowing no further chance of touch between them. As much as she wanted to feel that heat for the rest of all time, she needed to calm down. She was spending the night with the guy, for heaven's sake. She shouldn't be thinking about *kissing* him.

"Better?" Matthew asked, sitting down again, his chair creaking in protest.

"Yep," she lied. "Thank you."

She shoveled another bite into her mouth. It was a delicious cake. Just not as delicious as Matthew in his pajamas. Nothing could ever compare to that.

Except maybe Matthew in his pajamas on a *horse*.

A phone buzzed, and Winnie forced the ridiculous image away from her mind as he pulled out his phone from his pocket.

"Oops. It's Char. I forgot to call her back." He looked up at Winnie. "Do you mind if I...?"

She waved a dismissive hand, unable to speak due to her mouthful of cake. The food was working now, right? It had to be working now.

"Hey, Char," he answered. "Sorry. We made it to the inn and got a room."

"Oh, good. All right, I was just checking."

Her voice was perfectly clear to Winnie, despite Matthew not putting it on the speaker phone this time.

To avoid imposing without his knowledge, Winnie looked down at the street below, the orange lamp in front of the bed and breakfast casting a perfect halo beneath it. A couple walked past, their gentle whispers drifting up toward her as they walked beneath a single black umbrella together.

"Wait," Char said. "Did you say *a* room?"

Winnie took another bite, focusing outside all the harder.

"Yeah, there was only one available." Matthew leaned back in his chair, running his free hand through his wild hair that became even more unruly as it dried from the rain.

Would he let her touch it, smooth away one of the curls from his brow?

Pull yourself together, Winnie.

"Wow," Char said. "That escalated quickly. Didn't you guys hate each other, like, yesterday?"

"Hate's a strong word."

Winnie couldn't help herself. She glanced to Matthew, his eyes on her with a deep, lingering look.

"So...you like her, then?"

Matthew's smile faded, an unreadable expression stretching across his features. His eyes narrowed slightly, and she knew he was wondering if Winnie had heard Char's question. Still, Winnie couldn't look away.

"That," he began, "is a question for another day."

"Aww," came Char's disappointed response.

"Enjoy your date, Char," Matthew said.

"And you enjoy your night, Matty."

He hung up then, though their eyes remained locked.

Winnie's mouth dried, the cake turning to crumble as she

chewed. It didn't taste so sweet anymore. Not with Matthew's kiss on her mind.

Winnie.

She pulled her eyes away, chastising herself once again. "So," she said, finally pushing the cake away and carefully leaning back in her chair. She needed something else to distract herself—and there was something that *always* worked, even more than sugar. "About the festival..."

Her abrupt change in conversation didn't faze him, his smile remaining. "What about it?"

"Well, since this is a bonus night neither of us was expecting, I figured we could talk about it for a bit."

"Sound logic. If that's what you prefer to talk about, then let's get to it."

Winnie would *prefer* to talk about how Matthew had managed to obtain such formed muscles and how he looked better than half the men in New York City with their gym memberships and personal trainers.

But work would have to do.

She moved to the bed, sitting on the side of it as she rifled through her luggage and found her writing tablet.

"I've done really good with not thinking about work...when we're out and about." She opened her tablet and pulled up the document she'd been working on each night. "But once I'm alone and trying to sleep, my mind just wanders. I decided to make good use of that time by putting together a few ideas for the festival."

She stood with the tablet, walking toward him. "I realized," she explained, feeling more self-conscious and hesitant by the second, "that I was trying to turn the festival into a spectacle, basically a busy-book for adults and kids—always something to do, always something going on, super stimulative, super action-packed, super loud. But after this trip, I dunno. I guess I've just seen how different it is here. I realized that most people don't always want a busy, stimulating, action-packed event. With your festival, they expected what they receive from the rest of Yorkshire

—beautiful surroundings, things that help them feel active, moments that help them connect with history, time to process what's going on, and choosing what best they'd like to do."

Matthew looked up at her, his eyes soft and eyebrows raised.

She extended the tablet to him, and he reached for it, but she quickly pulled it back. "None of it is set in stone," she clarified. "And anything can change. And please, for the love of all things medieval, if something isn't going to work, *tell me*."

He smiled, still holding out his hand. "I promise."

She sighed, then finally handed him the tablet.

Be gentle, she prayed.

Over the next several minutes, she sat on the edge of the bed, chewing her thumbnail and watching his face carefully as he smiled, nodded, looked thoughtful, and sometimes even frowned, reading through her document of changes, suggestions, and ideas for his festival.

By the end of it, her nerves were shot. Matthew, who still sat on the fragile chair, lowered the tablet with a shake of his head. "Wow," he murmured.

Winnie hesitated. "Wow, as in, 'You've outdone yourself'? Or wow, as in, 'You're missing the boat again, Winnie, give up and go back to the States'?"

"No, wow, as in, you've entirely captured my original vision for the festival."

Relief flooded through her, pushing a smile on her lips and a giddy feeling across her body. "Really?"

"Really," he said with a look of sincerity. "All of these ideas are fantastic. Some of them might be a bit hairy to get sorted, but I think most of them will work." He pulled up the tablet again, reading off some of the ideas she'd had over the last couple of days. "No more rides, no loud music, no script for the jousting." He glanced up at her. "Those will go over so well with the others." He looked back down. "The food suggestions are a great compromise—beef and veggie stew, yes. Turkey legs! Sounds amazing. And purchasing tents that look medieval with flags and everything? I love it. Oh, and this one—having the kids dress as knights and princesses to fight off a dragon?" He gave her an impressed look. "It's not historically accurate, but that one is going to be such a hit. And the damsel! The damsel is back!"

She grinned. That had been the most difficult thing for her to finally get over. But after the trip, being the damsel in distress herself time and time again—being caught falling from a tree, being stuck atop a wall, being stranded in an old car, being lost within thoughts of her family—she figured, there was nothing inherently wrong with a man or a woman needing help from someone.

Especially if that someone was a knight willing and eager to help in return.

Still, she hadn't brought the damsel back without compromising. "She's not going to swoon from men sword fighting," she warned. "That I can't go back to."

"I would never expect you to," Matthew responded.

Winnie listened to him go on and on, describing his favorite ideas, sharing his concerns with others, and adding on to what she already had with his own suggestions.

They spoke of fortune tellers, fire breathers, double the falconry, knights jousting unscripted, sword fighting practice arenas, jugglers and jesters, magic shows and glassblowers.

"We can find local blacksmiths to teach their trade to kids, people who want to try their hand at archery, even ax throwing," Winnie said. "And what did you think of the idea of having one day a month be solely devoted to schools? Then kids can come in and have fun, yet educational experiences. You could even teach them dressed as a knight."

He shook his head with a grin, unable to say a word, which only made her all the more pleased.

"We can have souvenirs like wooden swords and mugs. Even magic wands like in *Harry Potter*."

He grinned. "You knew you'd get me with that."

She most certainly did. "There are quite a few things in there that aren't authentic or historically accurate," she warned. "Archery with the elves, wizards performing magic tricks. So how do you feel about that?"

He shook his head with a semi-amused smile. "I've been such a stickler for the rules, and what good has it done? I nearly lost the festival for good because of it." He held up the tablet with a nod. "But this holds some real magic. Really, *this* is why my dad hired you. This plan has all the heart he saw in you from the beginning, and I genuinely cannot wait to get started on it."

Winnie had to bite her lip to keep her grin at bay. She'd never been so proud of herself, never felt such joy from her work. To have it approved so wholeheartedly by someone who had practically hated her days before? She'd never known such satisfaction.

"Thank you," she said, looking away. "But I can't take all the credit. You were the one who decided to trick me into liking history by drowning me with medieval facts the last two days."

Matthew chuckled, leaning back on the chair again. "I did, didn't I? Well, you can't say it didn't work."

"No, I can't."

"You also can't say I wasn't smooth about the whole thing."

"Oh, you were so smooth," she returned. "My favorite was when you talked to me about the butchers in York. The mention of blood running down the street? Loved that."

"I bet you did." He grinned, reclining farther, this time with his hands behind his head. "Well, it just goes to show, a man with as much talent as me can get anything he wants. Even—"

A loud crack sounded, interrupting his final words, and all at once, the toothpick-legged chair crumbled to pieces, and he fell to the floor in a heap of wood.

CHAPTER THIRTY-SEVEN

WINNIE GASPED, RUSHING FORWARD. "OH MY GOSH, are you okay?"

Matthew let out an embarrassed chuckle, covering his face with his hands as he grunted. "Yeah, I'm all right."

She breathed out a sigh of relief, looking at the mess of wood strewn across the floor beneath him and doing her best not to laugh. Now that she knew he wasn't hurt, the image of his fall—his eyes widening in shock as he came down, arms and legs flailing about—was too funny to ignore.

"I can't believe that just happened," he said, still lying down, his features hidden behind his fingers.

Winnie bit her lower lip. "As they say, pride goeth before the fall. In your case, literally."

He raised his hands so he could meet her gaze, and she gave him an innocent smile, to which he responded with a hardly amused expression. Slowly, he stood, straightening from his position on the ground and groaning again as he rubbed his backside.

"Well, I guess I'll be adding this to my tab," he said, scooting a few pieces of the wood together with his foot. "Maybe I can fashion these scraps into a bed for myself tonight. Have any spare nails?"

"Only the ones on my fingers."

"That is entirely unhelpful, Miss Knox." He clicked his tongue, and Winnie grinned.

"Well," he began again, "how about instead of wasting away the evening trying my hand at carpentry, what if I ring Mrs. Kitchingside, confess my vandalism, and ask her if she has any spare VHS tapes lying around for us to watch? You know, end the evening on a high note instead of on the ground."

Excitement simmered in Winnie's chest. Watch a movie with Matthew? She could think of no better way to end their trip together.

Well, almost.

A few short minutes later, Matthew hung up the phone, having received grace from Mrs. Kitchingside, as well as instructions as to where to find the closet that held the movies. Sure enough, outside of their room, at the end of the hallway and past the bathroom, they found the stash of tapes.

And what a stash it was. As they opened the door, their mouths dropped at the sight of the hundreds of VHS tapes filling the entire closet from top to bottom.

"Wow," Matthew breathed. "That's a lot of movies." He moved forward, pulling out two of them. "But how are we ever going to choose between *Legends of the Fall* and"—He read the other—"*So I Married an Axe Murderer*?"

Winnie laughed. "Two very good choices."

"If you fancy that sort of thing, maybe."

He put the two tapes back, then together, they moved through the collection one-by-one, marveling at movies neither of them had ever heard before—though that wasn't a push for Winnie.

"I have no idea what's good and what isn't, so I'm leaving the choice up to you," she said.

"Oh, don't do that," Matthew said. "Or we'll end up with something like this."

He raised a copy of the live-action version of *The Flintstones*, and she laughed again.

"Okay," she said, leaning forward and choosing one herself, "how about *The Silence of the Lambs*?"

"Er, no. Do you know what that one is about?"

She shook her head, having only heard of the title before. She looked at the back and read the description, and her mouth dropped open in disgust.

Matthew laughed. "I take it that isn't your cup of tea."

"Not by a long shot."

He chuckled again.

A knocking on the side of the wall startled them both, followed by a gruff, "We're trying to sleep in here."

Winnie covered her mouth with her hand. "That's where the other guests are," she whispered.

Matthew clenched his teeth together in a half-wince, half-smile, though his eyes still shone with humor.

"Come on, let's pick something quick," Winnie said.

And yet, the more they looked, the more they laughed.

"*Godzilla*?" he asked. "Oh, no. *Lost in Space*. Oh, oh! *Hero and the Terror* with Chuck Norris! Ah, there are too many good ones to choose from."

Winnie continued laughing, the lateness of the night getting to her—and the fact that she found everything coming out of Matthew's mouth to be completely hilarious.

Eventually, he reached over, placing a few fingers on her lips as his eyes shone with mirth. "Quiet. You're going to get us into trouble again."

The thrill of his warm fingers against her lips was enough to finally settle her down, though now her heart raced instead.

She drew a deep breath, and nodded. "Seriously, just grab a few, and we'll head back to the room."

Matthew took another moment to decide, then reached for a few tapes before they headed back to their room.

She jumped onto the bed as he put the movie in and stood

back from the small screen, the warped sound of the tape warbling as the VHS warmed up to being played after who-knew-how-long.

"What did you choose?" she asked, watching the screen expectantly.

"*The Man from Snowy River*," he said, turning the volume a notch higher before looking back at her. "Have you seen it?"

She shook her head, and his smile grew. "I think you'll like it."

Intrigued, she watched the screen before noting Matthew moving to the chair he *hadn't* broken.

"What are you doing?" she asked.

He paused, motioning to the chair. "Sitting down to watch the movie."

She shook her head. "You can't break *another* one."

He propped his hands on his hips. "What makes you think I'm going to break this one, too?"

"What makes you think you *won't*?" she countered.

He pulled in his lips. "Fair enough."

He looked around the room, clearly in search of another place to sit, but Winnie sighed. It was inevitable. She'd known it from the start.

"Come on." She patted the bed beside her, the first movie preview being played across the screen. "You can sit here."

He gave her a sidelong glance, clearly unsure if her offer was made in earnest.

"I don't bite," she said, patting the bed again. "Come on. You're going to make me miss the movie."

He sighed, taking a few steps forward. "I just don't want to make you uncomfortable."

"You won't," she stated truthfully. "There's also no amount of pillows that we have that would make sleeping on that floor comfortable, so you can put that notion to bed, too."

Dad would be horrified with Winnie's suggestion.

"That is no way for a Knox to behave."

But tonight, his opinion didn't matter. Because she was just

Winnie now, and she was more than fine sharing a king-sized bed with a man she trusted wholeheartedly.

She leaned back against the headboard, but Matthew merely remained where he stood. "What do you mean?" he asked.

"I mean that you may as well sit here now because you're also going to be sleeping here."

"But we agreed to get the room on the premise that you would get the bed, and I would sleep on the floor," Matthew pressed, another preview playing on the screen.

She waved her hand across the length of the bed. "This bed is huge, Matthew. We're both adults. More importantly, we're friends. We can share the bed and perfectly respect each other still."

She'd never seen him so hesitant.

And she'd never liked him more.

"Look." She gathered a few of the extra pillows on the bed, lining them down the center so they both had a good twin-sized bed each to themselves. "See? More than enough room. And now there's a security barrier so you won't be nervous."

He looked slightly more at ease now, but still, he hesitated. "Are you sure?"

"Yes. I don't want you to be dinged for another chair broken," she teased. "And I definitely don't want to listen to you complaining for the next few weeks about how the floor was *so uncomfortable* when I got to sleep on the bed."

Finally, a smile cracked on his lips. "That does sound like something I would do."

"I know." The previews for the movie ended, and the "20th Century Fox" logo sounded weakly on the TV. "Come on, it's starting."

Matthew finally relented. "Fine. But you'd best keep your hands off of me. You may trust me, but I don't know if I can trust you after that slap."

She smiled. "Just don't try to scare me again, and you'll be fine."

He grinned, then he finally climbed onto the bed.

The mattress shifted. Even though they still felt miles apart, the intimacy of the moment increased, making the room feel closer than it was, cozier than it was.

"Comfy, huh?" she asked, trying to play off her palpitating heart as nothing out of the ordinary.

"So much so that I feel like I'm sitting on a sea of clouds," he returned.

She laughed, watching the screen as the tape created a line down the center of it.

"So what is this movie about?" she asked.

"You'll see," he said cryptically.

Soon enough, dozens of thundering hooves stomped across the television, and her heart jumped. She looked to Matthew, his blue eyes bright.

"Horses?" she asked.

His smile faded. "If you don't want to, we don't have to. I just thought..."

His words trailed off as Winnie shook her head. "No. This is perfect."

And it was. An excellent trip. An enthused response to her job proposal. A film about horses. Matthew seated beside her, creating an oasis of utter perfection. Now all they needed was...

Winnie paused, reaching for her suitcase. "Chocolate?"

"Ooh, yes. Only if it's British, mind."

She pulled out a few of the candy bars she'd purchased at the shop back in York. "Will these suffice, Sir Matthew?"

"Oh, yes. The good stuff," he cooed, reaching for a Mars Bar first.

Winnie could only smile. "Now stay on your side, and we'll have a good evening, okay?"

"Don't have to warn me twice," he said, then he took a bite of the candy bar and winked, his jaw working as he chewed.

Winnie looked away, focusing on the screen, though her eyes could have stared at his rolling jawline until the end of time.

They watched the movie in silence, and while Winnie was fully invested in the storyline and the gorgeous horses on display, nothing could pull her thoughts from her proximity to Matthew.

Especially when he rested his arm on the pillows between them.

She swallowed. "Are you crossing your line, sir?" she asked with a pointed brow.

"I daren't." He lifted his arm to reveal the pillow beneath. "See? I'm clearly on my side."

"All right, you just watch yourself," she warned half-heartedly.

"I will." He paused, then spoke again, his eyes remaining on the TV. "There's a lot of room on this pillow, you know? I reckon even your arm could fit on it...if you wanted it to."

Her pulse raced. He was asking to get closer to her. "I dunno. It looks pretty small."

"Cross my heart," he said.

"Don't finish that phrase. You might end up in the same place as Minnie."

Matthew sighed wistfully. "Ah, Minnie. She was a good lass."

They fell silent as the movie continued.

"You'll never know unless you try," he said after a minute.

"What?" she asked. Even though she knew exactly what he was talking about still.

"How big the pillow is."

She shook her head with a smile. Well, he was nothing if not persistent. And convincing—he was very convincing.

A few moments passed by before he leaned closer. "Still room," he muttered under his breath.

She glanced at him, but he looked around the room, pretending like he hadn't said the words, and she couldn't help but laugh.

"You're hopeless," she said.

He shifted closer, and she raised a forefinger at him. "I saw that."

"Saw what? I didn't do anything."

She looked at his arm that had now clearly crossed the imaginary line she'd made in the middle of the pillow.

"See?" She pointed to his arm. "You moved."

He raised his chin. "I did not. The ruddy feather pillow sank."

She laughed again.

She knew they couldn't kiss that night. No way. No chance. But surely just a touch would be enough to satisfy the flame in her heart, the longing in her soul to be near him.

Just...one touch.

She focused her gaze on the horses running across the screen, but after another moment, Matthew's arm drew closer to where hers rested only inches away.

"Just shifting," he said again.

She smiled, shaking her head, though the magnetism Matthew exuded from his sheer presence was undeniable. She didn't know how much longer she could keep away from him.

A few moments later, his eyes fell on her. She fought meeting his gaze for as long as she could before chancing a glance at him, only to have him look away before direct eye contact could be made.

She eyed him curiously, then focused again on the screen, only to have him immediately return to staring at her.

With a smile, she glanced at him again, but his eyes darted away once more. By the third time of her attempting to catch his stares, he leaned closer to her.

"Hey," he whispered. "Why do you keep staring at me?"

She turned to him with an open mouth, ready to defend herself and accuse him of the same thing, but the sheer delight in his blue eyes made her spirits fly.

"Fine," she said, pulling her arm away from the pillow altogether and folding it across her lap. "I *was* considering holding your hand until you did that, but now I don't think you deserve it."

He grinned. "That would've been very forward of you if you had, my lady."

"As if you weren't hinting and wanting to do the same the entire time."

"Not at all." He raised his chin, then shifted his arm on the pillow so his palm was face-up. "*This* would've been a hint."

She looked at his hand, his fingers wiggling discreetly as he kept his arm in place.

Her heart stuttered. *Now* he wasn't hinting. He was outright, blatantly requesting.

Excitement raced through her blood, her breath catching in her throat. Could she? *Should* she?

His fingers were callused and strong, long and masculine. Exactly as a knight's should be. She could only imagine how her smaller hand would feel, held securely in his own.

If she did hold his hand, that would be admitting outright that she felt something for him—an attachment, an attraction, a desire to be near him. Would that be so bad now, though, what with him basically admitting the same right now?

She waited a moment longer, focusing hard on the movie as Jim Craig continued his work with the horse, wondering if Matthew might just give in and take her hand instead of her having to do anything, but she knew deep down, he was giving her the option to choose for herself.

After another moment, her heart pounding against her chest, she couldn't take it any longer. With a sigh—if only to make it seem like she didn't want to be near him so badly—she unfolded her arms and laced her fingers through his.

An explosion of heat blasted through her skin, tingling sensations in every nerve up and down her arm sailing swiftly like a windsurfer across the sea.

And when he responded, his fingers wrapping around the back of her hand, holding securely and gently, she couldn't draw in a steady breath.

"Took you long enough," Matthew muttered.

Winnie snapped a look toward him, but he kept his eyes on the TV screen, his lips twitching with a smile.

Winnie pretended to pull her hand away, but he held steady. "No going back now," he said. "And no crossing this line with anything but your hand, Miss Knox. Otherwise there will be the devil to pay."

"As if I'm the one you need to be warning," she said pointedly.

He looked down at her, their eyes catching, and the look that passed between them told her enough. He *was* warning himself.

And that knowledge was enough to keep her satisfied. At least for now.

CHAPTER THIRTY-EIGHT

MATTHEW WAS DREAMING. IT WAS A LOVELY DREAM—
filled with wildflowers in a meadow, by the smell of it. Or maybe
he was in the rose garden at home. Wherever he was, the sun was
warm on his face and across his hand. It was soft. Comforting.
Gripping.

But, then, the sun didn't have fingers. So what was holding
him in such a pleasant way? Was it his own hand? Or...

A vague memory trickled through his mind like a babbling
brook, and his eyes fluttered open. He blinked as the sun's light
spilled out across his face, then he focused on what lay before him.

Instead of seeing his room, he was greeted by the sight of two
closed eyes, brown hair falling gracefully over a brow, and perfect,
pink lips just a few inches away from his.

Winnie.

How could he have forgotten? He was in bed with Winnie.
They'd fallen asleep watching the movie, shifting as they slept
throughout the night—always remaining on their respective side
—but each time, their hands had found each other's, as if unable
to handle being apart.

Truthfully, it had been one of the best nights of Matthew's

life. Like a dream. The whole *trip* had been like a dream—especially now, waking up beside her.

He remained still, taking the opportunity to observe her for a moment without her being aware.

When she'd first walked into the room last night, sweatpants, sweatshirt, and hair down, just like the night she'd almost left Foxwood, his breath had been snatched promptly from his chest.

He honestly had no idea how he'd kept his hands off of her, especially after he'd read her proposal for the next festival. The changes she'd made, not only to the event, but in herself, had been staggering.

But then, perhaps she *hadn't* changed. Perhaps she'd merely allowed the real Winnie Knox to be revealed. Would Winnie allow her to stay? Or would the New York Boss Lady return the second they made it back to Foxwood?

An unsettled feeling crept across him, but he managed to set it aside the very moment Winnie stirred.

She drew a deep breath, then sighed, her eyes still closed as she shifted to her back. As she did so, her hand slipped away from Matthew's.

The loneliness that followed rushed over him like a raging river.

As her eyes fluttered open, he refrained from reaching out to her again, watching instead as she took in her surroundings, confusion in her eyes until she settled her gaze on Matthew.

To his utter delight, a bright smile stretched across her lips. "Good morning," she said, her voice slightly husky.

How could she make even *that* attractive? "Good morning. Sleep well?"

She nodded, stretching her arms above her head, then covering her mouth as she yawned. "I think so. You?"

"Oh, yes."

Their eyes met, and a look of understanding passed between them. She glanced away with a soft blush across her cheeks.

He wanted to say something more, cause that appealing blush of hers to deepen, but his phone buzzed beside him.

"That's probably Char texting," he said, moving to sit up in the bed as Winnie did the same.

Sure enough, her name popped up on the front screen of his phone.

CHAR

You two lovebirds ready to be rescued?

Now it was Matthew's turn to blush. He swiftly moved the phone away, glancing at Winnie to ensure she hadn't seen his sister's ridiculous text.

Fortunately, she had shifted to pull up her own phone, seemingly unaware of Char's teasing.

MATTHEW

Yep. We're ready when you are.

He thought it best to ignore her "lovebird" comment altogether.

CHAR

I can be there in 45.

CHAR

Did Winnie see my lovebird comment?

CHAR

I hope so.

Matthew once more adjusted the screen to the side.

MATTHEW

No, and she's not going to.

CHAR

LOVEBIRDS LOVEBIRDS LOVEBIRDS

"Is she able to pick us up?" Winnie asked.

Matthew dropped his phone. He'd be sure to delete those texts before he was around Winnie again. "Yep. Forty-five minutes."

"I guess we'd better get up, then."

But both of them remained there. Was she as reluctant as he was to end the trip? Or was she ready to go back to real life?

That same feeling of worry tried to burgeon inside of him, but he batted it away as he would a bothersome fly.

"Hey," Winnie began softly, avoiding his gaze, "before Char gets here, I just wanted to say thank you. For the last few days, I mean. It was...it was really eye opening. Life-changing, even. So, yeah. Thank you for taking the time to help me as much as you did and bringing me along."

She ended with a shrug, clearly trying to play off her gratitude as nothing special. But to Matthew, it meant everything. And it was certainly enough to prompt him to prolong their time together.

"You're welcome," he said with a smile. "But the trip isn't over yet."

She looked at him with a questioning gaze.

"I still have one more thing for us to do at Foxwood. Just be sure to wear trousers this time."

Then he popped out of bed without another word, feeling Winnie's intrigue which made him all the more excited for what he had planned next.

WINNIE DIDN'T KNOW what to expect from Matthew after he'd said he'd had another surprise for her, but her excitement continued to grow throughout the day.

They'd had a full meal at the bed and breakfast, packed their belongings, then waited for Char and her daughters to pick them up. The drive home had been delightful, Matthew playing with his nieces and Char speaking of her date before they'd arrived home—rather, at Foxwood.

Matthew and Winnie had parted ways after, taking showers, sprucing up, and spending a few minutes recouping before meeting again in the afternoon.

Winnie would be lying if she'd said she hadn't been anxiously waiting to see him again. She was eager to discover what final surprise he had for her, but honestly, it didn't matter, so long as she could stare into his eyes and imagine herself touching his curls for longer.

When they did finally meet up in the main entryway of Foxwood—Matthew in his tan breeches, a navy-blue collared shirt, and black boots—every other thought fled her mind.

She knew what those clothes were for. "Matthew..." she began.

He must have already expected her response, raising his hands with a comforting smile. "It's okay. You don't have to do anything you're not ready for. I just thought, after seeing your face light up as you watched those horses on the movie last night, that if you *are* ready to ride, this might be the perfect opportunity to do so."

A rush of conflicting emotions blasted throughout her soul. She couldn't even begin to express how sweet his offer was, nor how it made her heart warm. But she'd sworn off riding horses more than ten years ago for a reason. She couldn't face the heartache of saying goodbye again to something she loved so deeply.

"Just come to the stables at least," Matthew said gently.

Winnie couldn't say anything, unable to dampen the hope in his eyes. In silence, she followed him through the woods until they emerged from the thick trees, the stables coming into view with two horses standing outside of them, all tacked up and ready to go.

Winnie stared at the geldings, then back at Matthew, who looked very much like he was regretting the idea to bring her out there.

The look in his eyes, his offer, his kindness, and his vulnerability softened her heart—*opened* her heart. So much so that a desire slipped by her defenses without her notice, expanding across her entire being before she could even recognize what was happening. That desire grew louder and faster and stronger. It pressed against her senses and prevented her from breathing.

It was a desire she'd suppressed for too long. A desire she never thought she'd feel again, yet a desire she'd longed to feel for ten years.

It was the desire to *ride*.

"I'm sorry," Matthew continued, clearly misinterpreting her silence. "I shouldn't have presumed, especially after what you told me before. We can forget this ever happened. Let's go...climb a tree or something."

He began to lead her away from the horses, but without thinking, Winnie reached forward, her hand resting on his forearm to stop him.

"Wait."

He turned to look back at her, his eyes wary. "Really, Winnie. I shouldn't have..."

His words trailed off when she shook her head. "No. This is the kindest, most generous thing anyone has ever done for me."

Relief shone in his eyes, and despite Winnie's continued reticence, she smiled.

"Are you sure you wish to?" he asked.

She looked back to the black and chestnut horses. "I'm sure."

And yet, as she spoke the words, her voice wavered. Perhaps her spirit was sure. But what about her mind? Her courage?

They moved forward, her heartbeat pounding in her ears.

"You remember Prince," Matthew said motioning to the chestnut gelding beside Nightshade, "Char's horse?"

Winnie nodded, moving to the front of the horse and

allowing him to smell her hand. Her fingers shook from the adrenaline that pulsated through her body. Prince responded with forward facing ears and a look of interest.

The sniff of the horse this time didn't send her spiraling, nor did she have recurring flashbacks of her father's actions. Instead, she was filled with different memories. Far less painful memories. Memories of tacking up Goldilocks. The palomino nibbling at the back of her hair she'd always worn down.

Matthew excused himself for a minute, disappearing within the stables, and Winnie took the time to allow Prince to get used to her—and for her to get used to him—rubbing his neck and forelock as he continued to sniff her.

Matthew returned a minute later. "These are for you. They're Char's. Should fit as perfectly as those wellies did." He extended toward her a pair of smart, black riding boots that matched his own.

"I'm gonna need to start paying your sister for all the clothes I'm borrowing from her," she joked.

She accepted the boots, placing them on one-by-one as more memories returned from her younger years. Donning black boots just like these, pulling on clean breeches, show coats, stock ties, and pins. She'd always looked clean and tidy at her performances, but today, her jeans and raincoat would have to do.

After all, she wasn't trying to impress any judges today. She was merely going to get on a horse for the first time in more than ten years.

Her stomach churned painfully, her nerves seeming to eat her from the inside out as Matthew finally faced her.

"Ready?" he asked.

She planted her feet securely on the ground and nodded.

"I can give you a leg-up," Matthew offered. "Unless you'd prefer a mounting block?"

Winnie shook her head, stepping around to the horse's left side where Matthew waited for her.

Her hands still shook, her legs as weak as jelly. She couldn't believe she was about to do this, to disregard her dad's direct orders—to sit atop this horse and to ride again.

She knew it had the potential to bring on a whole slew of issues. Craving riding day in and day out so she could no longer focus on work. Having Dad ridicule her for disobeying him and, worst of all, embarrassing him yet again by following this "childhood fantasy of becoming a horse girl."

And yet, Winnie knew if she *didn't* ride right now, she'd regret it for the rest of her life. So, with as much courage as she could muster, she moved toward Matthew.

He laced his fingers together and leaned low for her leg, but just before she placed her bent knee toward him, her breathing shallowed, and memories assaulted her.

The last time she'd ridden Goldilocks. The moment she'd been thrown. Dad's words. The feeling of freedom atop her beloved animal.

Tears sprung to her eyes, and she backed away. Matthew instantly straightened, concern filling his features. "It's all right," he said.

His understanding and compassion stabbed at Winnie's pride, and she turned away. "I just need a minute," she said, trying to calm her breathing. "Sorry. This is just..." She broke off with a sigh. "This is just so embarrassing."

"Hey," Matthew said at once, moving around to face her directly. "Please, don't be embarrassed. It's perfectly understandable. There is nothing harder than getting back in the saddle. There are literal books written about it."

But Winnie shook her head. "It's not about getting back in the saddle," she said, blinking away her tears. "It's...It's about *not* getting in the saddle again."

He didn't respond, allowing her time to continue.

"It's been so long," she whispered. "And I loved it *so much*. What am I going to do if I have to say goodbye to it all over again?"

His brow pulled together. "Why would you have to say

goodbye if you don't want to? I thought you *chose* to no longer ride."

She looked up at him, tears brimming again. This time, she didn't blink them away. This time, she allowed them to fall as she finally explained the truth.

CHAPTER THIRTY-NINE

MATTHEW LISTENED INTENTLY, FIGHTING OFF EVERY inch of him that wanted to reach forward and comfort Winnie with a hug, because he knew, in that moment, she needed a listening ear more.

"It was my dad," she said, sniffing as a tear trailed down her perfectly smooth cheek. "He never came to any of my shows. They were just silly and pointless to him. But as soon as I had the chance at reaching the Olympics, he invited all of his bigwig lawyer friends to watch me at the first event he ever attended. Of course that was the event I was thrown..." She trailed off, shaking her head. "He was so embarrassed. He couldn't take it any longer."

She looked away, and Matthew's heart broke at the sight of her own pain written so clearly across her creased brow and tear-filled eyes.

"That night, he told me I'd embarrassed him and our whole family," she said. "So he sold Goldilocks and told me I wouldn't be riding anymore."

Matthew's mouth dropped open, the breath rushing from his lungs. He'd thought her horse had died. But then, Winnie had merely mentioned that she'd lost her. Never in his wildest dreams would he have thought *this* would have occurred.

Anger stirred in his chest, pushing his heart rate higher and higher until he thought it might burst. How could her dad have done such a thing? And for one simple mistake? Worst of all, how could he have ever admitted to being embarrassed by his own daughter for something like this?

"I'm so sorry," Matthew said. "I had no idea."

She shrugged, wiping away another tear. "It's okay. It was just so painful to no longer ride. You always talk about having passion and heart in what you do." Her voice broke. "That was where my passion was. That's where my heart was—in riding. I begged and begged Dad to reconsider, but he said it was time for me to get a real job." She trailed off with another sniff. "It was bad enough to no longer have Goldilocks. But to no longer ride altogether? It took me years to become numb to it. To think of actually being on a horse again is terrifying because I don't want to go through the pain of *not* being on a horse again."

Matthew nodded with complete understanding. How she'd even considered saying yes to this venture blew his mind. And yet, hadn't she showcased her courage and tenacity throughout the entire trip? This woman would never cease to amaze him.

"I know it's not all my dad's fault," she continued. "I'm old enough to make my own decisions now. I could have ridden, but I've just been so afraid of embarrassing him again." She huffed out a soft, disbelieving laugh. "But that's going to happen no matter how hard I try not to."

A look crossed over her features, her brow furrowing.

Matthew longed to hear her thoughts, to know what she was working through in her mind—just as he longed to help. But as each moment ticked by, he could see her emotions shift, clarity rushing through her gray eyes.

She swiped at another tear, moisture smearing across her cheekbone like shining glass. "It's like, I just want to shut up and get on the dang horse, you know?"

He smiled, despite himself, her words so like her.

She looked up at him, her tears disappearing, her breathing steady, and brow setting. "So that's what I'm gonna do," she said, her words determined. "I'm gonna shut up and get on the dang horse."

Matthew couldn't help the pride swelling in his chest.

Before another moment could pass, he reached down, laced his fingers together, and lifted her into the saddle with ease.

And there she sat, tall and regal and ladylike.

In a word, she was perfect.

WINNIE ADJUSTED IN THE SADDLE, the seat comfortable, the stirrup irons steady at her feet, Prince firm in his footing. Her fears lingered, but only as a distant memory, replaced with her firm desire to ride.

"How does that feel?" Matthew asked from below, peering up at her with those caring eyes of his.

She took a moment before responding, closing her own eyes to immerse herself in the moment. The feel of the horse beneath her. The sound of Prince's soft nickering as he relaxed at her touch.

With a smile, she opened her eyes and looked down at Matthew. "It feels...amazing."

He grinned in response. In a matter of moments, he mounted Nightshade, then they were off.

The first few steps took Winnie's breath away. It felt like a life-time had passed by since she'd ridden, and yet, in that moment, it was as if no time had passed at all. For all she knew, she could have been that same eighteen-year-old girl, riding her heart out, moving fluidly with each step her horse took, at one with the animal, with nature. With *herself*.

Yet, she wasn't the same now. She was older. Wiser. She'd learned what heartache and loss were. She'd given up everything for her dad and for her family. And now? Now...she finally, for the first time in years, felt like herself. No more Winnie Knox of the Knox family.

Just...Winnie.

And she loved it.

"You were clearly born to ride," Matthew said beside her. "But how do you fare during a race?"

His eyes took on a challenge, and Winnie felt a burst of excitement.

Trotting, cantering, galloping. They all seemed like a distant dream. And yet, with a grin and a flash of recklessness she wasn't accustomed to, she clicked Prince forward. The horse didn't need much more encouragement, launching across the grass with fervor.

Winnie had been worried for the briefest of seconds that she might be thrown, that she wouldn't be able to handle Prince's obvious power. But then, how could she call herself a horse-woman without pursuing a little adventure?

If she was thrown, she was thrown. What was life without flying?

And so, she flew. She flew across the English countryside, the countryside that taught her to *be*. She flew atop Prince, his hooves pounding against the grass, digging it up as they raced for the horizon. She flew with young Winnie inside her heart, telling her to be brave, to be herself.

And she flew alongside Matthew, across the grounds of his family's estate, feeling a freedom she hadn't experienced—a *joy* she hadn't experienced—in far, far too long.

A HALF-HOUR INTO THEIR RIDE, rain began to fall, so Winnie and Matthew jumped down from their horses and led them nearby to the shelter of a large oak tree, the branches so thick, they could only hear the rain from above instead of feeling it.

With the horses grazing beside them, Winnie propped her hands on her hips, still breathing hard from the exhilaration of their ride.

"I forgot how it felt," she said, staring across the green expanse, mist blurring the trees in the distance. "Riding, I mean."

Matthew came to stand beside her. "There's nothing like it."

"There really isn't. And now I'm just mad at myself for waiting so long to do it again."

"Don't be," he said gently. "There are reasons you couldn't until now."

How true that was.

Silence settled around them, the two of them staring out across the gray-filtered world. Rain pattered on the ground before them, and the gentle footsteps of the horses' nearby marked the rhythmic sound with subtle thuds.

The days before this had been perfect, but right now, standing beneath the oak tree, she hadn't been this happy in years. And she had Matthew to thank for it.

She turned her eyes on him, already finding him watching her, though he averted his gaze to avoid being caught.

She smiled, moving to stand farther beneath the tree. "You know, I thought you'd be a faster rider than what I saw today, Matthew."

She faced him again, leaning against the trunk and propping her hands behind her back to give her a slight cushion.

"I let you win," he said, taking slow steps toward her.

"Really?"

"Yep. I wanted you to gain your confidence back."

While that was probably true, Winnie enjoyed teasing him too much to let it slide. "I dunno. I still think Prince and I could beat you and Nightshade any day of the week."

He held up a finger, his eyes narrowing as he was nearly upon her. "You'd best hold your tongue, Miss Knox. If there's one thing I'm more protective of than even Minnie, it's Nightshade."

"I should hope so. Minnie was a diva that—"

"Now, now," he said, taking another step toward her. He was so close now, Winnie had to lean her head back against the tree trunk in order to see him. "Let us not speak in such a way of the dead."

"You've written her off, then?"

He stared down at her, shrugging as he rested a hand on the thick branch that jutted out near her head. "I dunno. There's another woman who has come into my life recently and has made me rethink matters."

Winnie's heart stuttered. "Oh?" she asked, nearly breathless. "And who might that woman be?"

He leaned toward her, his eyes flicking to her lips. "Well, I've only just begun to get to know her. But what I've seen, I really enjoy."

"Is that so?" she asked.

She stared up at him, her pulse racing, hands still behind her back. She figured that was a good thing, or she'd reach up right that minute and pull his lips to hers.

"Mmm-hmm. She's quite a woman. Strong and brave. Intelligent and humble." His words cast a euphoric spell on her, causing her head to spin as he leaned closer, his blue eyes still shining as his voice dropped. "She also drives me absolutely bonkers."

Winnie scoffed in mock offense, reaching out a hand to swat him across his chest, but he caught it just in time, keeping hold of her wrist.

"You didn't let me finish," he said, grinning. "She drives me absolutely bonkers...in the best way possible."

Once more, she was wrapped up in his words as his thumb caressed the inside of her wrist.

"Because," he continued, his features sobering as sincerity touched his expression, "when I'm around her, I can't think straight. When I'm around her, nothing else exists in the world but the two of us."

He shifted his hold of her, pressing her own hand against his chest, where his jacket parted. His heartbeat tapped against her skin, the speed and strength matching her own heart.

"It wasn't always like this," he continued, his eyes focused solely on her lips, "but now that it is, I can't remember what life was like before she came into it. That is the effect this woman has on me." He paused, looking at her eyes once again. "That woman is you, in case I wasn't clear."

Winnie laughed. "I gathered."

He smiled in return, his throat bobbing as he swallowed. "I don't know what life will look like once we return to reality and our work starts again."

She nodded, her hair rubbing against the trunk. She'd thought the exact same thing across the course of the last few days, and it had kept her lucid. But now, with Matthew's arm propped next to her, his body so near to hers, she was ready to throw all caution to the wind. Was he?

"So I figured," he continued, "we ought to end this little business trip in a more memorable way."

She could hardly keep her eyes open. The tapping rain and Matthew's lulling accent were causing her to fall deeper and deeper into the dream she wanted to live in forever—the dream of being held in Matthew's arms.

"What did you have in mind, then?" she asked, slowly blinking up at him, though she couldn't focus on his eyes any longer.

Matthew licked his lower lip with a growing smile, and Winnie *officially* lost her mind. "I think you know, Miss Knox."

That nickname. Where once she'd despised the two words, now, her heart soared because of them. It was something only they shared. And now, it spoke measures of the change that had occurred between the two of them.

Slowly, he released his hold of her hand, though she kept it against his chest, and he reached forward to caress her cheek, allowing his fingers to slide back to the nape of her neck.

Chills sailed across Winnie's skin in droves, like water flooding the sand on a beach at high tide. She drew in a steadying breath, but it did nothing for the world spinning around her.

He leaned closer to her, inch by inch, her eyes on his until she could no longer see straight, and they drifted to a close.

For what seemed an eternity, she waited blindly, her lips parted, her heart reaching across the empty space between her and Matthew until finally, the warmth from his breath graced her lips, and his mouth pressed against hers.

Satisfaction she'd never known before filled her soul. She'd imagined what it would be like to kiss Matthew, to have his sole attention on her, but those dreams and imaginings paled so far in comparison to reality.

His lips were soft, yet firm, the whiskers of his beard tickling her mouth as he tipped his head to the other side and kissed her again. His heart thudded against her hand, and she pressed her palm flat against his chest to feel it better.

In response, Matthew removed his grip from the branch beside them, using both hands to cup her face in a gentle cradle that caused her legs to weaken.

Winnie had never felt such security, such peace in a person's embrace before, and that only intensified as their kiss grew. Soon, his arms wrapped around her, strong and firm and comforting.

She slid her own arms around his neck, feeling the movement of his upper back as he shifted his hold of her again and again, as if he was afraid to let go for too long.

In truth, she had that same fear. She didn't want him to let go of her—*ever*. Being in Matthew's embrace, being the recipient of his kiss, was everything she'd ever wanted.

Before, with Prince, she had flown.

Now, with Matthew...she *soared*.

MATTHEW WAS HOLDING BACK, though he didn't want to. He wanted to release everything within him into this kiss—his emotions, his fears, his feelings for the woman before him.

What he wouldn't give to keep her there in his arms forever. What he wouldn't give to share with her the feelings growing in his heart—feelings that were as real as they were confusing.

How had he been so wrong about her? How had they argued and fought for so long, only to now share their feelings for each other in such a way that would surely complicate their working relationship?

Then again, how could he care?

These moments with Winnie in his arms, her soft touch on his back, her smooth lips against his, were greater than anything he'd ever experienced. He couldn't be parted from her any longer. He couldn't pull back. He couldn't stop what was occurring between them because what if it didn't happen again? What if the planning for the festival got in the way of everything, destroyed the relationship budding between them?

The thought sobered him, and soon, the kiss weakened. He cursed his brain over and over again, trying to fight against it, but Winnie must have sensed his slowing down, as well.

A single moment later, they pulled apart, their breathing heavy as they tried to catch up from the exhilaration of their kiss.

He rested his forehead against hers, closing his eyes and praying for clarity, for peace, until finally, he dropped his hands from around her.

With a sigh he looked to the horses that had wandered out into the rain. "We should probably get back. It doesn't look like the rain is about to stop anytime soon."

Winnie nodded in silence. Was she as disappointed as he was to have their kiss end?

Together, they made their way out into the fields, gathered Prince and Nightshade, mounted the horses, then rode back to the stables in silence.

All the while, Matthew prayed that the time they'd spent together during their trip was a reflection for many more days to come—and not an indication of how their relationship would end.

CHAPTER FORTY

WINNIE STOOD IN FRONT OF THE STAFF IN THE assembly hall, recalling all too well the first time she'd done this. The uncertain glances, the subtle shaking of heads, Matthew's snarky comments from the back. It was all rushing back to her.

But this time would be different. Because this time, *she* was different.

"Hi," she said awkwardly, refusing to pull up her typical Knox exterior. How could she claim the power from the name when she'd decided to be just Winnie? "Thank you so much for coming here this morning. I'm sure you've all been wondering what's going to happen to the festival after last week's, um, okay event."

A few nods occurred around the room. Matthew, who sat on the front row, leaned forward, his eyes focused on hers with a soft, encouraging smile.

Her heart skipped a beat, as it had each time she'd seen him since their kiss the day before, but she tore her gaze away, not wanting anyone to notice their lingering attention on each other.

"I'm happy to say," she continued, "that Mr. Wintour has given us—has given *me*—another opportunity to prove the festival's worth with all of you. I'm even happier to share that this time, your opinions will take on more weight, the changes made will be approved by each member of the staff here, and Matthew and I will be working as a team to ensure this festival really goes off without a hitch."

Her eyes roved over the group, gauging reactions that ranged from excited smiles to wary brows. Inevitably, she returned to Matthew next, his knowing look and encouraging smile giving her the courage to continue until she saw Mrs. Birdwhistle glance between them with a curious gaze.

Winnie grimaced inwardly. She didn't want anyone to think that the only reason she hadn't been fired was because of her fraternizing with the boss's son. Matthew didn't seem bothered by revealing whatever this was between them, but *she* was.

She'd tried to speak with him about it the day before—and that morning after their plan had been approved by Mr. Wintour—but her courage had faltered each time because she worried Matthew wouldn't understand.

Either way, they couldn't carry on with their little looks and smiles, not if she wanted to prove that she'd come by her new position honorably. Until then, she would reinstate her will and force her eyes to focus on everyone *but* Matthew.

That became easier after a while, especially when she told the others that they would be reinstating the damsel in distress and unscripted winners for the joust. The looks of relief and joy across each face reaffirmed to her again that she had finally made the right decision in making the changes, and she was relieved because of it.

Finally, after an hour of Winnie explaining the new proposal, the staff agreed to accomplish the work in time to hold a two-day grand opening event, two weeks from Friday. If they were met with success, they'd continue on every other weekend after that until the summer ended.

To Winnie's relief, each of them appeared to leave the meeting with renewed spirits. Everyone, that is, but herself.

As Matthew remained behind, she geared up for another conversation, one she prayed would end up as good as the last.

Obviously unaware of her reluctance, Matthew grinned from ear-to-ear the moment the door clicked closed and they were left to themselves.

"Well," he said, raising his hands out to his sides, "is it just me, or did they all take those plans remarkably well?"

"No, it wasn't just you," she agreed, stacking up papers to avoid eye contact. "It's night and day compared to the last time."

Matthew didn't respond for a minute, his eyes boring into the back of her. "And yet...you're unhappy."

She straightened the rest of her belongings, then turned to face him. It was time. "No, I'm not unhappy with the meeting at all. It's just that..."

He looked at her, then nodded, as if he understood the turmoil within her mind. "It's just that...we need to chat."

She nodded slowly. "Yeah."

"About moving forward as professionals," he continued.

"Yeah," she repeated. "I just think it might be better if we kept our relationship...on the DL."

He tipped his head to the side, his eyes narrowing. "And by that, you mean..."

She sighed, leaning back so she half-sat on the table. "I'd like to keep seeing you. And spending time with you. But I think, right now, while things are so iffy with people trusting me, it might be smarter if we didn't do anything that led them to believe that I was given a second chance just because of you and I being...together?"

Her words were disjointed, as awkward out loud as they were in her mind.

Luckily, Matthew seemed to understand perfectly. "In short, you wish to keep our business ours."

"Yes, that's exactly what I want," she said.

"So..." He took a step closer to her. "That means no more secret looks."

She nodded.

"No more secret smiles." He drew a step closer.

That look in his eyes...She didn't know if she liked it. It was far too appealing. She tried to lean back, only then realizing she was stuck with the table right behind her.

"No more secret..." His eyes caught hers. "Kisses."

She swallowed hard, trying to remember what they'd been speaking about in the first place.

"Is that what you want?" he asked, his voice barely above a whisper.

"Yes?" The word had come out in a question. She cleared her throat, trying again. "Yes, that's exactly what I want."

He stood a breath away from her, their bodies so close to touching, a single movement would press their chests together.

That twinkle in his eye told her he was doing this on purpose, trying to call her bluff and test her resolve with these brand-new rules between them.

By giving in, she'd be revealing the truth—that she *had* no resolve. But then, why did she have to prove that she had none when she already knew she didn't? What if she *did* kiss him? No one else was in the room with them. Besides, once more wouldn't hurt. In fact, it would probably help her to get it out of her system.

She bit her lip, trying to talk herself out of it, but the more he stared at her in silence, the more her desire grew to wipe that gorgeous smirk off his lips with a kiss he wouldn't soon forget—a kiss that would put the ball back in her own court.

Without another thought as to why she most definitely shouldn't do it, Winnie grabbed his shirt and pulled him toward her, pressing her lips against his without notice.

He responded at once, and fire burst between them, embers from yesterday still simmering, making it easier for them to jump into the flames. She slid her hands up his arms, allowing her fingers free rein as they inched toward his curls—those curls she'd been dreaming of touching for weeks.

All that waiting was worth it, though, as the soft locks slipped easily through her fingertips. Matthew sighed deeply at her touch, and he wrapped his arms around her, his fingers splayed across her back as he pressed her against him.

Winnie deepened their kiss, all the while acutely aware of the location of the door, her ears homed in on any sound that may indicate anyone discovering them.

This kiss was different than the day before. It held more passion, more fire, more sparks. Gone was the timidity, the uncertainty of what the other felt, because they both knew now, as clear as the sun shining that morning, that their feelings were reciprocated.

And that was enough for her.

With as much strength as she could muster, she gave Matthew one final, long, lingering, satisfying kiss, then pulled abruptly away.

The dazed look in Matthew's eyes gave her just the boost her pride needed, his longing for her still emblazoned across his features.

She smiled, pretending to be unaffected.

"I..." Matthew began, his voice husky. He cleared his throat and tried again. "I thought you said no more kisses."

She shrugged. "That was just one last time to help us both get through the coming weeks." She smiled, wiping her lower lip for good measure. "Just like we promised."

"I think it did the opposite for me," he said, smoothing down his beard.

"I was hoping for that, too." She gathered her belongings and headed to exit the assembly hall. "Now come along, Matthew. We've got a lot of work to do."

She walked away, feeling his eyes on her until she left the room. Only then did she allow herself to admit how much trouble she was in. Because any chance she had before of focusing on the festival had now been swallowed up by the sheer and utter bliss she'd received from that kiss.

CHAPTER FORTY-ONE

WINNIE HAD THOUGHT SHE'D BEEN BUSY FOR THE FIRST festival, but that had been absolute circus peanuts compared to this one. Day in and day out, she was solving problems and creating solutions, trying to encourage others while still encouraging herself.

But what was wonderfully different about this one was the enormously altered detail of Matthew and his staff being proactive and genuinely supportive.

With every change made and every request given, each of them continuously jumped in to help. Winnie wondered if it was in part due to her humility or because they'd simply caught the vision of the festival. Whatever the reason, she would take it, as she needed all the positivity she could get.

Especially when Sunday rolled around. During her family chat, Dad had asked again about the estate. Instead of lying, Winnie used up what little courage she had to tell them the truth.

"But Arthur promised you that you wouldn't have to remain over the festival anymore," Dad had said.

"I know, but I didn't—"

"Did you remind him of that?" he'd interrupted.

"No, because this is what I wanted—"

"Never mind. I'm sure something else will come up soon."

His words had held a certain amount of intrigue that unsettled Winnie—Dad's scheming never turned out to be a good thing—but she'd done her best to push it aside.

She had been done speaking after that, slightly relieved that she didn't have the chance to tell them that this was the most satisfying job she'd ever had—or that she was head over heels for her coworker.

Ah, Matthew. The two of them had become nearly inseparable. Despite their best intentions, neither of them were true to their word, taking every opportunity they had to steal away on another horse ride, kissing beneath the oak tree that had swiftly become "their spot," and returning to Foxwood at different times to avoid looking suspicious.

At this point, however, Winnie didn't care if others found out about their budding romance. She was going to prove her abilities this time if it was the last thing she did—not because she wanted to but because she *had* to.

As the weeks flew by and her attachment to Matthew and his family grew, she began to feel the weight of what would occur if she didn't succeed.

She couldn't face the humiliation of begging for another chance from Mr. Wintour, which meant she'd have to go crawling back to New York, or worse, crawling back to Dad, who would take it upon himself to find her more work. She'd never hear the end of it from him or her family. She'd be the one who failed again. The one who embarrassed them *again*.

More than that, more than the stress of returning to her time as a New York consultant or facing her family, if Winnie failed, she also had to face her reality with Matthew sooner. What would happen if she was forced to leave early? Would they be able to stay together, her life in New York and his in Yorkshire?

She didn't know what sort of future she had—if any—at Foxwood or with Matthew. But what she did know was that if she wanted the chance to see what could become of the two of them, she *had* to succeed this time. She had to prove to everyone that she could make it at Foxwood. She had to prove to *Dad* that she could make it.

Because as much as she liked to pretend otherwise, as much as she'd grown in her efforts to ride horses, to trust Matthew, and to become humble enough to take advice for the festival, she was still absolutely out-of-her-mind with fear at the thought of embarrassing Dad again.

Every day the festival inched closer, she grew more and more unsettled, despite her desperate need to remain focused. Because she was still a Knox, no matter what she liked to pretend. And as a Knox, she could no longer accept failure.

THE FIRST DAY of the event arrived sooner than anyone was prepared for. And yet, somehow, as Winnie wandered the grounds of the medieval festival, she couldn't believe her eyes.

They'd done it. They'd actually done it.

Not only were the grounds filled with hundreds of guests, more than twenty booths, and dozens of opportunities for historical engagement, education, and enrichment, but the sun was shining after a week of rain, and smiles stretched across the guests' faces in countless numbers.

Things weren't perfect, of course. She still had hiccups to swallow and wrinkles to iron out, but overall, she couldn't believe how well the festival was turning out.

Taking a minute to herself for the first time in what felt like weeks, Winnie walked around to admire the work alone, greeting guests and workers along the way in her jeans and wellies—that Char had permanently gifted to her.

She loved those horrible little boots, each step making her

smile as she passed by the archery and the ax throwing, the maypole and the photo-op stalks.

Next, she observed the armorist, the female farrier, and the blacksmith who had come down from Scotland—thanks to a suggestion from Matthew's friend, Graham—their tents and beyond filled with guests asking questions about their processes.

Beside them were more booths with wood carvers, professional painters, calligraphy artists, storytellers, puppet shows, glass blowers, and a dozen more tents overflowing with local goods for sale from people who lived in Grassington and other neighboring villages.

Further up were the food tents. The cabbage chowder had been replaced with huge turkey legs and bread bowls, and the smell of roasted meat, warm beef stew, bread, and all manner of sweets—from plum tarts to sugared almonds—tickled her nose and caused her stomach to rumble in protest that it wasn't already being filled with such delectable foods.

It turned out that hiring a professional historical cook to help Mrs. Porter ended up being one of their saving graces, as the feedback for the food was already coming in as more than favorable.

Winnie paused behind a group gathered in the center of the booths, watching in delight as the juggler launched egg after egg into the air, handling them with ease.

The entertainment they'd found was stellar this time. Along with the juggler to occupy those waiting in lines, they'd also hired a flame breather, a few jesters, acrobatics, and even a fortuneteller, played by their very own Mrs. Birdwhistle—each entertainer and each actor dressed in bright costumes reminiscent of the medieval era.

One of Winnie's favorite activities was the dragon being fought off by children playing princesses and knights, each dressed in gowns or armor as they fought off the terror—who just so happened to be played by Char's now-boyfriend. The excitement on the kids' faces and the joy each parent clearly exuded was enough to make Winnie's day entirely.

After defeating the dragon, each of the children were rewarded with a complimentary plastic scepter, sword, or crown, making the day of both child and parent alike.

Fortunately, Winnie also had the foresight to hire a photographer—a freelancer from London, Liam Everhart—to capture those moments.

Winnie found him taking photos of the kids attacking the dragon, and she wandered up to him to see how things were going.

"Excellent," he said, his voice was buttery smooth. He flipped through some of the photos to show her. "My wife said the knights had come out now, so I'll be headed up that way shortly to capture them next."

"Perfect," Winnie said. "I'll go up there now myself."

She left the photographer to his business, then made her way to the booth where his wife, Claire, had set up flower crowns and small bouquets for sale—all items from a flower shop she ran down in London.

The husband and wife had come as a package deal, and Winnie was glad of it, as the line trailing out from the woman's booth was twice as long as anyone else's.

"Everything all right, Claire?" Winnie asked as she walked past.

Claire beamed. "More than all right," she said, her American accent standing out to Winnie after so long being surrounded by so many British ones.

The two had a great deal to chat about over the last couple of days, once they'd discovered they were both from the States, and Winnie had been glad to have found a new friend in someone.

"Liam said you spotted the knights?" Winnie asked next.

"Yes, up by the armory tent," Claire said.

Winnie nodded her thanks, then made her way toward the historical section of the festival, where exhibits of armor, shields, horse-wear, and other artifacts were put up on display.

Sure enough, as her eyes scanned the area, she found two of

the knights chatting with a group gathered around them, one of them posing for a picture with a gaggle of teenage girls, and the other, Matthew, speaking with a family with young children.

Winnie had been relieved when they'd all agreed to walk around the crowds before the tournament, hoping to ramp up the guests' interest in watching the joust.

By the looks of it, it seemed to be working.

She watched Matthew for a minute, admiring the armor covering every inch of his body, though he held his helmet in his hand.

As he moved from the family, the teenagers, who had been speaking to the other knight, came up to speak with him, saying he looked just like Sir Ulrick from Gelderland, and Winnie couldn't help but smile. That had been her first impression of Matthew, too.

She admired him for a minute, his shoulders in the armor, his curly hair styled to perfection, the smile on his lips as he posed for photo after photo. How had she, Winnie Knox, been so lucky to have won his favor?

She didn't know how long she'd been staring until Matthew turned his gaze on her, and her heart leapt.

His eyes remained on her. That same old sultry smirk that had filled her dreams for weeks were now filling her mind awake.

The girls asked for another picture, but Matthew rested his gauntleted hand on his heart and spoke with them. "Alas," he began, "I must bid you all adieu, as I speak with my fair lady boss yonder."

Winnie grinned. The idea for the knights to speak in such a way had been his, much to everyone's surprise. Well, everyone's surprise but Winnie's, of course.

To her delight, he strode directly toward her, his armor clanking as he passed by others, nodding his head to them before reaching her.

"Greetings, my lady," he said with as much of a bow as he could manage in his armor.

"Good morning, Sir Matthew," she said with as much of a restrained smile as *she* could manage. "You seem to be enjoying yourself."

"Ah how could a humble knight not, being treated with such love and wonder by everyone around him?"

"Particularly by the ladies?" she asked, raising a teasing brow.

He cleared his throat. "Ah, yes. I do apologize. I fear flattery sneaketh into my brain and muddleth my senses."

She almost laughed at his words.

"But allow me to make it up to you, my fair Lady Winifred." Without warning, he knelt down in front of her, taking her hand in both of his and peering up at her. "My mind of late hath been occupied solely by you, my lady."

"Oh?" she asked, glancing around as people stopped to watch them, thinking it was all part of the act.

Winnie couldn't even tell if he was in earnest or if he was still in character. Either way, this would hardly help the gossip that was no doubt already abounding between them.

Oh, well. If the staff hadn't figured out they were together by now, they wouldn't care anyway.

"Indeed," he continued, "so much so that I can hardly sleep due to images of thy matchless face. But I shan't gild the lily further. Sparest thou a moment of thy time to speak with I, a humble knight? Not this moment, of course. But later, perhaps? If thou wouldst be so willing."

She hesitated, leaning forward as the crowd continued to gather. "Are you being serious or is this part of the whole knight thing?" she asked in a whisper.

He stared, eyes mooning up at her. "Oh, I am in earnest, my lady, with all of my heart."

She couldn't help but smile at his dedication to his role, even if she was still slightly unsure if he was serious. "All right, sure. We can chat."

"Oh!" He delivered a deep sigh, closing his eyes. "How happy thou hast made me, my Lady Winifred. Words cannot express the joy thou has bestowed upon me with your mere smile. Now, I shall surely win this tournament for you."

"All right, great. Now get back to work." She tossed her head toward the tournament grounds with a look of amusement.

"Oh, yes, yes, of course, my lady." He rose, placing a kiss on the back of her hand. Her flesh tingled as he lingered a moment longer than necessary—though far, far less than what she would have preferred.

Finally, he straightened, winked in her direction, and sauntered away.

The crowd around her dispersed, as did her blush, and Winnie blew out a slow breath. What did he want to speak with her about? Something festival and work related? Or, dare she hope, did he wish to speak of their future?

How she wished for the latter.

CHAPTER FORTY-TWO

THE FESTIVAL WAS A SUCCESS. THAT WAS ALL THERE was to it. By the end of it, the guests were hesitant to leave and had to be ushered out with the promise of many more festivals to come.

The staff had been thrilled with the response, Mr. Wintour had been more than pleased, and nearly everyone in attendance had raved about the changes made. And Winnie, well, of course she was on cloud nine.

After praising the staff for their hard work, and receiving a great deal of praise from Mr. Wintour himself—"I knew you could succeed with your heart involved. I hope you're ready to help Foxwood now"—Winnie made her way back to the house floating with glee.

She'd done it. She'd pulled off a successful festival. She'd proven herself to Mr. Wintour. She would finally make her family proud.

And it was all thanks to Matthew.

She pulled out her phone and sent him a quick text, having not seen him with the rest of the staff after the event.

WINNIE

Hey! Were you serious about talking later today? I'm ready when you are! I've got some things I want to share with you, too. *wink emoji*

In an instant, he responded.

SIR MATTHEW

Ah, my fair Lady Winifred.

SIR MATTHEW

GIF of Mr. Bean bowing.

SIR MATTHEW

I was absolutely serious. Give me an hour to get out of character and shower. We can meet by the archery targets.

WINNIE

I'll be there.

SIR MATTHEW

Can't wait. xx

Winnie allowed an airy sigh to escape her lips. She was a total sucker for Matthew's fake kisses—almost as much as she was for his real ones.

And now...now they would be able to last that much longer. She'd have months now at Foxwood, which would allow them plenty of time to spend with each other—and plenty of time to decide on a future together.

Everything was perfect. Absolutely perfect.

She reached her room, ready to shower and wind down from the busy day, but her phone buzzed.

A smile caught her lips. Was Matthew calling to tell her he couldn't wait a minute longer to see her? To hear her voice?

She pulled up her phone, and her smile vanished. Dad. Why was he calling?

Usually, she'd ignore him until she had enough gumption to

deal with him, but right now she was absolutely ready. He would be relieved to hear that she was finally placed in charge of the estate. But would he be proud of her work for the festival, too?

She swiped the phone call to accept it. "Hey, Dad!"

"Winnie, you sound chipper."

"I am," she said with a smile, sitting down on her bed and propping her feet up. "I've just had an incredible day."

"Well, I'm about to make it even better."

She tried to inflate her spirits again, Dad's lack of interest in her words causing her to sink. "Oh?"

"Yep. I've just received word from my contacts in Chicago. You've finally got an out for working with the Wintours."

Winnie froze, her heart sinking so low, she could hardly feel it beating against her chest. "What? What do you mean?"

"Well, after Arthur pulled that switch on you, forcing you to prove yourself before giving you the job he promised, I couldn't take it," he said. "No one treats a Knox like that. Not even a ritzy Englishman."

Winnie's mind swirled. He and Mr. Wintour were friends. Why was he talking about him like that?

Dad continued. "Anyway, I called in a few favors from friends and, well, long story short, Kris & Sons wants to hire you. I promised them you'd be there by Sunday."

Winnie could hardly breathe. She sat upright in bed, her hand to her brow. "Wait...what?"

His sigh was audible. "Were you even listening to me?"

"Yes, of course I was. I just don't get it."

Kris & Sons was a highly reputable company that specialized in the software used for creating apps. Many of the businesses she'd worked for in New York used them, and not one of them had a bad thing to say about the company. If she worked for them, succeeded in her efforts, Dad would never have to find her work again. She would finally get that prestige he so desired for her.

But at what cost? Certainly nothing she wanted to pay.

"What don't you *get?*" Dad asked impatiently. "You were mistreated by someone I thought I could trust, so I found you another job with someone I *can* trust. It's all in writing. Kris & Sons will give you a trial run before hiring you for two months to help them out of the financial dilemma they've gotten themselves into."

The feeling of peace Winnie had before vanished, leaving behind a wake of fear, worry, and confusion. There was so much to say, so much to clarify, so much to defend.

"I wasn't mistreated here, Dad," she said, trying to respond to his accusations one at a time. "Mr. Wintour's been super nice. He gave me another chance when I couldn't pull off what he asked me to do the first time."

"You mean that ridiculous faire? I hate to tell you this, Winnie, but he wasn't doing you any favors by putting you over such an embarrassing event. If anything, it hindered your progress to actually becoming successful."

She winced at his words. How had she not come to expect this yet? Dad stepping into her life, into her business, just to avoid his own embarrassment.

"Winnie? Are you still there?"

"Yeah," she said.

"And? You have nothing to say about this good news? Nothing to say about all the work I put in to make it happen?"

Winnie swallowed. She had to play this carefully, almost like it was a business transaction. After all, that's all she was to Dad.

"I do have a lot to say," she began, pulling on her best consultant tactics and remaining calm. "But first, I wanted to talk to you about the festival and the success we found today. Mr. Wintour was so pleased that he'll be starting me up at Foxwood at the beginning of next week."

"If you can even trust what he's promised," Dad retorted. "Who's to say he wouldn't just change his mind and put you over some other menial task again?"

Dad was a lawyer for a reason. He was always so convincing,

knowing just how to plant noxious seeds of doubt into her heart, even though she knew he was wrong.

She stood from the bed and wandered toward the window, eying the grounds covered in the late evening sunshine. She tried to pull that sunshine into her heart, but her dad's words continued to darken the light around her.

"I can't believe you're not thanking me right now," he said. "I'm putting my neck on the line for you—*again*. Will you please, for once in your life, do the sensible thing?"

She chewed her lower lip. "But, Dad, I promised to help Mr. Wintour. How can I leave and completely ignore my agreement with him?"

"How? Because there's nothing holding you there."

Nothing holding her there? *Everything* was holding her there. Matthew. The Wintours. Her word.

But what would Dad know about any of that? "Won't that make things awkward between you and Mr. Wintour as friends?" she asked, hoping to play to his senses.

As if that could have ever worked.

Dad sighed, his voice taking on a slightly softer tone. "The only reason I reached out to him after all these years was to get you a job I had *hoped* would give you some prestige. Arthur is a very nice man. He always has been. And I'm glad you've been able to help him and his family. But working for him has done nothing for you."

She winced. That was the furthest thing from the truth. If only he knew all they had done for her—all *Matthew* had done for her.

"Dad..." she began, wanting to share with him the truth, but he interrupted.

"Listen," he said, "I've got to run, but we can chat about it later, okay?"

"Wait," she said, desperate to keep him a moment longer, to get him to see reason. "What if...what if I *want* to stay here?"

Silence met her on the other end.

"Are you serious?" Dad finally asked.

Winnie looked up at the ceiling as she prayed for strength. "I really like the work here...and those I work with."

More silence. Winnie shook her head, knowing Dad was already compiling all the reasons she ought to agree with him.

He sighed, his voice taking on a softer tone. "Look, I'm sorry to spring this on you all of a sudden. I know it's a lot to wrap your mind around, but I really thought you'd be excited about it. It's such an incredible opportunity."

She nodded, her defenses crumbling, just as they always did around Dad. "I know."

"I was going to wait to tell you this," he continued, "but I guess you may as well know. I have it on good authority that if you do this job, and do it well, I'll have an in with Kris & Sons. Your mom and I would become their go-to firm. I don't have to tell you how much credibility their company would lend to ours. Knox Family Law would be put on the map in ways we've only dreamed of. And it would be all thanks to you. Right? Winnie?"

Be like Fort Knox. She winced, discomfited by the phrase returning to her mind. "I guess."

"You're still not convinced?"

How could she be? How could she ever be convinced to leave the life she wanted to pursue in England, with the person she wanted to pursue it with?

"I guess I just don't get it," she said, doing her best to speak up, though her courage had all but fled. "Why would they bring you on as their permanent lawyers only if I agree to be their consultant? I'm nothing special."

Dad was silent for a minute. "It's complicated."

An inkling of indignation slid through her veins. "I'm sure I can understand it, Dad."

Again, he sighed. "I guess I came on a little too strong with Mr. Kris when we first met in person. I told him the vision of what I had for his company, and apparently, he was scared off by all of my ideas."

Winnie listened carefully, though she didn't find it difficult to believe that Dad had come on too strong. That had always been her issue with him, too.

"Anyway, I got the idea that he prefers a much less direct approach," he added.

"Which is where I come in?" she guessed.

"Exactly. You need to go in there and work your Winnie charm. Show them how wonderful we Knoxes are to work with, how they would be missing out on so many benefits if they *don't* work with us. All you'd have to do is your typical consultant magic while letting them know how lucky they'd be to have your mom and I work with them. Super simple."

Winnie reeled, and for a moment, a light beamed into her chest. Dad would never admit it, but he was essentially asking her for a favor. No, it was more than a favor. He was asking her to bail him out of something that *he'd* messed up. She'd never known him to ask for help before, and he'd asked *her*.

She had no qualms with the job at all. In fact, she knew she'd succeed with helping Kris & Sons because she'd previously excelled working with other software-based companies.

Did that mean Dad had that same faith in her?

"You do know who you're talking to, right?" she asked.

"Of course I do," he said, clearly impatient. "Win-Win-Winnie."

She grimaced, reality setting her firmly back on the ground. "You and I both know I never win at anything, Dad."

"That may be true," he readily agreed. "But you're a fine consultant. I have full confidence in your ability to charm the Kris family. Once they meet with you, there is no way they won't hire you."

Winnie pressed a hand to her pulsing brow. She knew how Dad worked—build someone up to get his way. It was his oldest trick.

So why was she falling for it? Why was she falling for his overdue compliments and his supposed faith in her?

Fortunately, there was one continual thought still grounding her.

What about Matthew?

She wanted to help her dad. Really, she did. But to give up so much of what was almost within her grasp—a potential future with a man she could see herself spending forever with, finding joy she'd sought for so many years? She couldn't agree to that.

"I don't know about this, Dad," she said softly. "I just...don't know."

Again, silence met her.

"Winnie," he began after a moment, his tone losing its softness from before. "How many times have I helped you find consultant jobs?"

The weight of the past few years settled on her chest, her bones pressing uncomfortably against her heart. "I—"

"How often did I support you in your endeavors?" he interrupted.

Winnie didn't bother responding now. He wouldn't hear her words.

"How frequently did I pull you under my wing," he continued, "urging you to keep going when you failed time and time again?"

The weight pushed down harder, her breath coming in labored bursts. Of course Dad would see his actions as supportive instead as oppressive. After all, he never did anything wrong.

"I don't wish to pressure you," he said, "but after everything your mother and I have done for you, after all the sacrifices we've made, if you can't do this one, simple thing to help us, your parents who love you more than anything...do you even wish to be a part of this family at all?"

She bit the inside of her cheek and closed her eyes. He didn't want to pressure her? That was exactly what he wanted to do because he knew pressure worked. It cracked even the hardest of metals and the strongest of desires.

It cracked even the happiest of spirits. And Winnie's had already suffered an irreparable fracture.

"So can I rely on you to help us, Winnie?" Dad asked.

Winnie pushed aside her feelings. She didn't have the right to them anyway. Just like she didn't have the right to her own dreams or her own life.

"Ah," Dad said, not even allowing her to answer. "Listen, honey, I've got another client calling. I really need to take this."

She barely heard his words, her heart numb. "Sunday," she murmured. "I wouldn't have time to go home first?"

Home. Home wasn't in New York. It certainly wasn't with her parents. In truth, she would be leaving the only place she'd ever really felt like she *was* home. She would be leaving the only person she'd ever felt at home *with*.

"No," Dad replied. "the deal is for you to arrive in Chicago by Sunday."

She nodded in silence.

"Winnie?"

"Yeah?"

"Can I tell them to expect you on Sunday?"

Sunday. That meant she had to leave tomorrow morning.

Leave? So that was it? She was just giving in?

A single tear rolled down her cheek, but she didn't bother to wipe it away. What was the point? She would just shed more anyway. That much was inevitable with her leaving Foxwood.

She didn't have any other choice. She'd stood up to Dad once before, and he'd sold Goldilocks to retaliate. She'd only *tried* to tell him now that she wanted to stay at Foxwood, and what had he done? Manipulated her until she'd agreed to leave.

She knew his actions were controlling. She knew they were wrong. But he needed her help. Maybe if she did this one thing for him, he would be satisfied. Grateful. Maybe even proud. Then she could create some distance between them, live out her life the way she wanted to.

"Winnie," Dad said, his tone strained. "I need an answer now."

"Yes," she said softly. "I'll be there on Sunday."

"Ah, that's my Winnie," Dad responded in a distracted tone. "I'll let them know. Thanks a bunch, honey. Your mom and I have to fly out to Florida tomorrow, but we'll stop by Chicago on our way back to Utah next weekend when we're done. That way we can catch up and see all your progress."

Winnie didn't bother saying anything back. He was done listening.

"Anyway," he continued. "Got to run. Love you, honey. See you soon. Bye."

Slowly, Winnie lowered the phone, staring out the window at the landscape of Foxwood that she'd grown so accustomed to. The green fields. The wild, tangled trees. The flags from the festival.

How could things change so suddenly? A few minutes ago, she was planning a future at Foxwood. And now? Now she was replacing those dreams with images of a life in Chicago, tethered to Kris & Sons. Tethered to consultant work for companies she didn't care about. Tethered to Dad with no hope of escape.

No hope and no joy, that's what awaited her outside of England.

That's what awaited her without Matthew in her future.

CHAPTER FORTY-THREE

MATTHEW PULLED BACK ANOTHER ARROW ON HIS BOW, lined up his shot, and released. The arrow whistled in the air for a split second, then thwapped straight into the bullseye of the target.

He smiled with satisfaction at his three arrows centered on the board nestled in a crook of trees seventy feet away. He was having the round of his life, and he knew who to thank for it.

Winnie's gray eyes appeared in his mind, and he smiled. She should be here any minute, then the two of them could finally chat.

But chat about what? Oh, he didn't care, really. So long as it involved them speaking about her future at Foxwood, him sharing his true feelings for her, and his desire to have their relationship finally out in the open.

All this sneaking around was amazing, but honestly, it was getting a little old when all he wanted to do was hold her close, stare into her eyes, and kiss her until they were both senseless. That was precisely what he had planned for that evening, and he couldn't wait for it.

Fortunately, he didn't have to for long, as Winnie's footsteps sounded behind him only a few minutes later.

He shot another arrow, this one hitting just outside the center before he turned to face her.

"Ah, my Lady Winifred. At last you have arrived."

He grinned at her, hoping she'd join in on the fun. But when she didn't smile in return, his racing heart slowed until it stuttered to a near stop. His smile faded away, and he set down his bow and arrow.

"Winnie," he said softly, noting the red in her eyes as he came up to meet her, "what's the matter?"

She shook her head, her chin raised and lips in a straight line. He hadn't seen her this dejected since the first festival hadn't surpassed her expectations.

"I just got off the phone with my dad," she stated simply.

His chest tightened. "Oh?"

She nodded, not a tear in her eye, not a flinching mark on her brow. "He told me of a new business opportunity he found for me."

Matthew could hardly breathe. "That sounds...promising."

"It is. It's with a client who can bring my dad's firm a lot of prestige, so long as I can succeed as their consultant."

Her eyes peered into his, as if warning him of what was to come.

Somehow, he already knew.

"I have to go," she said, her chin rising a degree higher.

When before, he wanted to reach out to her, now, Matthew's arms felt better at his sides. He'd been about to tell her he loved her. He'd been about to ask her to stay, not to continue on as a consultant, but to see if she wanted to make their relationship last.

How could he have been so stupid?

"When?" he said, turning away.

He reached for his bow and arrow again, facing the target. It was easier to look at than Winnie.

"Tomorrow morning."

Shock jolted through his body, followed swiftly by a deep ache that reached all the way to his bones. He tried not to be hurt, tried to remain impartial to the news, but the cut ran deep. He never should have allowed himself to trust her—to accept her help.

He tried to aim for the target, but unsurprisingly, the arrow bounced off a nearby tree instead.

Drawing a deep breath, he turned to face her. To her credit, a pained look had crossed her features, though she tried to blink it away the second he turned.

He couldn't understand why. Why could she not allow herself to look upset about having to leave—or rather, *choosing* to leave?

In an attempt to make himself feel better, Matthew drew his attention to something else, something more distant than his heart being pressed for juice like an apple with nothing left to give.

"What about the festival tomorrow?" he asked.

"It'll run just as smoothly as it did today," she said with a nod that looked like she was trying to convince herself of her words, too. "You can handle it all, I'm sure. And you have the staff and your family to help. You don't need me."

He almost scoffed. How had he fallen into this trap? How had he not seen this coming—her leaving him on his own to manage a festival he'd never been able to manage in the first place?

"Well, I guess that's it, then," he said.

That was it for her being at Foxwood—and that was it for Winnie being a part of his life.

Still, the niggling in his heart could not be removed. Slowly, he turned to face her, forcing his voice to remain level. "Are you willing to explain to me why you're doing this? Or do you expect me to just accept what's happening, no questions asked?"

"You can ask me anything, Matthew. You know that." Her voice was strong, though the look in her eyes was anything but.

"Then, why are you going?" he asked.

"Because...because my dad needs help."

Despite Matthew's desire and attempt to remain cool, indignation simmered in his belly. Not for Winnie, but for her father.

"Your dad is a grown man with an established firm. I'm sure he could handle this on his own."

"No, you don't get it." She broke off with a sigh. "He *asked* for help. He's been trying to build up his firm for years, and he finally found the company to help him do it, but he's worried that the deal will fall through. He's asked me to help him, Matthew. *Me.*" She took a step toward him. "Do you know how long I've waited for this? For him to see my value? For him to trust me? If I can make this work, I think he'll finally be proud of me."

Matthew longed to shout out how nonsensical she was being. They both knew she'd never be enough for her dad. He was just that sort of person. She'd said so herself.

But then, who was he to talk? From the time Winnie had arrived at Foxwood, Matthew had wanted to make his own dad happy—wanted to make him proud. Such was the prerogative of children and parents.

The difference was, though, that deep down, Matthew had always known that his father was proud of him, no matter how many mistakes he made. But Winnie? She'd never been given that luxury—no, that basic human right.

"Matthew?"

Winnie's voice pulled him from his thoughts.

"What are you thinking?" she asked, her voice holding a tentative tone to it, as if she was afraid to hear the truth.

He proceeded as carefully as he could, not wishing to injure her the way she'd already injured him. "Does your dad really need you...or is he just using you?"

Winnie tipped her head to the side, her lips pulled into a frown. "I'm not stupid, Matthew. I *know* he's using me. But after everything my parents have done for me, what kind of daughter would I be if I didn't help them?" She paused with an impatient sigh when he didn't respond. "Don't you get it? I think I can turn this around to benefit from the job myself. I'll get prestige, experience, and, like I said, I'll have finally earned Dad's pride and trust for myself."

"You shouldn't *have* to earn it," he said softly.

"Yeah, well, I wasn't lucky enough to have been born into a perfect family, Matthew." Her brow furrowed, her voice tense as she responded defensively. "That's what we Knoxes do. We come from a cutthroat environment. If we don't act how we're expected to, we get left behind, and that's exactly what will happen to me and to my dad if I don't do this."

"So that's what matters most to you, not getting left behind in a corporate world?"

She looked away. "No, helping my dad is more important." Her answer was weak, her tone unconvincing.

"Why?" he asked, desperate for her to admit the truth.

"Because not helping him would be selfish."

"That's not true. Not when it makes you sacrifice your *own* needs. Your hopes and dreams are just as valid as everyone else's, Winnie."

"Maybe in a perfect world. Not in mine."

He shook his head, trying to keep his frustration at bay because he knew it was only a mask for the pain pinching at his heart.

"Your intentions are honorable," he said. "But they're flawed. You're not leaving Foxwood to help your dad. You're leaving because you're scared."

Tears brimmed in her eyes. He'd found the truth.

His heart softened, and he dared a step toward her. "I get it. You're scared to stand up to him, to stand up for your own dreams. I would be, too. Giving up is easy. But following your heart? *That* takes courage."

He paused, praying his words would have some effect on her, but when she shook her head, all hope fled.

"I'm sorry," she said softly. "That is courage I don't have. And a choice I don't have either."

Her words pricked at his heart, his will to continue slipping through his fingers. "Everyone has a choice, Winnie. You can choose to stay here. Or you can choose to leave. It's as simple as that."

"Nothing is ever as simple as that," she replied.

Matthew didn't respond. What was the point? She'd already made her decision.

"I don't want to go," she whispered, her voice breaking. Their eyes connected, tears brimming in those gray pools he'd grown to love. "The last few weeks have been..."

Her words trailed off as Matthew shook his head. He couldn't bear listening to what she had to say. "It's fine," he said. "You don't have to do that."

She nodded, her shoulders slumped forward, her expression dejected.

Matthew wished he could step in, call her dad and demand that he release Winnie from his manipulative behavior and force him to acknowledge how he was ruining his daughter's life. But just like Matthew had told Winnie, it was *her* choice.

Without another glance, he turned away from her, unable to bear the sadness in her eyes any longer, his vision clouded by hurt.

"I really am sorry," she said, her broken voice breaking him.

"I know," he said, staring at the target as if the arrows were pierced into him. "I only hope you find the courage to seek your own happiness. Wherever that may be."

She didn't respond, but a few moments later, her retreating footsteps sounded across the pathway behind him.

With all his power, he fought the desire to look back at her. It was time to let her go. Time to move on. Time to remember that even though he may not be a disappointment to his father, he would always be a disappointment to himself. Because he'd failed to capture the heart of the only woman he'd ever truly wanted, the only woman he'd ever truly loved.

CHAPTER FORTY-FOUR

"Flight 311 will be boarding for Chicago at 11:31. Flight 311, boarding shortly."

Winnie stifled a yawn as the announcement sounded out across the airport's intercom again. She'd woken up at the crack of dawn, escaping Foxwood without running into a soul and zipping her way to Manchester Airport where she'd said her final farewell to the Aston Martin.

Of course, that was the easiest of her goodbyes. Mr. Wintour had been understanding, if not disappointed, and had suggested she return if she ever had the interest to. Mrs. Wintour had expressed her sorrow at not seeing her any longer. And Char had been straight-up confrontational—in the most loving way she could.

"I just don't get it," Char had said the night before, coming down to Winnie's room after Winnie had sent her a text, alerting her of her departure. "You're happy here. You're happy with Matty. Why would you give it all up?"

Winnie had tried to explain, but how could she in a way that made sense to Char when Winnie's own actions didn't even make sense to herself?

She shifted on the flat airport seat, trying to get comfortable once again as another announcement for yet another flight echoed across the busy terminal.

She'd been staring at her phone for the last two hours, trying to distract herself by reading over the proposal sent by Kris & Sons, but nothing was sticking. All these fancy words about software creation and app manipulation held nothing to medieval knights charging at each other with horses and lances.

And all of *that* held nothing to being with Matthew.

Tears once again threatened to prick the center of her eyes, but she promptly blinked them away. She'd never cried so much in her life, nor had she ever felt so terrible. At least, not since losing Goldilocks and riding altogether.

But this sort of ache was different. It ran deeper because it held with it the knowledge of all that could have been—*should* have been—with the man she loved.

Saying goodbye to Matthew, seeing the hurt and betrayal in his eyes, had shriveled her heart nearly past the point of feeling altogether. So that's how she remained now. Shriveled. Dry. Almost dead to the world with no more love to give.

So long as she had a brain to give Kris & Sons, though, Dad would be happy.

As if on call, her phone buzzed in her hand, and Dad's name lit up her screen as a FaceTime call, replacing the document from Kris & Sons she'd once again been too distracted to read.

She knew why he was calling—to make sure she was at the airport. Why couldn't he ever just trust her?

She shook her head and drew a deep breath, putting in her earbuds and pulling on her steely exterior before answering the call.

"Hey," she said.

She didn't bother smiling. Why pretend to be happy when she wasn't? That wouldn't get her a job, nor would it get her credit from Dad.

"Hey, Winnie," he said, clearly not looking at her as his eyes darted around his own screen. "Just a second. I'm bringing in a few more of the kids for a quick call."

Winnie nodded. It wasn't unheard of for Dad to schedule a random chat no matter the time of day for everyone else, and those who were available would pick up. He usually called when he had something to boast about that just couldn't wait to be shared.

What was today's good news? Finding another bigwig client? Succeeding in convincing his daughter to leave everything she loved behind just to succor his own pride?

In a matter of minutes, all but one of Winnie's siblings appeared across her screen. Spencer's service wasn't great in Nicaragua, but Sarah picked up at three in the morning in California—just finishing up the last details on a project—and Scott answered during a late-night shift at the hospital in Oregon.

"That's the Knox family for you," Dad praised. "Always working hard but willing to drop everything for family."

Winnie grimaced.

Most of them were bleary eyed, except for Samantha in Germany, who'd just sat down for a lunch break.

"Greetings from Florida," Dad said when they were all there. "Fortunately, I'm here and not in Utah, or I'd be as exhausted as Sarah and Scott."

Smiles stretched across her siblings' lips, but Winnie still couldn't even fake one. If only Dad *had* been in Utah, then she wouldn't have to be dealing with a call right now.

"Anyway," he continued, his own smile brightening her screen in a mocking gesture, "I just called you all to share some exciting news that couldn't wait for our usual chat." He paused, no doubt for dramatic effect. "As you all know, Winnie has been struggling in England for a few weeks now."

Samantha and Scott nodded their heads, and Winnie's frown punctuated her brow even more. Struggling? She hadn't been struggling. What lies had he been saying about her behind her back?

"That's all coming to an end, though," Dad continued. "She's agreed to take on a position as a consultant at Kris & Sons."

Words of congratulations and smiles sifted through her family.

"That's amazing, Winnie!"

"Well done!"

"That's one of the most prestigious companies in Chicago, isn't it?" Sarah asked. Her smile wasn't as bright as the others, though that could very well be due to the fact that she was half-asleep.

"It certainly is," Dad said with pride—no doubt more for himself than for Winnie. "That brings me to my next announcement. Kris & Sons are also considering Knox Family Law Firm to be their permanent lawyers for all their future needs."

More congratulations sounded for Dad, but Winnie looked up from her phone, staring out at the airplanes taxiing down the runways, rain speckling the windows of the airport in uniform patterns.

She'd miss the rain. Then again, she'd miss everything about England.

"So how did you get the job, Winnie?" Samantha asked. "Was the interviewing process super crazy?"

Winnie looked back to her phone, her spirits so low she could hardly breathe. "I wouldn't know. Dad got it for me."

Silence met her on the other end, and Winnie paused. What had she just said? She wasn't entirely sure. She was so tired, so miserable. So...*done.*

Her brow pursed, but not in a disappointing frown, as per usual. Instead, something strange bubbled inside of her, something she didn't recognize at all, but something she wanted to keep around.

"Now, that's not entirely true," Dad said with a strained

laugh. "You convinced them with your merit and track record, Winnie."

Winnie sniffed, nodding her head with an ironic smile. "Ah, yes. My stellar track record."

More silence. What on earth was going on with her? Why was she being so snarky? So vocal? And why was she *enjoying* it? Even Dad seemed stunned by her actions.

"So does that mean you finished with the festival, then?" Sarah asked.

She'd been the only one to have ever texted Winnie about the job at Foxwood. Of course she would be the only one to ask her about it now.

"Apparently," Winnie said. "Dad said I was done, so here we are."

There was that feeling again. That foreign feeling of...freedom? Lack of care? Whatever it was, it rose as she sensed her family's discomfort—discomfort that was only there due to her honesty. They were no doubt wondering what was going on with their baby sister.

"How did the Wintours take it?" Sarah asked next.

Winnie's joy dampened at the memory of the Wintours and their kindness to her, but instead of stamping out the feeling of freedom altogether, she kept hold of it, longing to feel that satisfaction again.

"They couldn't understand why I was leaving," she stated simply. "And I couldn't explain it to them either. Not in a way that made sense, anyway."

Dad gave another tense chuckle. "I'm sure they can all understand that business is business. You simply received a better offer and accepted it."

Oh, the Wintours knew business. But they knew *heart* more.

Winnie's own heart thudded against her chest. The freedom she clutched tightly in her hand grew, feeling stronger, more malleable. Could she maintain this feeling? Take it and run with it for longer?

"You know what, Dad?" she began, testing the waters further. "I'm not sure that I did receive a better offer."

Dad stared at her through the phone, her siblings deathly silent, each of them in shock. But their reactions, oddly enough, only proved to lend her more courage.

"In truth," she continued, "I loved working on the festival with the Wintours. I know you don't want to hear that because it's embarrassing for a Knox to admit enjoying a simple job and a simple life, but I don't care anymore. I *loved* it there."

Speaking the words aloud unleashed a current within her more powerful than she'd ever felt before. The freedom at her fingers was now so commanding, she could no longer maintain hold of it, and it spilled from her hands in droves like sunshine that couldn't be contained.

She was done. She was done being silent, of following exactly what Dad told her to, simply because he wanted to grow his own business for his own prestige. If she was being forced to do something she didn't want to do, she was going to let them know about it.

"I felt more joy there than I have in all of my other jobs, all of my other prospects combined," she said. "But now, I'm being—"

Dad sighed, cutting her off. "That's great, Winnie. I'm glad it was so good. But I've got some things to see to before my workday starts, so we're going to have to call it a day here."

Winnie scoffed, shaking her head in disbelief. Of course he'd end her words prematurely. He didn't want to hear how she really felt. He just wanted her to blindly agree with everything he said. Just like she always had.

But what if she didn't want to be that person anymore? What if she wanted to be...just Winnie?

She'd learned enough from interacting with her dad that chasing after money and acclaim led to nothing but stress and unwanted pressure. But from the Wintours, from Matthew, she'd learned that passion and heart, that sacrifice for those in real need, led to true happiness.

What she was doing for Dad wasn't that. What she was doing for him wasn't what she wanted to do, it was what *Dad* wanted her to do. And yet, following him had been...her choice.

All at once, something clicked within Winnie's mind, a light switching on and brightening the darkness she'd been trapped inside for years.

It was *her* choice. Just like Matthew had told her. How had it taken her so long to figure that out?

"Wait," she said, as if her voice was coming from a different person. Then again, it was. Because *she* was different. "You can wait a few more minutes for me to finish."

Dad stared at her in silence, as did the rest of her siblings on her small screen. Instead of those stares intimidating her like usual, strength poured into Winnie's heart.

"All right," Dad said after a moment, clearly struggling to give her permission. "Go on, then."

Winnie drew a deep breath. She wouldn't be rude, nor would she blame her dad for her struggles. Not anymore. That blame had held her back, had prevented her happiness, for too long. But now, Winnie was an adult. She was changed.

She was ready to be free.

"I rode a horse again," she stated simply.

Sarah smiled. Dad's jaw twitched. Everyone else merely watched in surprise.

"That was something I hadn't done in more than a decade," she continued.

"Because you chose to do something more sensible," Dad said.

"No," she corrected. "Because I was persuaded to do something you thought would bring the Knox family name more prestige than your daughter accidentally falling off a horse."

His lips thinned.

"I'm not going to blame you any longer, though, Dad," she said. "I know you were doing what you thought was best for the family. But I need you to know, that's not going to happen again.

From now on, I'm going to make my own decisions. And the first one I'm going to make right now is to stay in England. I'm going to keep working for Foxwood and not accept the offer by Kris & Sons."

Sarah's smile grew, though she tried to hide it behind her hands. Everyone else's mouths dropped open except for Dad's. He simply shook his head.

She rushed on before he could stop her. "I know I've been a huge disappointment to you over the years. I've done my best, but my heart hasn't been in anything I've tried over the last decade. And truth be told, I'm tired. I'm tired of trying to live up to the expectations of this family. I'll never be as adventurous as Spencer, as intelligent as Scott, as creative as Samantha, or as driven as Sarah. And I sure as heck will never be as persuasive as you, Dad."

She looked out to the window again, staring at the droplets of rain still speckling the glass—just how they'd looked that day she'd spun out on the road to Foxwood. On the day she'd met Matthew.

"But," she said with a smile, "I'm okay with that. I'm okay with not having a fancy job. I'm okay with being just Winnie. Average Winnie. The Winnie who wants to lead a simple life filled with horses...and spent with the man I love here."

The shock on each of their faces would have made her laugh, had her heart not pricked at the thought of Matthew again. She needed to see him, to speak with him.

"Is that what this is about?" Dad asked. "You've fallen for someone there, so you're going to give up everything?"

She looked at him, focusing hard to get her point across. "No. That's not why I'm refusing the job. I promised to stay with the Wintours and help at Foxwood, so that's why I'm going to do just that."

"You promised Kris & Sons you'd help *them*," Dad countered.

But Winnie shook her head. "I told *you* that I would, Dad. But I didn't promise them."

Dad shook his head, rubbing his fingers across his brow. "I can't believe this."

Her heart reached out to him. She had dropped a veritable bomb, destroying any hopes of the future he had with the prestigious company. But she couldn't do this any longer.

"You'll find new opportunities, Dad," she said. "You always do. But I might not have this opportunity to find joy again. I only hope you can be happy for me, even if my idea of happiness looks different than yours."

"I just can't believe we're going through this again with you," Dad said, anger in his eyes. "When are you ever going to learn to be sensible, Winnie Knox?"

A smile spread across her lips. "You know, I never *could* live up to our name, Dad." She stood from her seat and held her phone out in front of her. "Anyway, you'll have to excuse me. I've got a jousting tournament to get back to."

"Winnie—"

She shut off the video, ending her dad's words as a rush of adrenaline shot through her limbs. She reached for her suitcase and bag and charged through the airport, but she didn't make it far before her phone buzzed in her hand. At first, she ignored it, figuring Dad was trying to contact her, but after a moment, she glanced down to see Sarah had texted her instead.

SARAH

Oh my gosh, girl. That was the most amazing thing ever. I've NEVER seen Dad's face like that. Or anyone's! I'm so dang proud of you, and I'm so happy you've found so much joy in England. Maybe I'll quit and move there, too. Find a hot English beau for myself. Lol.

SARAH

Seriously, though, I don't think any one of us could have stood up to him like that. Go get that knight! Then tell me when the wedding is. *wink emoji* *wink emoji* Love youuuuuuuu

Winnie fairly beamed. She slipped her phone away, making a mental note to respond soon as she fled through the terminal.

She no longer had a plane to catch, but she had a car to rent, a festival to attend, and a knight to declare her love for.

Now the question was, would Matthew return that love, or had she missed out on her chance at happiness after all?

CHAPTER FORTY-FIVE

MATTHEW COULDN'T FOCUS. HE WALKED AROUND THAT morning in a sort of daze, greeting guests and speaking as knightly as possible, but his heart wasn't in it. Not when every single turn he took, every single object he looked at, every single thing he heard was a glaring reminder of Winnie's hand in his life.

Somehow, he and his staff and family had managed to get the festival off on the right foot with the guests happy and cared for, but not even that could help the sorrow deep within Matthew's chest, nor his desire to be with Winnie again.

All he wanted to do was see her bright smile. All he wanted to hear was her teasing about his worthless car. All he wanted to do was be by her side to tell her how her work on the festival had changed his life forever—and how her leaving had altered his *hope* forever.

But the time for that was gone. She was already on her way to Chicago, ready to meet with the next company she would no doubt help. Did she regret her decision? Or had she already moved on, forgotten about Matthew and Foxwood completely?

A voice spoke on the wind, originating from the speaker near the jousting grounds, and Matthew's stomach dropped. The tournament would begin soon. Somehow, he was supposed to ride

Nightshade along the tilt and joust with all his energy in front of a crowd of onlookers expecting a show that left them speechless. And yet, Matthew couldn't even find the gumption to put on his helmet.

With that same dazed feeling as before, he wandered through the crowds, trying to remember the guests and his staff who were all relying on his performance.

But he was in over his head. He couldn't keep this up any longer—the fake smiles, the forced conversations, pretending to feel some fervor in the joust when he wasn't even sure he could find the desire to raise his lance.

He couldn't do any of it. Not anymore. Not alone.

"Well, if you aren't the most wee adorable knight I've seen in donkey's years."

Matthew spun around at the sound of the Northern Irish accent behind him. "Finn?" he questioned, his brow pulling together.

Sure enough, his friend stood before him in the middle of the crowds.

"What the devil, man?" Matthew exclaimed, his heart instantly lifting. "What are you doing here?"

He moved forward, embracing his mate, though his armor didn't allow him to do so as fully as he wished.

"What do you think I'm doing here?" Finn asked, his grin broad as he eyed Matthew up and down. "You've been talkin' about how this festival was going to be a craic. I had to come see for meself. And, you know, I came to watch me mate make a fool of himself."

Matthew's smile faltered, his friend's words hitting too close to home.

Finn paused. "Hey, listen. It was only a joke..."

But Matthew shook his head. "No, I know. It's not that."

Finn wasn't often serious, but he'd always been able to read Matthew's moods, responding accordingly every time. "What's wrong? Your father?"

Again, Matthew shook his head. "No, I...You just came to the wrong festival. You're going to be disappointed." Just like the guests would be. Like his family would be. Like *Dad* would be.

Finn looked around him. "What are you on about? It looks incredible."

"For now."

Finn eyed him again, awaiting an explanation in silence.

"Winnie left," Matthew stated. "She found another job to go to, so I'm on my own. Which means the festival has no hope. Just like last time."

Finn stared for a minute, his face blank. "Catch yourself on, mate."

Matthew blinked. "What?"

"You aren't sad about the festival," Finn continued. "You're sad about your girl leavin'. So quit your gurnin', get your act together, and pay attention to your wee event."

Matthew stared. "Next time you're going through something, remind me to come support *you*."

Finn smiled broadly, then sobered as best as he could. "I *am* here to support you, mate. You're not alone, no matter how you feel. And I'm here to help. Just like everyone else."

His words settled on Matthew's mind, filling his thoughts with the truth. Finn was right. Matthew wasn't alone. Finn, himself, had come all that way to prove that fact. And his staff had sacrificed weeks out of their lives to show their support, while his family had been there to encourage him from day one.

So why did he still feel so low?

He didn't need to wonder long as Winnie's warm smile appeared in his mind's eye.

"Winnie did so much for the festival," Matthew explained. "I don't even have the desire to joust anymore with her gone. I just..." He looked up at his friend, his voice lowering as they stood near the busy booths of the festival. "I liked her, Finn. I liked her a lot."

Finn nodded, taking on a serious look. "I'm sorry for how

things turned out. I really am. But, mate, you can't give up on somethin' you've loved doin' for years. You just need to grasp the nettle and move on, least for the evenin'. After that, the two of us can commiserate together the proper way—over a couple o' pints. Of ice cream, mind. Just like the women do."

Matthew gave a short laugh. "I might need something more effective than ice cream."

"All right. Gelato. But that's as far as I'll take it."

Matthew smiled again, his mood picking up just enough to give him a nudge forward. "Thanks, Finn. For coming and for chatting."

"Ah, no bother. Now tell me what I can do to help." He rubbed his hands together, motioning to Matthew's armor. "Maybe I can get into one o' these wee suits. Imagine the ladies 'round me then."

But Matthew shook his head. "Naw. You've got to earn the right to wear one of these. You'll start as my esquire."

"And what do they do?"

Matthew motioned to the jousting area, leading the way forward for them both. "Clean up the dung from my horse."

Finn's smile faded. "Grand."

The two of them made their way through the crowds, Matthew feeling considerably better than he had moments before.

He still didn't know what the future held, nor how the festival would turn out that afternoon or in the weeks to come.

But right now, he would do his best to see its success, and that would be enough. Because all of them—himself and Winnie included—had put too much into this festival to see it come to ruin again.

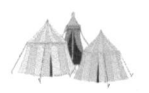

WINNIE ARRIVED at Foxwood and parked her car—this time, she was definitely *not* driving an Aston Martin—on the pea gravel drive. Her heart raced at the idea of seeing Matthew again. What would he say? Would he be happy to see her? Or would he tell her to leave, that she'd lost her chance to be with him for good?

She didn't have time to think about it for long. Just as soon as she pulled her suitcase out from the trunk, Char came running up to meet her.

"Winnie!" she greeted with a tight embrace. "What are you doing here?" She pulled back, taking Winnie's arms in her hands. "You'd best not have just forgotten something."

Winnie grinned. "No, I'm back. *Back*, back."

"Really?" Char said, her brow raised. "Please tell me you came back for my brother."

Winnie hesitated. "Well, I mean, I told my dad it wasn't because of Matthew, but let's be honest...it was."

Char squealed, reaching in for another embrace. "I knew it. I knew you'd come back. Just ask my mum. I told her you'd be back before long, and now you're here!"

Winnie's heart practically ached with joy. She'd made the right choice. "I'm so sorry for putting you all through that. Especially your brother. I just hope he'll forgive me."

"Oh, please. Of course he will."

"Is he still jousting?" Winnie asked.

"Yeah, the second half of the tournament is just about to start," Char explained. Then she paused. "Wait, did you not message Matthew to tell him you were coming back?"

Winnie smiled sheepishly. "No. I was kinda hoping to surprise him in person." She eyed the thick trees separating them from the view of the festival. "Although on second thought, maybe that wasn't a good idea."

Char's eyes brightened, and her mouth dropped open. "Oh my gosh, I have the perfect idea."

Winnie's heart jumped. "What?"

"Just follow me."

A SHORT THIRTY MINUTES LATER, Winnie stared at her reflection in the mirror in Char's room, shaking her head vigorously.

"Nope," Winnie said. "No, absolutely not. I can't believe I even let you talk me into putting this ridiculous dress on. There is no way I'm appearing in public like this—let alone in front of Matthew."

"Oh, come on, Winnie," Char said, straightening Winnie's headpiece. "He's going to *die* when he sees you."

"Die of second-hand humiliation," Winnie retorted.

She looked again at the reflection of her dark hair hanging past her shoulders, then peered down at the long, dark red dress Char had somehow encouraged her to put on. Apparently, Jess, their damsel, had left for home sick that afternoon after the first joust.

Char had been scheduled to take her place, but not anymore. Winnie would be the damsel instead.

Winnie. The damsel in distress. After all this time protesting the part in the festival, complaining about it being a twenty-first century faire, and now this.

What was she even doing right now? She looked like an elf from *Lord of the Rings*, with these long, drooping sleeves and low waistline. If she was being honest with herself, she didn't entirely mind the look. It was almost kind of fun. But she couldn't even stomach the thought of Matthew possibly rejecting her while she wore such clothes.

"Do you even know Matthew?" Char asked, smoothing out one of Winnie's sleeves. "He's going to jump on you when he sees you."

"Char!" Winnie said with a laugh. "I hardly think that'll be his reaction." She shook her head, looking down at the dress once more. "I can't. It's too much."

"No, you *can*," Char said. "He's going to love it. Trust me." She stood back and looked at her handiwork. "You can pull off this style, Winnie. You should become a regular at the festival."

As if Winnie would agree to such a thing. Then again, wasn't she a real-life damsel in distress right now? She was, after all, a young, unmarried woman who was suffering. Her dad was clearly upset with her, she didn't know if she still had a job at Foxwood, and she was about to appear before the love of her life and beg him to love her in return—all while in front of a huge audience.

If that didn't speak damsel in distress, she didn't know *what* did.

"So...are you ready to do this?" Char asked, still smiling at her.

Winnie's head swirled, but she nodded, nonetheless. "Yes. I'm ready. Let's go catch myself a knight."

MATTHEW CHARGED toward Hubert for their next round of jousting, Nightshade's hoofbeats pounding against the ground, the crowd cheering around him until his lance met contact with his friend and mentor's shoulder, the tip splintering across the grass.

The cheers grew louder, and the announcer's voice echoed around the area. "That is three points for Sir Matthew for splinterin' the tip of his lance. Did you see the speed they have runnin' down the tilt in the list? The list is what we call the field, my lords and ladies, and the tilt is the barrier between the horses."

Matthew couldn't believe the difference a good announcer made to the crowd. Funnily enough, Mr. Fogg—who had been more than happy to stand down as solely the score keeper—had told them all about his brother-in-law, Mr. Aiken, who was "far more enthusiastic" than himself. The change in the atmosphere was remarkable, and once again, it was thanks to Winnie for pushing a change in the first place.

Matthew rode his horse back toward his side of the tilt, trying to wipe the image of her from his mind again, but it was of no use. He couldn't help himself. He'd been seeing her throughout the day, too—or rather, imaginings of her. He just kept on hoping she'd show up around the tents or beneath a tree. At this point, he'd even take her in her pencil skirt, scribbling away on her tablet all the ways his festival had been terrible before she came along.

"Now Sir Matthew and Sir Hubert will be facin' each other again," Mr. Aiken continued. "Remember, where once the goal was to unseat the opponent, here, these knights must merely break their lance on the opposin' knight's body or shield."

Matthew faced Mr. Birdwhistle again, drawing in a deep breath. He needed to focus. While he no longer cared about winning the match, he still had to pay attention. The last thing he wanted to do was injure Mr. Birdwhistle or either of their horses accidentally.

"Oh, we have trouble a-brewin' on't other side of the tilt," Ed continued. "Who is that? Oh! Oh, no, it's the dreaded sorceress, Endora!"

Matthew waited at his side of the arena, listening to the script Ed had memorized—another imagining from Winnie—and recited from heart.

"Let's watch and see what she does," he whispered into the mic.

Just as they'd all rehearsed, Endora—or rather, Mrs. Birdwhistle who had set aside her fortune telling outfit for a long, gray wig and black robes—cackled at the end of the tournament area, appearing in a cloud of smoke.

She snuck toward the group of damsels—all actors hired and dressed up in their finest medieval ware—who remained unaware until one of them dressed in red was snatched by the sorceress.

He recalled Jess being assigned the role of damsel that afternoon, but he couldn't be certain, as Char had agreed to take charge over that part of the festival. Either way, due to his distance and his visor being down, Matthew couldn't see much of what was going on.

"Now you are mine!" Mrs. Birdwhistle shouted in a shrill voice.

"Oh, no!" Mr. Aiken exclaimed, narrating the event as Mrs. Birdwhistle grabbed the girl around her forearm and pulled her away from the other damsels. "Endora has taken a lovely lady from the rest. Who will rescue this damsel in distress now?"

The crowd was thoroughly engaged in the spectacle, and Matthew couldn't blame them. Everything Winnie touched was gold.

He watched as Jess was pulled away, the woman pretending to swoon into the sorceress, then he narrowed his eyes. His mind was playing tricks on him. It had been doing so all day long. And yet... Jess didn't look like Jess.

His heart flipped, but he pushed it down. He wouldn't allow himself to hope again. He couldn't handle the heartache.

But when the damsel in distress made eye contact with him from far down the list, he could no longer help himself. His breath was snatched away from him, and he threw open his visor.

He had been thinking about Winnie too much. There was no way Jess could have just magically turned into the love of his life. But as her eyes lingered on his, and he set aside his denial, he could no longer refuse the truth. That smile, that gorgeous, brown hair, that quintessentially Winnie expression of confidence mixed with uncertainty.

She *had* come back. Winnie had come back.

And she was dressed as a damsel.

Thoughts sped through his mind. Why *had* she come back? Was she to stay there for good or had she simply forgotten something?

A brief smile spread across her lips, no doubt from the look of utter shock on his features, but she pulled on an expression of fear and dismay as Mrs. Birdwhistle stole her away.

"We've heard rumors of Endora," Mr. Aiken said, Matthew barely registering the man's words. "She thieves unsuspectin' damsels often and turns them into toads for her magic spells. Will that 'appen to this fair lady yonder? Not if our king has anythin' to say about the matter."

Matthew continued to stare, unable to peel his eyes from Winnie, even when his dad—who had felt well enough to play the king of the tournament that day—stood at the center platform built to be raised above the rest of the grounds.

"My people!" he said, using another mic from his seated position. "We have witnessed something truly horrific this day. But I will not stand by and allow yet another one of our lovely damsels to be taken to fall prey to the ill will of the evil Endora. I will send our bravest knight to rescue her. Which of you shall go?"

"I will!" Mr. Birdwhistle shouted, raising his lance from the other end of the list.

"Nay, send me!" David—Jess's husband—cried out.

"I will fight for her!" shouted James.

Then, silence. Blast. Matthew had forgotten his cue.

"I am the bravest knight! I shall rescue the lady!" he shouted.

His words had sounded less convincing than the others, but could he be blamed? He was still too focused on Winnie being dragged away to the outskirts of the event, standing near another platform they'd built beneath a tree—the very tree she'd stood under that first festival so many weeks ago. Her hands were bound behind her back, and Mrs. Birdwhistle was crouched low beside her in a menacing stance.

Winnie's eyes were still on Matthew.

"So many brave knights," Mr. Aiken chimed in. "Which will our king choose?"

"Whomever wins the tournament," Dad said, "will win the right to fight for the lady's rescue—and her hand."

Matthew looked back to Winnie, her eyes still on him, and his heart leapt. That look she was giving him...she had to be staying. She had to have changed her mind about leaving. Right?

His mind swirled, his heart beating against his chest. He needed to speak with her. To ask her flat out what had happened between her leaving him the night before—and her returning this very moment.

And he needed to see her closer in that dress.

But he couldn't very well leave the joust right in the middle of it, not with all those people watching.

Mr. Aiken continued, but Matthew didn't hear his words until the man shouted, "Let the tournament commence!"

Matthew didn't take his eyes off Winnie, his chest swelling. There was only one thing left to do. He had to follow through on his word, to win the tournament for the love of his life.

He slammed his visor down and faced forward, gripping his lance with a firm grasp.

Now he had something to fight for.

CHAPTER FORTY-SIX

WINNIE HAD NEVER SEEN MATTHEW JOUST SO WELL. She'd watched him in training, in practice, and in actual tournaments, but never had she witnessed his form so perfect, nor his passion so evident.

She couldn't help but hope that it was due to her coming back.

Time after time, with each of the knights he competed against, his lance splintered into pieces, gaining him more and more points as the tournament went on, until finally, the last match arrived.

Winnie stood beside Mrs. Birdwhistle still, both of them staying in character for the better part of the tournament, despite Winnie growing antsier by the minute.

She'd been unable to stop the pride welling in her heart, the look of shock on Matthew's face having been well-worth all the effort and all the uncertainty. Gone were her insecurities from before, dressed in the medieval gown and wearing a heart-shaped hennin headpiece, replaced with a burning desire to speak with the man she loved.

She really couldn't believe her life in that moment, watching the man she loved jousting. *Jousting*. Of all the things. She'd always pictured herself being with some executive of a fancy business who was obsessed with work and money—not because she wanted to, but because she would have no other options.

But a knight on a horse with a lance in his hand? Now *that* was unbeatable.

The final joust was run, Matthew's lance once more splintering against James's armor, and Mr. Aiken—that blessed brother-in-law who showed so much excitement—shouted into the mic.

"Three cheers for the victor, Sir Matthew of Foxwood!"

The crowd roared, Mr. Aiken playing a short music clip of "Low Rider" over the speaker before Mrs. Birdwhistle pretended to drag Winnie back to the arena where the final event would take place.

Her heart raced as she watched Matthew riding around the area for his victory lap, a fresh lance in his hands being raised in the air. How she wanted his helmet removed so she could see his features again. She wanted to be with him—to speak with him, to explain.

But they had to wait, no matter how her heart yearned to be with him.

"Ah, the sorceress has returned!" Mr. Aiken declared. "What will our brave knight do now?"

Winnie, with her hands still bound behind her back—albeit very loosely—was situated in the center of the arena when Matthew launched off his horse and charged toward the sorceress, and together, the two battled out in a pretend clash of magic and swords.

Winnie stood on the sidelines, watching the event play out, knowing the sorceress would eventually pretend to be struck by Matthew before disappearing into a cloud of smoke.

But Winnie couldn't wait any longer. She hesitated, biting her lip and hoping her actions wouldn't upset Mr. Aiken or the other staff members. Then she moved toward Matthew herself.

"And now, we have…Uh…" Mr. Aiken hesitated, unsure of what to say off script. "Well, we have the damsel in distress racin' toward the knight. Not exactly sure what she's up to."

Winnie ripped free from her loosely tied ropes, and Matthew stood still, clearly in shock as she ran toward him, his visor still down. She stripped his sword directly from his hands, then turned toward Mrs. Birdwhistle and charged toward the sorceress herself.

"Ah, the damsel…" Mr. Aiken continued, "looks like she's taking matters into her own hands. Apparently, the knight was takin' too long to rescue her." He chuckled, and the crowd cheered.

Winnie reached Mrs. Birdwhistle in a matter of seconds, pretending to strike her side with the blunted weapon. Mrs. Birdwhistle's eyes twinkled before she shrieked as part of the act, then she launched into a cloud of smoke and ran away through the crowds.

"Ah, and the damsel has defeated the evil sorceress!" cried Mr. Aiken. "But will she accept the brave knight's hand…even though she sort of rescued herself?"

The crowd laughed and cheered again, and Winnie's heart swelled. Would she accept Matthew's hand? Oh, yes, she would.

Standing in the middle of the list, she waited as he strode directly toward her. She could hardly breathe, his clanking armor music to her ears. She waited in place, holding his sword with the tip pointed in the grass, then he stopped just before her.

His face was still covered by his helmet, just like when they'd first met, and he knelt down on one knee before her, reaching for her hand.

"Winnie," he breathed, only loud enough for her own ears to hear.

She couldn't help herself. She just had to. "Sorry," she said, "I can't hear you with all of…" She paused, waving her hand in front of her face like she had when they'd first met. "This."

To her utter joy, he laughed within his helmet, then raised the visor, looking up at her. "You came back," he said, still kneeling down.

Winnie peered down at him, the love in his eyes matching her own. "I did."

"Why?"

Tears brimmed in her eyes. "Because I've fallen in love with a knight. The only knight who could ever rescue a damsel in distress like me."

His lips spread into a smile, and he blinked as his blue eyes shone with tears. "But I didn't rescue you."

Her chin trembled. "Oh, yes, you did." She sniffed away her emotion, her voice soft as she continued. "I'm so sorry, Matthew. I'm sorry for leaving, for abandoning the festival and your family. For abandoning *you*. I never should have left, but I want you to know that I'm finally choosing who *I* want to be—and with *whom* I want to be." She stared down at him, wiping away another tear. "And that is you, Matthew...I just hope I'm not too late."

A moment passed by, and Winnie held her breath, fearing her apology wouldn't be accepted before Matthew stood, threw off his helmet and hood, and closed the distance between them.

She dropped his sword to the side of them and wrapped her arms around his neck, standing on the tips of her toes as he bent down and kissed her.

Her breath was stolen away, every inch of her heart and soul invested in the knight holding her as firmly and as gently as only Matthew could.

They'd shared many kisses over the last few weeks, each one better than the last, but this one was different. This one answered the questions they'd had from the beginning. This one made their feelings clear, their love for each other apparent.

The crowd cheered around them, thinking this was all part of the show, but Winnie didn't care. Because she knew this was real. Their *love* was real. And it would be a love that would last through the ages.

AFTER THE TOURNAMENT HAD ENDED, the festival had come to a close, and Matthew and Winnie had both changed out of their period clothing, the two of them returned to the house.

"Dinner tonight?" he asked, his arm around Winnie's shoulders as they crossed the grounds. "The White Hart, perhaps?"

"Sounds amazing," Winnie said, wrapping her arm around his waist and holding his hand that draped over her shoulder.

"Would it sound as amazing if Finn were to join us?" Matthew asked, glancing at her sidelong. "He just came all this way and is only here for the weekend..."

"Of course! I'd love to hear that accent of his again."

"Hey," Matthew warned, and she laughed.

"Where is he now, anyway?" she asked, looking around.

"I believe he's already snuck inside," Matthew responded. "Shirking his esquire duties, no doubt."

Winnie smiled, staring ahead of them as the house came into view. "Do you mind if I drive tonight?"

Matthew sighed. "We don't really have another option now. At least not until Minnie gets out of the shop. Your emerald steed will have to do."

"Oh, didn't you hear?" she asked, looking up at him. "I turned that one in."

He peered down at her in surprise. "Did you?"

She nodded, then motioned up ahead to where her new car was parked on the drive. A minivan as round and as red as could be sat proudly in front of them.

"I like to call her, Minnie 2.0," Winnie said.

Matthew let out a burst of laughter, stopping to face her as he wrapped his arms around her waist. "Who am I even dating right now? First you're a damsel in distress, now you're driving a people carrier. What's next for you, jousting?"

She laughed. "No, I think I'd prefer being a damsel to anything. I quite like being rescued by you. Although next time, I expect you to speed things up a bit."

He laughed. "You have changed, Miss Knox...in some ways more than others."

She stared into his eyes, her heart swirling with warmth and love for the man in front of her. "The biggest change is how much happier I am now. And it's all thanks to you." She looked to the side with a shrug. "And of course, to England."

He grinned, leaning down to kiss her before pulling back. "Well, the happiness looks good on you." He paused. "As did that medieval dress. You know...I wouldn't mind if you put that on again."

She gave him a saucy smile. "Oh? Well, maybe I will, if you promise to win another tournament for me."

"Then you shall have thy wish, my fair Lady Winifred," he said, putting on his ancient accent. "Anything you so desire is yours, so long as thou dost promise to share thy love with me forevermore."

She stared into his eyes. "I dost promise."

He looked to the side, then whispered, "'*I dost promise*?' I don't think that's right."

"Hey, at least I'm trying."

"I mean, they speak more accurately on *A Knight's Tale*," he teased again.

She swatted his chest. "You just can't help but correct me, can you?"

"'Tis a curse that I take great pleasure in," he said with an air of feigned pride. "But forgive me. I shall give it up if I must." He smiled, dropping his knightly façade as he continued. "Because nothing makes me happier than winning Winnie's hand...and her love."

"Well, *that* you have, sir," she said. "But I think I'll stick to speaking like this from now on, if you don't mind."

"Whatever suits your fancy," he said with a wink.

Then he leaned down for another kiss that Winnie heartily returned.

EPILOGUE

ONE WEEK LATER

> **MATTHEW**
> Well, lads. It's official.

FINN
You've lost the plot?

GRAHAM
Minnie is dead?

CEDRIC
You admit you're terrible at running?

Matthew grinned. They just couldn't help themselves.

> **MATTHEW**
> Just for that, I'm not coming to the next charity run.

FINN
You have to. I've got a craic lined up in Belfast.

> **MATTHEW**
> We'll see. But your guesses are all wrong.

GRAHAM

Come on. Tell us, then.

MATTHEW

Winnie and I are officially dating.

FINN

...All right, how much are you paying her?

GRAHAM

Whatever the amount, it's not enough.

CEDRIC

Wait, I thought you hated her.

FINN

No, remember? He only said he hated her.
Obviously, he was in denial.

GRAHAM

So much denial.

FINN

Anyway, this isn't much of a surprise. When I
was there, you two were all over each other.

Matthew smiled again. He had such supportive friends.

FINN

So when's the wedding? Don't tell me next
month. I've got me next bus tour starting then.

MATTHEW

Ha. Ha. No wedding yet. But I'll be sure to
keep it to myself, seeing how well THIS news
was received.

They laughed at his text, though Matthew set aside the image
that their own messages had prompted. Winnie in a white gown.
Matthew in his top hat and tails. The two of them dancing with
loved ones around them.

It was way, way too early to be thinking about such things—even if they were exactly what Matthew wanted in his future.

CEDRIC

Proper chuffed for you, Matt. Really.

GRAHAM

She's great. Hope you are happy together.

FINN

Yeah, congrats, mate. You both deserve all the happiness!

FINN

Bring her along to the next race. It'll be good to catch up with you both.

MATTHEW

Will do. If you can all promise to behave yourselves this time.

FINN

Yeah, that's not an option for us. Sorry.

"Texting your friends?"

Matthew looked up as Winnie joined him in the stables, her hair hanging loosely down her shoulders.

"Yep," he said, putting his phone away, though the buzzing texts continued.

He'd much rather pay attention to Winnie, but his friends couldn't possibly understand. None of them had a girl like *her* in their lives.

"I can always tell you're messaging them when you have that smile on your face," she said, encircling her arms around his waist.

"Well, you should know, then, I was smiling because I finally told them about us." He leaned down and kissed the tip of her nose.

"Did you? How did they take it?"

"Not as excitedly as Char," he said.

He drew up the memory of his sister hugging them both over

and over again throughout the evening the night of that first festival together.

"But they're well happy for us," he said, "which is nice to hear."

"Very nice."

Matthew peered down at her, admiring her features in silence.

A mere week had passed since her decision to stay at Foxwood and nearly two months since they'd first met. In a way their time together seemed brand new, but in other ways, it seemed like she had been there forever, a permanent fixture in his home, a permanent figure in his life.

Not only did the festival continue to thrive under her watchful care, but the ideas she had to keep Foxwood prosperous had been better than any of the Wintours could have dreamed— and she still had two months left.

Of course, after that, who knew what would happen? The only thing Matthew *could* say for certain was that he would do whatever it took to keep his relationship with Winnie alive and well. She truly was one-of-a-kind, and he could never say enough prayers of gratitude that she had chosen to stay with him.

They stood in the same manner for a minute, staring at each other in the stables until her eyes clouded over, and he knew where her thoughts had strayed.

Winnie had received a call from her dad only a few minutes before—the first since she'd chosen to stay in England. She'd slipped out to take it while Matthew had stayed behind to finally message his friends.

"How was it?" he asked gently.

"It was all right," she replied with a shrug. "He was still clearly upset with me, but he actually apologized for making me feel like I had to do whatever he wanted me to. I don't know if he was sincere, but it's a step in the right direction." She looked away. "Of course he ended the call with sharing how well everyone was doing in their own jobs, so that was the same as usual."

Matthew tightened his hold of her. Standing up to her dad

had been a long time coming for Winnie, but that didn't mean it was any less difficult to do. In truth, it had taken its toll on her. He could see it in her eyes.

He would never be able to fully understand having a father like Mr. Knox. Only yesterday, Matthew's own dad had pulled him and Winnie aside, telling them both yet again how pleased he was.

"You both did such a wonderful job with the festival," he'd said. *"I still can't express how proud I am of both of you."*

Matthew had never been more grateful for his father's kindness. He and his whole family would give anything to have Winnie experience the same sort of love and acceptance from her own father, but until she did, Matthew would be there for her, every step of the way.

"Anyway," Winnie said, pulling on a smile as Matthew departed from his thoughts. "Sarah's been awesome throughout the whole thing. I told her she needs to find herself a boyfriend now and stand up to Dad next. Oh, and did I tell you Scott messaged me?"

Matthew shook his head. "What did he say?"

"He told me he was proud of me for standing up for myself and that he hoped I would be happy."

"That's kind of him," Matthew said.

Winnie nodded, her eyes taking on a distant look before returning to Matthew. "Well, are you ready to ride?"

"I'm ready if you are," he said, and he returned her smile.

Matthew was hesitant to so readily set aside something that still clearly pained her, but he trusted her. She would talk to him when she was ready to, just like she always did.

In a matter of minutes, the two of them set off across the countryside, taking a break near their tree and admiring the effect the sunshine had on the green grass, brightening each blade like glass and warming the very air around them.

Of course, Matthew was more taken with Winnie. Her long

hair blowing in the soft breeze. Her eyes taking in the world around her.

He couldn't believe his luck. He couldn't believe the blessing she was in his life.

"What are you staring at, Sir Matthew?" Winnie asked, watching him from the corner of her eye.

"Only the most beautiful lady I have ever beheld."

She rolled her eyes, though a smile spread across her lips. She directed Prince to face Matthew, her legs brushing against his as she leaned forward, placing a hand to his cheek and kissing him soundly on the lips.

When she pulled back, a wistful look had taken root in her eye. "Thank you," she said.

"For the kiss?"

She laughed. "No. For being there for me. And for always wanting my happiness."

He sobered, nodding his head. "I'll always want that for you, Winnie."

"I know."

Then the two of them shared another kiss, relishing the love between them and the future before them—because they both knew their future together would be as bright as the sunshine after an English rain.

One Month Later

Finn O'Meara pulled out his phone to text his mates. He was already behind schedule, but there was nothing he could do when he was still waiting for the last straggler.

There was always one on every bus tour.

FINN

Wish me luck, mates. Another tour starts this morning. If these folks are more boring than the last, I might just leave them stranded at Giant's Causeway.

His last tour had been abysmally, mind-numbingly dull. Not a single soul on the bus had laughed at his jokes or responded to his stories. What was the point of doing these things if none of them—himself included—enjoyed it?

MATTHEW

Maybe you should be less boring, then.

Finn almost laughed out loud at his friend's joke. He did like a good tease.

MATTHEW

Winnie tells me to apologize for that. I suppose I should.

But no apology came. Finn smiled all the brighter.

FINN

Tell Winnie thanks for the support. She's some yoke.

MATTHEW

She says you're welcome but wanted me to tell you that you spelt yolk wrong.

Finn smiled again, about to send another quick text before footsteps sounded up the bus.

"I'm so sorry I'm late," an airy voice said.

A flash of a blue dress and waves of blonde curls passed him by before he even had the chance to look up at the woman who'd just entered his bus, dropped her ticket on his lap, and scurried to the seats behind them.

He turned off his phone, tucking it away in the slot to the right of his seat as he glanced at the ticket. This was the

straggler he'd been waiting for, the girl from the States—
Maisie King. He could only hope her late arrival wasn't a
forecast for how she'd be throughout the duration of the
tour. Americans were usually his favorites to travel with,
being the most fun and the most vocal. Would she turn out
like that, too?

He ticked her name off on his now-finalized list, then stood to
greet the new group who would be his closest companions over
the next few weeks.

"'Bout ye," he greeted with a friendly smile, tipping his flat
cap to them as he scanned the group.

A few of them responded, most of them nodding. Maisie
King had her head ducked as she situated her belongings beside
her, obviously unaware that he was even speaking.

It was no matter. He didn't need one hundred percent attention from every single person on the bus.

At least, not all the time.

He clapped his hands, then rubbed them together. "Right,
now that we're all here, I think we should head out, aye?"

More nods, but the blonde still didn't look up.

"First, we have a few wee rules to go over," he said, swiftly
going through them as the small group nodded their understanding.

They may prove boring yet, but at least they all seemed atten-
tive. Except for the one, of course.

Setting aside the lack of attention he was receiving from her
once more, he turned around and started the bus.

"Let's get on our way, then, aye?" he said through the intercom. "We're going to have quite the craic over the next few weeks,
so I hope you're ready."

A few cheers were heard, and he breathed a sigh of relief. This
group was *bound* to be better than the last. Now if he could just
get that American's attention.

He reached across to turn up the radio, not planning to speak
again until the group got settled in, but his hand froze on the

volume knob when he glanced in the rearview mirror and finally caught sight of her.

The American.

Maisie stared out the window with a perfect profile, perfect blonde wavy hair, and perfect dark eyelashes. He'd honestly never seen anyone so beautiful. Not in a fake, plastic kind of way either. In a real sort of way. Natural and stunning.

His wheel ran across a dip in the road he hadn't seen, and his hand suddenly jerked forward, launching the speakers far louder than he'd intended.

Irish music blasted out across the bus, and gasps sounded behind him.

Boys a dear, he was in trouble. Swiftly, he turned the music down, then pulled up his intercom.

"My apologies, ladies and gents, I thought we were in a wee pub for a minute there. Don't worry. Won't 'appen again."

He glanced back, and to his surprise, the one person watching him in the rearview mirror, the one person with a smile on her lips, was Maisie.

Their eyes connected, and his heart stuttered. She really was a looker. He grinned, then pulled his gaze away to focus on the road.

Well, this tour might just end up being his best one yet if she kept smiling at him like that. Maybe Matthew could give him a pointer or two on how to keep the attention of a lovely woman from the States. His mate seemed to have done fairly well in that regard with Winnie.

Either way, Finn would definitely be messaging the lads about *this* American.

THE END

AUTHOR'S NOTE

I can't believe it's been a solid year since I wrote the last author's note. In some ways, the year has flown by, in other, it has been the longest of my life! Either way, I hope it was worth the wait for you to now have this book in your hands!

Now sit back and enjoy a bit of behind-the-scene facts about *Winning Winnie's Hand*! (I promise to keep it shorter than the book itself...)

THE BEGINNING OF WINNIE

I first had the desire to write a story involving knights when I went to a medieval festival in England way back in 2015. But it wasn't until last year at a ren faire in Idaho that I was finally inspired to write *Winning Winnie's Hand*.

While the idea came easily, the writing did not, and I struggled for the better part of nine months to get this bad boy on paper. I realized only when I finished the book that one of the main reasons it was difficult for me to write was because of my complete and total lack of connection with Winnie Knox. Funny, huh??

I seriously have never had such a hard time connecting with one of my main characters before, and I still don't know why it was so difficult with her. I had to dig deep before I finally found something that she and I had in common, and fortunately, I found two things—her love of horses and her love of Englishmen. Thank heavens I discovered our similarities, or this book might not have seen the light of day!

ENGLISH PHRASES

Speaking of Englishmen...Here are some English phrases. (Okay, weakest segue ever. But what did you expect? I just spent countless hours writing this book and my brain is fried.)

Here are some of my favorite phrases and words that I used throughout the book:

- *"It's a good job"* - "it's a good thing"
- *"Quid"* - "money"
- *"Whinging"* - "whining"
- *"Slippy"* - "slippery"
- *"People carrier" (or MPV)* - "minivans"
- *"How are your family?"* - "How is your family?"
- *"Well happy"* - "They're very happy"
- *"Trousers"* - "pants"
- *"Pants"* - "worthless"
- *"Muppet"* - "lighthearted word for fool"

A KNIGHT'S TALE

All right, I saved the best for last.

One of the biggest pulls I had to write this book was being able to give several nods to one of my all-time favorite movies, *A Knight's Tale*. Seriously. This movie, guys. It's just too good. Heath

Ledger, the jousting, the horses, the romance, the humor, the music. Everything about it is amazing. I have quoted the heck out of it my entire life, ever since seeing it as a kid. This year alone, I've watched it dozens of times to get myself in the jousting mindset. I've loved every second of it!

Here are my favorite nods to the movie that I included in *Winning Winnie's Hand*:

- Mentioning the movie itself a number of times
- Mentioning a female farrier
- Matthew promising to win the tournament for Winnie
- Mentioning Geoffrey Chaucer, who is one of my favorite characters in the film
- Including multiple songs like "We Will Rock You," "Golden Years," and "Low Rider"
- This quote being a nod to a side character's quote speaking with Count Adhemar about William's success: "But a knight on a horse with a lance on his hands? Now that was unbeatable."
- Adding in these random words and phrases that are reminiscent of the film: "trudge," "my people," "gild the lily," "oh my giddy aunt," "cat's meat," "found wanting," and "there will be the devil to pay."

Did you catch them all? Or did you find even more that I didn't mention? I wouldn't be surprised if I missed some, what with how engrained this movie script is in my lifelong vocabulary!

THANK YOU

Well, if you made it this far, I just have to say thank you! Thank you for reading my book, and thank you for reading this author's note Only the most dedicated of people would get through both.

As Matthew would say, "I must commend your stamina, my fair lads and ladies!"

You are truly why I write.

Now, if you haven't already, join me on Instagram and Facebook, then sign up for my newsletter to never miss a new release. I'd love to have you join me!

Also, if you enjoyed this book, please consider leaving a review here. Reviews help authors out so much because that is how people hear about our books.

Until next time!
Deborah

ACKNOWLEDGMENTS

I love writing. But sometimes, it can really get an author down. Luckily, I've had a slew of people behind me, pushing me on and helping me find my way as I navigated through the ups and downs that inherently come while writing a novel.

First, thank you to my editor, Jacque, for your initial feedback on the story. Your detailed advice and suggestions were just what I needed to get through that first round of edits!

Thank you to my beta readers who put in so much work reading through the HORRIBLE draft I gave you. Joanna Barker, Jess Heileman, Brooke Losee, Arlem Hawks, Ruth C., and Maren S., thank you so much!

Thank you to my cover artist, Ink & Laurel. You are an absolute master cover creator. I'm so grateful for your work and talent! You understood my vision and multiplied it by one hundred. Thank you!

Thank you to Winnie's Influencers (you know who you are) for being with me every step of the way! Your patience as I've strung you along and your willingness to help me get the word out about this book were unmatched. You are all my favorites!!

Thank you to my ARC readers for always dropping everything to read my books. You are why I do what I do!

Thank you to my family for your encouragement and support, especially through the last couple of months. I couldn't get through life without you all. Thanks for being Wintours and not Knoxes...

Thank you to my children, including our brand-new addition. You all have helped me find more purpose in life than I'd ever dreamed possible. Your smiles sustain me!

Thank you to my husband, for supporting me as I spent months writing and brainstorming. You're always my go-to, the one who helps me through plot holes, the one who encourages me, the one who digs me out of the pits I fall into time and time again. You have been the answer to my prayers countless times. You have always been there for me. I'm so grateful to have you as my eternal companion.

Finally, I want to express my gratitude for my Savior. He alone knows exactly how I feel, and He alone knows exactly how to succor me. I'm so grateful for His sacrifice, His unending love, and His ever-present support. The song that has kept me going this past year has been "There is Peace in Christ," and it has supported me for a reason. I can never thank Him enough for what He has done for me.

BOOKS BY DEBORAH M. HATHAWAY

A Cornish Romance Series
On the Shores of Tregalwen, a Prequel Novella
Behind the Light of Golowduyn, Book One
For the Lady of Lowena, Book Two
Near the Ruins of Penharrow, Book Three
In the Waves of Tristwick, Book Four
From the Fields of Porthlenn, Book Five

Belles of Christmas Multi-Author Series
Nine Ladies Dancing, Book Four
On the Second Day of Christmas, Book Four

Seasons of Change Multi-Author Series
The Cottage by Coniston, Book Five

Sons of Somerset Multi-Author Series
Carving for Miss Coventry, Book One

Christmas Escape Multi-Author Series (Contemporary)
Christmas Baggage

Castles & Courtship Multi-Author Series
To Know Miss May, Book Two

Men of the Isles Series
Winning Winnie's Hand's, Book One

ABOUT THE AUTHOR

Deborah M. Hathaway graduated from Utah State University with a BA in Creative Writing. As a young girl, she devoured Jane Austen's novels while watching and re-watching every adaptation of Pride & Prejudice she could, entirely captured by all things Regency and romance.

Throughout her early life, she wrote many short stories, poems, and essays, but it was not until after her marriage that she was finally able to complete her first romance novel, attributing the completion to her courtship with, and love of, her charming, English husband. Deborah finds her inspiration for her novels in her everyday experiences with her husband and children and during her travels to the United Kingdom, where she draws on the beauty of the country in such places as England, Ireland, Scotland, Wales, and of course, her beloved Cornwall.

Made in United States
Troutdale, OR
11/28/2024

25393102R20260